# MARIANNE
## *The Stranger from Tuscany*

# MARIANNE
## *The Stranger from Tuscany*

### *Juliette Benzoni*

## Book 2: Marianne Series

First published in English as *Marianne and the Masked Prince*
in 1971 by Heinmann.

This edition: Telos Publishing
139 Whitstable Road, Canterbury, Kent CT2 8EQ,
United Kingdom.

www.telos.co.uk

ISBN: 978-1-84583-214-8

Telos Publishing Ltd values feedback. Please e-mail any comments you
might have about this book to: feedback@telos.co.uk

British Library Cataloguing in Publication Data.
A catalogue record for this book is available from the British Library.

# CONTENTS

# Principal Characters

*Marianne Elisabeth d'Asselnat.* The daughter of a French marquis and his English wife, both of whom perished in the French Revolution. She was rescued as a baby by her godfather, Gauthier de Chazay, and taken to England to be brought up by her spinster aunt, Ellis Selton. In 1809, she married Francis Cranmere who, on her wedding night, gambled away both her fortune and her virginity. Marianne saved herself and fled to France where, after many adventures, she fell in love with Napoleon and became his mistress. She lives in the Paris mansion which had belonged to her family under the name Signorina Maria Stella, an Italian singer.

*Adelaide d'Asselnat.* A French cousin of Marianne's, an elderly spinster. Marianne found her living in hiding in the attics of her house and prepared to burn it down rather than see it occupied by an upstart. She became Marianne's companion.

*Fortunée Hamelin.* A Créole lady, and a leading figure in Parisian society. Passionately devoted to the Emperor, she was entrusted by him with the task of introducing Marianne to the polite world and the two women became great friends.

*Francis, Lord Cranmere.* Marianne's dastardly husband, whom she had left for dead in the burning wreck of Selton Hall after forcing him to fight a duel with her. Marianne believed she saw him, scarred but alive, on the night of her debut as a singer.

*Jason Beaufort.* The American sea-captain to whom Francis lost Marianne's fortune and virginity at cards. He generously failed to claim the second and reappeared later in Paris to become one of the few people Marianne felt prepared to trust.

*Arcadius, Vicomte de Jolival.* A French aristocrat and one of Marianne's staunchest friends, as well as her theatrical manager.

*Gracchus-Hannibal Pioche.* A former Paris errand boy, now, at the time of the action, Marianne's devoted coachman.

*Gauthier de Chazay.* A French Abbé, Marianne's godfather, and the man who rescued her as a baby from the Revolution.

*Duroc.* Napoleon's Grand Marshal of the Palace.

*Joseph Fouché, Duke of Otranto.* Napoleon's cunning Minister of Police.

*Dorothée de Périgord, Princess of Courland.* The wife of Talleyrand's nephew; Marianne became friends with her while engaged as a reader in Talleyrand's household.

*Charles Maurice de Talleyrand, Prince of Benevento.* Napoleon's Grand Chamberlain, and ex-Foreign Minister. Fouché used Marianne as a spy in his household.

*Nicolas Mallerousse, alias Black Fish.* One of Fouché's secret agents operating in England. Marianne escaped from England in his boat and he developed a deep and fatherly affection for her. She took his name in her first days in Paris.

*Baron Surcouf.* A sea-captain, famous for his free-lance activities against English shipping off the coast of Brittany.

*Morvan the Wrecker.* Leader of a band of Royalist ship-wreckers; Marianne was once his prisoner when her ship was wrecked on the coast of Brittany.

*Gwen.* Morvan's Bretonne mistress.

*Fanchon Fleur-de-Lis, alias the Dame Désormeaux.* A hideous old woman in whose hands Marianne was once a prisoner. At the time of the action, a figure in the Paris underworld and fiercely anti-Revolutionary.

# PART I

# The Man with the Scarred Face

# CHAPTER ONE
## Appointment at *La Folie*

Abruptly, Napoleon ceased pacing up and down the room and came to a stop in front of Marianne. The girl huddled in the big arm-chair by the fire gave a sigh of relief. Even deadened by the thick carpet, that regular pacing racked her nerves and made her head throb. So much had happened in that fantastic evening that she was too exhausted to be conscious of anything beyond the splitting ache in her head. There had been the thrill of her first appearance on stage at the Théâtre Feydeau, her stage-fright and, above all, the inexplicable appearance in one of the stage boxes of the man she believed she had killed, followed by his equally mysterious disappearance. Enough to overcome a much stronger constitution than Marianne's!

With an effort, she opened her eyes and saw that he was watching her, his hands clasped behind his back and an anxious look on his face. Was he anxious, or just vexed? The pressure of his smart, silver-buckled shoe was digging a hole in the pale carpet, while the quiver of his thin nostrils and a certain steely glint in his blue eyes betokened an incipient burst of temper. Marianne asked herself suddenly if the man before her was her lover, the Emperor, or an examining magistrate. In the ten minutes that had elapsed since he burst in on her, he had said little, but she could sense the questions in the air. The quiet room with its blue-green watered silks, bright flowers and sparkling crystal, so peaceful and reassuring a few moments before, had taken on a fragile, transitory air. Sure enough, the peace was shattered in an instant by his curt voice.

'Are you sure what you saw was not a hallucination?'

'A hallucination?'

'Yes. You could have seen someone who looked like … like this man. Someone quite different. It is hardly likely that an English nobleman could be at large in France, going to theatres, even sitting in the Chancellor of State's own box and no one any the wiser! My police are the best in Europe.'

Despite her shock and exhaustion, Marianne bit back a smile. So that was it: vexation rather than anxiety was uppermost in Napoleon's mind, for the simple reason that the efficiency of his police force was in question. Yet God alone knew how many foreign spies were loose in France at that moment! Marianne sighed wearily.

'Sire, I know the vigilance of your Minister of Police as well as you do, better perhaps, and I meant no reflection upon them. But there can be no doubt the man I saw was Francis Cranmere and no other.'

Napoleon made a movement of irritation but controlled it at once and came to sit at the foot of Marianne's sofa. His tone was markedly softer as he asked: 'How can you be sure? You told me that you barely knew this man.'

'One does not easily forget the face of a man who has destroyed one's life. Besides, the man I saw had a long scar on his left cheek.'

'And what does that prove?'

'Only that I gave it him, with the point of a rapier, to make him fight,' Marianne said quietly. 'I scarcely think any accidental resemblance would go so far as to reproduce a scar known here only to me. No, it was he and from now on I am in danger.'

Napoleon laughed and drew Marianne into his arms with a movement of spontaneous tenderness.

'Now you are talking nonsense. *Mio dolce amor*, how could you be in danger while I love you? Am I not the Emperor? Do you know how powerful I am?'

The terror which had been gripping Marianne's heart miraculously relaxed its hold. Once again she was conscious of the extraordinary sense of security which only he could give her. He was right when he said that nothing could touch her while he was there but – that was just the trouble. He was going away. With an impulse of childish fear, she clutched his shoulder.

'You are the only one I trust. But you are leaving me, leaving Paris. You will be far away.'

She had a vague, momentary hope that he would offer to take her with him. Why shouldn't she go to Compiègne too? True, the new Empress was due to arrive in a few days but surely, he could install her in a house in the town, away from the palace but not too far? She might have broached her desire but already he had laid her back against the cushions and risen to his feet with a swift glance at the ormolu clock on the mantelshelf.

'I shall not be away long. I will send for Fouché when I get back and give him strict orders concerning this house. In any case, he must scour

Paris for this Cranmere. Give him a complete description of the man tomorrow morning.'

'The Duchess of Bassano said she saw a Flemish gentleman, the Vicomte d'Aubécourt, in the box. Perhaps Francis is going by that name?'

'Then the Vicomte d'Aubécourt shall be found and Fouché shall report to me in detail. Don't worry, *carissima mia*, I will be watching over you, even from a distance. And now I must leave you.'

'So soon! Can't you stay with me tonight, at least?'

Marianne regretted her plea as soon as the words were out. If he was in such haste to leave her, she should not have pleaded with him to stay, as if she did not trust him or herself. But in her heart, she was a prey to all the demons of jealousy. In a moment he was leaving her to go to another woman. There were tears in her eyes as she watched him cross to pick up his grey coat from the chair where he had flung it as he entered. Only when he had put it on did he look at her and answer.

'I had hoped so, Marianne, but when I got back from the theatre, I found a host of dispatches waiting to be answered before I leave. Do you know I left six people waiting in my antechamber to come to you?'

'At this time of night?' Marianne's voice held disbelief.

He moved swiftly to her side and tweaked her ear.

'Always remember, little one, the official daytime visitors are not always the most important. I hold more nocturnal audiences than you might imagine. Now, good-bye.'

He bent and kissed her lightly on the lips but Marianne did not respond. She uncoiled herself from her chair and went to fetch a branch of candles from her dressing-table.

'I will escort your majesty,' she said, a little chill of formality in her voice. 'All the servants except the porter will be in bed.'

She had opened the door and was about to precede him to the stairs when he caught her back.

'Look at me, Marianne. You are cross with me, aren't you?'

'I should not presume so far, sire. I am honoured that your majesty can spare your valuable time to remember your humble servant.'

Before she could complete her stately curtsey, Napoleon laughed and, taking the candles firmly from her hand, pulled her roughly to her feet and into his arms.

'My love, I swear you are jealous. It suits you. I told you once before you should have been a Corsican. God, but you are beautiful like that, with your eyes blazing like emeralds in the sun! You are dying to abuse me roundly, only you dare not. I can feel you trembling ...'

The laughter died out of his face as he spoke. Marianne knew from his sudden pallor and the tightening of his jaw how much he wanted her. Then his head was buried in her neck and he was covering her shoulders and her breast with kisses. It was he who was trembling now while Marianne, her head thrown back, her eyes closed, listened to her racing heart, and gave herself to his caresses. A wild thrill of happiness, made up of pride as much as love, surged through her at the realization that her power over him was as great as ever. At last, he swept her up into his arms and carried her to the big bed and dumped her down unceremoniously. Moments later the exquisite white dress, which had dazzled all Paris so short a time before, lay in ruins on the carpet, while Marianne lay in Napoleon's arms, gazing up at the canopy of sea-green watered silk rippling over her head.

'Those people waiting for you at the Tuileries,' she whispered, between kisses, 'I hope they won't be bored – and are not too important?'

'A courier from the Tzar and a papal envoy, you little devil. Happy?'

For answer, Marianne twined her arms more closely round her lover's neck and closed her eyes with a happy sigh. It was moments like these that made up for all the disappointments, fears and jealousies. Listening to his frenzy of passionate endearments, Marianne was comforted. Surely this Austrian female he was about to take into his bed in place of Joséphine, this Marie-Louise, could never win so much love from him? Probably she was nothing more than a frightened little ninny commending her soul to God with every minute of the journey that was taking her closer to her country's enemy. Napoleon to her must seem a kind of Minotaur, a contemptible upstart. If she had anything in common with her aunt Marie-Antoinette, she would treat him with all the hauteur of her imperial blood, while if, as it was whispered in the *salons*, she was merely a silly girl with as little intelligence as beauty, she would submit passively.

Even so, an hour later, as she watched through a hall window the porter shutting the massive gates behind the imperial coach, all Marianne's fears and uncertainties came flooding back. The next time she saw the Emperor, he would be married to the Archduchess and meanwhile, under one name or another, Francis Cranmere was at liberty in Paris.

Shivering in the lace dressing robe which she had slipped on in haste, Marianne picked up the candlestick and made her way back to her own room with a disagreeable feeling of isolation. The sound of the carriage carrying Napoleon away echoed in the distance, a melancholy counterpoint to the words of love still ringing in her head. But for all his tender protestations of affection, Marianne was too honest to conceal from herself that a page had been turned and however great the love that bound her to Napoleon, nothing could ever be quite the same again.

When Marianne got back to her room, she was surprised to find her cousin there. Mademoiselle Adélaïde d'Asselnat, dressed in a loose wrap of puce velvet with an immense fluted cap adorning her head, was standing in the middle of the room contemplating, with interest but no apparent surprise, the glorious debris of the white dress left lying crumpled on the carpet.

'Adélaïde, you're here? I thought you were asleep long ago.'

'I always sleep with one eye open and something warned me you might need a little company when "he" had gone.' The old maid sighed and picked up the scrap of pearly satin. 'Ah, now there's a man who has a way with women! I do not wonder you should fall for him. I did myself, you know, when he was only a shabby, underfed little general. But tell me, how did he take the sudden resurrection of your late lamented husband?'

'Badly,' Marianne said, rummaging among the ravages of her bed for the nightgown which Agathe, her maid, must have laid out to await her return from the theatre. 'He is half-convinced that I was seeing things.'

'You were not?'

'No! Why should I suddenly see Francis's ghost when he was a hundred miles from my thoughts? I thought him dead. No, I am sorry, Adélaïde, but there could be no mistake; it was Francis for sure ... and he was smiling, smiling at me in a way that terrified me! God knows what he means to do.'

'Time will tell,' the spinster said placidly, moving in a purposeful way towards the small table with a lace cloth on which a cold supper had been left ready for Marianne, although neither she, nor the Emperor, had eaten a mouthful. Calmly, Adélaïde uncorked a bottle of champagne and filled two tall glasses. One of these she emptied at a draught, the other she carried over to Marianne, after which she returned for her own glass, selected a wing of chicken from the dish, and settled herself comfortably on the foot of the bed in which her cousin was by now ensconced.

Marianne sat propped up on her pillows, glass in hand, and regarded Adélaïde with an indulgent smile. The amount of food which that frail, bird-like creature could absorb was quite amazing. All day long Adélaïde was nibbling, sipping or toying with 'a little something', none of which deterred her in the least from sitting down to table with undiminished enthusiasm when the time came. Yet for all this she never seemed to put on an ounce of weight or lose one jot of her dignity.

The strange, nervous, cantankerous creature whom Marianne had found in the *salon* late one night about to set fire to the house had completely disappeared. She had been replaced by a woman no longer young but whose backbone had recovered all its innate rigidity. Well-dressed, her soft grey hair neatly combed into long, silky ringlets that peeped below her voluminous lace caps and velvet hoods, the erstwhile revolutionary who had been sought by Fouché's police and kept under house arrest had become once again Adélaïde d'Asselnat, a great lady. Now, however, she was sitting with half-closed eyes, aristocratic nostrils quivering with greed, consuming chicken and champagne with the dainty self-satisfaction of a contented cat. Marianne could not help smiling. While not perfectly sure that her cousin's conspiratorial instincts were altogether buried, Marianne had grown very fond of Adélaïde.

She sipped her champagne slowly, waiting for the old lady to speak. She guessed that Adélaïde had something to say to her, and, sure enough, having reduced the chicken to bare bone and drunk the champagne down to the final drop, Adélaïde wiped her lips with satisfaction and bent her blue gaze earnestly on her cousin.

'Dear child,' she began, 'I think you are looking at your problem from the wrong angle. I gather that your late husband's unexpected resurrection has thrown you into a dither and now that you have seen him you are living in terror of his appearing to confront you again. Is that it?'

'Of course, it is! But I don't understand, Adélaïde. Do you think I ought to be overjoyed at the return of a man I believed I had punished as he deserved for what he did to me?'

'Well, yes, in a way.'

'But why?'

'Because now that he is alive you are no longer a murderess and need not fear pursuit from the law in England.'

Marianne smiled. 'I was not much afraid of it,' she said. 'Apart from the war, the Emperor's protection is more than enough to remove all my fears. But you are right in a way. It is nice to know there is no blood on my hands.'

'Can you be sure of that? There is still the pretty cousin you stunned so neatly ...'

'I can hardly have killed her. If Francis is alive, I would wager that Ivy St Albans is alive as well. Besides, Francis means nothing to me now and I have no reason to desire her death.'

'He is still your lawfully wedded husband, my dear. That is why, if I were in your shoes, instead of running away from your ghost, I should do my best to meet him again. When citizen Fouché calls on you in the morning —'

'How did you know I was expecting the Duke of Otranto?'

'I shall never become accustomed to calling that unfrocked priest by that title. But, of course, he is bound to come tomorrow ... Oh, don't look at me so! Naturally I listen at keyholes when I want to know what is happening inside.'

'Adélaïde!' Marianne was genuinely shocked.

Mademoiselle d'Asselnat stretched out her arm and patted Marianne's hand.

'Don't be such a little prude. Even an Asselnat may listen at doors. It can be very useful, as you will find. Where was I?'

'You were saying that the – the Minister of Police would call.'

'Ah yes. Well, instead of begging him to lay hands on that precious husband of yours and send him back to England on the first frigate, you must ask him, on the contrary, to bring him to you so that you may inform him of your decision.'

'My decision? Have I decided anything?' Marianne was more and more confused.

'Of course, you have. I wonder you should not have thought of it yourself. And while you have the minister to hand, ask him to try and find out what has become of your reverend godfather, that Jack-of-all-trades, Gauthier de Chazay. We shall be wanting him shortly. Even while he was still a little nobody of a priest he had the Pope in his pocket, and you can't imagine how useful the Pope can be when it comes to dissolving a marriage. Are you beginning to understand now?'

Marianne was indeed beginning to understand. Adélaïde's idea was so brilliant and so simple that she scolded herself for not thinking of it sooner. The marriage was never consummated and besides it had been contracted with a Protestant: it should be possible, even easy, to get it annulled. Then she would be free, wholly, wonderfully free, without even her husband's death upon her conscience. But even as she called to mind the grave little figure of the Abbé de Chazay, Marianne was conscious of a creeping uneasiness.

She had thought of her godfather so often in the time since she had stood on the quayside at Plymouth and gazing after the little vessel's fast-disappearing sails. She had thought of him sadly but hopefully at first, but a slight anxiety had grown with the passage of time. What would he say, that man of God, so fiercely upright in all matters of honour, so blindly loyal to his exiled king, if he knew his god-daughter was masquerading as Maria Stella, an opera singer and the Usurper's mistress? Would he ever understand what it had cost Marianne in suffering and blighted hopes to reach her present state and the happiness it held for her? If she had caught up with the Abbé on the *Barbican* at Plymouth her destiny would have been a very different one. He would probably have gained admittance for her to some convent where she would have been given every opportunity, in prayer and meditation, to expiate what she had never ceased to regard as the righteous execution of her husband. But although she had often thought of her godfather's affection and goodness with real regret, Marianne understood she did not in the least regret the life that would have been hers in the convent.

Finally, Marianne put something of her doubt into words by saying to her cousin:

'It would make me happy to see my godfather again, cousin, but don't you think it would be selfish of me to seek him out merely to get my marriage annulled? Surely the Emperor —'

Adélaïde dapped her hands.

'But what a good idea! Why did I not think of it? Of course, the Emperor is the very man!' She went on in an altered tone: 'The Emperor on whose orders the Pope was put under arrest by General Radet, the Emperor who kept the Pope a prisoner at Savona, the Emperor who was excommunicated by His Holiness last June in his splendid bull *"Quum memoranda"* – the Emperor is the very man we need to present a request for annulment to the Pope. He could not even procure the dissolution of his own marriage to that poor, sweet Joséphine!'

'Oh,' Marianne said, crestfallen. 'I had forgotten. But do you really think my godfather … ?'

'Will get you your dissolution for the asking? I don't doubt it for an instant. We have only to discover the dear Abbé and all will be well. Liberty!'

Adélaïde's rush of enthusiasm inclined Marianne to attribute some of her optimism to the champagne, but there was no doubt the old lady was right and that their best recourse in this situation was to rely on the Abbé de Chazey, although it was disappointing to discover a field in which Napoleon was not all-powerful. But how soon could the Abbé be found?


Fouché snapped shut the lid of his snuff-box, restored it to his pocket and shook out his lace ruffles with old-world grace.

'If, as you seem to think, this Abbé de Chazay forms one of the entourage of Pius VII, he must be at Savona and it will be an easy matter to trace him, and bring him to Paris. Your husband, however, is another matter.'

'Is it so difficult?' Marianne said. 'If he and this Vicomte d'Aubécourt are one and the same?'

The Minister of Police had risen to his feet and was pacing the room slowly, his hands clasped behind his back. His progress had none of the Emperor's nervous energy. It was slow and thoughtful but, even so, Marianne found herself wondering why men felt it necessary to walk about in order to conduct a conversation. Was it a fashion started by Napoleon?

Fouché's perambulations brought him to a stop in front of the portrait of the Marquis d'Asselnat which brooded arrogantly over the gold and yellow harmonies of the *salon*. He stared at it for a while, as if waiting for an answer, then turned his heavy eyes on Marianne.

'Are you so sure?' he said slowly. 'There is no evidence to connect Lord Cranmere with the Vicomte d'Aubécourt.'

'I know that. But I should at least like to see him, to meet him.'

'Even yesterday, that would have been simple. The handsome Vicomte lodged in the rue de la Grange-Batelière, at the Hôtel Plinon. Since his arrival here he has been a constant visitor at the house of Madame Édmond de Périgord, having come armed with a letter of introduction from the Comte de Montrond who is at present in Anvers.'

Marianne nodded, a frown forming between her eyebrows. She experienced a twinge of doubt. Ever since the night before she had been acting on the assumption that Francis was the Vicomte d'Aubécourt. She had clung to the idea, as though to prove to herself that she was not suffering from hallucinations. But Francis as a visitor in the house of Talleyrand's niece? Madame de Périgord, by birth Princess of Courlande, and the richest heiress in all Europe, had been a real friend to Marianne when she was living as reader to Madame de Talleyrand. It was true that Marianne was not in her friend's company so often that she was familiar with all her connections, but she felt that she would have known if Lord Cranmere had begun to form part of Dorothée de Périgord's court.

'If it was at Anvers,' she said at last, 'that the Vicomte became acquainted with Monsieur de Montrond, that proves nothing. There have always been close ties between the Flemish and the English.'

'I agree, but I doubt whether, as an exile under police surveillance, the Comte de Montrond would dare to cover for an Englishman disguised as a Fleming, and therefore a spy. Surely, that would be taking too great a risk? I do not doubt that Montrond is capable of anything but only if it is worth his while and, if I remember rightly, the man you married gambled away your fortune on the spot. I have little reliance on Montrond's goodwill unless bolstered by financial incentives.'

It was all too logical, as Marianne was obliged to concede. Very well, Francis might not be concealing his identity under the name of the Flemish Vicomte, but he was certainly in Paris. At last, with a weary sigh, she said: 'Have you heard of any vessel come secretly from England?'

Fouché nodded. 'An English cutter put in by night a week ago on the isle of Hoedic to pick up a "friend" of yours, the Baron de Saint-Hubert, whom you met in the quarries of Chaillot. Naturally, I did not hear of it until after the cutter had sailed out again, but the fact that it took someone off does not mean that it could not previously have landed another passenger from England.'

'How can we find out? Is ...' Marianne paused, struck by a sudden thought which made her green eyes shine. Then she went on, more quietly: 'Is Nicolas Mallerousse still in Plymouth? He might know something about the movements of ships.'

The Minister of Police grinned wickedly and made her a mocking bow.

'Do me the kindness of believing that I thought of our worthy Black Fish long before you did, my dear. However, it so happens that just at present I am ignorant of the whereabouts of our remarkable son of the seas. There has been no news of him for a month past.'

'For a month?' Marianne exclaimed in a voice of anxious protest. 'One of your agents! And you are not worried about him?'

'No. If he had been caught or hanged, I should have known. Black Fish has disappeared because he has found out something. He is following a trail, that is all. You must not worry so. Faith, my dear, I shall be thinking that you have a genuine kindness for your adopted uncle!'

'You may believe it,' Marianne told him curtly. 'Black Fish was the first person to offer me the hand of friendship when I was in trouble, without asking anything in return. That I cannot forget.'

The implication was sufficiently obvious. Fouché coughed, and held his handkerchief to his lips, then took a pinch of snuff from his tortoiseshell box and finally changed the subject abruptly, saying: 'At all events, my dear, you may rest assured that I have put my best sleuths on the trail of your phantom in blue: Inspector Pâques and my agent Desgrée. They are making inquiries about all foreigners in Paris even now.'

Marianne asked hesitantly, reddening a little at her own persistence: 'Have they – have they called on the Vicomte d'Aubécourt?'

Fouché's expression did not alter. Not a muscle moved in his pale face.

'They began with him. But the Vicomte left the Hôtel Plinon yesterday with all his luggage, leaving no address.'

Marianne sighed. Unless he showed himself, Francis was now about as easy to trace as a needle in a haystack. And yet he must be found at all costs. But to whom could she turn when Fouché confessed himself beaten?

As though he had read her thoughts, the minister gave her a thin smile and bowed to take his leave.

'Do not look so downhearted, Marianne, my dear. You know me well enough to know that I dislike admitting defeat. And so, without echoing Monsieur de Calonne's words to Marie-Antoinette: "If it is possible, it is done already, if impossible, it shall be done," I will be more modest and merely advise you not to lose hope.'

Despite Fouché's soothing words, and Napoleon's kisses and assurances, Marianne spent the next few days in a state of gloom and ill-temper. Nothing and no one could please her and herself least of all. Tormented, day and night, by the fires of jealousy, she prowled about her great house like a trapped animal. Yet she dreaded going out even more. At that moment she hated Paris.

The capital was a hive of preparations for the imperial wedding. Everywhere was festooned with garlands, streamers and fairy lights. On every public building, the black eagle of Austria nestled alongside the gold eagles of the Empire with a familiarity that raised growls from the veterans of Austerlitz and Wagram. With the aid of endless buckets of water and vigorous wielding of brooms Paris put on her holiday dress. The coming event hung over the city, fluttered in the depths of its innumerable streets, echoed through barracks and drawing-rooms to the music of fanfares and violins, filled shops and stores where the imperial portraits, presided over piles of food and bales of silks and laces, brooded over tailors' and barbers' shops and dawdled with the idlers along the *quais* beside the Seine, where preparations for firework displays and illuminations were already under way. Most of all, it filled the sentimental hearts of the Parisian working girls for whom the Emperor had been suddenly transformed from the invincible god of battles to a Prince Charming. To Marianne, so much fuss made for a wedding which brought her nothing but grief seemed shocking and only depressed her more. Paris, which had lain at her feet a moment before, was now making ready to purr like a great, tame cat for the benefit of the hated Austrian, and she felt doubly betrayed. She preferred to stay shut up indoors, waiting for goodness knows what: perhaps for the peals of bells and salvoes of guns that would tell her the worst had happened and the enemy was inside the city?

The court had left for Compiègne, where the Archduchess Marie-Louise was expected on the twenty-seventh or twenty-eighth of March but the round of parties still went on. Marianne, now one of the most sought-after women in Paris, was showered with invitations but nothing could have persuaded her to accept. She would not even go to Talleyrand's, in fact there least of all because she could not bring herself to face the subtle irony of his smile. On the pretext of a non-existent cold, she stayed obstinately at home.

Aurélien, the porter at the Hôtel d'Asselnat, had strict instructions: except for the Minister of Police or anyone sent by him and of Madame Hamelin, his mistress would see no one.

For her part, Fortunée Hamelin disapproved strongly of this behaviour. With her insatiable love of amusement, she was at a loss to understand her friend's voluntary retreat from the world merely because her lover was about to contract a marriage of state. Five days after Marianne's historic recital, she renewed her attack on her friend.

'Anyone would think you had been widowed or deserted!' she declared roundly. 'When in fact your position is a most enviable one. You are the adored and all-powerful mistress of Napoleon, yet without being a slave to him. This marriage releases you from the yoke of fidelity. Good God, you are young and ravishingly lovely, you are famous ... and Paris is full of attractive men asking nothing better than to help you while away your solitude! I know at least a dozen who are wild for you. Shall I tell you their names?'

'No need,' protested Marianne, who found herself both shocked and amused by Fortunée's complete absence of moral principles. 'No need. I do not want to meet any other men. If I did,' she added, pointing to a small rosewood writing-table on which was a pile of letters, 'I would only have to answer some of those.' The post brought them every day, along with great masses of flowers.

'Don't you even open them?'

Fortunée swooped on the pile and, using a slender Italian stiletto for a paper-knife, slit open several of the letters and, after a rapid glance at the contents, found the signatures and sighed.

'This is pitiful! My poor dear, half the Imperial Guard is in love with you! Look here: Canouville ... Tobriant ... Radziwill ... even Poniatowski! Flahaut, the exquisite Flahaut himself is your slave! And you sit by the fire sighing at the clouds and the rain while his majesty rides to meet his Archduchess! Do you know who you remind me of? Joséphine!'

The name of the repudiated Empress managed to get through the wall of bad temper with which Marianne had wilfully surrounded herself. Her green eyes flickered for a moment to her friend's face.

'Why should you say that? Have you seen her? What is she doing?'

'I saw her last night. She is still in a wretched state. She should have left Paris days ago. Napoleon has given her the title of Duchess of Navarre and the vast estates around Évreux that go with it ... on the unspoken understanding, naturally, that she withdraws there when the wedding takes place. But she has returned to the Elysée and is clinging to it like a drowning woman. Day after day goes by and Joséphine is still in Paris. Yet she must go in the end, so why delay?'

'I think I understand her,' Marianne said with a melancholy smile. 'And isn't it hard to take her house away from her and send her away to a strange place, like an object one has no further use for? Surely, he might have left her Malmaison when she loves it so?'

'Too close to Paris. Especially when the daughter of the Austrian

Emperor is arriving. As for understanding her,' Fortunée continued, 'I don't know that you should. Joséphine is clinging to the shadow of what she was – but she has already found consolation for her bruised heart.'

'What do you mean?'

Madame Hamelin burst out laughing, displaying the brightness of her small, sharp teeth. Then she sank into a chair beside her friend, enveloping them both in an overpowering scent of roses.

'That she has done what you should do, my pet, what any woman in her right mind would do in her case – and in yours. She has taken a lover!'

Too dumbfounded to answer, Marianne merely stared at Fortunée, making the gossip-loving Creole almost purr with satisfaction.

'You need not look so shocked,' she said. 'In my view, Joséphine was quite right. Why should she be forced to spend her nights alone, which was already her fate for the most part at the Tuileries? She has lost a throne and found love. And if you ask me, it is no more than justice.'

'Perhaps. Who is he?'

'Count Lancelot de Turpin-Crissé, a magnificent, golden-haired Greek god of about thirty. He is her chamberlain which makes it more convenient.'

Marianne was forced to smile at her friend's comments.

'Novels are not always right, you see,' Fortunée went on. 'Why don't you do the same? Find someone to console you. Wait, I'll help you —' She was making for the writing-table again but Marianne stopped her with a gesture.

'No. It is no good. I don't want some young man muttering inanities into my ear. I love him too much, don't you see?'

'What does that matter?' Fortunée persisted. 'I adore Montrond but if I had to remain faithful to him all the time he is in Anvers, I should have gone mad by now.'

Marianne abandoned the attempt to make her friend see her point of view. Fortunée's warm-blooded nature made her more in love with love than with men. The tale of her lovers was endless, the latest being the financier Ouvrard who, if his looks were inferior to those of the handsome Casimir de Montrond, amply made up for this deficiency by a vast fortune in which Madame Hamelin was revelling with innocent enjoyment.

Marianne said with a sigh: 'Despite this marriage, I would not break with the Emperor.' Thinking that this would be an argument Fortunée could understand, she added quickly: 'He would be sure to hear of it and would never forgive me. Besides, let me remind you that somewhere I have a husband who may reappear at any minute.'

With an instant change of mood, Fortunée returned to her seat by

Marianne and asked seriously: 'You have heard nothing?'

'Nothing. Only a note from Fouché last night telling me he had found no trace. Even the Vicomte d'Aubécourt seems to have vanished. Yet I believe Fouché is really looking for him. And Arcadius is scouring Paris and he knows the city as well as any professional sleuth.'

'It is odd, all the same —'

The door of the *salon* opened as she spoke and, as if conjured up by Marianne's words, Arcadius de Jolival appeared and bowed gracefully to the two ladies. He held a letter in his hand. He was dressed, as ever, with exquisite taste in a blend of olive green and grey relieved by the snowy whiteness of his shirt-front, above which twinkled the bright-eyed inquisitive countenance, with its small moustache and goatee, of Marianne's indispensable friend.

Fortunée greeted him amicably. 'Our friend has been telling me how you spend your time scouring the Paris underworld, yet here you are looking for all the world as if you have just sprung from a bandbox!'

'Today,' Arcadius said, 'I have been nowhere more dreadful than Frascati's, eating a great many ices and listening to the chatter of a number of pretty girls. My greatest peril was from a pineapple sorbet which Madame Récamier let slip within an inch of my pantaloons.'

'Still no news?' Marianne's strained face formed a striking contrast to the smiling looks of her companions. Ignoring the anxiety in her voice, Jolival cast the letter he held negligently on to the pile of those already waiting and subjected the cameo ring on his left hand to a critical scrutiny.

'None,' he said casually. 'The man in blue seems to have vanished into thin air like the genie in the Persian fables. I did meet the director of the Théâtre Feydeau, however, and he is somewhat surprised to have heard nothing from you since Monday evening's triumph.'

'I sent a message that I was unwell,' Marianne interrupted pettishly. 'That ought to have satisfied him.'

'Unfortunately, it did not. Put yourself in his place. The man discovers a new star of the first magnitude, only to have her vanish instantly. He is full of plans for you, each more Austrified than the last, naturally. He means to put on *Die Entführung aus dem Serail* followed by a concert composed entirely of *lieder* and —'

'Impossible,' Marianne snapped. 'Tell the man that to begin with I am not a regular member of the company of the Opera Comique. I was engaged for that one performance only —'

'As our friend well knows,' Arcadius sighed. 'Especially since he is aware of the other offers that have been made to you. Picard wants you for the Opera, for the celebrated *Bardes* which so delighted the Emperor, and Spontini makes your – what shall I say? – your Italianate quality his excuse for demanding you for Paesiello's *Barber of Seville* with the Italian company. Then there are the *salons* ...'

'That's enough!' Marianne interrupted him irritably. 'I want to hear no more of the theatre for the present. I am quite incapable of working. I may confine myself to concerts.'

'I think it is better not to plague her,' Fortunée intervened at this point. 'She is in no state to bear it.'

She rose and kissed her friend affectionately before going on: 'Are you sure you will not sup with me tonight? Ouvrard is bringing some excellent company – including some very pretty young men.'

'No, really. I don't want to see anyone except yourself, and I don't feel frivolous. Come again soon.'

While Arcadius was seeing Madame Hamelin to her carriage, Marianne threw a cushion on to the floor in front of the fire and sank on to it with a weary sigh. She felt chilled and wondered if from pretending to be ill she was really becoming so. But the sickness was all in her heart, racked by doubts, anxieties and jealousy. Outside, a cold, wet night was setting in, so much in tune with Marianne's own mood that for a moment she glanced almost gratefully at the dark windows framed in gold damask curtains. Why must they talk to her of work? She was like a bird, only able to sing when her heart was light. Besides, she had no wish to fall into the conventional pattern of opera singers. Perhaps the truth was that she had no real vocation for the theatre. The offers made to her held no temptation. Or was it the absence of the man she loved that had caused this curious reluctance to accept?

Her gaze wandered from the window to the hearth and came to rest on the portrait that hung above it. Again, she shivered. All at once she seemed to read in the handsome colonel's dark eyes a kind of ironic pity, not unmixed with contempt for the wretched creature sitting at his feet. In the warm glow of the candlelight, the Marquis d'Asselnat seemed to be stepping out of his smoky background to shame his daughter for proving unworthy of him and herself. The silent condemnation of the portrait was so clear that Marianne blushed. She muttered: 'You cannot understand. Your own love was so simple that I dare say to die together seemed to you a logical conclusion, the perfect consummation. But for me –'

Her attempt to justify herself was interrupted by the sound of Arcadius's soft footfall. He stood for a moment watching the slim figure in black velvet, a dark spot in the bright room, even lovelier perhaps in melancholy sadness than in the fullness of joy. The firelight fell on her high cheekbones and awakened a gleam of gold in her green eyes.

'You must never look back,' he told her softly, 'or look to the past for counsel. Your empire lies before you.'

25

He trod briskly over to the writing-table, picked up the letter he had brought with him and held it out to Marianne.

'You should at least read this one. A courier, mud to the eyebrows, was handing it to your porter when I came in. He said it was urgent. He looked as if he had travelled a long way in bad weather.'

Marianne's heart missed a beat. Could this be news from Compiègne at last? Snatching the letter, she glanced hurriedly at the superscription. It told her nothing. The writing was strange to her, and the seal was plain black. Nervously, she slipped her finger underneath the wafer and opened the missive. It was unsigned and contained only one short paragraph.

'If the Signorina Maria Stella will condescend to come on the night of Tuesday the twenty-seventh to the chateau of Braine-sur-Vesle she will be conferring untold happiness upon her ardent admirer. The name of the domain is De la Folie and folly perhaps is the presumption of him who will await her there. Prudence and discretion.'

The letter was strange and stranger still the appointed meeting place. Without a word, Marianne handed the letter to Arcadius and watched him raise one eyebrow as he glanced at the contents.

'Odd,' was his comment, 'but not incomprehensible.'

'What do you mean?'

'That now that the Archduchess is actually on French soil, the Emperor is obliged to exercise the utmost discretion. And that the village of Braine-sur-Vesle is on the road between Rheims and Soissons – and it is at Soissons that the new Empress is to spend the night of the twenty-seventh.'

'You think the letter comes from him?'

'Who else would ask you to meet him in that way in such a place? I think—' Arcadius paused, reluctant to name the man whose identity must be concealed. 'I think he means to give you the final proof of his love by spending a few moments with you at the very moment of arrival of the woman he is marrying for reasons of state. That should allay your fears.'

Marianne needed no further persuasion. Her eyes were sparkling and her cheeks on fire, her whole being absorbed in her love, and she could think of nothing but that in a little while now she would be in Napoleon's arms again. Arcadius was right. Despite all his elaborate caution, he was giving her this one, great, wonderful token of his love.

'I will set out tomorrow,' she announced. Tell Gracchus to have my horse ready.'

Will you not take a carriage? The distance is nearly a hundred miles and the weather appalling.'

'I am advised to be discreet,' she smiled. 'A single rider will attract less attention than a smart carriage with a coachman and outriders. I am an excellent horsewoman, you know.'

'So am I,' Jolival retorted. 'I will tell Gracchus to saddle two horses. I am going with you.'

'Is there any need? You don't think – ?'

'I think you are a young woman and the roads are none too safe. Braine is only a village and this rendezvous of yours is to take place after dark in a place not known to me. You must not be thinking I suspect – well, you know who – but I shall not leave your side until I see you in good hands. After that, I shall find a bed for myself at the inn.'

His tone admitted no argument and Marianne did not insist. All things considered, she would be glad of Arcadius's company on a journey that would take three days there and back. But she could not help thinking that it was all rather complicated and would have been much easier if the Emperor had taken her to Compiègne and installed her in a house in the town. However, rumour had it that the Princess Pauline Borghese was at Compiègne with her brother and that she had her favourite lady-in-waiting with her: the very same Christine de Mathis who had preceded Marianne in Napoleon's affections.

*What am I thinking?'* Marianne asked herself suddenly. *I am seeing rivals everywhere. I must be jealous. I will have to watch myself.*

The sound of the front door slamming shut gave her thoughts another turn. It was Adélaïde returning from the evening service which she attended on most days, less out of piety, in Marianne's secret belief, than to take a good look at her neighbours. Mademoiselle d'Asselnat had a cat-like curiosity which ensured that she always had some titbits of gossip and observation to bring home which proved that her Maker had not held her undivided attention.

Taking the hand Arcadius held out to her, Marianne got to her feet and smiled.

'Here is Adélaïde,' she smiled. 'We shall have all the latest gossip while we dine.'

# CHAPTER TWO
# A Little Country Church

Sometime the next afternoon, Marianne and Arcadius dismounted before the inn of the Soleil d'Or at Braine. The weather was horrible: a steady downpour had been drowning the country round about since daybreak, and despite their heavy cloaks, the two riders were drenched to the skin and in urgent need of shelter and something hot to drink.

They had been travelling since the previous day, making as much speed as possible; Arcadius wanted to see the lie of the land before the time set for the strange meeting. They took two rooms at the inn, the one modest hostelry the village boasted, and then made their way to the coffee room, empty of customers at this hour, to partake respectively of a bowl of soup and a cup of mulled wine. In a little while, an hour or two at most, the new Empress of the French was to pass through Braine on her way to Soissons where she was to dine and stay for the night.

Rain or no rain, the whole village was out of doors, dressed in its holiday best, gathered under the garlands and the fairy lights that were sizzling out one by one. A dais draped in the colours of France and Austria had been set up near the church where the local dignitaries would be taking their places under umbrellas to address the new Empress as she passed through. Through the open door of the fine old church came the sound of the choir practising its hymn of welcome to the cavalcade. Only Marianne felt more miserable than ever, although her gloom was shot through with curiosity. When the time came, she would go out with the rest to catch a glimpse of the woman she could not help thinking of as her rival, that daughter of the enemy who, simply because she was born on the steps of a throne, dared to steal her place beside the man she loved.

Unusually for him, Arcadius was as silent as Marianne. He leaned his elbows on the coarse-grained wooden table, polished by generations of other elbows, staring into the deep purple wine steaming in the pottery bowl before him. He seemed so abstracted that Marianne was impelled to ask what he was thinking.

'About your assignation for tonight,' he told her and he sighed.

'Now that we are here, it seems stranger than ever. So strange that I am beginning to wonder if the message can have come from the Emperor.'

'Who else? And why not from him?'

'What do you know of the chateau of *La Folie?*'

'Why, nothing. I have never been here before.'

'I have, but so long ago that I had almost forgotten. The landlord refreshed my memory just now when I called for our order. The chateau of *La Folie*, my dear, is the charming pile you may perceive from where we sit. It seems to me a rather sombre setting for an amorous tryst.'

As he spoke, he pointed to a wooded eminence rising steeply from the far bank of the River Vesle where the massive, half-ruined shape of a thirteenth-century castle loomed in medieval decay through the grey curtain of rain. Walls blackened by time and warfare presented a sinister appearance which the budding green of the surrounding trees was powerless to dispel. Marianne frowned, conscious of a strange wave of foreboding.

'That Gothic ruin? Is that the castle I am to visit?'

'That and no other. What do you think of it?'

For answer, Marianne stood up and swept up the gloves she had placed on the table by her place.

'That it may well be a trap. I have seen them before. Remember the circumstances of our first meeting, my dear Jolival, and our tender treatment at the hands of Fanchon Fleur-de-Lys in the quarries of Chaillot. Will you go and fetch the horses? We'll pay a visit to this unlikely love nest here and now, although I would give much to be mistaken.'

She had been in a strange mood ever since leaving Paris. All along the road that was bringing her nearer her lover, Marianne had been unable to repress a sense of reluctance and uneasiness which may have been because the all-important letter had not been written in his own hand, and because the place appointed was on the very road the Archduchess must take. This last objection had been partly done away with at Soissons where she learned that the place where the Emperor was to meet his betrothed for the first time, on the afternoon of the twenty-eighth, was at Pontarcher, some seven or eight miles from Soissons on the road to Compiègne, yet not, after all, so very far from Braine. Napoleon would have plenty of time to rejoin his suite early in the morning.

Now, the prospect of activity was doing her good, dragging her out of the slough of uncertainty and vague disquiet in which she had wallowed for the past week. While Arcadius went for the horses, she drew from her belt the small pistol which she had taken the precaution of bringing with her from Paris. It was one of those which Napoleon himself had given her, knowing her familiarity with fire-arms. Coolly, she checked the priming. If Fanchon Fleur-de-Lys, the Chevalier de Bruslart or any of their unpleasant followers were waiting for her behind the ancient walls of *La Folie*, they would be in for something of a surprise.

She was about to leave the table which stood near the room's only window when something drew her attention to the other side of the street. A large, black travelling coach, bearing no arms on the panel but drawn by a team of very fine greys, was drawn up outside the blacksmith's shop. The coachman, muffled in a vast, green overcoat, was standing with the smith by one of the lead horses and both men had their heads bent over what was no doubt a faulty shoe. There was nothing unusual in this sight but it held Marianne's attention. It seemed to her that the coachman was familiar.

She leaned forward to catch a glimpse of the occupants of the coach but could see nothing beyond two vague, but undoubtedly masculine, figures. Then, suddenly, she bit back a cry. One of the men had leaned forward for a second, probably to see how the coachman was getting on, revealing through the window a pale, clear-cut profile surmounted by a black cocked hat, a profile too deeply engraved in Marianne's heart for her to fail to recognize him. It was the Emperor.

What was he doing in that coach? Was he already on his way to the rendezvous at *La Folie*? If that were so, why was he waiting in the coach for the shoe to be repaired? This struck Marianne as so improbable that her sudden gladness at seeing him, at the very moment when she was losing faith in this mysterious meeting, was short lived. She had seen Napoleon in the coach make a quick, frowning movement, the gesture of a man in a hurry. But where was he going at such speed?

Marianne had no time to ask herself more questions. The smith stepped back, the coachman climbed back to his box and cracked his whip. With a clatter of harness, the vehicle was away. In a moment Marianne was outside and found herself face to face with Arcadius who was leading out the horses.

Without a word of explanation, Marianne sprang into the saddle, rammed the felt hat which covered the coiled mass of her hair hard down over her eyes, and shot away in pursuit of the travelling coach which was already disappearing into the muddy spray thrown up behind it. Arcadius followed automatically but when he realized that they were travelling in the opposite direction from *La Folie*, he spurred his horse to catch up with the girl.

'Hey! Where are we off to?'

'That coach —' Marianne flung into the wind over her shoulder. 'I want to know where it is going.'

'What for?'

'The Emperor is inside …'

It took Jolival a moment to assimilate this news, then, abruptly leaning forward in the saddle, he seized hold of Marianne's bridle and, with a strength surprising in a man of his slight build, succeeded in bringing her horse to a walk while at the same time retaining control of his own mount.

'What do you think you're doing?' Marianne flung at him furiously. 'Are you mad?'

'Do you want his majesty to see that he is being followed? On a straight road we can hardly miss him. If, on the other hand, we were to take the path you see there on the right, we should be on a short cut which will get us to Courcelles before the Emperor.'

'What is Courcelles?'

'Merely the next village. But if I am not mistaken, the Emperor is simply going to meet his bride, which he will do before very long.'

'Is that what you think? Oh, if I could be sure —'

Marianne had gone white to the lips. The frightful pangs of jealousy returned, more fiercely tormenting than ever. Arcadius nodded with a small, unhappy smile.

'But you are, quite sure. Be honest with yourself, Marianne. You know where he is going and you want to see her for yourself first, and then witness their meeting.'

Marianne gritted her teeth and looked away, turning her horse's head at the same time towards the narrow lane. Her face had hardened but she did not contradict him.

'Yes, it is true. And nothing and no one shall stop me.'

'I did not think of stopping you. Come if you must, but you are making a mistake. It can only bring you useless suffering.'

The two riders resumed their gallop, regardless of the mud and rain. They followed the track along the course of the Vesle, now swollen to twice its normal volume by the torrential rains. The weather seemed to get worse as they advanced. The fine drizzle had become a solid downpour, out of a dismal, lowering sky. The riverside track proved quicker, even so, and it was not long before the first houses of Courcelles came in sight.

Marianne and Arcadius emerged on to the high road in time to see the coach racing towards them, its great wheels throwing up fountains of spray.

'Come,' Arcadius said. 'We must not stay here, unless you want him to see you.'

He was trying to draw her aside into the little church which stood close by but Marianne would not be drawn. Her eyes were riveted on the approaching vehicle and she was conscious of a dreadful urge to stay where she was and let him see her, to meet that masterful gaze and read in it – just what precisely, she could not have said. But there was no time for further thought. The coach swerved suddenly, it may have been on account of the already faulty shoe, and the off-side fore wheel caught the steps of the small shrine erected at the entrance to the village. The wheel was wrenched off and Marianne cried out involuntarily, but the coachman, acting with great skill, managed to bring his horses under control and stop the coach.

Two men jumped out. One was tall and dressed with a degree of finery strangely out of keeping with the weather. The other was all too easily recognizable. Both were furiously angry. Marianne saw the taller of the two men point towards the church, then both began to run quickly through the rain.

Arcadius seized her arm. 'Now come,' he told her firmly, 'or you will come face to face with him. They appear to intend to take shelter here while the coachman goes in search of a wheelwright.'

This time she suffered him to lead her where he would. Jolival hurried her out of sight round the back of the church. Here there was a clump of trees, to one of which they tethered their horses. Arcadius guessed that since the Emperor was stranded here, nothing would persuade Marianne to ride on. She had already spotted a small door in the side wall of the building.

'Come inside,' she said. We shall be able to see and hear without being seen.'

Inside the little chapel the air was cold and damp, smelling strongly of mildew. It fell about their wet shoulders like a leaden cloak.

'We'll catch our deaths in here!' Jolival muttered but Marianne took no notice. The place was in semi-darkness and seemed to have fallen into almost complete disuse. Numerous broken window-panes had been replaced with oiled paper. In one corner there was a heap of broken pieces of statuary; only two or three pews remained and the pulpit and churchwardens' pew were draped in cobwebs. But the main door beneath the tiny gallery was slightly open, allowing a view of what was happening in the porch as Napoleon and his companion hurried in out of the rain. A dipped, impatient, all-too-familiar voice broke the silence of the little church.

'We'll wait here. How much farther, do you think?'

'Not far,' the other man answered. He was a large, floridly handsome fellow with brown, curly hair. At present he was occupied in doing his best to shield a vast, plumed hat beneath his cloak. 'But why wait here with water dripping down our necks from these abominably leaky, rustic gutters when we might seek shelter in some farm-house?'

'Your stay in Naples has done you no good, Murat,' the Emperor said mockingly. 'Are you frightened of a few drops of rain?'

'Not for myself, but for my dress. I shall be obliged to greet the Empress wearing sodden plumes, like a wilting palm tree!'

'If you dressed more plainly, you would have nothing to worry about. You should do as I do.'

'Your style of dress is deplorably sober, sire, as I have always said. You cannot go to meet an Archduchess dressed like a shopkeeper.'

This remarkable exchange gave Marianne time to regain control of herself. The breathless pounding of her heart had stopped and jealousy was giving way to sheer feminine curiosity. So this was the famous Murat, the King of Naples and the Emperor's brother-in-law. Despite his impressive height and the splendours of the blue uniform glimpsed beneath the enveloping black cloak, Marianne thought there was a vulgarity in his features and an excessive swagger in his bearing. He might be the finest horseman in the Empire but if that were so he should take care never to be seen without his horse. On foot, he seemed only half a man. But Napoleon was speaking again.

'I told you; I wish to take the Archduchess by surprise and show myself to her without frills. And I want to see her in her plain travelling dress. We'll step out into the road when the Cortège comes in sight.'

A sigh loud enough to reach Marianne's ears indicated Murat's opinion of this plan but he said resignedly: 'Very well, we'll wait.'

'Now don't look so gloomy. All this is very romantic, you know. Must I remind you that your own wife is with Marie-Louise? Aren't you glad to see Caroline again?'

'Oh yes, but we have been man and wife long enough for the first shock to have worn off. Besides —'

'Hush! Don't you hear anything?'

All the occupants of the church, the watchers and the watched, strained their ears. There was a rumbling in the distance, like an approaching storm, still faint and very far away but coming slowly nearer.

'Ah yes,' Murat agreed, with evident relief. 'That must be the coaches. Yes, surely —' The King of Naples plunged bravely out into the rain and after a quick glance along the road came running back, crying: 'I can see the leaders of the escorting hussars! Your bride approaches, sire!'

In an instant, Napoleon had joined him, while Marianne, drawn by a curiosity she could not help, crept forward into the church doorway. She was in no danger of being seen. The Emperor's attention was all on the long string of carriages now coming at a smart pace down the road towards them, led by a mounted escort in colours of blue and mauve. Marianne could feel the tension in him from where she stood, and it came to her suddenly how much it meant to him, the arrival of this daughter of the Habsburgs to whom he looked for his heir and through whom he would ally himself at last with the blood royal of Europe. To fight back her growing anguish, she strove to remember his contemptuous words: 'I am marrying a womb.' It was no good. Everything in her lover's attitude (gossip even said that he had insisted on learning to dance in his new bride's honour) betrayed how impatiently he had been waiting for the moment when his future wife would come to him. Even this schoolboy prank in which he had indulged in the company of his brother-in-law! He could not bear to wait for the next day's official, ceremonial meeting at Pontarcher.

Napoleon stood in the centre of the road and the hussars were already reining in their mounts at the sight of his familiar figure, crying: 'The Emperor! It is the Emperor!' The words were echoed a moment later by the chamberlain, M. de Seyssel, who came riding up, but Napoleon ignored them all. Oblivious of the driving rain, he was running towards the big coach drawn by eight steaming horses and tugging open the door without waiting for it to be opened for him. Marianne caught a glimpse of two women inside before one leaned forward and exclaimed: 'His majesty, the Emperor!'

But Napoleon, it was clear, had eyes only for her companion, a tall, fair girl with a pink and white complexion and round, somewhat protuberant blue eyes, now bulging more than usual with alarm. Her pouting lips were trembling as she tried to smile. She was dressed in a plain green velvet cloak but on her head, she wore a startling confection of multicoloured feathers that resembled the crest of a moulting parrot.

Marianne, standing a few yards away devouring the Archduchess with her eyes, experienced a fierce spasm of joy at the realization that Marie-Louise, if not precisely ugly, was certainly no more than passable. Her complexion was good enough but her blue eyes held no intelligence and the famous Habsburg lip combined with an overlong nose to produce a face lacking in charm. And then she was so badly dressed! She was fat, too, too fat for a young girl: in ten years she would be gross. Already there was a heaviness about her.

Eagerly, Marianne looked at the Emperor who was standing with his feet in a puddle gazing at his future wife, trying to gauge his reactions. Surely, he must be disappointed. He would bow formally, kiss his bride's hand, and then return to his own carriage which was already undergoing repairs — but no, his voice rang out gaily:

'Madame, I am delighted to see you!'

Oblivious of his drenched clothes, he sprang into the coach and caught the fair girl in his arms, kissing her several times with an enthusiasm that drew a prim smile from the other occupant of the vehicle, a pretty, blonde woman whose pearly skin and dimpled charms were not destroyed by the fact that her face was over-fleshed and her neck too short. The innocence of her expression was belied by a sardonic glint in her eye which Marianne did not quite like. This must be Napoleon's sister, Caroline Murat, one of the most notorious harpies in court circles. Her husband, having first kissed the Archduchess's hand, returned alone to the plain travelling coach while Napoleon settled himself in the seat facing the two women and addressed the coachman who still stood beside the vehicle with a beaming smile.

'Drive on to Compiègne, and don't spare the horses!'

'But sire,' the Queen of Naples protestes, 'we are expected at Soissons. There is to be a supper, a reception.'

'Then they can eat their supper without us. It is my wish that my lady wife spends tonight in her own house! Drive on.'

Caroline's lips tightened at the snub but she retired into her corner and the carriage moved off, affording Marianne a last glimpse through her tears of Napoleon smiling blissfully at his bride. A shout of command and the escort quickened their pace to a trot. One by one, the eighty-three vehicles of the new Empress's train moved past the church. Marianne leant on the wet stones of the Gothic porch and watched them unseen, so deep in her own miserable thoughts that Arcadius had at last to shake her gently to rouse her.

'What now?' he asked. We ought to go straight back to the inn. You are soaked to the skin, and so am I.'

Marianne looked at him strangely.

'We are going to Compiègne …'

'What for?' Jolival sounded suspicious. 'You're up to some foolishness, I don't doubt. What can you do in all this?'

Marianne stamped her foot. 'I wish to go to Compiègne, I tell you. Don't ask me why because I don't know. All I know is that I must go there.'

She was so pale that Arcadius frowned. All the life seemed to have drained from her, leaving only a mechanical creature. To rouse her from her frozen stupor, he objected wildly: 'But what about the rendezvous tonight?'

'That no longer concerns me. He did not make it. Surely you heard? He is going to Compiègne. He does not mean to return to this place. How far are we from Compiègne?'

'About forty miles.'

'You see! To horse, and fast. I want to be there before them.'

As she spoke, she was running towards the trees where they had tethered the horses. Hard on her heels, Arcadius persisted in trying to make her see reason.

'Don't be a fool, Marianne. Come back to Braine and let me go and see who is waiting for you tonight.'

'That does not concern me, I tell you. When will you understand that there is only one person in the world I care about? Besides, it is bound to be a trap. I am certain of that now … But I do not ask you to come with me,' she added cruelly. 'I can very well go alone.'

'Don't talk nonsense.' Arcadius shrugged and cupped his hands to throw her into the saddle. He did not blame her for her ill-temper because he knew what she was suffering at that moment, but it grieved him to see her punishing herself in a situation which she was powerless to alter.

He merely said: 'Very well, let's go if you insist.' Then he sought his own mount.

Without answering, Marianne dug her heels into her horse's sides and the creature shot off, making for the little track along the river. The few people who had emerged to witness the scene went back indoors and Courcelles sank back into its accustomed quiet. The damaged coach, provided with a fresh wheel by the local wheelwright, had also disappeared.

Although it had the advantage of them by several minutes, Marianne and Arcadius emerged on to the main highway at Soissons in time to see the imperial coach pass by at the head of the column, having thundered through the town before the shocked and astonished eyes of the Sous-Préfet, the town council and the military who had waited for hours in the pouring rain merely to have the pleasure of seeing their Emperor dash away under their noses.

'Why is he in such a hurry?' Marianne muttered through clenched teeth. 'Why does he have to be in Compiègne tonight?'

She was swinging into the saddle again after a change of horses at the Hôtel des Postes when she saw the imperial carriage come to a sudden stop. The door opened and the Queen of Naples, recognizable to Marianne by the pink and mauve ostrich feathers adorning her pearl-grey bonnet, stepped out into the road, and marched with an air of offended dignity towards the second coach, the chamberlain trotting at her heels. The steps were let down and, like a queen going into exile, she disappeared within, and the procession continued on its way.

Marianne looked inquiringly at Arcadius. 'What was that about?'

Arcadius was bending over his horse's neck, apparently having some trouble with the bit, and did not answer. Irritated by his silence, Marianne burst out: 'Have the courage to tell me the truth at least, Arcadius! Do you think he wants to be alone with that woman?'

'It is possible,' Jolival conceded cautiously. 'Unless the Queen of Naples has been indulging in one of her unfortunate fits of ill-humour —'

'In the Emperor's presence? Unlikely, I think. Ride fast, my friend. I want to be there when they alight from that coach.'

The mad career began again, splashing through icy puddles, brushing aside the low branches that obscured the unfrequented ways.

It was dark by the time they entered Compiègne and Marianne's teeth were chattering with cold and exhaustion. She kept herself in the saddle only by a prodigious effort of will. Her whole body ached as if she had been thrashed. Even so, they were only moments ahead of the Cortège; the rumble of the eighty-three vehicles had never been out of earshot on that endless ride except at moments when they had plunged deep into woods far off the road.

Now, riding through the brightly-lit streets, decorated from top to bottom, Marianne blinked like a night-bird caught suddenly in the light. The rain had stopped. The news had run through Compiègne that the Emperor was bringing home his bride that very night instead of on the morrow as expected, and in spite of the darkness and the weather all the inhabitants were out in the streets or in the inns. Already a large crowd had gathered outside the railings of the big white palace.

The building glittered in the darkness like a colony of fireflies. A regiment of grenadiers stood to attention in the courtyard, ready to march out and line the streets. Marianne dashed the water that dripped from her hat brim out of her eyes.

'When the soldiers come out, we'll take our chance to make a dash for it,' she said. 'I want to get close to the railings.'

'Marianne, this is madness. We will be trampled and crushed to death! There is no reason why anyone should let us through.'

'No one will even notice. Go and tether the horses and then hurry back.'

As Arcadius hurried back towards the lighted doorway of a large inn, all the bells in the town were already ringing.

The Cortège had reached Compiègne. At the same time a great shout went up in the darkness. The palace gates opened to make way for the solid mass of grenadiers who carved an orderly furrow through the very thickest of the crowd and formed up in a double line to allow a passage for the coaches. Marianne seized her chance and ran, with Jolival on her heels. The backward movement of the crowd was just enough to let her slip behind the guardsmen's backs right up to the palace railings. One or two voices were raised in protest at the impudence of people who pushed themselves forward where they had no right to, but Marianne was oblivious of everything outside her own purpose. Besides, the first of the hussars were already cantering into the square, reining in their sweating horses. A great roar went up from the crowd:

'Long live the Emperor!'

Marianne had climbed on to the low wall at the base of the gilded railings and was clutching at the wet ironwork with both hands. Now there was nothing but a vast, empty space between her and the great staircase lined with footmen in purple livery bearing torches that flickered brightly in the cold air. The palace windows were filled with a brilliant crowd of people, more people were swarming on to the balconies above and an orchestra appeared on the central balcony overlooking the courtyard. Torches were everywhere. The noise was deafening, its volume swelling as the drums began to roll.

Pages, outriders, officers and marshals clattered up the lane between the grenadiers; then came a coach, followed by another, and another, and another. Marianne's heart was beating wildly under her sodden riding-habit. She stared wide-eyed at the carpeted steps, seeing the broad perron below the triangular pediment fill up with ladies in sweeping gowns and tiaras flashing multicoloured jewels, with men in dashing uniforms of red and gold or blue and silver. She made out several Austrian officers, their white dress uniforms a foil for the orders glittering on their chests. Somewhere a clock struck ten.

Then, as the shouting and cheering rose to fever pitch, there came in sight the travelling coach drawn by eight horses which Marianne remembered all too well. The brass band on the balcony struck up a patriotic tune and the vehicle swept through the open gates and described a graceful curve to draw up before the steps. Footmen hurried forward, torch-bearers streamed down into the courtyard, the drums rolled and all the satins and brocades lining the entrance swept the ground in stately reverence. Through a mist of tears, she was no longer able to restrain, Marianne saw Napoleon spring out and turn triumphantly to help the other occupant of the coach with the tender care of a devoted lover. A spasm of rage dried Marianne's tears at the sight of the Archduchess, very red in the face with her absurd, parrot-feathered bonnet askew and a curious suggestion of confusion in her manner.

Standing, Marie-Louise was taller than her bridegroom by half a head. They made an ill-assorted couple, she all soft, Germanic heaviness, he with his pale skin and Roman nose and all the superficial nervous energy he owed to his Mediterranean blood. Perhaps the only thing that did not jar was the great difference in age, for Marie-Louise was too big to convey any impression of delicate youth. Moreover, neither seemed aware of any incongruity. They were gazing at one another with an apparent rapture that made Marianne suddenly long to commit murder. Only a few days ago this man had been making passionate love to her, swearing with all sincerity that she alone possessed his heart: how could he stand there looking at that great blonde cow like a child gazing on his first Christmas present? She ground her teeth and dug her finger-nails into the palms of her hands to stop herself from screaming aloud.

On the other side of the railings, the newcomer was exchanging kisses with the ladies of the imperial family: the exquisite Pauline, barely able to preserve her countenance in the face of that appalling hat; sober Elisa with her stern, classical features; the darkly beautiful Queen of Spain and fair, graceful Queen Hortense, dressed with faultless elegance in a white silk gown and softly-glowing pearls that stood in glaring contrast to the tasteless clothes of the new Empress.

For an instant, Marianne forgot her own grief in wondering what Joséphine's gentle daughter, Hortense, must be thinking, seeing this woman dare to seat herself on her mother's still-warm throne. Surely it was unnecessarily cruel of Napoleon to have forced her to be present to welcome this stranger into a French palace? Unnecessary, yes, but characteristic of the

Emperor. Not for the first time, Marianne realized that his native kindness was sometimes marred by a streak of inhuman coldness.

'Now will you let me take you indoors out of the cold?' Arcadius's friendly voice spoke in her ear. 'Or do you mean to spend the night clinging to these railings? There is nothing more to see.'

Marianne came to herself with a shiver and saw that he was right. Except for the carriages, the grooms and servants already leading the horses away to the stables, the court was empty. The windows were closed and the crowd in the square was drifting slowly, almost regretfully away, like an ebbing tide. The face she turned to Arcadius was still wet with tears.

'You think I am mad, don't you?' she said softly.

He smiled affectionately and slipped a brotherly arm about her shoulders.

'I think you are wonderfully and terribly young. You rush to wound yourself with the blind determination of a frightened bird. When you are older you will learn to avoid the iron spikes that life strews in the path of human beings to tear and wound them, you will learn to keep your eyes and ears shut to preserve your illusions and your peace of mind at all events. But, not yet …'

The hostelry known as the Grand-Cerf was full to bursting point when Marianne and Jolival entered it. At first the landlord, running hither and thither like a frantic chicken, was too busy even to attend to them. In the end Arcadius had to lose patience and arrest the worthy man in mid-career by putting out a hand and getting a firm grip on the knotted handkerchief he wore about his neck.

'Not so fast, my friend. There is a time for everything and now you will kindly listen to me. This lady' – he indicated Marianne who had wearily removed her hat, allowing her hair to tumble down her back – 'is, as you can see, extremely tired, wet and hungry. And since she is a person close to His Majesty you will be well advised to exert yourself to find her a place to rest and dry herself, even if it must be your own bedchamber.'

There was strength in Arcadius's slender fingers and the poor man turned all colours of the rainbow. At the mention of the Emperor, he let out an anguished moan. His short, fat arms flailed desperately and he rolled his eyes at Marianne like a drowning man.

'But, my prince, I have no bedchamber. I was obliged to give up my own room to the aide-de-camp of the Duc de Rovigo. At this very moment Madame Robineau, my wife, is making a bed up for me in the pantry. It would not be proper to offer that to madame – or should I say Her Highness?' His evident distress wrung a smile from Jolival. The unhappy landlord was clearly asking himself feverishly if this could be yet another of the Emperor's sisters: the Bonapartes were so numerous.

'Madame will do, but find something.'

Just as the unfortunate Robineau was contemplating the desirability of unconsciousness as a way out of his dilemma, an Austrian officer in the handsome light brown uniform of the *Landwehr*, who for some moments had been studying Marianne's beautiful pale face with some intentness, approached and clicked his heels. Marianne, her eyes closed, was leaning back against the wall, paying no attention to the discussion.

'Allow me to present myself: Prince Clary und Aldringen, special envoy of his Majesty the Emperor of Austria. I have taken two rooms in this hostelry: the lady will do me a favour by accepting one ...'

Jolival was bowing stiffly as this speech was interrupted by an exclamation from Robineau.

'*Mon Dieu!* Milor' returns so soon! I understood milor' to be dining at the palace?'

The Austrian prince laughed easily. He was a tall man in his early thirties with a fine-boned, intelligent face surmounted by thick fair hair.

'Well, my good landlord, I am afraid you will have to find me something to eat. I do not dine at the palace because there is no dinner at the palace for anyone.'

'Has the cook committed suicide?' inquired Jolival with a smile.

'No, indeed. The whole court was assembled in the great *salon* ready to go in when Marshal Duroc came to tell us their majesties had retired to their own apartments - and there would consequently be no dinner. But if I was cursing a moment ago, now I bless the unexpected turn of events which has allowed me to be of some small service to madame.'

The last words were addressed, of course, to Marianne who, oblivious of the gallantry implied, did not even remember to thank him. One thing only had she grasped from what the Austrian had said and the question it raised in her mind impelled her to ask:

'Their majesties have retired? Does that mean - but surely —' The words died on her lips, but Clary was laughing again.

'I fear it does. It appears that the Emperor's first action was to inquire of his uncle, Cardinal Fesch, if he were truly married - that is, whether the proxy wedding in Vienna made the Archduchess lawfully his wife.'

'And?' Marianne's throat was dry.

'And the Emperor informed the - the Empress that he would shortly do himself the honour of visiting her in her apartments. He merely wanted time to take a bath.'

Every vestige of colour drained from Marianne's face.

'So —' Her voice was so hoarse that the Austrian glanced at her with surprise and Arcadius with alarm.

'So their majesties retired and I promptly came here to your service, madame – but how pale you are! You are not ill? You, Robineau, let your wife at once conduct this lady to my own room, it is the best in the house … Good God!'

This last exclamation was caused by Marianne who, drained of her last ounce of strength by the blow which he had unwittingly dealt her, had suddenly swayed, and would have fallen if Jolival had not caught her in time. A moment later, carried by Clary and preceded by Madame Robineau in a starched muslin cap and armed with a large brass candlestick, Marianne ascended the well-polished staircase of the Grand-Cerf in a state of total unconsciousness.


When, some fifteen minutes later, she emerged from this blissful state, Marianne found herself looking at two faces side by side. One was Arcadius's mouse-like countenance, the other, which was highly-coloured and surmounted by a lofty cap from which some wisps of brown hair escaped, belonged to a woman. Seeing that Marianne had opened her eyes, the woman ceased bathing her temples with vinegar and observed with satisfaction: 'that was better now'.

To Marianne it did not seem in the least better, worse if anything. She was frozen to the marrow yet every now and then she felt bathed in great waves of heat, her teeth were chattering and there was a vice tightening on her head. Even so, the returning memory of what she had heard was enough to make her try and spring up from the bed where they had laid her fully dressed.

'I must go!' she said, trembling so much as she spoke that she could hardly get the words out. 'I want to go home, at once!'

Arcadius put both hands on her shoulders and forced her to lie down again.

'Out of the question. Ride back to Paris in this weather? It would be the death of you, my dear. I am no doctor but I know a little of the subject. I can tell from your flushed cheeks that you have a temperature –'

'What does that matter? I cannot stay here! Can't you hear it – the music, the singing, the fireworks? Can't you hear the whole city going mad with joy because the Emperor has bedded the daughter of his greatest enemy?'

'Marianne, I beg you –' Arcadius was looking at her haggard face in alarm.

Marianne gave a strident peal of laughter that was painful to hear. Brushing Arcadius aside, she jumped off the bed and ran to the window. With a furious gesture she flung back the curtain and stood holding on to it, looking out at the brightly-lit palace which stared challengingly back across the wet and empty square. Inside that building Napoleon was holding that

Austrian woman in his arms, possessing her as he had possessed Marianne, murmuring perhaps the self-same words of love ... Rage and jealousy combined with the fever in her already burning head to torment her with the flames of hell. Her memory recalled with ruthless clarity all her lover's ways, the way he looked – oh, if she could only see through those bland, white walls, if she could only know which of those shuttered windows hid that betrayal of love in which Marianne's own heart was the victim!

'*Mio dolce amore* –' she muttered through clenched teeth. '*Mio dolce amore*! Is he saying that to her, too?'

Arcadius had not dared to go to her or touch her, fearing that in her delirium she would begin to scream aloud. Now he spoke softly to the horrified landlady.

'She is very ill. Fetch a doctor, quickly.'

The woman did not need telling twice. She whisked herself off down the passage in a flurry of starched petticoats while very quietly, one step at a time, Jolival approached Marianne. She did not even see him. Standing taut as a bowstring, and staring with dilated eyes at the great, white building, it seemed to her as if the walls were made of glass, enabling her to see right into that inner room where, beneath a canopy of gold and purple velvet, an ivory body lay embracing another whose plump flesh was overlaid with tints of rose. In that moment of crucified agony, nothing existed for Marianne save the picture of a love scene which her imagination conjured up the more vividly because the reality had so often been hers, Arcadius, standing within an arm's length of her, heard her murmur:

'How can you kiss her as you kissed me? Yet, the lips are your own. Have you forgotten indeed? You cannot – you cannot love her as you loved me. Oh no, I implore you – do not hold her so close! Let her go ... She will bring you bad luck, I know it. I can tell. Remember how the wheel broke on the steps of the wayside shrine. You cannot love her – no, no – NO!'

She uttered one, brief, heartbroken cry, then sank to her knees beside the window, racked by shuddering sobs. Even so, the tears released the nervous tension which had so alarmed Arcadius so that now he found himself trembling with relief.

Realizing that he might safely touch her now, he bent and reached out with infinite tenderness to raise her to her feet. Hardly daring to hold the slender form that trembled against his shoulder, he guided her faltering steps towards the bed. She did not resist but suffered herself to be led like a little child, too deep in her own misery to be aware of what was happening. By the time Jolival had her lying on the bed once more, the door had opened to admit Madame Robineau with the doctor. That this should be none other than Corvisart, Napoleon's own doctor, did not surprise Arcadius in the least. After the events of that day, nothing would have had the power to surprise him. None the less, it was a remarkable comfort.

'I was downstairs,' he said, 'sharing a bowl of punch with some friends, when I heard madame here calling for a doctor. Prince Clary was hard on her heels, bombarding her with questions, and it was he who informed me of the invalid's identity. May I ask what the Signorina Maria Stella is doing here and in this condition?'

Frowning severely at the still-sobbing Marianne, the doctor folded his arms and his black-dad bulk seemed to tower over Arcadius. Jolival made a helpless gesture.

'She is your patient,' he said, 'and you must know her a little. She was set on coming —'

'You should not have let her.'

'I'd have liked to see you try and stop her. Do you know, we followed the Archduchess's convoy from the other side of Soissons? When Marianne heard what had happened at the palace, her feelings overcame her.'

'All that way in the pouring rain! It was madness. As for what happened at the palace, that was nothing to go into convulsions over. Good lord, to throw a fit because his majesty was in haste to see what kind of a bargain he had got!'

While the two men were talking, Madame Robineau, with the help of a maidservant, had been expeditiously undressing Marianne, now quiet as a baby, and tucking her into the big bed which the maid had warmed hastily with a copper warming-pan. The girl's sobs were quieter now although she was growing increasingly feverish. Her mind seemed calmer, however, and the violent outburst of grief which had shaken her had done something to relieve the worst tension, so that she was able to listen almost with indifference to Corvisart's rumbling voice berating her on the imprudence of riding about in the icy rain.

'You have a carriage, I think, and some very fine horses? What made you go on horseback in this weather?'

'I like riding,' Marianne said obstinately, determined to reveal nothing of her real motives.

The doctor snorted, 'And what do you think the Emperor will say when he hears what you have been up to, eh?'

Marianne's hand emerged swiftly from the bedclothes and was laid on Corvisart's.

'But he will not hear. Doctor, please say nothing to him! Besides – I dare say he will not be interested.'

Corvisart gave a mighty roar of laughter.

'I see. You do not wish the Emperor to know, but if you could be sure it would make him very angry to hear what you have been doing, you would send me to him straight away, is that it? Well then, you may be happy: I will tell him and he will be furious.'

'I don't believe you,' Marianne said bitterly. 'The Emperor is —'

'The Emperor is busy trying to get himself an heir,' the doctor interrupted her ruthlessly. 'My dear girl, I find you quite incomprehensible. You must have known that this was inevitable – that it was the Emperor's sole purpose in marrying.'

'He need not have been in such a hurry! Why tonight –'

'Why take the Archduchess into his bed tonight?' Corvisart seemed bent on finishing her sentences for her. 'Because he is in a hurry, of course. He is married, he wants an heir, he sets about the business right away. What could be more natural?'

'But he is not properly married! The real marriage service is to take place in Paris in several days' time. Tonight, the Emperor should have –'

' – slept at the Chancellory, I know. He is merely making sure of his bargain. And there is nothing for you to upset yourself about. Lord, my dear, you've only to look at yourself in your mirror, even now, when you look more like a sodden spaniel than a celebrated *cantatrice*, and then cast an eye at that poor little dumpling who is to give us an heir to the throne. Nearly every man in Paris is at your feet! Yes, even that Austrian fellow is hanging about downstairs for news of you! You let the Emperor get on with his job. If you'll permit me to say so, you won't find him a worse lover because he's a husband.'

Marianne did not answer. What was the use? No man could ever understand what she felt at that moment. She was not such a fool, nor Fortunée Hamelin sufficiently discreet, that she could believe herself the first woman who had tried to hold the master of Europe. Napoleon had adored his first wife and betrayed her time after time. Even when he was deeply in love, this craving for change, this irresistible urge to polygamy, was part of the very essence of the man. And yet, however much she reasoned with herself, Marianne could not ease the dull pain in her heart. Did the physical shape of the woman he held in his arms matter so little to him? If that were so, why had he chosen her, Marianne? How deeply had she really stirred him? What place did she hold between his memories of Joséphine and those of the golden-haired Marie Walewska with whom he was said to have been so wildly in love in Warsaw?

Thinking that she was falling asleep, Corvisart softly drew the curtains round the bed and departed, accompanied by Arcadius. He had given her a cordial to drink and prescribed mustard plasters, rest and warmth. Before the door closed, Marianne heard him say in a low voice: 'The crisis is past and I think the chill will lead to no ill effects. It will keep her quiet at least.'

Marianne chuckled underneath her blankets. Quiet! When she could feel fresh forces bubbling up inside her, strengthened, perhaps, by her fever? She was not the woman to waste time lamenting her fate. She was a born fighter and now on this, another woman's wedding night, she suddenly found a new sense of purpose in her own life. Dislike was the first motive, a dislike so strong that it almost amounted to hatred for this Austrian – this great, indolent pink and white doll. There followed, naturally, the urge to cross swords with her, and measure her power over Napoleon's mind, heart and senses.

Why not deal her fickle lover tit for tat? Why not use against him the oldest weapon of all those with which the Devil has stocked the feminine arsenal: the self-same jealousy which had been tormenting Marianne herself for the past week? Already, she was famous. All Paris knew her name, her voice, her face. She had every means at her disposal to get herself talked about, from Fouché down to the news-sheets and Fortunée's witty gossip. How would the Emperor react to hear her name persistently coupled with that of some other man? It might be interesting to see.

'The whole of the Imperial Guard is in love with you,' Fortunée had said. It would be silly not to use their infatuation to penetrate a little further into the mysteries of Napoleon's heart. Of course, the experiment must be only in appearance, not in fact.

When Arcadius, on tiptoe, crept back into the room to see that all was well, she fixed him suddenly with her bright green eyes.

'That Austrian – the prince – is he still downstairs?'

'Er – yes. It was he who insisted on my coming up to see if you needed anything. At this very moment he is earnestly questioning the doctor about your condition. Why do you ask?'

'Because he was very kind and I did not thank him as I should. Will you do that for me tonight, Arcadius, and tell him that I shall be happy to see him tomorrow?'

Clearly, this request came as a surprise to Jolival. He stared.

'I will do that certainly, but —'

Before he could finish, Marianne had wriggled down into the bedclothes and, turning on her side, gave an obvious yawn.

'Good night, dear friend. Go and get some rest. You must need it. It is very late.'

The church clock, not far away, was striking midnight and Marianne's sleepiness was not altogether feigned. The fever was making her drowsy. Tomorrow she would see the Austrian and be very nice to him. He might even offer her a seat in his own carriage for the journey back to Paris, and once back in the city she would feel better placed to win her battle with the two men in her life: the fight for freedom from Francis Cranmere and the fight for love with Napoleon.

Strong in this resolution, Marianne closed her eyes and sank into a restless sleep, broken by confused dreams. Strangely enough, neither the Emperor nor Francis Cranmere entered into those dreams. Marianne was struggling for breath in the green depths of some infernal jungle, enmeshed in silvery tentacles of weird vegetation, in flowering lianas that opened gaping mouths: she tried to cry out but no sound came from her lips. The more desperately she fought, the more terrifying became the feeling of suffocation. The green jungle rose and filled her mouth and covered her, and instantly it had changed into a raging sea with mountainous waves looming above her head. Marianne felt her strength failing, she was drowning. Then suddenly a hand appeared, groping down, down through the greenish depths, growing larger and larger until it held her in a warm grip and drew her back abruptly into the light. The figure of a man was there, etched against an angry sky, and Marianne knew quite suddenly that it was Jason Beaufort. He was looking at her with an expression of mingled sorrow and anger.

'Why are you so bent on destroying yourself?' he said. 'Why ... why ... why ...?'

The voice dropped and faded away until it was no more than a whisper; the black cloak swirled about the retreating figure which suddenly became a bird and flew away into a livid purple sky.

With a scream and a sob, Marianne awoke. The fire had gone out and the room was dark except for the faint glow of a night light. Outside, all was still, the only sound the steady rattle of torrential rain upon the window-panes. Marianne shivered. She was bathed in sweat but her fever seemed to have abated.

Sleep in that sopping bed being out of the question, she got up and stripped off the sodden sheets and the nightgown that clung damply to her body. Then, wrapping herself in the blankets, she lay down on the bare mattress and pulled the big red eiderdown over her. Not once had she turned to look at the white shape of the palace opposite. Her strange dream still had her in its spell and her mind reached back to it almost with regret. She had not thought of the American for a long time but now it came to her suddenly that her present trials would have been easier to bear if he had been there. Despite all that had occurred to drive them apart, she had grown to value the feeling of quiet strength that clung to him, the love of adventure and excitement, even the cool, unromantic practicality which had so repelled her at first. With a wry smile, she thought that if there was one man with whom she might have enjoyed making Napoleon jealous, that man was Jason. But would she ever see him again? Who could tell where on the high seas his fine new ship might be sailing at that moment? A ship whose name she did not even know.

Better to try and put him out of her mind. Besides, the Austrian Prince would serve her purpose just as well, or any one of her many admirers.

Sighing, Marianne fell asleep again, to dream this time of a tall ship flying under full sail over a grey sea. And the figure carved at the prow bore the hawk-like features of Jason Beaufort.

# CHAPTER THREE
# Imperial Wedding

Marianne returned home the following evening in the carriage of Prince Clary und Aldringen, having left Arcadius de Jolival to see to the horses. She was not yet fully recovered from the high fever brought on by her long ride in the rain but she was possessed by a frantic haste to leave Compiègne behind her. The mere sight of the palace was so intolerable to her that she would have faced another long ride in the wet if necessary to escape from a town which had been buzzing since daybreak with speculation about Napoleon's amazing disregard of protocol.

She was so distraught that Arcadius set out immediately after breakfast to find her a carriage. He had no need to go farther than the inn yard. The Emperor had kept Léopold Clary at his side until the arrival of his new bride, but now the Prince was bound with all speed for Paris, carrying despatches from his sovereign to the Austrian ambassador, Prince von Schwartzenberg. Hearing that the beautiful songstress who had aroused his admiration on the previous evening was in search of a vehicle to carry her to Paris, the young Austrian's delight knew no bounds.

'Say to Madame Maria Stella that my carriage and myself are hers to command.'

An hour later, Marianne drove out of Compiègne in the young diplomat's company while Jolival directed his steps somewhat gloomily towards the stables. The fact was that Marianne's faithful mentor was more than a little perplexed. There was nothing inherently suspicious in this sudden friendliness towards a young man who, only a few hours earlier, had been a total stranger to her, and yet it was so unlike Marianne's usual behaviour that Arcadius could not help wondering if there were more behind it than met the eye.

Meanwhile, Clary's big travelling chaise was speeding through the wet and dripping woods on its way to Paris. The rain showed no signs of slackening. The low sky overhead was a depressing yellowish grey colour but neither of the vehicle's occupants appeared to notice it. Marianne, still very tired, sat huddled against the soft, red cushions, wrapped in the black, hooded cloak which Jolival had procured for her that morning, staring at the rain with unseeing eyes, her mind full of the scenes of the previous day. She recalled Napoleon's rapturous expression when he flung open the carriage door and beheld the Archduchess's plump cheeks framed by the absurd parrot feathers. She recalled the way he had held out his arms to hand her out into the courtyard at Compiègne.

Clary sat silently contemplating his companion's exquisite face, now white with exhaustion, the dark smudges round her green eyes, so touchingly shadowed by the soot-black lashes, and the perfection of the gloveless hand lying like a pale flower on her dark cloak. The diplomat could not help a feeling of surprise that this Italian nobody, an opera singer, should show such evident signs of breeding. The girl carried herself like a duchess, and her hands were those of a queen. And this air of secret sorrow, as if she bore some mysterious grief in her heart – it was this sense of mystery as much as Marianne's beauty which attracted Clary, and inspired him to behave towards her with the utmost respect. Throughout the long journey, he spoke only to assure himself that she was not cold or that she would not prefer to make a short stop, feeling almost absurdly pleased if she only smiled at him.

Wrapped in her own angry misery, Marianne was grateful to him for not intruding and she did not need any speeches to measure her effect on him: his eyes spoke eloquently enough.

It was long past nightfall when they entered Paris by way of Saint-Denis but Clary had not taken his eyes off Marianne, even when her face was no longer more than a vague blur in the dim interior of the chaise. He longed to know where his fair companion lived but, faithful to his self-imposed discretion, he said: 'Our way leads past the embassy. With your permission I will leave you there but my carriage will take you wherever you wish to go.'

His eyes said so clearly what he would not permit his lips to utter that Marianne could not resist a tiny smile.

'I thank you, Count, for your chivalry. I live at the Hôtel d'Asselnat in the Rue de Lille … and I shall be happy to receive you if you should care to call.'

The chaise was drawing up outside the Austrian embassy at the junction of the rue du Mont-Blanc[1] and the rue de Provence. Blushing furiously, the diplomat bowed over the hand held out to him and brushed it with his lips.

---

[1] Now the Chaussée d'Antin.

'Be sure I shall give myself that pleasure tomorrow, madame. I trust I shall find you fully restored to health.'

Again, Marianne smiled. She had felt the young man's lips tremble against her hand and she was sure, now, of her power over him. She meant to make the fullest use of it. So it was with a great deal more cheerfulness that she re-entered her own house, to find Adélaïde entertaining Fortunée Hamelin.

The two women were sitting in the music room talking earnestly when Marianne entered. Clearly, they had not expected her and both turned to stare at her in amazement. Madame Hamelin was the first to recover herself.

'Now, where have you sprung from?' she cried, hurrying to embrace her friend. 'Do you know everyone has been looking for you for a whole day?'

'Looking for me?' Marianne said, removing her cloak and hanging it on the big, gilt harp. 'Who has been looking for me, and why? Adélaïde, you knew that I was obliged to go out of town.'

'Yes, indeed!' the old maid said indignantly. 'You were remarkably discreet about it, too, hinting that you were called away on the Emperor's business. So you may imagine my surprise when a messenger came here yesterday from the Emperor himself, inquiring after you.'

Feeling as if the ground had opened under her feet, Marianne sank down on the piano stool and stared at her cousin.

'A messenger from the Emperor? Inquiring after me? But why?'

'Why, to sing, of course! You are a singer are you not, Marianne d'Asselnat?' retorted Adélaïde, with such a sting in her voice that Fortunée could not help smiling. It was clear that the thing which galled the aristocratic old lady most about Marianne's new life was the fact that she earned her living as a singer. To cut short these recriminations, the Creole stepped quickly over to Marianne and sat down, putting an arm about her friend's shoulders.

'I don't know what you have been up to,' she said, 'and I do not wish to pry into any secrets, but one thing is quite certain: yesterday an official request came from the Grand Marshal of the Palace for you to sing before the Court at Compiègne today.'

Marianne sprang to her feet with a sudden spurt of anger.

'Before the Court, was it? Or before the Empress? Because she is the Empress, you know, ever since last night, even before the wedding ceremonies have been completed!'

Fortunée blinked at this outburst. 'What are you saying?'

'That Napoleon took the Austrian to his bed last night! He slept with her! He couldn't wait for the wedding ceremony and the cardinal's blessing! He was so besotted about her, it seems, that he could not help himself! And now he dares – he dares to order me to go and sing before that woman! I, who only yesterday was his mistress!'

'And are still,' Fortunée observed placidly. 'My dear child, you must understand that to Napoleon there is nothing in the least shocking, or even unusual, in the idea of bringing his wife and his mistress face to face. Let me remind you that he has chosen more than one of his bedfellows from among Joséphine's own ladies, and our Empress was obliged on numerous occasions to applaud the performance of Mademoiselle Georges – to whom, moreover, he even made a present of his wife's diamonds. Before your time no concert was complete without Grassini. Our Corsican Emperor has something of the Turk in him. Besides, I dare say he had a secret urge to see how you reacted to his Viennese. Well, he will have to be satisfied with la Grassini!'

'La Grassini?'

'Oh, yes, Duroc's messenger had orders, if the great Maria Stella were unavailable, to settle for the usual stand-by. You were absent, and so it is the opulent Giuseppina who was obliged to sing at Compiègne today. Mind you, I think it may have been just as well. There was to be a duet with Crescentini, the Emperor's favourite castrato, a dreadful, painted creature. You would have loathed him on sight, but Grassini adores him. In fact, she admires him as she does everything Napoleon chooses to honour, and he decorated Crescentini.'

'I wonder why?' Marianne said absently.

Fortunée gave a tinkling laugh which relaxed the atmosphere a little.

'That is the funny part! When Grassini was asked the same question, she said quite seriously: "Ah, but you forget his disability!"'

Adélaïde generously echoed Fortunée's laughter but Marianne merely smiled automatically. She was not sorry that she had not been at home. She found it hard to picture herself making her curtsey to the 'other woman' and indulging in a musical flirtation with a man who, apart from his exceptional voice, was no more than a hollow sham and could only make her ridiculous. Besides, she was too much a woman not to hope that, for a few seconds at least, it might occur to Napoleon to wonder where she was that she was unable to attend. Yes, all things considered, it was better so. The next time she beheld the man she loved, it would, she trusted, be in the company of someone who might well give him some anxious moments – supposing him capable of feeling jealousy on her account. The thought made Marianne smile despite herself and drew a waspish comment from Fortunée.

The delightful thing about you, Marianne, is that one can say anything to you and be quite sure you are not listening to a word of it. What are you thinking of now?'

'Not what, who. Of him, of course. Sit down, both of you, and I will tell you what I have been doing these last two days. But for heaven's sake, Adélaïde, get me something to eat. I am starving.'

While she addressed herself with an energy remarkable in one who had been so ill only the night before to the sumptuous meal which Adélaïde conjured up from the kitchen, Marianne described her adventures. But although the account contained a good deal of humour at her own expense, it did not make her two hearers laugh. Fortunée's expression, when she had finished, was extremely serious.

'But this assignation?' she said. 'It might have been important. Should you not have sent Jolival, at least?'

'I thought of it, but I did not want to part from him. I felt – so very desolate and unhappy. Besides, I am convinced it was a trap.'

'All the more reason to be sure. What if it were your – your husband?'

There was silence. Marianne set down the glass she had just drained with a bang that snapped the delicate stem. Her face was so white that Fortunée took pity on her.

'It was only an idea,' she said gently.

'But one that might have been checked. All the same, I don't see what motive he could have for getting me to that ruined castle, although I admit I did not think of him. I was thinking rather of the people who kidnapped me once before. What can I do now?'

'What you should have done straight away: inform Fouché and then wait. Whatever the attempt on you was to have been, whether it was a trap or a genuine rendezvous, there will certainly be another. By the way, let me congratulate you.'

'On what?'

'On your latest Austrian conquest. I am delighted to see you have decided to take my advice. You will find the faithlessness of men much easier to bear when you have another all ready to hand.'

'Not so fast,' Marianne said, laughing. 'I have no intention of doing more than being seen in Prince Clary's company. His great attraction, you see, is that he is Austrian. I like the idea of amusing myself with a countryman of our new sovereign.'

Fortunée and Adélaïde laughed gaily.

'Is she really as ugly as they say?' Adélaïde asked eagerly, selecting one of the preserved fruits provided for her cousin.

Marianne did not answer at once. She half-closed her eyes, as if it helped her to conjure up the vision of the intruder, and a wicked smile curved the soft lines of her mouth. The smile was all woman.

'Ugly? No, not exactly. It is hard to say, really. She is more – commonplace.'

Fortunée sighed exaggeratedly. 'Poor Napoleon. What has he done to deserve that! A commonplace wife, when he loves only the exceptional!'

'If you ask me, it is the French who have done nothing to deserve it,' Adélaïde exclaimed. 'A Habsburg is bound to be a disaster.'

'Well, they do not seem to think so,' Marianne said with a laugh. 'You should have heard the cheering in the streets at Compiègne!'

'At Compiègne, maybe,' Fortunée said meditatively. 'They have very little excitement there, except for hunting parties. But something tells me Paris will not be so easily impressed. The only people who will welcome her arrival here will be those circles who see her as the Corsican's doom and the avenging angel of Marie-Antoinette. The people are far from delighted; they worshipped Joséphine and they have no love for Austria.'

Gazing at the crowd filling the Place de la Concorde on the following Monday, the second of April, Marianne reflected that Fortunée might well be right. It was a holiday crowd, dressed in its smartest clothes and rippling with excitement, but it was not a happy crowd. It stretched all along the Champs-Élysées and was thickest around the eight pavilions which had been erected at the corners of the square. It washed up against the walls of the Garde-Meuble and the Hôtel de la Marine but there was none of the throbbing gaiety of a great occasion.

Yet the weather was fine. The depressing downpour had ceased quite suddenly at dawn, the clouds had been swept away and a bright spring sunshine bathed the opening buds of the chestnut trees in sparkling light. Straw bonnets and hats trimmed with flowers burgeoned on the heads of the Parisiennes and their male escorts were resplendent in pale pantaloons and coats of innumerable subtle shades. Marianne smiled at the outburst of seasonable elegance. The population of Paris seemed bent on demonstrating to the new arrival that the French knew how to dress.

Seated with Arcadius and Adélaïde in her carriage near one of the prancing stone horses, Marianne had an excellent view of the scene. Flags and fairy lights were everywhere. The Tuileries railings had been newly gilded, the fountains were running with wine and free buffets loaded with food had been set up in red – and white-striped tents under the trees of the Cours La Reine, so that everyone might have a share in the imperial wedding feast. Orange trees, glowing with fruit, stood in tubs round the square in readiness for the night's illuminations. Later, when the wedding ceremony had been performed in the great *salon carré* of the Louvre, the Emperor's loyal subjects would be free to consume four thousand eight hundred pies, twelve hundred tongues, a thousand joints of mutton, two hundred and fifty turkeys, three hundred and fifty capons, the same number of chickens, three thousand or so sausages and a host of other things.

Jolival sighed and helped himself delicately to a pinch of snuff. 'By tonight, their majesties will reign over a nation of drunkards, not to mention the overeating there will be.'

Marianne did not answer. She found the holiday atmosphere both entertaining and irritating. All up and down the Champs-Élysées was a sea of little booths containing attractions of all kinds, tiny open-air theatres, dancing, peepshows, and shies. From Marianne's carriage, as from any of the others which had come to view the spectacle, it was possible to overhear an endless succession of vulgar jokes which were a clear indication of the prevailing mood. What had passed at Compiègne was common knowledge and no one doubted that Napoleon was about to lead to the altar a woman whose bed he had been sharing for a week, although the civil ceremony had taken place only the day before at Saint-Cloud.

It was noon and the cannon had been roaring for a good half-hour. At the far end of the long vista of the Champs-Élysées, lined with the pale green haze of the young chestnut leaves, the sun fell on the huge Arc de Triomphe made of wood and canvas which had been set up in place of the yet unfinished monument to the glory of the Grande Armée. The imitation arch looked well in the spring sunshine, with its brand-new flags and the great bouquet placed there by the workmen, the *trompe l'oeil* reliefs on the sides and the inscription to 'Napoleon and Marie-Louise' from The City of Paris'. The thing was amusing enough, Marianne thought, but it was by no means pleasant for her to see the names of Napoleon and Marie-Louise so coupled together.

The red plumes on the tall shakos of the Grenadier Guards waved all along the route, alternating at the intersections with the red and green cockades of the Chasseurs. Orchestras and bands everywhere were playing the same tune, a popular song called 'Home is where your Heart is' which soon got on Marianne's nerves. It seemed an odd choice for the day when Napoleon was marrying the niece of Marie-Antoinette.

Suddenly, Arcadius's hand, gloved in pale kid, was laid on Marianne's.

'Don't move and don't turn round,' he said softly. 'But I want you to try and take a peep into the carriage that has just drawn up beside us. The occupants are a man and a woman. The woman is a stranger to neither of us but I do not know the man. He has an air of breeding and is very handsome, despite a scar on his left cheek – a scar that might have been caused by a sword cut –'

With a supreme effort, Marianne sat still, but her hand trembled under Jolival's. She raised the other to her lips and yawned ostentatiously, as if the long wait for the bridal procession were becoming tedious. Then, slowly and with perfect naturalness, she turned her head very slightly, enough to bring the interior of the neighbouring carriage within her field of vision.

It was a black and yellow curricle, brand new and extremely smart, bearing the obvious signature of Keller, the fashionable coach-builder in the Champs-Élysées. There were two people inside. The elderly woman was splendidly dressed in black velvet trimmed with fur, and Marianne was not surprised to recognize her old enemy, Fanchon Fleur-de-Lys. It was the woman's companion, however, who drew her eyes and although her heart missed a beat the cause was not surprise but an unpleasant sensation more akin to revulsion.

This time, there could be no mistake. It was Francis Cranmere and no phantom conjured up by a fevered imagination. Marianne saw the familiar, almost-too-perfect features, set in an expression of perpetual boredom; the stubborn brow and the rather heavy chin supported by the folds of the high, muslin cravat; the powerful body, exquisitely dressed and preserved, as yet, from corpulence by physical exercise. His clothes were a blend of subtle dove-grey shades, relieved by a dramatic black velvet collar.

They must have followed us,' Jolival murmured. 'I will swear they have come for no other purpose. See, the man is looking at you. It is he, is it not? Your husband?'

'It is,' Marianne agreed. Considering the turmoil within her, her voice was curiously calm. Her proud, disdainful green eyes met and held Francis's grey ones without flinching. She was discovering, agreeably, that now that she was face to face with him in fact, the vague terrors which had haunted her ever since his appearance at the theatre had melted away. It was the sense of some obscure, unspecified menace which had frightened her. She was afraid of the unknown but the prospect of an open fight left her in full possession of her faculties.

She read the mockery on the faces of Francis and his companion but the steadiness of her gaze did not falter. She was conscious of no great astonishment at seeing them together, or at finding the hideous crone dressed up like a duchess. Fanchon was cunning and dangerous, a kind of female Proteus. However, Marianne had no intention of discussing her affairs in front of Fanchon Fleur-de-Lys. Her self-respect would not permit the interference in her life of a woman who had been publicly branded a criminal. She decided that it would be wiser to postpone her desire to be done with Lord Cranmere once and for all.

She was already leaning forward to tell Gracchus-Hannibal, at present lording it in his new livery on the box, to extricate them from the crowd and drive home when the door was pulled open and Francis himself appeared, hat in hand, bowing with mocking courtesy. He was smiling but the eyes that rested on Marianne's face were hard as stone.

'Permit me,' he said lightly, 'to pay my respects to the queen of all Paris.'

Beneath the bonnet of lilac silk and white Chantilly lace that matched her expensively-tailored carriage dress, her face was very white but she put out one gloved hand to restrain Arcadius who had started forward to bar Francis's way.

'No, Arcadius. This is my affair.' Then, with only a slight quiver in her voice, she asked: 'What do you want?'

'I told you – to pay my respects to Beauty and, perhaps, to talk a little, if you please …'

'I do not please,' Marianne cut him short disdainfully. 'If you have anything to say to me, you may write to Monsieur de Jolival who deals with all my letters and engagements. He will tell you when I am able to receive you. We cannot talk in this crowd. I live –'

'I know where you live and, flattered though I am that you should prefer the delights of a tête-à-tête, I must remind you, my dear,' Francis countered sardonically, 'that one is never more alone than amidst a crowd, and this one is getting bigger with every minute. In a little while it will be quite impossible to stir at all, and so I am afraid you will be compelled to endure my company whether you like it or not. In which case, we may as well talk business, don't you think?'

The crowd had, in fact, become so dense that all vehicles in the square had been brought to a standstill. There was a good deal of noise, swollen by distant sounds of music, but the hubbub was not so great as to make conversation impossible. Francis, who had remained standing in the doorway, poked his head into the carriage and addressed himself to Jolival.

'If this gentleman will be good enough to allow me to usurp his place beside you for a moment …' he began, but Marianne spoke sharply, her hand still on her friend's arm:

'I have no secrets from the Vicomte de Jolival. He is, as I have told you, more than a friend to me. You may say what you wish before him.'

'I thank you,' Francis said dryly. 'You may have nothing to hide but my own nature is less trusting. I should infinitely prefer our conversation to be private.'

'If we were to consult our own preferences, Monsieur,' Jolival retorted, unable to contain himself any longer, 'I should infinitely prefer to throw you out of this lady's carriage forthwith.'

Francis laughed softly. 'I see your friend cherishes some prejudice against me, my dear,' he said. 'I can only suppose that you must have put it into his head. I do believe he takes me for some kind of highwayman.'

'What I think is neither here nor there,' Arcadius said stiffly. 'However, I may say that I have seen nothing in your behaviour to cause me to change my mind.'

'As you so rightly say,' the Englishman agreed smoothly, 'that is neither here nor there. But, my dear sir, if you fear to find the time hang heavy on your hands, I know there is a lady in my own carriage who will be delighted to renew her acquaintance with you. See, she is smiling at you.'

Marianne's eyes went automatically to the black and yellow chaise and she frowned as she realized that, in so far as it was possible for her, Fanchon was indeed directing a winning smile at Jolival. Jolival, however, merely shrugged and moved to the box to speak to Gracchus, without taking his eyes from the two inside the vehicle. Marianne spoke abruptly.

'Since you say you wish to talk with me, my lord, you need not begin by insulting my most faithful friend. Not everyone shares your taste for dubious company. And indeed, that seems to me a generous description of the lady in question.'

Without answering, Francis dropped heavily on to the green velvet cushions next to Marianne who moved instinctively to avoid touching him. He sat for a moment in a silence broken only by the faint rasp of his breath. Marianne wondered, not without some private satisfaction, if that were a legacy of the sword thrust she had put through his chest; yet even that seemed poor consolation for the disappointment of finding him still alive. For a moment, she studied the man she had once loved, as dispassionately as if he had been a stranger. She had believed in him as a god, had sworn joyfully to love, honour and obey him … It was the first time that she had been alone with him since that terrible wedding night. So many things had changed. Then, she had been a child to be coldly sacrificed, a helpless victim in the hands of a heartless and unscrupulous man. Today she had the Emperor's love for strength and protection. This time, it was she who would call the tune.

Francis, she saw, had altered very little except, perhaps, for the cynical curl which had replaced the twist of boredom at the corner of his full mouth. Lord Cranmere was still a handsome man; the thin scar down one cheek only served to add a touch of tragic glamour to the nobility of his perfect features. Remembering how she had loved him; Marianne was amazed to find that she felt nothing in his presence beyond a dislike amounting to loathing. Seeing that he did not seem anxious to break the silence but was apparently engaged in earnest contemplation of the gleaming toes of his highly-polished boots, she decided to take the initiative at last. She wanted to get it over quickly. His very presence in that confined space was painful to her.

'You wished to speak to me,' she said coldly. 'Say what you have to say. I have no wish to prolong this interview.'

He turned his head and smiled at her under drooping eyelids.

'Why not? Surely this is a most affecting moment: a husband and wife together again after such a long absence – especially after believing themselves parted for ever? My dear Marianne, you should be glad to be reunited with the man you loved – for you did love me, my dear. You were quite devoted to me on our wedding day. I can still see your great, swimming eyes when the dear old Abbé –'

Marianne had had enough.

'That will do!' she said sharply. 'You are amazingly impertinent. Have you forgotten the charming circumstances attending our marriage? Do I have to remind you that you had no sooner sworn to God to love and cherish me than you set about gaming away not merely the little you had left but also the considerable fortune which I had brought you – and for which you had married me? And as if that were not enough, you dared to stake the innocent love I bore you on the turn of a card, you staked my innocence and my virginity, my honour itself. You have the audacity to talk about the night when you destroyed my life as if it were merely another of those delightful escapades you men discuss over your brandy!'

Lord Cranmere shrugged contemptuously, but his eyes shifted to avoid Marianne's sparkling gaze.

'If you had not been such a little fool, that's all it would have been. It was you turned it into high tragedy.'

'Indeed! And what should I have done, pray? Welcome your substitute with open arms?'

'You need not have gone so far as that. Any woman worth her salt would have been able to hold him off while leading him on. The fool was mad for you –'

'Rubbish!' Marianne said briskly, repressing a sudden pang at this reminder of Jason Beaufort. 'He had not set eyes on me before that day.'

'Do you think that is not long enough to desire a woman? You should have heard him sing your praises, your grace and charm, the splendour of your eyes. "If sirens existed," he said, "Lady Marianne must be their queen …" Good God!' Francis exploded with sudden violence, 'you could have done what you liked with him! He might well have given the lot back to you in exchange for one hour of love! For one kiss, even. And instead of that you enacted a Cheltenham tragedy and sent packing the man who held our whole fortune in his hands.'

'Our fortune?'

'Very well, your fortune, if you insist. Even more reason for you to fight for it, try and redeem some remnant of it at least …'

Marianne was no longer listening. What was the use? She had no illusions about Francis's character and it was not surprising that he should sink to the depths of reproaching her for failing to trick Jason out of his winnings. She stopped listening and recalled instead those last moments with Jason in her room at Selton. She had not given him that kiss, but he had taken it all the same and Marianne discovered to her astonishment that, even after all this time, she could still taste the sweet violence of it, strange and overpowering despite the anger which had filled her at the time. It was her first kiss, something not easily forgotten.

She had closed her eyes for a second, remembering, but now she opened them. What was Francis saying?

'I protest you are not even listening!'

'You have ceased to interest me. I will not waste my time pointing out to you how an honourable man might have acted in such circumstances, but if it concerns you, I will say I am amazed that you should dare to approach me. I believed that I had killed you, Francis Cranmere, but whether or not the devil has looked after his own, to me you are dead and will remain so.'

'I can see that might be more comfortable for you, but the fact remains that I am alive and intend to remain so.'

Marianne turned away with a shrug.

'Then keep away from me and try to forget that Francis Cranmere and Marianne d'Asselnat were ever made man and wife. That is, if you wish to continue, if not alive, then certainly at liberty.'

Francis was looking at her curiously.

'Indeed? Do I detect a threat, my love? What do you mean by that?'

'Do not pretend to be more stupid than you are. This is France and you are an Englishman, an enemy of the Empire. I have only to point you out, to say the word, and you will be arrested. And once arrested, it would be child's play to see to it that you disappeared forever. Do you think the Emperor would deny me your head if I were to ask for it? Be a sportsman, for once, admit that you have lost and do not try to see me again. You must know that you cannot harm me.'

She spoke quietly but firmly and with immense dignity. She did not relish making a parade of her power over the Master of Europe but in the present instance it seemed best to lay her cards fairly on the table at the outset. Let Francis vanish from her life forever and she was sure to forgive him one day. But instead of meditating on her words as might have been expected, Lord Cranmere only burst out laughing, and Marianne found her fine confidence wavering a little.

'What have I said to amuse you?'

'My dear, you are truly priceless! I swear you think yourself the Empress. Boney has not married you, you know, but that wretched Archduchess.'

Francis's mockery, combined with the contemptuous English epithet for Napoleon, pricked Marianne's temper.

'Empress or no,' she ground at him through her teeth, 'I will show you I am not afraid of you, and that no one insults me with impunity.'

She leaned forward quickly to call Arcadius, meaning to send him for one of the police officers whose black figures, clad in long overcoats and beaver hats, with stout truncheons on their wrists, could be seen dotted about the gaily-dressed crowd. But before she could open her mouth, Francis had grasped her by the shoulder and thrust her roughly back against the squabs.

'Stay where you are, you little fool! Besides, you are wasting your time. No one can get in or out of the carriage in this crowd. I cannot leave you, even if I would.'

This was true. The crowd surged so thickly around them that nothing was visible beyond a sea of heads. Even Arcadius had been obliged to retreat for safety to the box alongside Gracchus. In the distance, rising above the murmur of the crowd, was a sound like thunder, mingled with the elusive strains of music. Perhaps the procession was approaching at last. But for Marianne, all the interest of the day had fled. She felt stifled, although she could not have said exactly why. It must have been the poisonous presence of the man she hated.

She shook off the hand that still rested on her shoulder and gave him a glance filled with loathing.

'You may as well wait. When you leave this carriage, it will be for Vincennes or La Force.'

But Francis only laughed again and once more Marianne felt the cold pricking on her skin.

'If you were as much a gamester as I am,' he said with disquieting coolness, 'I would lay you odds it will be nothing of the kind.'

'What is to prevent me?'

'Yourself, my dear. For one thing, it will do no good to denounce me, for I should be released with apologies immediately, and for another, you will have no desire to do so when you hear what I have to say.'

Marianne stiffened, fighting off a creeping fear, struggling to think. He seemed so sure of himself. Was it his borrowed name that gave him his assurance? What was it Fouché had told her? The Vicomte d'Aubécourt was a frequent visitor at the house of Dorothée de Périgord? But surely that was not enough to make him immune from Fouché's ceaseless quest for potential spies and conspirators? What then? Oh God, if she could only shake off the terror he inspired in her!

Once more, Francis's mocking voice brought her back to reality, saying, with terrifying softness: 'You know, you make me almost sorry for the past. You are very beautiful, my dear. No man could help but desire you. It suits you to be angry, it makes your green eyes sparkle magnificently, your bosom heaves …'

He let his eyes dwell appreciatively on the lovely face, now shadowed by the bonnet, and caress the long, graceful throat and the proud curves revealed by the low-cut bodice of silk and lace. There was no softness in his gaze, only the calculating greed of a horse-dealer looking over a promising filly. Marianne's cheeks flamed darkly at the naked lust in his face, undressing her and putting a price on her at the same time. The Englishman leaned closer, as though hypnotized by the proximity of so much beauty. He was about to take her in his arms. She shrank back against the side of the chaise and spoke through clenched teeth:

'Don't touch me! Don't come near me! If you do, I'll scream, do you hear, whatever the consequences! I'll scream so loud that everyone will hear me.'

He shuddered and drew away from her. The lust died out of his eyes and was replaced by his habitual bored expression.

Leaning back in his own corner of the seat, he sighed and closed his eyes.

'A pity ... a pity, too, that such riches should be reserved for Boney's pleasures. Or do you make him share them? I hear that half the men in Paris are in love with you.'

'Will you be quiet,' Marianne said furiously. 'Say what you have to say and make an end. What do you want?'

He opened one eye and smiled at her.

'If I were a gentleman, I ought to answer: you. And it would be no more than the truth. But we can discuss that later – at our leisure. No, for the present my wants are more practical. I need money.'

'Again!' Marianne cried. 'Do you suppose that I will give it to you?'

'I do not suppose, I know.' His voice was cynical. 'Money has always played a great part in our relations, Marianne. I married you for your fortune. Unfortunately, I dissipated it somewhat speedily, but you are still my wife and as you are clearly rolling in money, I find it quite natural to turn to you.'

'I am no longer your wife,' Marianne said, her anger slowly giving way to a vast weariness. 'I am Maria Stella, a singer, and you are the Vicomte d'Aubécourt.'

'Ah, you are aware of that? Well, I am delighted. It gives you an idea of my position in Paris society. I am much in demand.'

'You will be much less in demand when I have done with you. Everyone will know what you are: an English spy.'

'Perhaps, but in that case, they will know who you are also, and since you are my lawful wife, you will become Lady Cranmere again, an Englishwoman, and therefore why not also a spy?'

'No one would believe you,' Marianne said indifferently, 'and as for giving you money –'

'You will arrange to have fifty thousand livres to hand immediately,' Francis interrupted her smoothly. 'If not –'

'Yes?' Marianne said evenly.

Lord Cranmere felt unhurriedly in his pockets and produced a sheet of yellow paper, folded in four. Unfolding it, he laid it on her lap, before continuing: 'If not, all Paris will be deluged with these.'

The yellow sheet, printed in heavy, black letters, fluttered in the light wind that entered through the lowered windows, as with growing horror, Marianne read: 'The enemy in the Emperor's bed! Napoleon's beautiful mistress, the *cantatrice* Maria Stella, is in reality an English murderess, at present sought by the representatives of the law in England ...'

For a second, Marianne thought she must be going mad. There was a red mist before her eyes and a storm of utter fury in her heart such as she had never felt before, drowning that other impulse of sickening fear.

'Murderess!' she gasped. 'I have killed no one. You are still alive, alas!'

'Read on, my love,' Francis purred softly, 'and you will see it is no more than the truth. You are indeed a murderess. You forget my charming cousin, Ivy St Albans, whom you hit so effectively on the head with a heavy candlestick beside what you imagined to be my own dead body. Poor Ivy! She was less lucky than I. Thanks to my friend Stanton, I am still of this world, but she was so frail, so delicate. Unfortunately for you, however, she recovered consciousness before she died – just long enough to accuse you. There is a price on your head in England, my fair Marianne.'

Marianne's mouth was filled with a taste of ashes. In the shock of finding Francis alive, she had not given a thought to his cousin, the tiresome Ivy. Until this moment, moreover, she had always regarded the duel and what followed as a kind of divine judgement. Yet, despite her horror, she managed to say boldly: 'We are not in England now, but in France. Although I suppose your reason in coming here is to carry me back for the sake of the reward.'

'Faith, I'll admit I thought of it,' Lord Cranmere agreed pleasantly. 'It is hard times with me. But finding you so comfortably situated at the heart of the Empire gave me a better idea. You can be worth a great deal more than a few hundred guineas to me.'

This time, Marianne let the words pass. She was still staring at the yellow broadsheet feeling that she had reached the very limits of disgust. The accusation was that she had cold-bloodedly murdered her husband's pretty, gentle cousin. Nothing had been left to chance and the mire into which she was to be dragged down was made as sordid and disgusting as possible.

'My next thought,' Francis continued, apparently oblivious of her silence, 'was simply to abduct you. I arranged a rendezvous in a ruined castle belonging to a friend of mine, but you must have suspected something, for you did not come, although I am glad of that now. Driven by necessity, I imagined that Boney would pay handsomely to have his fair mistress restored to him unharmed, but it was a hasty thought and consequently a bad one. There was a better plan.'

So he had been behind the appointment at *La Folie*! Marianne felt little surprise. She had gone beyond all power of feeling or of lucid thought. Trumpets blared out a fanfare close at hand, backed by a swelling roll of drums that seemed to come from the inmost heart of Paris. The wedding procession must have been approaching for some minutes but, wrapped in her own troubles, Marianne had been deaf to the sounds of mounting excitement in the crowd around her. In a way, she had not wanted to hear:

the contrast was too poignant between the gay, laughing throng outside and the duel, even more desperate, perhaps, than that earlier duel at Selton, which was taking place within the carriage.

'Here comes the procession,' Francis observed, settling himself more comfortably, in the manner of one intending to remain. We shall have to continue our talk later. It is impossible to converse in this uproar.'

This was true. An incredible river of dazzling, coruscating colour was flowing down the Champs-Élysées, advancing majestically towards the Tuileries amid a clamour of brass bands playing, drums rolling and cannon roaring, greeted by waves of cheering and cries of 'Long live the Emperor!' The whole great square, so packed with people that the bright colours had all merged into a uniform, grey blue, appeared to give one mighty heave. Around her, Marianne could hear those nearest exclaiming as the procession passed by.

'Those are the Polish Light Cavalry in front!'

'How handsome they are! Some of them must be thinking of Marie Walewska today!'

Red, blue, white and gold, snowy plumes waving on their square shakos and the tips of their long lances gleaming fiery red and gold, Prince Poniatowski's troops rode past in perfect formation, holding the powerful white horses that were a familiar sight on every road in Europe well in hand. After them came Guyot's Chasseurs in purple and gold, alternating with troops of Mamelukes, girded with shining steel, their dark skins and white turbans surmounted by black aigrettes, and the panther skins over their saddles adding a touch of barbaric splendour. Next came the Dragoons, commanded by the Comte de Saint-Sulpice, dark green and white, magnificently whiskered, their black-plumed helmets shining in the sun. Next, red, green and silver, the Guards of Honour, preceding a long file of thirty-six gorgeous golden coaches bearing the imperial family and the highest officers of the court.

As though in a dream, Marianne scanned the amazing kaleidoscope of colour that was the Emperor's staff, his marshals, aides-de-camp and equerries, picking out Duroc, a blaze of gold, Massena, Lefebvre and Bernadotte, all of whom she had seen more than once in Talleyrand's house. She saw Murat in a purple uniform thickly encrusted with gold braid, sable-lined cloak swinging from his shoulder, glittering like a firework display from his spurs to his diamond cockade. Despite his overweening pride in his own magnificence, he was a figure that compelled admiration for the consummate horsemanship which enabled him to manage his mettlesome Arab stallion with such apparent ease.

The shimmering cavalcade moved on, a tide of men and horses and splendid carriages. Most sumptuous of all, drawing a gasp of admiration from the crowd, was the great, gilded coach drawn by six white horses that rolled on its stately way surmounted by an imperial crown. This was the Empress's state coach. But although the harness gleamed and the windows flashed with reflected sunlight, no figure waved from within. The coach was empty. For this day the imperial pair had elected to ride together in an open carriage. The barouche that carried Napoleon and Marie-Louise followed immediately after this gilded monument to imperial grandeur. Marianne stared at it with eyes grown suddenly round with amazement, while the crowd were hushed. All were stunned by the vision that met their eyes.

Marie-Louise sat in the carriage smiling vaguely about her and waving in an ungainly, mechanical way. Her face, under the massive crown of diamonds, was very red and she was dressed in a masterpiece of Leroy's handiwork, a magnificent gown of silver tulle literally covered in diamonds. As for Napoleon, seated beside her in the carriage, his appearance was so different from that he normally presented that for a moment Marianne was startled into forgetting Francis.

Accustomed to the extreme simplicity of his habitual dress, the black or grey coat of a colonel in the Chasseurs or the Guards, Marianne could hardly believe that the figure waving and smiling from the barouche was indeed the man she loved. He was dressed in the Spanish fashion with a short cloak of white satin liberally sprinkled with diamonds and he, too, had on his head an incredible confection of black velvet and white plumes, circled with eight rows of diamonds, which seemed to maintain itself upright in defiance of gravity. The head-dress had an impromptu, vaguely Renaissance air which Marianne found preposterous, and wholly unsuited to the pale, clear-cut features of the latter-day Caesar. How could he ever have consented to dress himself up like that and what —

A shout of laughter broke in on her thoughts. She turned on Francis wrathfully, not altogether sorry to have someone on whom to vent her rage and disappointment. He was lying back against the squabs, laughing unrestrainedly.

'May I ask what you find to amuse you?'

'What – oh no, my dear. Don't tell me you don't find Boney's fancy dress very funny? It is so dreadful, it is sublime! I've never seen anything so comical! I could weep with laughter! It's – it's unbelievable!'

Marianne fought back the impulse to fly at him tooth and nail and wipe the smile from his insolent face. Her fury was all the greater because, in her heart of hearts, she knew that he was right, that for all its wealth of gems this astonishing costume turned her warrior into a dandified figure of fun. If there had been a weapon to hand at that moment, she would have used it with no more hesitation than on that night at Selton. She had longed so desperately for Napoleon to appear before her enemy in all the stern and sombre majesty of his military uniform, to strike terror into his heart or at least to make him think twice before assailing her, Marianne, his accredited mistress. But instead of that, he had got himself dressed up as a protégé of King Henry III to marry this great, red-faced lump of a girl. Even so, she knew she must silence that hateful laughter which mocked at the only thing she had left in the world, her love.

Marianne drew herself up and turned on Francis, her green eyes blazing in her bloodless face, who was still laughing helplessly.

'Get out!' she told him fiercely. 'We have no more to say to one another. Get out of my carriage before I have you thrown out. Do you think I care what you may do? You can scatter your filthy broadsheets to the winds for all I care. Do as you please, but go! I never wish to see you again, and you will not get a penny from me!'

Her voice rose to a scream and regardless of the hubbub in the square heads were beginning to turn to look at them. Francis Cranmere had stopped laughing. His hand fastened on Marianne's arm, gripping it so that it hurt.

'Be quiet,' he commanded. 'Stop this nonsense! It can do no good. You will not escape me.'

'I am not afraid of you. As God is my witness, if you threaten me, I will kill you and this time no human aid will save you! You know me well enough to be sure that I mean what I say.'

'I told you to be quiet. I understand. You think yourself very strong, do you not? You think *he* loves you enough to defend you even against calumny, that he is powerful enough to protect you against any danger? Well, look at him! Bursting with joy and satisfied ambition! This, for him, is the crowning moment of his life. Think: he is marrying a Habsburg, he, a mere Corsican upstart! A niece to Marie-Antoinette! All this dazzling display of wealth and jewels, however preposterous, is laid on to impress her. Her wishes will be law to your Napoleon because he hopes that she will give him the heir who will establish his dynasty. And do you still believe that he will risk the displeasure of his precious Archduchess to protect a murderess? His spies in England will very soon tell him that you are indeed sought by the law for killing a defenceless woman and grievously wounding myself. What then? Believe me, Napoleon's watchword from now on will be: "No scandal, at any price!" '

Marianne felt an aching bitterness creep over her as he spoke. In an instant, all the confidence which she had based on the power of her love, on her influence with Napoleon, collapsed and fell in ruins. She knew that he cared for her, loved her perhaps as much as he could love any woman, but no more. The love the Emperor might feel for a woman of flesh and blood could not compete with the love he bore his Empire and his name. He had loved Joséphine, had married her, crowned her, yet Joséphine had been forced to step down from the throne and make way for this pink Austrian cow. He had loved the Polish countess, she had borne his child, and yet

Marie Walewska had been packed off back to Poland in the depth of winter to bring the fruit of that love into the world. What were Marianne and all her charms beside the one to whom he looked for an heir to inherit his Empire and his name? Bitterly, Marianne recalled the careless tone in which he had said to her: 'I am marrying a womb!' That womb was more precious to him than the greatest love on earth.

Her eyes filled with tears and she saw through a glittering mist the bright forms of the newly-married pair, apparently borne up upon a sea of heads. Francis's voice came to her, persuasive and insinuating, as though out of a dream.

'Be sensible, Marianne, and be satisfied with your own power – a power it would be foolish to throw away for the sake of a few hundred ecus! What are fifty thousand livres to the queen of Paris? Boney will have given you as many again within the week.'

'I have not got them,' Marianne said shortly, angrily snuffing out an impending tear with the tip of her finger.

'But you will have in – shall we say – three days? I will let you know where and how to get them to me.'

'And what assurance have I that if I give them to you this will be the end of your infamous demands?'

Francis stretched his long arms with the lazy grace of a big cat and smiled a sleepy smile.

'None, I grant you, unless it be that I shall not need money – for a while. One can always write a new pamphlet …'

'Which I shall have to face sooner or later? Oh no. If that is how it is, Lord Cranmere, you get nothing from me! Sooner or later, you will attack me, when I have no more money, perhaps. No. You may do your worst. You shall not have your fifty thousand livres!'

Marianne was thinking hard as she spoke. She would go to see Fouché, or even the Emperor, if that were possible, this very night. She would tell them of the danger threatening her and then she would go away, anywhere, so that if Fouché's men failed to stem the tide of pamphlets, at least there would be distance enough between her and Napoleon to prevent their names being linked again. She would go, perhaps, to Italy, where her voice would enable her to earn a living and where she might possibly find her godfather and get this dreadful marriage annulled. Then, when she was Marianne d'Asselnat again (she had noticed that her maiden name was not mentioned in the pamphlet), she might be able to approach Napoleon afresh. For the second time, Lord Cranmere's voice interrupted her plans.

'Ah, I was forgetting,' he said, on a note of gentle mockery. 'Knowing the impulsiveness of your character and your regrettable passion for disappearing without trace, I have taken additional precautions – in the person of the eccentric female who seems to act towards you as a mother and a chaperon but who is, I believe, your cousin.'

Marianne's heart missed a beat and she found herself suddenly at a loss for air.

'Adélaïde?' she gasped. 'What is this to do with her?'

'Why, a good deal, I think. If you knew me better, my dear, you would know that I am not the man to start a game without several trumps in my hand. Mademoiselle d'Asselnat received a message purporting to come from you and by this time should be safely in the care of friends of mine. If you wish to see her again alive ...'

Marianne realized suddenly, from the anguish that tore her heart, just how fond she had grown of Adélaïde. She closed her eyes so that he should not see the tears which started into them. The devil! He had dared to lay hands on that kindly, devoted old maid! Marianne knew now that he was hand in glove with Fanchon Fleur-de-Lys and her gang, and felt sickened at the thought of her cousin in their hands. She knew them, knew how cruel and unscrupulous they were and their hatred for all those connected, however remotely, with the imperial regime.

'You dared!' she muttered through clenched teeth. 'You dared to do that and you think by this means to bring me to agree? Well, I shall find her. I know the den of that evil creature who sits grinning at us.'

'You may find her,' Francis retorted coolly, 'but I warn you, if Fouché's spies start poking their dirty noses into my friend Fanchon's territory, they will find only a corpse.'

'You would not dare!'

'Why not? On the other hand, if you behave sensibly, as I hope, and do as I ask nicely, then I can promise to restore her to you unharmed.'

'Do you expect me to believe the word of a —'

'A scoundrel,' Francis finished for her. 'I know. It seems to me you have no choice. First find the fifty thousand livres I need, my sweet Marianne. I promise I will not call on your generosity again for – a year, let us say. And now —'

He heaved himself up from the velvet cushions and took the hand which Marianne was still too stupefied to withdraw and carried it to his lips. At the last moment, her slim fingers slipped from Francis's gloved hand, as though instinctively.

'I hate you,' she said dully. 'Oh, how I hate you!'

He gave his twisted smile. 'That does not disturb me. With some women, hatred has more spice than love. I shall have my money!'

'You shall have it, but take care. If you of harm one hair of my cousin's head, there is no hiding-place in all Europe safe enough to keep you from my vengeance. That I swear by my father's memory, I will kill you with my own hands, even if I die for it!'

She shook her gloved fist in Lord Cranmere's face. The smile left

Francis's lips and he flinched before the cold fury in her glittering green eyes. The pallor of that lovely face, the anguish so clearly written there, had their effect on the Englishman, touched, perhaps, some forgotten chord in his selfish, cynical nature. He opened his mouth to say something, then thought better of it, shrugged, like a man seeking to shift a burden from his shoulders, and stepped down from the carriage. When he stood beside it, he muttered without looking up: 'If you do as I require, nothing unpleasant will happen. And you can forget these tragedy airs – they reek of the boards, you know.'

He was gone before Marianne could recover enough to retort. What was the use? Through the tears she was no longer able to restrain, she saw him climb in to the curricle, take the reins, and back the vehicle away. The wedding procession had moved out of sight past the swing bridge by the Tuileries and the crowd was already dispersing among the side-shows, the sweetmeat stalls and the open-air buffets, and the fountains which would soon begin to flow with wine. But Marianne saw none of this.

Overwhelmed by a terrible feeling of defeat and helplessness, she sat motionless in her seat, her hand clenched on the shining handle of her parasol, her cheeks wet with tears that dropped unheeded on to her lace gown. It did not occur to her to summon Arcadius or to command the carriage to drive on. Her whole mind was concentrated on her cousin and what that elderly woman might be enduring at the hands of Fanchon Fleur-de-Lys and her minions. Jolival, however, had seen Lord Cranmere leave the carriage and had instantly leaped down from the box to rejoin Marianne.

'By all the saints in heaven, what has happened?' he exclaimed, seeing her transformed into a statue of grief. 'What has that man done to you? Why did you not call me?'

She turned her tear-drenched eyes to him and made a little movement to smooth out the crumpled yellow paper which she held between her hands before she gave it to Arcadius.

'Read it,' she said with difficulty. 'All Paris will read it unless I give him the money he wants. And – to make sure – he has abducted Adélaïde. He has me, Arcadius, and he will not let me go. He knows the Emperor will not endure a scandal, nor see his name linked to that of a murderess.'

'A murderess? There is no truth in this filth.'

'Yes. Without intending it, in self-defence, I did kill Ivy St Albans and the runners are searching for me in England.'

'Oh.'

Arcadius lowered himself heavily on to the squabs. Marianne saw, to her distress, that he had gone very pale and she wondered momentarily if he too were about to shrink from her in horror. But Jolival merely extracted a large and spotless handkerchief from his pocket and, putting one arm in a brotherly fashion round Marianne's shoulder, began patiently drying the tears which still flowed from her eyes. A comforting smell of tobacco filled the carriage.

'And what are the – er – gentleman's demands?' Arcadius asked matter-of-factly.

'Fifty thousand livres – within three days. He will tell me where and how to hand it over.'

Arcadius whistled softly.

'The devil! He is greedy. And that, I dare say, is only the beginning. He will not stop there.' He returned the now useless handkerchief to his pocket.

'You think he will want more? I think so too, but he engaged himself, if I give him what he asks, not to demand more money for a year – and to restore Adélaïde to me unharmed.'

'Kind of him. I imagine you do not mean to trust him?'

'Not for an instant, but we have no choice. He has Adélaïde and he knows that I will do anything to save her life. If I set the police on his track, he will kill her without mercy. If that were not so, we should already be on our way to call on the Duke of Otranto –'

'– who would not be able to receive you since he is attending the Emperor's wedding. Besides, there is nothing to say that he could prevent the spread of this dirt. It is almost impossible to suppress a pamphlet of this kind. They appear every day. No, I am wondering if we cannot make shift to recover Mademoiselle d'Asselnat for ourselves. I cannot think there are so many places where Fanchon Fleur-de-Lys can have hidden her, for you may be sure she is in her hands.'

'Can she be in the quarries of Chaillot?'

'Quite certainly not. The Dame Désormeaux is no fool. She knows that charming spot has no secrets from us. No, she will have her somewhere else, but we will need to take great care in finding where because I agree that this Englishman will not hesitate to kill his prisoner as he threatened. I only hope he will honour his agreement and restore her to us on payment of the ransom.'

'Suppose – suppose he does not?' Marianne said faintly.

'That is why we must try and find out where he has hidden her. Besides, as you say, we have no choice. First, we must pay, after that –'

He paused and Marianne saw his jaw tighten under the short beard. She was suddenly conscious that beneath the pleasant, willowy exterior of this little man with his precise, almost feminine elegance, was a will every bit as strong as Francis's.

'After that?' she breathed.

'Take advantage of whatever breathing space we are allowed to attack in our turn. We must render Lord Cranmere harmless for the future.'

'You know that my one desire is to get my marriage annulled so that I may become myself again?'

'That may not be enough.'

'What then?'

'Then,' Jolival said, very softly, 'supposing the Emperor is unable to offer you his head, I think we may have to take it ourselves.'

With the utterance of this cool sentence of death, Arcadius leaned forward and tapped with his cane on the glass.

'Ho there, Gracchus!'

The coachman's round, youthful face appeared.

'Monsieur le Vicomte?'

'To the Tuileries, my lad.'

The words roused Marianne from her contemplation of her friend's pronouncement. She started.

'The Tuileries? What for?'

'Have you forgotten you are engaged to meet Count Clary? He has promised to take you into the grand gallery of the Louvre to see the imperial pair leave the chapel?'

'Do you really think,' Marianne burst out, glad of the chance to relieve her feelings, 'that I have any intention of taking a closer look at this – this masquerade?'

Arcadius threw back his head and laughed.

'I see you have duly appreciated our Emperor's efforts at sartorial splendour. Yet it will be a fine sight, even so ...'

'... and you may as well tell me straight out that you wish to be rid of me! What are you up to, Arcadius?'

'Nothing very much. I have a little business to attend to and I was hoping that if you did not require the carriage, you would let me take it.'

'Take it, but take me home first. Gracchus! We are going home.' Marianne rapped on the glass in her turn. She was curious to know just what it was that Jolival had found to do so urgently but she knew from experience that it was practically impossible to make him talk when he had made up his mind to say nothing.

Marianne's carriage swung round to make its way back across the Concorde bridge. The crowd, which had been so dense while the procession was passing, had thinned a little and most of the people were drifting away through the gardens or along the river towards the palace of the Tuileries, where the imperial couple were to show themselves on the balcony. Marianne, however, had no wish to see the ill-assorted pair again. Had Napoleon taken to wife a princess who matched up to her ideas of what a princess should be, a thoroughbred worthy to be the mother of an emperor, the aristocrat in Marianne would have taken a kind of painful pride in the event. But this blonde pudding with her cow-like expression! How could he gaze at her with such apparent joy and pride? Even the people had sensed it. Perhaps because the graceful and delicate image of Joséphine was still before their eyes, the crowd had given the newcomer only a perfunctory acclaim. The cheering had been scattered and lukewarm. How many were there in that crowd, moreover, who were now greeting Marie-Louise in the very spot where, seventeen years earlier, they had watched the execution of Marie-Antoinette? How could the people of Paris feel anything but uneasy suspicion for this new Austrian, so pitiful a caricature of that radiant princess of an earlier day?

Marianne and Jolival sat in silence as the carriage proceeded across the bridge, and then past the new classical façade of the Palais du Corps Législatif[2], still shrouded in scaffolding, to the Rue de Lille. Both were locked in their own thoughts and each respected the other's silence.

When the vehicle drew up before the newly restored front entrance to the Hôtel d'Asselnat, however, Marianne could not help asking as she gave her hand to Jolival to descend from the carriage: 'Are you sure you would not like me to come with you on this – this urgent business?'

'Quite sure,' Arcadius answered smoothly. 'Go in and sit by the fire like a good girl and wait for me, and do try not to worry. We may not be altogether as helpless as Lord Cranmere likes to think.'

An encouraging smile, a bow, a nourish and the Vicomte de Jolival had disappeared into the carriage which was already turning back towards the street. Marianne gave a little shrug and trod up the steps to where a servant was holding the door for her. Wait like a good girl – not to worry – it was like Jolival to give her that advice. But it was dreadful to have to return to the house when Adélaïde was not there, dear, irritating, wonderful Adélaïde, with her insatiable appetite and never-ending fund of gossip.

As it turned out, she had no time to wonder what she should do with herself until Jolival's return. As she reached the marble staircase that led to her own room she was met by her butler, Jérémie, stiff and solemn as ever in his dark green livery. Marianne was not over-fond of Jérémie, who never smiled and always seemed to have some unwelcome news up his sleeve, but Fortunée, who had chosen him, maintained that to employ a person of such lugubrious and distinguished bearing lent tone to a house. Jérémie bowed, his aquiline features a mask of boredom and gloom.

'Monsieur Constant awaits madame in the music room,' he murmured apologetically, as though confiding some shameful secret. 'He has been waiting for rather more than an hour ...'

A sudden wave of happiness swept over Marianne. Constant! Napoleon's faithful valet, the man most in his confidence and now, to Marianne, the guardian of what seemed a kind of Paradise Lost. Surely fate could have offered no better answer to her present anxiety and the agonizing days ahead? Constant's presence in her house meant that even on

---

[2] The Palais Bourbon

this day of days, Napoleon had thought of her in her loneliness and perhaps the Austrian's hold on him was after all less than Parisian gossip would have it.

Marianne cocked an eyebrow quizzically at her butler.

'I may as well tell you, Jérémie, that M. Constant's visit is very welcome, so there is no need to announce it as if it were a disaster of the first magnitude. You should smile, Jérémie, when you announce a friend, smile – do you know what that is?'

'Not altogether, madame, but I will endeavour.'

# CHAPTER FOUR
# Madame Hamelin's Lovers

With the patience that characterizes the northerner, Constant had sat down to wait in what comfort he could for Marianne's return. He even fell into a doze, ensconced beside the fire with his feet on the fender and his hands clasped on his stomach. He was roused by the sound of Marianne's quick footsteps on the tiled floor outside and by the time the girl entered the music room he was on his feet, bowing respectfully.

'Monsieur Constant! I am so sorry to have kept you waiting. I am so glad to see you, and today of all days! I should have thought no force on earth would have dragged you from the palace.'

'No occasion is important enough to outweigh the Emperor's orders, Mademoiselle Marianne. He commands – and behold, I obey. As for keeping me waiting, think nothing of it. I have been enjoying the peace of your house as a change from all the excitement.'

'He thought of me,' Marianne said involuntarily, shaken by this unexpected happiness, coming on top of the horror she had experienced in the Place de la Concorde.

'Indeed – I believe his majesty thinks of you very often. At all events,' he continued, declining the seat to which his hostess waved him, 'I am charged to deliver my message to you and return to the palace forthwith.' He moved across to the harpsichord and picked up the heavy canvas bag which lay there. 'The Emperor instructed me to hand you this, Mademoiselle Marianne, with his compliments. It contains twenty thousand livres.'

'Money?' she exclaimed, flushing. 'But —'

Constant allowed her no time to protest.

'It occurred to his majesty that you might be in need of funds at this present time,' he said, smiling. 'Moreover, this is in the nature of a remuneration for your services which I am to engage for the day after tomorrow.'

'The Emperor wishes me to —'

'To sing at the reception to be held at the Tuileries. I have the invitation here.' He drew the card from his pocket and presented it to Marianne. Ignoring it, the girl clasped her arms across her breast and went slowly to one of the windows overlooking the small garden. The fountain pattered softly into the grey stone basin, under the smiling gaze of the cupid on the dolphin. Marianne watched it for a moment without speaking. Disturbed by her silence, Constant came towards her.

'Why don't you answer? You will come, of course?'

'I – Constant, I do not want to! To be obliged to curtsey to that woman, sing for her – I couldn't.'

'I am afraid you must, however. The Emperor was far from pleased that you did not come to Compiègne and Madame Grassini suffered for his displeasure. If you fail him this time you must be prepared for his anger.'

'His anger?' Marianne swung round suddenly. 'Can't he understand how it feels to see him with that woman at his side? I was in the Place de la Concorde just now and I saw them ride past, smiling and triumphant and so full of happiness that it hurt. He makes himself ridiculous to please her! That absurd dress, that head-dress —'

'Oh, that dreadful head-dress,' Constant said, laughing. 'It certainly gave us some trouble. Half an hour it took us to set it at a reasonable angle – and even then, I confess, it was not a success.'

Constant's good humour did something to relax Marianne's nerves but her evident distress had not escaped the Emperor's valet and it was in a more serious tone that he continued:

'As for the Empress, I think that you, like all of us, must regard her simply as the symbol and promise of a future dynasty. It is my sincere belief that the Emperor is inclined to value her birth above her person.'

Marianne shrugged.

'Indeed!' she said sullenly. 'I have heard that after that famous night at Compiègne, he took one of his associates aside and told him: "Marry a German, my friend, they are the best women in the world: sweet, kind, innocent and fresh as roses!" Did he say that or no?'

Constant shifted his eyes and moved away to pick up his hat from a chair. He stood for a moment turning it between his hands but he looked up at Marianne at last and there was a touch of sadness in his smile.

'Yes, he said that, but it means little beyond an expression of relief. Remember, she is a Habsburg, the daughter of the man he defeated at Wagram. He might have looked for pride, resentment, even rejection. This placid princess is reassuring, she is a little awkward and nervous, like a country cousin. I think he is profoundly grateful. As for love, if he was as much in love with her as you would like to imagine, would he have thought of you today? No, Mademoiselle Marianne, believe me, come and sing for him, if not for her. And tell yourself that it is Marie-Louise who should fear comparison, not you. Will you come?'

Defeated, Marianne bowed her head in consent.

'I will come. You may tell him so. And tell him,' she added with an effort, indicating the bag of coins, 'that I thank him.' It hurt her to accept the money but as matters stood at present it was very welcome and Marianne could not afford the luxury of refusal.

Arcadius weighed the bag in his hands and laid it back on the writing-table with a sigh.

'The Emperor is generous. It is a good sum, but not nearly enough to satisfy our friend. We need more than twice as much and unless you ask his Majesty to prove himself more generous still ...'

'No!' Marianne cried, flushing. 'Not that! I could not! Besides, I should have to explain, tell him everything. Then the Emperor would set the police on Adélaïde's track – and you know what will happen when Fouché's men come on the scene.'

Arcadius felt in his waistcoat pocket and produced a pretty snuff box of tortoiseshell bound with gold, a present from Marianne, and helped himself luxuriously to a pinch of snuff. The time was nearly nine o'clock and he had just returned to the house, apparently no more ready to explain his mission than he had been at the start. He restored the box to his pocket and smoothed the little bump it made there with his fingers, dreamily, as if in contemplation of a particularly agreeable idea. At last, he said: 'We need have no fear of that happening. None of Fouché's agents will lift a finger to find Mademoiselle Adélaïde, even if we were to ask them.'

'What do you mean?'

'You see, Marianne, when you described your conversation with Lord Cranmere, one thing struck me: the fact that this man, an Englishman travelling under a false name and in all probability a spy, was able not merely to go about Paris in broad daylight – and in the company of a woman notoriously suspect – but seemed to be in no dread of apprehension by the police. He told you, did he not, that if you had him arrested, he would be released at once, with apologies?'

'Yes, I told you.'

'Did it seem odd to you? What did you make of it?'

Marianne clasped her hands and took two or three quick turns about the room.

'Well, I don't know – I did not think about it at the time.'

'Not then or later, I think. But I was curious to know a little more and so I paid a visit to the quai Malaquis. I have some – er – connections among the minister's staff and I found out what I wanted to know, the reason the Vicomte d'Aubécourt is not afraid of the attentions of the police. Quite simply, he is hand in glove with Fouché, perhaps even in his pay.'

'You are mad!' Marianne gasped. 'Fouché would never be hand in glove with an Englishman.'

'Why not? The Duke of Otranto has, at this present moment, excellent reasons for remaining on good terms with an Englishman. He has certainly extended a warm welcome to your noble husband.'

'But – he promised to find him for me?'

'Promises cost nothing, especially when you have no intention of keeping them. I think I can promise you that Fouché not only knows quite well where the Vicomte d'Aubécourt is to be found but also who is passing under that name.'

'This is absurd – fantastic!'

'No. It is politics.'

Marianne felt the world reeling about her ears. She clapped her hands to her head to steady her whirling thoughts. What Arcadius was saying was so shattering that she felt lost on the roads which were suddenly opening out before her, filled with lurking shadows and traps laid before her feet at every step. She made an attempt to see sense in the confusion.

'But this is impossible – the Emperor —'

'Who said anything about the Emperor?' Jolival broke in roughly. 'I said Fouché. Sit down for a moment, Marianne. Stop fluttering about like a frightened bird and listen to me. At this present moment, the Emperor has reached the peak of his success and power. Almost nothing stands against him. Ever since Tilsit, the Tzar swears he loves him like a brother. The Emperor Franz has given him his daughter to wife. He holds the Pope in his hand and his Empire stretches from the Elbe and the Drava to the Ebro. His only enemies now are the wretched Spaniards and their ally, England. Now Joseph Fouché has one burning ambition, and that is to be, after the Emperor, the most powerful man in Europe. He means to become Napoleon's understudy, his right-hand man, and in order to achieve this he has conceived a plan of almost suicidal boldness. His aim is to bring about a reunion between France and England, her last and most deadly enemy. For several months he has been secretly employing trusted agents to negotiate with the Government in London, through the medium of the Dutch king. Let him once find any basis for agreement with Wellesley and he will be able to say to Napoleon: "I have brought you England, willing at last to come to terms with you, on this or that condition." Of course, Napoleon will be furious at first – or pretend to be, because in fact it will remove the biggest thorn from his hide and set his dynasty securely on the throne. Morally speaking, he will have triumphed. That is why Lord Cranmere has nothing to fear from Fouché. He is certainly sent from London.'

Marianne had listened attentively to Jolival's long explanation. Now she said quietly: 'But there is still the Emperor and, to make Fouché do his duty, which is to pursue enemy agents, it is enough to tell his majesty what is in the wind ...'

Her old resentment against Fouché, as the man who had cold-bloodedly made use of her when she was a friendless fugitive, made her by no means reluctant to inform Napoleon of the secret machinations of his trusted Minister of Police.

'I think you would be making a mistake,' Arcadius said seriously. 'I realize, of course, that you are shocked to find one of the Emperor's ministers so exceeding his authority, but an agreement with England would be the best thing that could happen for France. The continental blockade has brought a host of troubles: the war in Spain, the imprisonment of the Pope, incessant levies of troops to defend our ever-growing frontiers.'

Marianne had no answer to this. She never ceased to be surprised at Arcadius's extraordinary ability to acquire information on all subjects, yet, this time, he seemed to her to be going a little far. To have such knowledge of state secrets, he must have been intimately concerned in them. Unable to conceal her thoughts, she said point blank: 'Tell me the truth, Arcadius. You yourself are one of Fouché's agents, are you not?'

The Vicomte laughed outright, but it seemed to Marianne that there was something guarded in his laughter.

'But my dear girl, all France dances to the minister's piping: you, me, Fortunée, the Empress Joséphine ...'

'Don't laugh at me. Tell me the truth.'

Arcadius stopped laughing and, crossing to his young friend's side, gently patted her cheek.

'My dear child,' he said softly, 'I am no one's agent but my own, except perhaps for the Emperor and yourself. But when I need to know something, I take steps to find it out. And you cannot imagine how many people are involved in this business already. I would swear, for example, that your friend Talleyrand is not unaware of it.'

'Very well,' Marianne sighed irritably. 'In that case, since Lord Cranmere is so powerful, how can I protect myself against him?'

'For the present, I have told you: pay up.'

'I shall never find thirty thousand livres in three days.'

'Exactly how much have you?'

'Beside these twenty thousand, a few hundred livres. There are my jewels of course – those given me by the Emperor.'

'Out of the question. He would never forgive you if you sold them, or even pledged them. The best thing would be to ask him to make up the sum. As for your day to day expenses, you have a number of engagements offered you which will take care of that.'

76

'I will not ask him for the money at any cost,' Marianne broke in, so decisively that Jolival did not press the point.

'In that case,' he sighed, 'I see only one way —'

'What?'

'Go and put on one of your prettiest dresses, while I get into knee breeches. I think Madame Hamelin gives a party tonight and you are invited.'

'But I do not mean to go.'

'But you are going, that is, if you want your money. For there we shall certainly find our charming Fortunée's lover, Ouvrard, the banker. Apart from the Emperor, I can think of no quarter where you are more likely to obtain money than from a banker's coffers. This one, moreover, is extremely susceptible to the charms of a pretty woman. He may agree to advance you the sum and you can repay him with the next proof of the Emperor's generosity, which will soon be forthcoming.'

Marianne could not like Arcadius's plan. The idea of using her charms to extract money from a man was repugnant to her, but she told herself firmly that Fortunée would be there to oversee the transaction. Besides, she had no choice. Meekly, she departed to her room to change.


Marianne had never thought that it could take so long to travel the distance from the Rue de Lille to the Rue de la Tour d'Auvergne. The streets were crowded and the carriage moved forward at walking pace through a city illuminated by fairy lights and the coloured sparks of towering firework displays.

'We should have done better to go on foot,' Jolival remarked. 'It would have been quicker.'

'It is much too far,' Marianne retorted. 'It would be morning by the time we got there.'

'I am not sure it won't be, as it is.'

Yet even they yielded at last to the beauty of Paris that night. The Pont de la Concorde was a flaming avenue, its eighty columns garlanded with coloured baubles and surmounted by shining crowns of stars, linked by more lights. All the trees in the Champs-Élysées were decked with multicoloured lights and strings of lights bordered every alley. The noble buildings were illuminated and the streets were bright as day. It was thanks to this, as they crossed the Place de la Concorde, Gracchus was able to avoid running down a few drunkards who had been rather too freely patronizing the fountains running with wine. Things were a little quieter in the Rue Saint-Honoré but they were held up for some time in the vicinity of the Conseil d'État where the wedding banquet was in progress.

The Emperor and his bride actually appeared on the balcony,

accompanied by the Austrian chancellor, Prince Metternich. Amid scenes of wild enthusiasm, the Prince raised his glass and cried:

'I drink to the King of Rome!'

'The King of Rome?' Marianne said petulantly. 'Who is that?'

Arcadius laughed. 'Have you never heard of the Act of the seventeenth of February last? That is the title which the Emperor's son will bear. You must confess that for a minister of the erstwhile Holy Roman Empire, Metternich displays a grandeur of ideas.'

'He displays a total want of tact! A strange way of reminding that poor little goose that she has been married only for the children she may be expected to bear. See if we can get on a little faster, do. We shall never get there!'

Jolival refrained from comment, guessing that this fresh view of the newly-wedded pair had done nothing to calm Marianne's excited nerves. Gravely, he urged the youthful coachman to 'spring the horses', to which Gracchus replied, with equal gravity, that short of driving over the heads of the crowd this was impossible, but that the stream of traffic was beginning to move again. They reached the boulevards where a new form of distraction intervened. Heralds in gilded livery were throwing handfuls of commemorative coins among the crowd, so that it was impossible to shift the mob that surged about their horses, trying to catch hold of the medals. Marianne's carriage was trapped in the centre of a human tide.

'We shall never get through,' Marianne exclaimed, finally losing patience. 'And we must be almost there. I would rather go on foot.'

'In a satin gown, through that mob? You will be torn to pieces.'

But as she spoke, Marianne had flung open the door and, whipping the pink and gold train of her satin dress over one arm, leaped down among the crowd. She slipped away like a snake, without heeding the frantic cries of Gracchus from his box.

'Mademoiselle Marianne! Come back! Don't do it!'

Jolival had no alternative but to leap out after her, but a handful of medals cast at random by one of the young heralds bounced off the brim of his hat and instantly he found himself buried by dozens of loyal subjects of the Emperor, all avid for medals. As he disappeared from view, Gracchus sprang down and rushed to his assistance, brandishing his whip and shouting.

'Hold on, Monsieur le Vicomte! I am coming!'

Marianne, meanwhile, had succeeded in reaching the entrance to the Rue Cerutti without any other damage than the ruin of her coiffure and the loss of her long scarf of quilted satin. However, the evening was exceptionally mild for the time of year, so she ignored this and began to run as fast as the uneven cobbles and the filth in the street allowed to one whose feet were shod in dainty pink satin slippers. The crowd here was much thinner than on the boulevard but even so there were plenty of people walking up and down. However, no one paid much attention to the young woman in her low-cut evening gown. Groups passed by with linked arms, singing for the most part bawdy songs at the tops of their voices, all, directly or indirectly, urging the Emperor to greater prowess in his matrimonial exertions. A few prostitutes in daring gowns with outrageously painted faces roamed from group to group in search of custom and Marianne hurried past, hoping not to be mistaken for one of them.

Once past the Hôtel de l'Empire, she came to a darker patch by the house of the banker Martin Doyen, when suddenly a garden door opened and Marianne ran straight into a man just coming out. He grunted with pain.

'You bloody fool!' he said, pushing her back roughly. 'Can't you look where you are going?'

Then, almost at once, he saw who his assailant was and chuckled.

'My apologies. I did not see you were a woman. But you hurt me.'

'Do you think I enjoyed it?' Marianne retorted. 'I am in a hurry.'

Just then another group of revellers passed by, armed with a lantern. The light fell on Marianne and on the unknown man.

'By God!' the man said, 'you're a beauty! Perhaps this is my lucky day, after all. Come here, my sweeting, you are just what I've been looking for.'

Dazed by his sudden change of tone, Marianne saw that the stranger, who wore a black coat flung hastily over an ill-fastened white shirt, had a military air, that he was tall and lithe with an arrogant, slightly plebeian cast of features, framed by thick, dark hair, so curly as to be almost frizzled. Too late, she realized that the sight of her low-cut bodice and the black curls round her brow had made him take her for a woman of the streets. His hand drew her irresistibly through the door from which he had emerged while with the other he slammed it fast behind them, thrusting her back against the wooden panels, his body close to hers. He was kissing her ardently, while his hands were restlessly exploring the fastenings of her dress.

Angry and half-stifled Marianne reacted instantly, biting the lips that forced themselves on hers and pushing desperately at her assailant. She struck out as hard as she could with what little strength she had left and found to her surprise that the man stepped back with another gasp of pain.

'You little bitch! That hurt —'

'Good,' Marianne said grimly. 'You brute!'

With all her might, she delivered a ringing slap to her attacker's cheek. He staggered under the blow, allowing Marianne, who was feeling for the latch with her other hand, to wrench the door open and tumble out into the street. As luck would have it, a band of students and their girls from the boulevard were passing, filling the street, and tossing about the medals they had won. Slipping among the noisy throng, she managed, at the cost of a few knocks and kisses, to find herself at last outside the doors of Notre-Dame de Lorette, with her attacker nowhere in sight. From there, she was able to make her way painfully up the steep hill, arriving, somewhat out of breath, at Fortunée's house.

All the windows were ablaze with light. Crystal chandeliers shone through the windows between the long, golden-yellow curtains. The sound of voices and laughter wafted out into the street against a soothing background of violins. Casting her eye over the waiting carriages to see if hers was among them, Marianne, with a sigh of relief, hurried up the steps to where Madame Hamelin's enormous major-domo, Jonas, stood impressively on the steps, dressed in his handsome suit of purple and silver.

'Jonas, take me to madame's room and tell her I am here. I cannot appear in public like this.'

The elegant pink dress was torn and crumpled and stained in several places. Marianne's hair was coming down and she looked, indeed, very much what the unknown gallant had taken her to be. The big man rolled his eyes at her.

'Mademoiselle Marianne. You are surely in some state!' he exclaimed. 'Whatever happened to you?'

Marianne laughed lightly. 'Oh, nothing very much. I came here on foot, that is all. Take me upstairs, quickly. I should die of shame if anyone were to see me.'

'Yes, mademoiselle. Come this way, quick.'

Jonas led her through a doorway and up a set of back stairs to his mistress's room where he left her to go in search of Fortunée. With a sigh of relief, Marianne sank down on to a soft stool, cushioned in apple green silk, that stood before a tall mahogany pier glass inlaid with bronze. The image reflected back at her from the mirror was pitiable indeed. Her dress was ruined, her hair in a tangled mass of unruly dark curls, and the rouge which she had used on her lips smeared all over her face by the stranger's greedy kisses.

Angrily rubbing her cheeks with a handkerchief which she found lying on the floor, Marianne scolded herself for a fool. A fool to have jumped out into the crowd in her passion for haste, and still more a fool for listening to Arcadius in the first place. It would have been far better to have gone to bed and waited until the morning to visit Fortunée, rather than embarking on this crazy journey across a city full of revellers. How could she hope to find thirty thousand livres tonight of all nights! The only result was that she was tired to death, her head ached and she looked a fright.

Madame Hamelin came hurrying in to find her friend on the verge of tears, scowling at herself in the mirror. Fortunée promptly burst out laughing.

'Marianne! Have you been in a fight? Was it the Austrian, perhaps? If so, she must be in a fine state, and you are heading for the Vincennes prison!'

'I've been fighting his majesty's worthy subjects,' Marianne retorted, 'and with some maniac who tried to rape me behind a garden door!'

'My dear, what fun!' Fortunée clapped her hands delightedly. 'Tell me all.'

Marianne glared at her friend. Fortunée was looking more than usually radiant tonight. Her dress of yellow muslin trimmed with gold embroidery set off the warm colour of her skin and her rather full lips to admiration. Her dark eyes were shining like coal-black stars beneath her long, sweeping lashes. Her whole being radiated warmth and happiness.

'There is nothing to laugh at,' Marianne said bitterly. 'Apart from my wedding day, this has been the worst day of my life! I – I am half-dead with worry and so dreadfully unhappy –'

Her voice broke and great tears rolled from her eyes. Fortunée stopped laughing instantly and put her arms around her friend, enveloping her in a powerful scent of roses.

'You are crying? And I was laughing at you! Oh, my poor pet, I am sorry. Quickly, tell me what has happened. But first, you must take off that rag and let me find you another dress.'

She was unfastening the ruined dress as she spoke when all at once she paused with a cry, pointing to a dark stain on the crumpled fabric.

'Blood! You are hurt?'

'Good heavens, no,' Marianne said in surprise. 'I don't know where it can have come from. Unless –'

Suddenly, she recalled the exclamations of pain which she had drawn from her attacker, and the disorder of his dress, with his coat flung over his half-open shirt. He could have been wounded.

'Unless what?'

'Nothing. It does not matter. Oh, Fortunée, you must help me or I am lost.'

In quick, broken sentences, but growing calmer as she talked, Marianne described her terrible day, Francis's threats and demands, the abduction of Adélaïde and, finally, the impossibility of laying hands on thirty thousand livres in the next forty-eight hours, short of selling her jewels.

'I can lend you ten thousand,' Madame Hamelin said soothingly. 'As for the remainder ...' She paused for a moment, regarding Marianne's reflection in the mirror through half-closed eyes. While Marianne had been talking, Fortunée had stripped off the rest of her friend's clothes and, fetching a sponge and a flask of Cologne from her dressing-room, had busied herself wiping away the dust of the streets and rubbing her friend down comfortingly.

'What of the remainder?' Marianne asked, when Fortunée still said nothing.

Madame Hamelin gave a slow smile and, picking up a huge swan's-down puff began gently powdering her friend's breast and shoulders.

'With a fine body like yours,' she said coolly, 'that should not be difficult to come by. I know a dozen men who would give that much for a single night with you.'

Marianne gasped. 'Fortunée!' She had recoiled instinctively and was scarlet to the roots of her hair. Her indignation had no effect on the Creole's smiling calm. She only laughed.

'I keep forgetting your obsession with the idea of a single love and your regrettable faithfulness to a man who, for the present, is doing all he can to get another woman with child. Little fool, when will you learn that your body is a wonderful instrument of pleasure and that it is a crime against nature to neglect it so tragically? It is senseless!'

'Senseless or not, I will not sell myself!' Marianne declared hotly. Fortunée shrugged her beautifully-rounded shoulders.

'The trouble with you aristocratic people is that you feel obliged to use grand words for the simplest things. Well, I will see what I can do for you.'

She went to the wardrobe and brought out a charming white silk dress adorned with huge appliquéd tropical flowers.

'Put this on, you chaste little guardian of the sacred flame of love, while I go and see whether I can sacrifice myself in your place.'

'What are you going to do?' Marianne inquired uneasily.

'Don't worry, I shan't sell myself to the highest bidder. I am merely going to ask my friend Ouvrard to be so obliging as to lend us the twenty thousand that we need. He is shockingly wealthy and I dare say he will deny me nothing. He is downstairs. Moreover, since he has not been in high favour with the Emperor, he will probably be delighted to serve one as close to his majesty as yourself. Sit down and rest. I will tell Jonas to bring you up some champagne.'

'You are a darling!' Marianne said, and meant it.

She kissed her hand to the disappearing cloud of yellow muslin, then turned her attention to the dress which Fortunée had bestowed on her. She slipped it on hastily, in case Jonas should come in and catch her unawares, then, finding a silver brush and ivory comb upon the dressing-table, she proceeded to untangle her dark hair. A sense of peace stole over her, divinely restful after the miseries of the preceding hours. Fortunée's morals might leave a good deal to be desired, but her whole personality breathed a vitality and a warm humanity that could cheer the chilliest soul. The beautiful Creole was one of those simple, uncomplicated people endowed by nature with the power of giving without asking for anything in return. She would give of her help, her time, her affection, money and sympathy all with the same generosity and saw not the slightest reason why she should not give as freely of something as natural as her body. She was not one of those women who use their virtue as an excuse for treating men with a coldness and cruelty that could drive them to despair. No one had ever killed themselves for Fortunée. She could not bear to see anyone suffer, especially when that suffering could be eased by a few hours of love. Moreover, she had the rare talent of being able, once love was past, to make faithful friends of her often-inconstant lovers. Certainly, in the present instance, Marianne had no doubt that she would use all her charms to extract from her rich lover the huge sum of money needed by her friend.

Smiling inwardly at the thought of this friendship, Marianne was busy winding her newly-plaited hair in a crown about her head when she heard the door click shut behind her. Thinking it was Jonas bringing the promised champagne, she did not turn but went on with her task.

'I don't know who you are – ' a voice spoke gaspingly from the other side of the room – 'but for pity's sake – fetch Madame Hamelin.'

For an instant, Marianne sat rigidly, her arms frozen above her head, then she turned. It seemed to her that the voice was in some way familiar. A man was leaning back against the closed door. His face was very white and he seemed to be struggling against an overwhelming faintness. His eyes were closed and his mouth set in a grim line, his breath came in hoarse gasps, but still Marianne made no move to help him. She sat staring in amazement. The man was dressed in dark blue pantaloons and hessians, with a white shirt. A heavy, black coat was flung over his shoulders and his brown hair was very curly, while to her horror Marianne had no difficulty in recognizing his face. It belonged to her attacker of the rue Cerutti.


Marianne had been correct in her idea that the man was hurt. The explanation of the bloodstains on her dress was now clearly visible on the white shirt, just below the left shoulder, as the man slid to the floor, unconscious.

She watched, petrified, as he collapsed and would probably have sat there wondering still, without doing a thing to help him, if Jonas's voice had not sounded outside the door.

'It is Jonas, mademoiselle. The door is stuck, can you open it?'

The spell was broken. Marianne saw that the man had fallen in such a way as to obstruct the opening of the door.

'Just a moment, Jonas, I will do it.'

She seized the unknown man by the feet and tugged with all her strength to drag him into the middle of the room. He was heavy and it was all she could do to shift him enough to allow Jonas to enter.

'Leave the tray outside. I can't get it open any more,' she told him, pulling on the handle as she spoke. The butler eased himself through the narrow space.

'What is the trouble, Mademoiselle Marianne?' Then, seeing the obstacle. 'Monsieur le Baron! Lordy, he badly hurt!'

'Do you know this man?'

'Surely. He what you might call one of de family. It is de General Fournier-Sarlovèze. Has Madame Fortunée not spoken of him? He can't stay here. We better put him on de bed.'

While Jonas picked up the wounded man as easily as if he had weighed nothing at all and laid him on the bed, Marianne gathered her scattered thoughts. General the Baron Fournier-Sarlovèze? Of course, she had heard of him from Fortunée who had spoken of him with a soft, cooing intonation that spoke volumes to anyone acquainted with the Creole. This was the handsome Francois, one of her three accredited lovers, the other two being the no less attractive Casimir de Montrond, at present an exile in Anvers, and the much less seductive but vastly wealthier Ouvrard. But what else was it that Fortunée had said? Why had Marianne never yet met him in her friend's house? Ah yes, that was it: the man was impossible, 'the worst fellow in the whole army' but also the 'finest swordsman' in that same army. He divided his time between dashing feats of arms and interludes on half-pay brought about by his innumerable affairs of honour. This must be one of those times when he had been sent home until the Emperor was pleased to forget his latest indiscretion.

The thought of Napoleon reminded Marianne of something else her friend had told her and which at the time had shocked her profoundly. Fournier was a child of the Revolution, into which he had thrown himself with enthusiasm, but he hated the Emperor, who cordially returned his dislike. Nevertheless, Napoleon continued to offer the hothead employment in his service for the sake of his military prowess, a prowess which had earned him the rank of general and the title of baron. To Fournier, however, these seemed small things beside the fortunes and the honours lavished on the marshals. All in all, considering her own recent experience, Marianne felt little concern or liking for the man. To some extent, he could even be dangerous and she felt little desire to further her acquaintance with him. It was bad enough to know that Fortunée, for all her devotion to Napoleon, could retain a soft spot for the fellow merely because he was handsome and a tireless lover.

Seeing Jonas occupied, with many exclamations of grief and horror, in pulling off the wounded man's boots and administering some rough first aid to his wound, Marianne turned away and moved towards the door. She would have gone down to warn Fortunée but hesitated to do so, not knowing how her friend meant to approach the banker. Before she could make up her mind, the door was flung open and Madame Hamelin swept in saying: 'I have done all I can and I think —'

She broke off as her eyes went past her friend and widened with horror as they fell upon Jonas, busy by the light of a branch of candles beside the bed.

'François! My God, he is dead!'

She darted past Marianne and ran quickly to the bed, pushing aside Jonas who, with his sleeves rolled up, was beginning to clean the wound with lint. With a cry like a tigress, she flung herself upon her lover's motionless body.

'Gentle Jesus, Madame Fortunée!' Jonas exclaimed. 'Don't shake him like dat, or you'll kill him right enough. He not dead. He fainted. His wound not grave.'

Fortunée, who Marianne suspected had a secret fondness for high tragedy, paid no attention and continued to shriek and lament at the top of her voice, covering her lover's face with so many passionate kisses that, coupled with the smelling salts applied by Jonas, they finally persuaded him to open his eyes. This sign of life drew a triumphant scream from Madame Hamelin.

'Heaven be praised! He is alive!'

''Course he alive,' Jonas said scornfully. 'He only fainted from exhaustion and loss of blood. Don't you maul him like dat, Madame Fortunée. Monsieur le Ba'on he do ve'y well. You see —'

The injured man was endeavouring to raise himself on one elbow. He groaned but managed to smile at his mistress.

'I must be getting old,' he said. 'Dupont got me this time, damn him, but I'll be even with him.'

'Dupont again!' Fortunée exclaimed wrathfully. 'You never set eyes on the man but you must fight him! How long is it? Ten years? Twelve?'

Fournier grinned. 'Fifteen. And since we are well matched with swords, this will not be the last. Haven't you anything to offer a wounded man who —' He broke off as his gaze went past Madame Hamelin to where Marianne was standing with folded arms staring into the fire, waiting for these first transports to be over. 'But - I know you!' he said, clearly searching his memory for a recollection which could not be long in coming. 'Surely, you are —'

'Well, I do not know you,' Marianne declared firmly. 'But I should be grateful if you would spare Fortunée to me for a moment, since I ask nothing better than to leave you to one another's company.'

'Oh my God, my poor darling, I was forgetting you! The shock —' She sprang up and fled with equal impetuosity back to her friend and flung her arms about her. 'I have spoken to Ouvrard,' she whispered. 'I think he will agree but he wants to talk to you. Will you go down to him? He is waiting in the little drawing room. Jonas, go with Mademoiselle Marianne and bring me a decanter of brandy for the general.'

Without further urging, Marianne turned on her heel, glad to be out of range of Fournier's gaze, in which she could now read a very evident mockery. It seemed that he had recognized her and felt not the slightest shame at the memory of his unforgivable effrontery. As she left the room, she heard him remark thoughtfully to Fortunée: 'I am not acquainted with the name of your charming but strait-laced friend, and yet, I don't know how it is, but I have a vague feeling that I stand somehow in her debt ...'

'You are feverish, dearest,' cooed Fortunée. 'I can assure you; you have never met my dear Marianne before. You can't have done.'

Marianne restrained herself from comment with an effort. The wretch knew very well that she could never bring herself to tell her friend the truth about their stormy meeting and, besides, it was of no importance because she was determined that matters should go no further between them. It was not necessary for her to know that this man, with his odious self-assurance, hated the Emperor. She had already ranged him among the people she had no wish to meet again, and she was determined that it should be so. Curiously, as if he had read her thoughts, Jonas murmured in her ear as they went down the stairs: 'If de general stay here some time, Mademoiselle Marianne, we not see much of madame. De last time she and de general not leave their room for mo' dan a week.'

Marianne frowned but said nothing. She was not shocked by the length of time itself, but it seemed to her that such behaviour could not be much to the taste of the banker Ouvrard, Fortunée's lover of the moment. It would be disastrous for her, Marianne, if the man on whom she depended should take serious offence in the days to come.

Sighing, she made her way to join the banker in the little room that was already familiar to her as one of Fortunée's favourite apartments because it was lined with tall Venetian mirrors set in moulded frames of grey and gold in which she could contemplate her own charming image multiplied to infinity. Pleasantly reflected likewise were the dull pink drapes and the soft glow of the delicate directoire furnishings, and the single note of brilliant colour in the room, the huge turquoise-blue Chinese vase filled with tulips and irises. The presence of the mistress of the house lingered in the faint scent of roses that mingled with the smell of a wood fire.

Coming into the room and seeing Ouvrard leaning against the chimney-piece, Marianne reflected that, for all his fortune, the man did not fit into his surroundings. Apart from his money, she could see little in him to attract women. He was in his early forties, short, foxy-faced and greying, dressed with extreme care and rather exaggerated opulence. Yet Gabriel Ouvrard was popular with women, and not only with Fortunée, who made no attempt to conceal her love of money. It was rumoured that the divinely languorous Juliette Récamier herself had bestowed her favours on him, and other beauties besides.

Although feeling herself no more drawn to this second lover of Madame Hamelin's than she had to the first, Marianne forced herself to smile in a friendly fashion as she advanced to meet the banker, who had turned at the sound of the door. With a satisfied 'Ha!', Ouvrard took both her hands in his and placed a kiss on each before leading her over to the pink sofa on which, when she had nothing better to do, Fortunée was in the habit of lying for hours at a time nibbling sweets and devouring the few novels which passed the strict imperial censorship.

'My dear, dear lady,' he said on a note of earnest familiarity filled with reproach, 'why did you not come to me at once. You should not have troubled our friend with such a trifle.'

Marianne appreciated the mention of a 'trifle'. Twenty thousand livres seemed to her a considerable sum and she supposed that only a banker could talk so airily, yet it gave her fresh heart. However, Ouvrard had not finished.

'You should have come to me, to my house, at once. It would have saved a great deal of trouble.'

'Indeed – I should not have dared,' Marianne confessed, endeavouring to extricate her hands from the banker's kneading grasp.

'Not dared? A pretty woman like you? Surely you have heard that I am a slave to beauty? And who in Paris is more beautiful than the Emperor's Nightingale?'

'The Emperor's Nightingale?'

'But yes, adorable Maria Stella, that is what they are calling you. Did you not know?'

'No, indeed,' Marianne said, feeling that her companion was lavishing all too fulsome praise on someone preparing to borrow a large sum of money from him. But Ouvrard was continuing.

'I was present at your performance at the Feydeau. Ah, a miracle indeed! Such a voice, such grace, such beauty! I can truthfully say I was in transports! I fell beneath your spell! The exquisitely moving tone, the purity of the sounds that sprang from that delicate throat, those rosy lips! Who would not be at your feet? Myself –'

'You are too kind,' Marianne said quickly, beginning to feel some alarm in case the banker should suit the action to the words and go down on his knees before her, 'but I beg you, say no more about that evening, it – it was not all I could have wished.'

'Ah, to be sure, your accident! That was –'

'Extremely disagreeable and the consequences are by no means finished. I ask you to forgive me if I seem rude and impatient, but I must be sure. You can imagine how reluctantly I have been compelled to appeal for assistance –'

'From a friend – a loyal and devoted friend. I hope you do not doubt that?'

'I should not be here else. And so – I may count on such a sum, the day after tomorrow perhaps?'

'Indeed, you may. In the afternoon, shall we say?'

'No, that will not be possible. I am to sing at the Tuileries before – before their majesties.'

She stumbled on the plural but she got it out somehow. Ouvrard listened with a beatific smile.

'In the evening, then? After the reception? I will expect you at my house. That will be even better. We can talk – get to know one another.'

The colour flamed in Marianne's cheeks. She rose quickly, snatching back her hands which the banker still held. It had dawned on her suddenly on what conditions Ouvrard was prepared to advance her the money. Quivering with anger, she burst out: 'Monsieur Ouvrard, I do not think we understand one another correctly. This is a loan merely. I will repay you the twenty thousand livres within three months.'

The banker's pleasant face was crossed by a momentary frown. He shrugged.

'Who spoke of a loan? A woman such as you may make what demands she pleases. I will give you more if you wish.'

'I do not want any more – and that only as a loan.'

The banker sighed and getting to his feet moved heavily to where Marianne had prudently retreated to the chimney-piece. His voice had lost its honeyed tones and there was a strange flicker in his eyes.

'Leave such matters to men, my dear, and take what is offered you in good faith.'

'In return for what?'

'For nothing – or nothing to signify. A little friendship, an hour of your company, the right to look at you, breathe in your fragrance …'

Again, his hands groped towards her eagerly, ready to hold and caress. The banker's sallow face had turned brick red above his snowy cravat and his eyes rested greedily on the beautiful, bare shoulders before him. A tremor of disgust ran through Marianne. How could she have been such a fool as to apply to this man with his dubious history, and who had barely emerged from prison? It was madness!

'What you ask,' she said hastily, in a desperate attempt to frighten him, 'is impossible. The Emperor would never forgive either of us. You must know that I am – an imperial perquisite.'

'Perquisites cost money, signorina. Those who enjoy them must be aware of this and take steps to see that no one can outbid them. In any case, think about it. You are tired tonight, and clearly under some stress. Today's wedding must have been very trying for a – perquisite! But do not forget that twenty thousand livres, or more, will be waiting for you at my house the day after tomorrow, all night if need be, and all the next day.'

Without a word or even a glance, Marianne turned on her heel and went to the door. Her pride and dignity made her look like an insulted queen, but there was despair in her heart. What had seemed her last remaining chance to obtain the money was gone, for she would never, never agree to accept Ouvrard's conditions. She had thought, in her innocence, that he would make her a friendly loan but now she realized once again that with men all transactions came down to the same thing, when the woman concerned was young and pretty. 'I know a dozen men who would give as much for one night with you,' was what Fortunée had said and Marianne had thought she was joking. How much had Madame Hamelin known about Ouvrard's intentions? Was it in order that the proposition could be put to Marianne directly that she had not concluded the matter herself? Marianne found it hard to believe that her friend could have led her so cruelly into a trap so repugnant to her, knowing her as she did.

Her question was answered sooner than she expected. She was on the point of leaving the room when Ouvrard's voice made her pause.

'Do not forget: I shall be waiting. You understand, of course, that there is no need to tell our friend Fortunée about our little agreement. A delightful creature, but inclined to be jealous!'

Jealous? Fortunée? At that moment, Marianne almost forgot her anger and laughed in his face. Did this absurd little man really believe that he had power to attach that exotic creature to himself alone? She had an irresistible urge to throw in his face the information that this 'delightful' but 'jealous' creature was in all probability even then revelling in the arms of the handsome soldier who was her heart's delight. Just to see what he would say.

But Madame Hamelin conducted her life according to her own rules and not for anything would Marianne have caused her the slightest trouble. Besides, it was a relief to know that she was unaware of Ouvrard's little plan and of the terms of the bargain he meant to offer. Marianne was beset by a fresh temptation: to go and warn her instantly, and this she would most probably have done, had Fortunée been alone. But Marianne had no wish for a fresh encounter with the insolent Fournier, much less to interrupt the lovers' tête-à-tête.

'Tell Madame Hamelin I will see her tomorrow,' was all she said to Jonas when he appeared at her side, 'that is, if she is receiving callers.'

'But Mademoiselle Marianne, you are not going out like that? Wait while I call for the carriage.'

'No need, Jonas. I can see my own carriage arriving.'

It was true. A glance through the hall windows had shown her Gracchus-Hannibal bringing the chaise round in sweeping style to draw up at the steps. But even as Jonas tenderly arranged a handy cashmere shawl about Marianne's shoulders, his eyes widened at the sight of Arcadius descending from the carriage.

His black coat was torn, shreds of lace hanging from his shirt front, his fine silk hat completely stove in, one eye blackening nicely and countless scratches on his face: the Vicomte de Jolival showed all the signs of a glorious combat, while Gracchus sat upright on his box, hatless and dishevelled, extremely red of face and bright of eye, wielding his whip with a triumphant flourish.

'Well,' Marianne said, 'so here you are! Where have you been?'

'In the crowd, where you left us,' Jolival growled. 'You look a good deal fresher than we do, but I thought you were wearing a pink dress when we started out?'

'That met with some adventures, too. But let us go home, my friend. You need a bath and some attention to that eye. Home, Gracchus, as quick as you can.'

'If you want me to spring 'em, mademoiselle, we'll have to go through the wall by the Fermiers Généraux and half-way round Paris.'

'Go which way you please, but take us home and avoid the crowd.'

As the carriage swept out of the courtyard once more, Arcadius held his handkerchief to his swollen eye again.

'Well?' he asked. 'Did you get anything?'

'Ten thousand livres which Madame Hamelin offered me at once.'

'That was kind – but not enough. Did you try Ouvrard as I suggested?'

Marianne pursed her lips and frowned at the recollection of what had passed.

'Yes. Fortunée paved the way for me, but we could not agree. He – his charges are too high for me, Arcadius.'

There was a short silence, spent by Jolival in weighing up the implications of these words, which he had no difficulty in interpreting correctly.

'Ah,' was all he said. 'And – does Madame Hamelin know the terms of this bargain?'

'No. Nor is it intended that she should. I would have told her at once, of course, only she was very much occupied.'

'With what?'

'With a certain wounded soldier who dropped on her like a chimney-pot in a gale and who seems to hold a high place in her affections.'

'Fournier, I know. So, the hussar has returned? For all his dislike of the Emperor, he can never bear to stay long away from the field of action.'

Marianne uttered a small sigh. 'Is there anything you do not know, my friend?'

Jolival achieved a painful grin regardless of his scratches, and stared gloomily at the ruins of his hat.

'Yes, such as, for instance, how we are to procure the twenty thousand livres that we need?'

'There is only one way left. My jewels. Even if it does mean trouble with the Emperor. You must see if you can pledge them tomorrow. If not, they must be sold.'

'You are making a mistake, Marianne. Believe me, you had better go to the Emperor. Ask for an audience and, since you are to sing at the Tuileries the day after tomorrow ...'

'No! Definitely not! He questions too shrewdly and there are things I would not have him know. After all,' she added sadly, 'it is true I am a murderess. I killed a woman, unintentionally, but I killed her. I cannot tell him that.'

'Do you think he will not ask questions if he hears that you have sold his emeralds?'

'Try and arrange to buy them back in two or three months' time. I will sing wherever I am asked. You find me the contracts.'

'Very well,' Jolival sighed. 'I will do my best. Meanwhile, take this.'

He felt in the pocket of his battered white waistcoat and extracted something round and shining which he slipped into Marianne's hand.

'What is this?' she said, leaning over to see it more clearly in the darkness of the chaise.

'A little souvenir of a memorable day,' Jolival said sardonically. 'One of the medals they were throwing to the crowd. I won it in fair fight. Take care of it,' he added, dabbing once more at his swollen eye, 'it cost me dear.'

'I am sorry about your eye, my poor friend, but one thing you may be sure of: even if I live to be a hundred, I shall never forget today.'

# CHAPTER FIVE
# Cardinal San Lorenzo

Faithful to his self-appointed role of *cicisbeo*, Prince Clary presented himself on the following Wednesday ready to escort Marianne to the Tuileries. But as the ambassadorial carriage drove them there, Marianne did not fail to notice that her companion seemed preoccupied. The young man's forehead was wrinkled below his fair hair in an anxious frown and his candid smile was without its usual gaiety. When she taxed him gently with it, he made no effort to deny it.

'I am uneasy, my dear Maria. I have not seen the Emperor since the night of his marriage, the day before yesterday, and I fear this reception may not go altogether smoothly. I am not yet well-acquainted with his majesty, but I saw him in such anger the other day as he came from the chapel —'

'Anger? Coming out of the chapel? But what happened?' Marianne asked, her curiosity aroused at once.

Léopold Clary smiled and dropped a rapid kiss on her hand.

'Of course, you were not there, you deserted me. Well, I must tell you that as the Emperor entered the chapel he noticed that only twelve of the twenty-seven cardinals invited were actually present. Fifteen had failed to appear and, believe me, their absence was extremely noticeable.'

'But why should they deliberately stay away?'

'That it was deliberate, there can be no doubt, alas. And it has caused us at the embassy a good deal of embarrassment. You know how the Emperor stands with the Pope? He holds his Holiness a prisoner at Savona and did not feel himself bound to apply to him for a dissolution of his previous marriage. It was all done here in Paris. Now the absence of these princes of the Church casts some doubt on the legality of our Archduchess's marriage. It is all most unpleasant, and Prince Metternich was far from pleased at those fifteen empty stalls.'

'Bah!' Marianne retorted, not without a certain satisfaction. 'You knew all this before your Princess ever left Vienna. You could have insisted that his Holiness should authorize the Empress Joséphine's divorce. Don't tell me you did not know the Pope had excommunicated the Emperor a year ago?'

'I knew,' Clary agreed gloomily. 'We all knew. Since then, we have been defeated at Wagram, we needed peace, a breathing space, and we were simply not strong enough to refuse Napoleon's request.'

'You mean this marriage was more than you dared hope for?' the young woman countered with a cruelty regretted as soon as it was out, when she saw her friend's unhappy face and heard him sigh.

'It is never much fun to be beaten. In any case, this marriage is a fact and however painful it may be to us to see the Church treat one of our princesses in this cavalier fashion, we cannot entirely blame her. That is what worries me. All the bishops and cardinals have been invited to this concert, you know.'

Marianne did know and had dressed accordingly. Her gown of heavy, dull-blue silk, embroidered with palm-leaves in silver, was made high to the throat, framing the rows of pearls which she had inherited from her mother and which were the only jewels she had kept, all the rest having been handed to Jolival the day before. The dress had long sleeves, half-concealing her hands. She waved those hands now, carelessly.

'You are tormenting yourself for nothing, my friend. Why should these cardinals come to the concert any more than to the wedding?'

'Because your Emperor's invitations are more in the nature of commands and they may not dare to absent themselves a second time. But I fear the reception they will get from Napoleon. If you had seen the way he looked at the empty seats in the chapel, you would be as anxious as I am. My friend Lebzeltern said it sent cold shivers down his spine. If it comes to an open breach, our position will be highly uncomfortable. The Emperor Franz is on close terms with his Holiness.'

This time, Marianne said nothing. She felt little interest in the qualms of conscience suffered by Austria. Besides, they were arriving. The carriage had passed the Pont des Tuileries and the guards outside the Louvre and was approaching the high, gilded railings enclosing the Cour du Carrousel. But from here, progress became increasingly laborious. A large crowd had collected round the palace and was pressing up against the railings. Some people had even climbed up to get a better view, against all efforts to restrain them. There were sounds of exclamations and laughter.

'Crowds, whether Viennese or Parisian, are always equally strange and uncontrollable,' observed the Prince. 'I hope they will let us pass.'

But the ambassador's groom had already announced his master's carriage and the guards were busy clearing a way for it. The coachman urged his horses inside and the occupants of the carriage were able to see for themselves the extraordinary spectacle which had been attracting the laughter of the Parisian crowd. There, in the great courtyard, among the soldiers standing to attention, the palace officials and the grooms and servants controlling the arrival of the guests, were fifteen cardinals in ceremonial dress, the skirts of their purple robes thrown over their arms, wandering about at random, their secretaries trotting at their heels like a flock of terrified black chickens. Only a Parisian crowd could have found anything humorous in the sight of these stately, red-robed figures, moving about apparently aimlessly; neither soldiers nor officials seemed to pay them the slightest attention.

'What does it mean?' Marianne asked. Turning to Clary, she saw that he had gone very white and that his heavy side-whiskers were trembling uncontrollably.

'I am afraid that this is the way the Emperor has chosen to manifest his displeasure. What else does he intend, I wonder?'

The carriage drew up at the steps. A footman opened the door. Clary got out and held out his hand to his companion.

'Come inside, quickly. I would give a great deal not to have seen this.'

'To spare your conscience further qualms?' Marianne said, with irony. 'What is the creature which behaves so? An ostrich, is it not? Perhaps we should call you Ostrichians?'

'What a dreadful pun! There are times when I wonder if you hate me.'

This was a question Marianne had already asked herself many times but at that moment it had ceased to interest her. Her eyes had come to rest on one of the cardinals, a small man whose billowing red robes made him look like an overblown rose. He had his back to her and was standing on the bottom step, apparently talking earnestly with a thin, dark Abbé who was bending his tall figure to hear what was being said. Something about the little cardinal fascinated Marianne. The shape of his head, perhaps, above the ermine collar, or the colour of the grey hair under the round red cap? Or then again, was it the exquisitely-shaped hands as he waved them in the heat of his argument? All at once, he looked round and at the sight of his profile a cry was torn from Marianne.

'Godfather!'

The blood rushed to her face as she recognized the man who, throughout her childhood, had shared her heart with her Aunt Ellis, and although she had no more than a brief glimpse of his face, she could not be mistaken now. The little cardinal was Gauthier de Chazay.

'What was that?' Clary said anxiously regarding her. 'You know—'

But Marianne was no longer listening. She had forgotten his presence as she had forgotten the place where they stood, even the person she now was. She was, as she had been long ago, little ten-year-old Marianne, running as hard as she could the whole length of the park at Selton when she saw the Abbé de Chazay coming slowly up the avenue. She felt no surprise, even, at finding the little Abbé, perpetually short of money, now dressed in the red robes of a cardinal. With him, all things were possible, even the most improbable. In a sudden rush of joy, she did quite naturally what she had always done, she picked up the skirts of her magnificent dress in both hands and hurried after the two priests who were already beginning to move away, careless of the curiosity she aroused. A moment later, she had caught up with them.

'Godfather! Oh, this is wonderful – wonderful!'

Laughing and crying at once, she threw herself into the arms of the little cardinal who had barely time to see who it was before she had her arms round his neck.

'Marianne!'

'Yes, it is I, indeed! Oh, godfather, this is wonderful!'

'Have I taken leave of my senses? Marianne? Here? What are you doing in Paris?'

He had extricated himself and was now holding her at arm's length gazing at her in a delighted astonishment much stronger than concern for his dignity. His homely features shone with joy.

'I am not dreaming! It is really you! Good heavens, child, how lovely you have grown! Let me kiss you again.'

And before the horrified gaze of the thin priest and of Prince Clary who had followed his companion automatically, the cardinal and the girl began hugging one another again with an enthusiasm which left their mutual feelings in no doubt.

The thin priest must have formed his own ideas about these unorthodox transports, for he coughed gently and tapped the cardinal's shoulder.

'Forgive me, your Eminence, but it might perhaps – that is – er – the circumstances – your Eminence must be aware that people are staring.'

This was true. Palace servants, guards and prelates were all staring transfixed at the odd little scene: the black-clad priest and the splendid Austrian officer watching the little cardinal and the richly-dressed girl. There were smiles and whispers. Léopold Clary alone seemed conscious of embarrassment. Gauthier de Chazay shrugged magnificently.

'Don't be a fool, Bichette. Let them look if they care to. Do you realize that I have found my long-lost child, the child of my heart, I mean. Allow me to introduce you. Marianne, my child, this is the Abbé Bichette, my faithful secretary. And you, my friend, meet my god-daughter, Lady Marianne –'

He stopped short, realizing what he had been about to say in his delighted enthusiasm. The smile faded, as if a curtain had been drawn across by some invisible hand and he looked at Marianne in sudden disquiet.

'This is impossible,' he muttered. 'How is it you are here, in France, entering this palace in the company of an Austrian?'

'Prince Léopold Clary und Aldringen,' the young man introduced himself promptly, clicking his heels and bowing.

'Charmed,' the cardinal responded automatically, still pursuing his own thoughts. 'What I mean is, how do you come to be in Paris, when the last time we met ... Where is —'

Marianne broke in hurriedly, guessing with horror what he was about to say. As it was, Clary had certainly heard that unfortunate 'Lady Marianne', so much was clear from his expression, and that was sufficiently alarming.

'I will explain everything later, godfather. It is a long story and too complicated to explain here. But tell me what you are doing yourself. You were about to leave on foot, if I guess rightly?'

'I shall do as the others do, of course,' the cardinal declared. We came here, my brothers and I, and were informed by the Grand Marshal of the Palace that we were to leave again at once, since his majesty churlishly refused to receive us!'

'Eminence,' begged the Abbé Bichette, rolling his eyes in horror, 'be careful what you are saying.'

'What's that? I shall say what I please! I was shown the door, was I not? They even paid us the compliment of sending away our carriages so that we might present the riff-raff of Paris with the amusing spectacle of fifteen cardinals trotting home on foot, like grocers, with their robes tucked up out of the dust! I hope the good people of Paris appreciate their Emperor's courtesy!'

Monsignor de Chazay's face was as red as his robe and his usually well-modulated voice was growing alarmingly shrill. Clary intervened.

'If I understand correctly,' he said stiffly, 'your Eminences saw fit to absent yourselves from the wedding of our Archduchess? Naturally, the Emperor could not allow such an affront to go unpunished. I confess, I had expected the worst.'

'You need have no fear, the worst will certainly come. As for the Archduchess, I assure you, monsieur, we regret it deeply, but it is our duty to his Holiness to adhere to the position which he has adopted. The marriage between Napoleon and Joséphine has not been annulled in Rome.'

'In other words,' Prince Clary said, 'in your eyes, our Princess is not married?'

Marianne, horrified at the prospect of a fresh scandal, hastened to intervene.

'For pity's sake, gentlemen! Not here – godfather, you cannot walk home like this. Where are you living?'

'With a friend, Canon Philibert de Bruillard, in the rue Chanoinesse. I do not know if you are aware of it, my child, but our family's house is now in the possession of an opera singer who enjoys the favour of Napoleon.

Consequently, I am unable to live there.'

Marianne felt as if she had been struck. Each word seemed to wound her to her very soul. She drew back, white to the lips, groping for Léopold Clary's arm and leaning on it heavily. Without that support she would probably have fallen in the dust that was already marking the red slippers of the prince of the Church. Those few words measured the gulf which had opened between her and her childhood days. She was seized by a sudden terror that, in his innocence and old-world chivalry, Clary would spring to her defence and utter the truth that she was that very opera singer in person. Marianne meant to tell her godfather the truth, the whole truth, but in her own time, not among a crowd.

Fighting desperately to control herself, she managed a pale smile, while her grip tightened on the Prince's sleeve.

'I will visit you tonight, if you will let me. Meanwhile, Prince Clary's carriage will take you home.'

The young Austrian stiffened.

'But – my dear, what will the Emperor say?'

At this she lost her temper, finding in her anger a release for her deepest emotions.

'You are not the Emperor's subject, my dear Prince. And may I remind you that your own sovereign is on excellent terms with the Holy Father. Or did I not understand you correctly?'

Léopold Clary drew himself up, as if in the presence of the Emperor Franz himself.

'You understood quite correctly. Eminence, my carriage and my servants are at your service. If you will do me the honour …'

Without turning, he clicked his fingers to summon the coachman. The carriage rolled obediently up to the little group and one of the grooms sprang down to open the door and let down the steps.

The cardinal's bright eyes took in the pale-faced girl in the blue dress and the Austrian prince, nearly as white as she in his white uniform. His clear gaze held a world of questions, but Gauthier de Chazay uttered none of them. Royally, he extended his hand with the great sapphire ring for Clary's lips to kiss, then turned to Marianne who sank to her knees, heedless of the dust.

'I will expect you this evening,' he said, as she rose. 'Ah, I was forgetting. His Holiness, Pius VII, has conferred a cardinal's hat on me. I am known, and admitted to France, by the name of San Lorenzo-Fuori-Muore.'

Moments later, the Austrian carriage passed the gateway of the Tuileries, followed by the envious gaze of the remaining princes of the Church who, one by one, were resigning themselves to departing homewards on foot, their followers at their heels, with the hope of finding a public vehicle for hire on the way.

Mechanically, Marianne dusted the silver embroideries of her dress with her gloves, then turned to her companion.

'Shall we go in?'

'Yes, although I wonder what our reception will be. Half the people in the palace saw us offer a carriage to a man whom the Emperor regards as his enemy.'

'You wonder too much, my friend. Let us go in and we shall see. There are many things in life, believe me, which are infinitely more to be feared than the Emperor's anger.' She spoke the words through clenched teeth, thinking of what her godfather would say that evening when he heard the truth.

The prospect threw a slight shadow over the joy which she had felt a little while before at seeing him again, but could not altogether destroy it. It was so good to find him, especially at a time when she had such urgent need of his help. What he would say would hardly be pleasant, she knew, he would not look kindly on her new career as a singer, but in the end he would surely understand. No one had more understanding and human sympathy than the Abbé de Chazay and why should the Cardinal San Lorenzo be any different? Marianne remembered suddenly how her godfather had always distrusted Lord Cranmere. He would surely pity the misfortunes of one who, as he himself had said a moment ago, was as dear to him as his own child.

No, all things considered, Marianne found herself looking forward to the evening with more hope than foreboding. Gauthier de Chazay, Cardinal San Lorenzo, would have no difficulty in persuading the Pope to annul a marriage which dragged like a heavy chain round his goddaughter's neck.

This was the first time Marianne had entered the state apartments of the Tuileries. The salle des Maréchaux, where the concert was to be held, overwhelmed her with its size and magnificence. Once the guardroom of Catherine de Medici, it was a vast chamber rising to two storeys below the dome of the central section of the palace. On the level of the upper storey, facing the dais where the performers were to stand, was a huge box in which the Emperor and his family would soon take their places. This box was supported on four gigantic caryatids completely covered in gold leaf, representing armless female forms in classical draperies. From either side of the box, balconies ran right round the room, entered by means of archways draped, like the doors and windows elsewhere in the hall, in red velvet scattered with gold bees. The roof was a rectangular dome, the corners occupied by massive, gilt trophies, with, in the centre, a colossal chandelier of cut crystal. The dome itself was adorned with allegorical frescoes and, to enhance the warlike aspect of the room, the lower walls were decorated with full-length portraits of fourteen marshals, interspersed with busts of twenty-two generals and admirals.

Although the vast room and the balcony were full of people, Marianne felt lost, as though in some huge cathedral. The noise was like an aviary run mad, drowning the sounds of the musicians tuning up their instruments. So many faces moved before her eyes that for the moment, in the shifting blur of colours and flashing jewels, she was incapable of recognizing any that she knew. At last, she saw Duroc, magnificent in the violet and silver of the Grand Marshal of the Palace, coming towards her, but it was to Clary that he spoke.

'Prince Schwartzenberg is asking for you, monsieur. If you will be good enough to join him in the Emperor's private office.'

'In the Emperor's —'

'Yes, monsieur. I should not keep him waiting, if I were you.'

The young Prince met Marianne's eyes with a look of alarm. This summons could mean only one thing: the Emperor was already aware of the incident of the carriage and poor Clary was in for a dressing down. Unable to let her friend bear the blame for her action, Marianne intervened.

'Monsieur, I know what the Prince is summoned to his majesty for, but as the matter concerns myself alone, let me be allowed to go with him.'

The Duke's frown did not lighten and the look he bent on the young woman before him was stern.

'Mademoiselle, it is not my place to admit to his majesty's presence those who have not been sent for. I am in fact instructed to escort you to Messieurs Gossec and Piccini who await you with the orchestra.'

'Monsieur le Duc, I beg you. His majesty may be committing a grave injustice.'

'His majesty is aware what he is about. Prince, you are expected. Will you go with me, mademoiselle?'

Marianne was obliged to part from her companion and follow the Grand Marshal. A faint rustle of applause greeted her as she passed but, absorbed in her own thoughts, she paid no attention to it. She placed one hand timidly on Duroc's arm.

'Monsieur, I must see the Emperor.'

'You shall see him, mademoiselle. His majesty has condescended to say that he will see you after the concert.'

'Condescended – you are very stern, monsieur. Are we no longer friends?'

Duroc's face relaxed into a faint smile.

'We are still friends,' he murmured hurriedly, 'but the Emperor is very angry, and my duty forbids me to show it.'

'Am I – am I in disgrace?'

'That I cannot say. But it looks a little like it.'

'Then you may safely resign her to me for a moment, my dear Duroc.' The pleasant, drawling voice came from behind Marianne. 'We disgraced persons should support one another, eh?'

Even before that final 'eh?', Marianne had recognized Talleyrand. Exquisite as always in an olive-green coat glittering with medals, knee breeches and white silk stockings, his lame leg supported by a gold-headed stick, he was smiling impishly at Duroc as he offered his arm to Marianne.

Not wholly unwilling, perhaps, to be released from his embarrassing charge, the Grand Marshal bowed with a good grace and resigned Marianne to the Vice-Grand Elector.

'I thank you, Prince, but do not take her far. The Emperor will be here soon.'

'I know,' Talleyrand purred. 'Just time to wash poor Clary's head and teach him not to succumb too readily to the wiles of a pretty woman. Five minutes, I am sure, will suffice.'

As he spoke, he was leading Marianne gently towards one of the tall window embrasures. His manner was that of a man enjoying an agreeable polite flirtation but Marianne soon saw that what he had to say was far more serious.

'Clary will probably be getting a severe scold,' he remarked quietly, 'but I fear that the Emperor's chief anger will fall on you. What possessed you? To fling your arms round a cardinal on the steps of the Tuileries, and a cardinal very much out of favour into the bargain? It was scarcely wise – unless that person was very close to you, eh?'

Marianne said nothing. It was not easy to explain her action without revealing her true identity and as far as Talleyrand was concerned, she was only Mademoiselle Mallerousse, from Brittany, a person of no consequence whatever, certainly not on familiar terms with a prince of the Church. While she cudgelled her brains in vain for a likely explanation, the Prince of Benevento spoke again, his tone more detached than ever.

'I was at one time closely acquainted with the Abbé de Chazay. He began life as deputy to my uncle, the ducal archbishop of Rheims, at present chaplain to the king in exile.'

Marianne was conscious of a stab of fear, as if the Prince's words were drawing a net tighter about her. She recalled her wedding day and the tall figure and long face of Monsignor de Talleyrand-Périgord, chaplain to Louis XVIII. It was true, her godfather had been on the best of terms with the prelate. It was he, in fact, who had lent the liturgical ornaments for the ceremony at Selton Hall. Without apparently noticing her agitation, Talleyrand continued in the same light voice, smooth and untroubled as a windless pool.

'In those days, I used to live in the Rue de Bellechasse, not far from the Rue de Lille, then called the Rue de Bourbon, and I was on excellent, neighbourly terms with the Abbé's family.' The Prince sighed. 'Ah, those were delightful times! No one who has not lived in the days before 1789 knows anything of the pleasures of life. I do not think I ever met a more handsome couple, or one more tenderly devoted, than the Marquis d'Asselnat and his wife, whose house is now your own.'

Despite her self-control, Marianne felt her mind reeling. Her hand tensed on Talleyrand's arm, gripping tightly as she fought to conquer her emotion. She was gasping for breath and her heart was pounding. She felt as if her knees were about to give way under her, but the Prince's face was as serene and expressionless as ever and his heavy lids still drooped incuriously. A tall and very lovely woman dressed all in white, with flaming red hair and a passionate, wilful face, passed close by them.

'My dear Prince,' she said, with the insolence of the very well-bred, 'I did not know you had such a taste for opera.'

Talleyrand bowed gravely.

'My dear Duchess, all forms of beauty have a claim on my admiration, surely you know that, who know me so well?'

'I do know it, but you had better escort the young person to the dais. The little – the imperial couple, I should say – are about to make their entrance.'

'Thank you, madame. I was about to do so.'

'Who was that?' Marianne asked as the beautiful red-head left them. 'And why does she treat me with such contempt?'

'She treats everyone so, and herself most of all since she has finally accepted a post as lady-in-waiting merely to serve an archduchess. She is Madame de Chevreuse. She is, as you see, a great beauty. She is also extremely spirited and far from happy. She suffers from her own passionate nature. You see, she is obliged to say "the Emperor" and "his majesty" in referring to someone who, in private she calls "the little wretch". You may have noticed that she almost let it slip just now. As for her contempt of you –' Talleyrand's bland gaze was turned suddenly on Marianne. 'Your own actions are the reason for that. A Chevreuse will necessarily look down on a Maria Stella – whereas she would have opened her arms to the daughter of the Marquis d'Asselnat.'

There was silence. Talleyrand leaned down a little, his pale eyes staring deep into the green ones, which did not flinch.

'How long have you known?' Marianne asked, feeling suddenly very calm.

'Ever since the Emperor gave you the house in the Rue de Lille. It was then I understood the vague feeling of familiarity which I had been unable to place before, a resemblance I had failed to grasp. Then I knew who you really were.'

'Why did you keep quiet?'

Talleyrand shrugged. 'What would have been the use? You had, quite unpredictably, fallen in love with the man of all men whom you were born to hate.'

'Yet it was you drove me into his bed,' Marianne said brutally.

'I have regretted it sufficiently! But I decided the remedy was best left to time and chance. Neither this love affair, nor your career as a singer, was ever made to last.'

'Why, may I ask?' Marianne interrupted coldly.

'For one very good reason. You were never made for Napoleon or for the theatre. However much you may try to persuade yourself otherwise, you are one of us, an aristocrat of the highest birth. You are so like your father — '

'Am I? You knew him?' Marianne asked with sudden eagerness born of her deep longing to know the truth about this man whose flesh and blood she was, yet of whom she knew no more than his portrait. 'Tell me of him!'

Gently, Talleyrand removed the clutching fingers from his sleeve but held them a moment in his own.

'Not now. His spirit would be ill-at-ease in these surroundings. The Emperor is coming. You must be Maria Stella again, for a little while.'

He quickened his pace and led her over to the group of musicians. She saw Gossec beckoning, Piccini arranging the scores on the instrument and Paer, the imperial choir-master, carefully wiping his baton. As they came up to them Marianne, moved by an irrational impulse, caught at Talleyrand's sleeve.

'If I was not made for – for the Emperor, or for the theatre, then what am I for?'

'For love, my dear.'

'But – we are in love!'

'I said for love and that is something different. For the great love which overthrows empires and founds undying dynasties, the love which lasts beyond death, and which most men never find.'

'Then why should I find it?'

'Because if you do not find it, Marianne, it does not exist. And it must exist, so that people like me may continue to disbelieve in it.'

Troubled, Marianne watched him limp away with his uneven, yet oddly graceful gait. It seemed to her that these words, so out of keeping with the character and legend of Talleyrand, contained an offer of friendship, or at least of help. Help, how she needed help at that moment! But how far was the Prince of Benevento to be trusted? Marianne had lived under his roof and knew, better than most, the peculiar charm of his personality, the more powerful in that it seemed to be quite unconscious. She remembered suddenly something the Comte de Montrond had said about him and which Fortunée had gleefully repeated one day: 'Who could help liking him? He is so thoroughly vicious.'

What was his motive now? A disinterested attempt to recall her to a life more fitting for her birth, or simply to divide her a little further from the Emperor, whom, it was rumoured, he was himself in the act of betraying to the Tzar?

A fanfare of trumpets, a solemn banging of his staff by the master of ceremonies, the Comte de Ségur, and the enormous room lapsed into a respectful silence. All heads were turned towards the great balcony where, amid a flutter of dazzling dresses and braided uniforms, the imperial couple were making their entrance. Marianne saw two figures detach themselves from the shimmering background of court ladies and aides-de-camp: Napoleon in his green uniform and Marie-Louise in pink. Then she saw nothing more as, like the rest of the ladies present, she sank into a deep curtsey.

Marianne wished that curtsey might never end. When at last she lifted her eyes to the newly-wedded pair, the picture of happiness which they presented cut her to the heart. Without a glance for the brilliant assembly, Napoleon was leading his wife to her seat with every sign of the most tender consideration, even dropping a kiss upon the hand which he retained in his own as he too seated himself. Moreover, he continued to lean towards her, talking privately, with a complete disregard of his surroundings.

Marianne stood by the piano, stupefied, uncertain what to do. The court was seated now, waiting for the Emperor's signal for the concert to begin.

But Napoleon continued his smiling tête-à-tête and it seemed to Marianne that the low dais on which she stood was a kind of pillory to which she had been bound by the cruel whim of a neglectful lover. She had a wild impulse to run from that opulent room and its hundreds of pairs of eyes. If only it had been possible. Up above, in the royal box, the Comte de Ségur was bending respectfully before the Emperor, asking for a sign. It was given him, carelessly, without so much as a look, and translated instantly into a solemn rap of his staff.

At once, like an echo, there came the sound of Paer's baton tapping on the desk. Alexandre Piccini at the piano struck up the opening chords, taken up a moment later by the violins. His anguished glance told Marianne that her distress was evident. She caught sight of Gossec in his corner, looking anxious, his face intent, as if in prayer. Surely no one had ever seen the Emperor treat a famous artiste with such contempt?

Fortunately, anger came to Marianne's rescue. Her first song was to be the great aria from *La Vestale*, the Emperor's favourite. Taking a deep breath to calm the frantic beating of her heart, she attacked the piece with a passionate energy that left her audience gasping. Her voice soared with such a fierce intensity as she expressed the despair of Julie, the vestal virgin condemned to burial alive, that even this worldly audience was shaken. In her determination to make the Emperor attend to her, she sang better than she had ever done. On the final notes, her voice rang with such poignant misery that a chorus of spontaneous, frenzied applause broke out, in defiance of protocol which decreed that the sovereign alone should give the signal for it. But the skill of the singer had electrified her audience.

She looked up at the royal box, eyes sparkling with hope, but no, not only was Napoleon not looking at her, he did not even appear to have noticed that she had been singing. His head was bent towards Marie-Louise, talking softly to her. She was listening to him downcast, a simpering smile on her lips and her face so flushed that Marianne could only conclude with rage that he was making love to her. She nodded sharply to Paer to begin the second piece, an aria from *The Secret Marriage* by Cimarosa.

Never, surely, was the Italian composer's light and delicate music sung with such grim feeling. Marianne's green eyes were fixed on the Emperor, as if they would force his attention. Her heart swelled with uncontrollable anger, depriving her of all sense of proportion, all self-control. How dared that stupid Viennese sit there smiling like a cat at a cream pot? How could anyone have the nerve to claim that she liked music?

Marie-Louise's love of music must have been confined to the airs of her own country for she was not only not listening but, right in the middle of the aria, she giggled suddenly. It was a childish giggle but too loud to escape notice.

Every drop of blood left Marianne's face. She stopped singing. For a moment, her glittering eyes swept the rows of heads before her, all with the same expectant expression, then with her own head held proudly erect, she marched off the dais and, in the astounded pause which followed, she left the salle des Maréchaux before anyone, even the men at the doors, could think to stop her.

Her head on fire and her hands like ice, she walked stiffly on, ignoring the storm which broke out behind her. The one idea in her fevered brain was to depart for ever from the place where the man she loved had dealt such a cruel blow to her pride, to go home and bury her grief in the old home of her family and wait, wait for what was bound to follow such an act: the Emperor's wrath, arrest, perhaps even imprisonment. But for the moment, nothing mattered to Marianne. So furious was she that she would have walked to the scaffold without so much as a glance.

A voice called after her.

'Wait! Mademoiselle! Mademoiselle Maria Stella!'

She went on down the grand staircase as if nothing had happened. Not until Duroc caught up with her at the foot of the stone steps did she finally stop and turn with an expression of complete indifference to face the Grand Marshal, who seemed on the verge of an apoplexy, his face as scarlet as his splendid uniform.

'Have you gone mad?' He gasped, struggling to regain his breath. 'Such conduct – in the Emperor's presence!'

'Whose conduct was the more shocking, mine or the Emperor's – or that woman's, at least?'

'That woman? The Empress? Oh —'

'I know no empress other than the one consecrated by the Pope, at Malmaison! As for that caricature you call by the name, I deny her right to make a fool of me in public. Go and tell your master that!'

Marianne was beside herself with rage. Her voice rang coldly among the stone arches of the old palace with a clarity that, to Duroc, was highly embarrassing. Was that a shadow of a smile under the moustaches of the grenadier on duty at the foot of the stairs? Forcing a sternness into his voice which he was far from feeling, he took Marianne's arm and began: 'I am afraid you will have to tell him yourself, mademoiselle. My orders are to take you to the Emperor's private office to await his pleasure.'

'Am I under arrest?'

'Not to my knowledge, not yet at any rate.'

The implication of this was not reassuring but Marianne did not care. She expected to pay dearly for her outburst but if she were to be given the chance to unburden herself to Napoleon once and for all, she meant to do so without mincing words. If she were going to prison, it might as well be worthwhile. At least it would save her from the machinations of Francis Cranmere. The Englishman would have to wait until she was released to pursue his plans, since he would gain nothing by destroying her altogether. There remained Adélaïde, but here Marianne was confident she could rely on Arcadius.

It was, therefore, with a degree of serenity that the Emperor's rebellious subject entered the familiar room, calmed for the moment by the prospect of an interview with its owner, and heard Duroc give orders to Roustan, the Mameluke guard, to permit no one to enter, nor to allow Mademoiselle Maria Stella to communicate with anyone. This last recommendation even drew a smile from her.

'I am a prisoner, you see?' she said gently.

'No, I have told you. But I would rather not have young Clary yapping outside the door like a lost lapdog. I must warn you to be prepared for a long wait. The Emperor will not come until the reception is over.'

With no other response than a faint but highly impertinent shrug of her shoulders, Marianne sat down on the little yellow sofa drawn up to the fire where she had first set eyes on Fortunée Hamelin. The thought of her friend succeeded in finally calming Marianne. Fortunée was too experienced in the ways of men ever to have feared Napoleon. She had convinced Marianne that to show fear was the worst mistake she could make, even, or indeed especially, if he were in one of his famous rages.

A deep silence, broken only by the crackling of the fire, descended on the room. It was warm and cosy, regardless of its absence of luxury. This was the first time Marianne had been alone there and feminine curiosity impelled her to take stock of it. It was comforting to be there, where every object reminded her of the Emperor. Passing over the files of documents, the red Morocco folders with the imperial arms stamped on them, the large map of Europe flung down on the desk, she took pleasure in handling the long white goose quill that stood in the porphyry inkstand, the ormolu watch-stand in the shape of an eagle, and a chased gold snuff-box with an ill-fitting lid from which the fragrance of the contents escaped. Each object proclaimed his presence, even the crumpled black cocked hat thrown down in a corner, in a temper probably, and not long ago either, since Constant had not yet retrieved it. Was it the matter of the carriage which had provoked that outburst? For all her courage, Marianne could not help feeling an unpleasant tingling sensation up her spine. What would he be like later?

The time passed slowly. Marianne had the scent of battle in her nostrils and she wanted it to begin. Tired of roaming about the padded silence of the room, she picked up a book that lay on the desk and returned to her seat. It was a much-worn copy of *Caesar's Commentaries*, bound in green leather stamped with the imperial arms. It was so thumbed and annotated, the margins so heavily scored and filled with a cramped, nervous hand, that it had become wholly unreadable for anyone but the author of those notes. Marianne let it fall onto her lap with a sigh, although her hand continued to caress the worn leather, as though unconsciously searching for the trace of another hand. The cover grew warm, almost human under her touch. Marianne closed her eyes, the better to savour the feeling.

'Wake up.'

Marianne started and opened her eyes. Candles had been lighted in the room and outside it was dark. Napoleon stood before her with folded arms, a brooding anger in his eyes.

'I congratulate you on your courage,' he said with heavy irony. 'You were very sound asleep. Apparently, the knowledge that you had incurred my displeasure weighs little with you.'

The tone was loud and bullying, clearly calculated to overwhelm someone starting out of sleep, but Marianne possessed the faculty of coming instantly and completely awake, however deeply she had been sleeping.

'The Grand Marshal warned me I should have a long wait,' she said quietly. 'Sleep seems the best way of shortening a period of waiting.'

'It seems to me decidedly impudent, madame – moreover I have not yet seen your curtsey.'

Napoleon was clearly seeking a quarrel. He had been prepared to find Marianne agitated and alarmed, trembling and red-eyed perhaps. The woman who woke so calmly could not fail to rouse him to annoyance.

Ignoring the ominous spark in the grey eyes, Marianne risked a smile.

'I am ready to fall at your feet, sire, if your majesty will step back sufficiently to permit me to rise.'

He turned on his heel with an exclamation of fury and marched over to the window as if he meant to go straight through it.

Marianne slipped from the sofa straight into the deepest and most respectful of curtseys. 'Sire.'

There was no response. Napoleon continued to stare out of the window in silence, his hands clasped behind his back, for what seemed to Marianne an eternity, obliging her to remain in her uncomfortable, semi-kneeling position. Realizing that he was deliberately seeking to humiliate her, she gathered her courage for what was to come, knowing that it was bound to be unpleasant. She had only one desire, and that was to save her love.

Abruptly, without turning, Napoleon spoke.

'I await your explanation, if you have one to offer, of your astounding conduct. Your explanation and your apologies. It would appear that you were suddenly bereft of your senses, and of the most elementary notions of respect towards me and towards your Empress. Have you gone mad?'

Marianne was on her feet at once, the blood rushing to her cheeks. The words 'your Empress' had struck her like a blow.

'Apologies?' she said clearly. 'I think it is not I who should apologize.'

He did turn round at this, his eyes alight with anger.

'What did you say?'

'That if anyone here has been insulted, it is I! What I did was for the sake of my own dignity.'

'Your dignity? You are ridiculous, madame. Do you forget where you are? You forget that you came here at my command, by my good pleasure, with the sole object of providing entertainment for your sovereign.'

'My sovereign? If I had thought for one moment that you had brought me here for her sake, I would never have crossed this threshold.'

'Indeed? In that event, I should have had you brought here by force.'

'Maybe. But you could not have forced me to sing! Besides, how edifying for your court to see your mistress dragged onto the stage under guard! A spectacle to match the one you presented to them earlier of eminent churchmen dragged through the dust, exposed to vulgar mirth – as if it were not enough to have laid hands on the Vicar of Christ himself!'

In a couple of strides the Emperor was on her, and Marianne knew from his dreadful pallor that she had gone too far, but it was not in her power or her nature to draw back now. She tensed to meet his wrath as his face was thrust into hers.

'You dare to say that!' he flung at her. 'Those men insulted me, mocked me, should I have spared them? You should be on your knees in gratitude for my forbearance and mercy. I could have flung them into prison, or worse, you know that!'

'And given more substance to your own legend? No, you did no worse because you dared not and you are angry with me because, by offering a carriage to my godfather, I refused to take part in your petty revenge!'

For a second curiosity overcame the Emperor's fury.

'Your godfather? That Italian cardinal —'

'Is no more Italian than I am. His name is Gauthier de Chazay, Cardinal San Lorenzo. He is my godfather and I owe him my life because it was he, who saved me from the hands of the Revolutionaries. In helping him, I was doing no more than my duty.'

'That's as may be. But my duty is to put down all opposition to my throne, my family, my marriage. I command you to go to the Empress and beg pardon on your knees.'

The picture he conjured up succeeded in casting Marianne into a rage equal to Napoleon's own.

'No,' she said flatly. 'Have me thrown into prison, executed if you like, but such an abject submission you will never get from me, never, do you hear! I, on my knees to that woman ...'

Transfigured with fury, rigid with all the accumulated pride and rebelliousness of her race, it was she who dominated now. Unable to bear the sight of her arrogance and disdain, Napoleon let out a growl of rage and seized her by the arm, twisting it in a cruel grip that made her cry out with pain.

'More of this and you will be on your knees to me, you crazy vixen! On your knees begging my forgiveness! I was right, you are mad —'

He made a move to throw her to the ground. Fighting desperately to keep her balance and stave off the pain, Marianne managed to gasp out:

'Mad? Yes, I am mad – or I was! Mad to have loved you as I did! Mad to have believed in you! To think I trusted your love! It was all words, smoke! Your love is given to the newest. That fat, red-faced creature had only to appear to make you her slave, you – the master of Europe, the Eagle – at the feet of that cow! And I hid my grief because I believed the things you said to me! A political marriage, indeed! When you flaunt your love openly in the eyes of all, a love which kills me, tears me apart! Well, you have played with me enough. You are right, I was mad – and I am mad still because in spite of everything, I love you. I wish I could hate you, yes, hate you, as so many others do! It would be so easy, so wonderfully easy ...'

Overcome by her grief and the pain of her bruised arm, she fell to the ground, collapsing with the abruptness of a summer storm, and buried her head in her hands and wept. It was all over, she had said it all and now she wanted nothing but final, blessed oblivion. The terrifying anger which had lifted her out of herself and driven her to defy the Master with such insensate daring had gone, leaving only a horrible wretchedness. Careless of what he might do to her now, Marianne wept over the ruins of her broken love.

Napoleon stood rigidly staring at the figure in blue and silver lying in a crumpled heap on the carpet, hearing the heartbroken sobs. Perhaps he was wondering how to react, or trying to maintain his anger in the face of this dreadful display of grief, these cries of love which strove to transform themselves to cries of hate. Perhaps, too, his private love of the dramatic made him secretly relish the theatrical aspect of the scene. But suddenly the door opened and a plump, pink female form appeared. A childish, somewhat whiny voice, complained in a strong German accent:

'Vot are you doink? I am ze bored without mein veery naughty gallant! Come to me, Nana!'

The effect of this voice on Marianne was like acid on an open wound. She jerked up her head and stared at the Emperor and his wife. The Habsburg girl, was staring now at her in horror, stammering.

'Oh, you beat ze bad voman, Nana?'

'No, Louise. I have not beaten her. Leave me, sweet, and I will come to you soon. Go now ...'

He led her to the door with a smile that sat badly on his drawn face, and kissed her hand as though embarrassed by the domestic interlude which had fallen like a bucket of cold water on the fires of tragedy. Marianne herself was too dazed even to rise to her feet. Nana! She called him Nana! It was funny, if Marianne had had the heart for laughter.

But now they were alone again. The Emperor turned slowly back to his desk. He was breathing hard, as though with difficulty. The gaze that fell on Marianne was blank, as if all life had vanished with his anger. He leaned with both hands on the massive table and hung his head.

'Get up,' he said dully. He raised his head again and looked at her with unexpected softness but when, surprised by the change in his tone, she opened her mouth to speak he stopped her and, taking a deep breath, continued: 'No, don't speak. You must not say anymore, you must never anger me again as you have done. It is too dangerous. I – I might have killed you and I should have regretted it all my life. It may be hard for you to believe it but – I do love you. There are some things you cannot understand.'

Marianne got to her feet, as slowly and painfully as if she had been fighting. She was obliged to hold on to the sofa for support. Every muscle in her body ached. Even so, she tried to go to Napoleon, but he restrained her with a gesture.

'No. Stay where you are. Sit down and rest. We have hurt one another cruelly tonight, have we not? It must be forgotten. Listen, I am leaving Paris tomorrow for Compiègne. From there, towards the end of the month, I go to the northern provinces. I have to show my – the Empress to my people. It will give us time to forget – and I shall not be obliged to send you away, as I should be if I were to remain here. I will leave you now. Stay here a while. Constant will come for you and take you to the carriage.'

He turned to the door; his step curiously heavy. Unable to help herself, Marianne held out her arms to him, her eyes full of tears, trying instinctively to hold him back. Her voice, when she spoke, was low and pleading.

'Do you forgive me? I did not mean –'

'You know you meant every word, but I have forgiven you because you were right. But do not come near me. I must not touch you or I shall fail the Empress. We shall meet again.'

He went out, quickly, and Marianne returned to her seat by the fire. Her heart and mind felt empty, and she was suddenly chilled to the marrow. Something told her that things could never be the same again between them. There were the words which had been spoken, words which would be followed by absence, and silence. She experienced a piercing regret for the miraculous days at the Trianon when all quarrels had been dissolved at last in kisses. But nothing could bring back the Trianon. From now on, love would have a bitter taste of loneliness and renunciation. Would there ever be a return to the state of pure happiness which had been hers for those few weeks? Or must she learn from now on to give without looking for anything in return?

Around her, the palace had grown silent as a desert. Constant's footsteps, approaching across the bare wooden floor outside, seemed to come from the depths of time. She felt suddenly faint. Her heart was beating fast and a cold sweat had broken out all over her body. She tried to rise but a dreadful feeling of sickness made her sink back, panting, on the couch. It was there that Constant found her, her eyes enormous, her face like wax, her handkerchief to her lips. She stared up at him desperately.

'I don't know what is the matter with me. I feel so ill, dreadfully ill. I was all right a moment ago.'

'You are very pale. What is wrong?'

'I am so cold, my head is spinning, but worst of all, I feel so dreadfully sick.'

The valet busied himself silently, fetching eau-de-Cologne, bathing Marianne's temples and making her drink a cordial. The sickness went as swiftly as it had come. Little by little, the colour came back into her cheeks and before very long she felt as well as ever.

'I can't think what came over me,' she said, smiling gratefully up at Constant. 'I thought I was dying. Perhaps I should see a doctor.'

'You should see a doctor, mademoiselle, but I do not think the matter is very serious.'

'What do you mean?'

Constant picked up the bottles and napkins he had brought with studious care, then he smiled kindly, with a hint of sadness in his smile.

'I mean it is unfortunate that mademoiselle was not born to the purple. It would have saved us from this Austrian marriage, which promises nothing but trouble. All the same, I trust that it will be a boy. It would give the Emperor so much pleasure.'

# CHAPTER SIX
# The Bargain

The revelation of her condition overwhelmed Marianne and, at the same time, gave her fresh courage and an extraordinary sense of triumph. She was not so innocent as to imagine that if the discovery that she was expecting a child had come a few months earlier it would have prevented the Austrian marriage. Napoleon had known, after Wagram, that Marie Walewska was carrying his child and it had made no difference. He could have married her: he loved her and she came of a noble family. Yet he had made no move because, however nobly born, Marie, like Marianne herself, was not a princess and so not sufficiently well-born to found a dynasty. Yet it gave Marianne a strange, rather agonizing joy, to think that the imperial blood was at work somewhere deep inside her, while Napoleon was exerting himself to impregnate his plump Viennese and obtain the heir he longed for. Whatever he did now, he was bound to Marianne by ties of flesh and blood, and so nothing could destroy her exultant happiness in the knowledge that she bore his child, not even the stigma attached to the word 'illegitimate'. Marianne was prepared to confront gossip, scorn and social ostracism for the sake of the few ounces of humanity slowly forming within her.

These thoughts sustained her as she drove, in the carriage which had been brought for her, towards the rue Chanoinesse, prepared to face what would undoubtedly be one of the hardest battles of her life.

She was all too familiar with her godfather's uncompromising royalism, his rigid moral principles and the inflexibility of his private code of honour, and she knew that her confession would have its painful moments.

At this late hour, the rue Chanoinesse was in darkness, except for two street lamps hung on cables across the road. The metal-shod wheels rang on the big cobblestones that paved the road between the silent, secretive houses where the canons of Notre Dame lived behind their barred windows. The twin shadows of the cathedral towers stretched, grotesquely elongated, across the ancient rooftops, making the dark night seem darker still.

A belated priest, accosted politely by Gracchus-Hannibal, pointed out the house of Monsieur de Bruillard which was easily recognizable by the tall, slender tower rising from its courtyard. It was also one of the few houses that still showed a light. The canons went early to bed, leaving the streets free for the ruffians who infested the old part of the city.

Considerably to Marianne's surprise, the canon's house breathed none of that smell of cold wax and musty papers which she associated with a churchman's dwelling. A footman in dark livery with nothing monkish about him conducted her through a pair of *salons* furnished with a discreet elegance, and brought her to a closed door before which the Abbé Bichette was standing guard, head hunched between his shoulders and hands clasped behind his back. At the sight of the visitor, the faithful secretary hurried forward with an exclamation of relief which told Marianne she was expected.

'His Eminence has asked three times if you had yet arrived. His impatience is so great that he will have no one near him, not even myself.'

'Especially yourself,' Marianne thought, deciding that she could not have borne with the Abbé's company for more than fifteen minutes.

'You must know,' Bichette continued, lowering his already hushed voice still further, 'that we are to leave Paris before dawn.'

'What? So soon? My godfather said nothing of this to me.'

'His Eminence was not then aware of it. Early this evening Monsieur Bigot de Preameneu, the Minister concerned with religious affairs, informed us that we were no longer welcome in the capital and should prepare to leave.'

'But where to?'

'To Rheims, where the refractory members of the Curia are – er – detained. It is most unfortunate and quite unjust.'

At that moment the door before which they were standing was thrown open and the cardinal appeared, looking now much more like Marianne's recollections of the Abbé de Chazay in a suit of black somewhat shabbier than the footman's.

'Bichette!' he said severely. 'I am old enough to recount my misfortunes to my goddaughter in my own way. You waste time with your chattering, when you would be better employed sending a message to the kitchen for coffee, a great deal of coffee, very strong, and do not disturb me again until Monsieur Bruillard tells you he is ready. Come in, my child.'

The last words were addressed to Marianne. She entered and found herself in a small but comfortable library, its pale woodwork, rich bindings and bright Beauvais tapestries no more ecclesiastical in feeling than the rest of the house. The portrait of a pretty woman smiled mischievously from a fine oval gilt frame, flanked by a pair of tall ormolu candlesticks, while over the fireplace the young Louis XV in coronation robes seemed to invest the whole room with his royal presence.

The cardinal observed Marianne's surprise at the sight of the portrait and smiled.

'De Bruillard is the natural son of Louis XV and the fair lady you see above the desk. Hence this portrait, which is not often seen in Parisian houses nowadays. But never mind that now. Come and sit by the fire and let me look at you. I have been striving ever since I left you to think what miracle could have brought you to Paris and how it comes about that I, who married you to an Englishman, now find you on the steps of the Tuileries in the company of an Austrian.'

Marianne smiled a little nervously. The moment she dreaded had arrived. She was determined to face up to it at once, without any attempt at prevarication.

'Do not try, godfather dear, you will never guess. No one could ever imagine the things that have happened to me since we parted. Indeed, there are times when I wonder if it is all true and not just a dreadful nightmare.'

The cardinal drew up a chair facing Marianne's. 'What do you mean? I have had no news from England since your wedding day.'

'Then you know nothing – nothing at all?'

'No, I assure you. First tell me, what has become of your husband?'

'No,' Marianne said quickly. 'Please, let me tell you in my own way. It will not be easy.'

'I thought that I had taught you not to be put off by what is difficult.'

'And I shall not be. But first you must understand one thing. The Hôtel d'Asselnat belongs to me. The Emperor gave it to me. I – I am that opera singer you mentioned.'

'What – ?'

The cardinal had risen to his feet in astonishment. His homely face was a stone mask, devoid of all expression. But despite the shock she knew it must be to him, Marianne felt suddenly lighter. The most difficult part was over.

Without a word, the cardinal crossed to a corner of the room where an ivory crucifix hung in a red velvet frame and stood for a moment, upright and not obviously praying, but when he turned and made his way back to Marianne some of the colour had returned to his face. He sat down again, only this time, perhaps in order to avoid looking at his goddaughter, he turned towards the fire, holding out his thin hands to the blaze.

'Tell me,' he said quietly. 'I will hear you to the end.'

Marianne began her story …

The coffee brought by the impassive footman, reverently escorted by the

Abbé Bichette, arrived just as Marianne reached the end of her recital. Faithful to his promise, the cardinal had not uttered a word all the time she was speaking, although he stirred restlessly more than once. Now he greeted the arrival of the coffee tray with the relief of a man granted a truce amid a fierce battle.

'Leave it there, Bichette,' he said as the Abbé showed signs of being about to pour for them, no doubt as an excuse to remain in the room. 'We will serve ourselves.'

The Abbé withdrew, disappointed but submissive, and Gauthier de Chazay turned to Marianne.

'It is a long time since you poured tea or coffee for me, Marianne. I hope you have not forgotten.'

Tears sprang to Marianne's eyes at the recollection the words conjured up of home and childhood. She stripped off her gloves and dropped them on the floor, then went to the little table and began carefully pouring out the fragrant, steaming beverage. Absorbed in her task, she did not look up at her godfather. Neither spoke until, as she handed him his cup, she plucked up courage to ask: 'You – you do not judge me too harshly?'

'I have not the right. I did not like Lord Cranmere, or this marriage, and yet I went away. I know now that I should have stayed to watch over you instead of leaving you as I did. No doubt it was God's will, for a few minutes earlier and you would have caught up with me on Plymouth quay and everything would have been very different. You had no choice. You had to follow your fate and I am not without my part in the way things have gone.'

He paused.

'No, I have no right to say one word of blame, for that would be to blame you for having survived.'

'Then, help me, godfather. Save me from Francis Cranmere!'

'Save you? How can I?'

'Lord Cranmere has never touched me. My marriage to that base man was never consummated. Ask the Holy Father to annul the marriage so that he will have no more rights over me. Let me be myself again and forget that Lord Cranmere ever existed.'

'Will he permit you to forget him so easily?'

'It will not matter when I am no longer bound to him. Save me, godfather! I want to be Marianne d'Asselnat once more.'

The echo of her words lingered in the room as the cardinal drained his cup. Still without speaking, he set it down and remained for a while in contemplation of his clasped hands. Marianne respected his silence, stifling her painful anxiety. Why did he not answer? What was in his mind?

At last, he raised his eyelids and looked up at her and Marianne shivered at the unhappiness in his blue eyes.

'It is not in order to become yourself again that you ask for my help, Marianne. Indeed, that is no longer possible, the change in you goes much deeper than the name you bear. You want your freedom in order to belong more fully to the man you love. That is something I cannot countenance because to do so would be to permit you to live openly in a state of sin.'

'What difference would it make? At present I am Napoleon's acknowledged mistress,' Marianne cried, a note of defiance in her voice.

'No. Napoleon's mistress is a woman named Maria Stella, not the daughter of the Marquis d'Asselnat. Make no mistake, child, the post of royal favourite has never been considered an honour in our family. Still less the favourite of a usurper. I will never allow your father's name to be linked with that of Bonaparte!'

A touch of anger came to add to the bitterness of Marianne's disappointment. She knew, as she had always known, that Gauthier de Chazay was a fanatical royalist, but it had not occurred to her that he would allow his loyalty to his king to affect his dealings with her, his goddaughter, the child of his heart.

'I have told you what this man has done to me and means to do even now, godfather,' she said wretchedly. 'Will you force me to remain tied to such a villain for the sake of some kind of political morality?'

'Not at all. I merely wish in saving you from Cranmere to save you from yourself. Like it or not, you were not born to join your fate with that of Napoleon. Neither God nor the simple, everyday morality of ordinary life, nor what you call political morality, will have it so. This man is about to destroy himself. I will not permit you to destroy yourself with him. Promise me that you will give him up for ever, and I promise you that I will have your marriage dissolved within a fortnight.'

'What a bargain!' Marianne exclaimed, more bitterly hurt because the cardinal was merely repeating, with the same calm assurance, what Talleyrand had said to her earlier.

'Perhaps,' the cardinal admitted equably, 'but if you must dishonour your real name, as well it should be that of the Englishman. One day, you will thank me.'

'That I do not believe! Even if I were willing to give you this promise, even if I would destroy with my own hand the love that is my very life, I could not do it. You do not know all, Eminence. Well, you shall learn the whole truth. I am going to have a child, his child! A Bonaparte!'

'Unhappy girl! More foolish than wretched. You dared to talk of becoming little Marianne of Selton once again! What you have done has placed an irrevocable barrier between you and yours.'

At this revelation, Gauthier de Chazay's composure had finally snapped, but Marianne was conscious of no special dismay. Her only feeling was one of sudden, fierce joy, a triumphant exultation, as if the child that lay

JULIETTE BENZONI

mysteriously inside her body had succeeded in that moment in avenging all the hatred and disdain endured by its father at the hands of the royalist émigrés. Her voice was cold as she answered.

'Perhaps, but it is also my chief motive for wishing for a final separation from Francis Cranmere. The Emperor's child must not bear the name of a scoundrel. If you refuse to untie the knot which still binds me to him, I will stop at nothing, nothing, do you hear, not even cold-blooded murder, to erase Francis Cranmere from my life.'

The cardinal must have realized that she meant what she said for even as she saw him blench, she was aware of something else, a curious pride glowing in his usually gentle eyes. Marianne had expected anger, violent protests, instead of which there was a sigh and a faint, sardonic smile.

'The exhausting thing about your family,' Gauthier de Chazay observed, 'is your determination. As soon as your will is crossed, you start spitting fire and sparks and threatening to kill everyone. The worst of it is that you not only generally keep your promises but that you are perfectly right.'

'What?' Marianne was aghast. 'You tell me to —'

'To send Francis Cranmere to join his noble forbears? As a man, I see no objection to it, I might even applaud it. As a priest, however, I am obliged to deprecate violence of any kind, however well deserved. No, Marianne, when I say you are right, I mean that you are right to say this unborn child must not bear that man's name, but only because he will be your son.'

Marianne's face glowed suddenly as she felt victory within her grasp.

'Then you will ask for an annulment?'

'Not so fast. Answer me one question first. How long have you known – about the child?'

'Not until today.' In a few words, she told him about the faintness which had come over her at the Tuileries.

'Have you – I am sorry to have to ask you such a question but this is no time for delicacy – have you any idea when it happened?'

'Not long ago, I think. Not more than a month at most, less perhaps.'

'A curious way to anticipate the arrival of a new bride,' was the cardinal's comment. 'However, no more of that. Time presses. Listen to what I have to say and do not argue because this is my last word. This is the only way that I can help you without betraying either my conscience or my duty. First, you will keep what you have told me strictly to yourself. Do you understand? Keep it absolutely secret for the present. Francis Cranmere must not get wind of it. He could ruin everything and with such a man one must take no chances. Not a word, therefore, not even to those closest to you.'

'I will remember. What else?'

'The rest is up to me. In fifteen days, the time it will take me to reach the Holy Father at Savona, your marriage will be annulled. But in a month, you will be married again.'

Marianne wondered if she had heard aright.

'What did you say? I do not understand —'

'No, you heard me quite correctly. I said that in a month you will be married again.'

He spoke in such decisive tones that for the moment Marianne could find nothing to say. She could only stammer, helplessly: 'But that is impossible! Do you know what you are saying?'

'I am not in the habit of talking nonsense and I must remind you of what I said a moment ago. No argument. However, I will make myself perfectly plain. If you are a month pregnant, then in another month you must be wedded to some suitable man whose name both you and your child may bear without blushing for it. You have no alternative, Marianne. And don't talk to me about your love, or your Emperor or your freedom. Think of the child, since child there is to be. He must have a name, and a father, since the man who fathered him can do nothing for him.'

'Nothing?' Marianne said rebelliously. 'He is the Emperor! Surely, he is sufficiently powerful to provide for the future of his child?'

'I am not denying his power, although I believe him to have feet of day, but how can you be sure that the future is his to dispose of? What will happen if he should ever fall? And what will happen to you and to the child? Our house will own no bastards, Marianne. You must make this sacrifice to your parents' memory, to the child, to yourself, even. Do you know how society treats an unmarried mother? Does the prospect attract you?'

'Ever since I realized, I have been prepared to suffer, to fight —'

'For what? For whom? To keep your hold on a man who has just been married to another?'

'He was obliged to marry – but I cannot.'

'And why not?'

'He would not permit it!'

The cardinal smiled at that.

'No? You do not know him. Foolish child, he would be the first to marry you off without delay, the moment he knew you carried his child. When one of his mistresses has been without a husband, he has always made it his business to provide one. No trouble and no complications, that has always been his motto in affairs of the heart. He has enough of that at home.'

Marianne knew that what he said was true, yet she was loth to admit the horrifying prospect which he laid before her.

'But, godfather, think! Marriage is something so important, so serious. Can you expect me to walk into it blindly to trust my whole life to a complete stranger, to put myself wholly in his power, day after day, night after night? Can't you see that my whole being would rise in revolt?'

'I understand first and foremost that you mean to do your utmost to remain Bonaparte's mistress, against all reason, and that you are no stranger to the realities of love. But it is possible to marry a man and live apart from him. From what I hear, the beautiful Pauline Borghese spends little enough of her time with poor Camillo. But I repeat, within a month you must be married.'

'To whom? To speak with such certainty, you must have someone in mind. Who is it?'

'That is my affair. You need not be afraid, the man I will choose for you, have already chosen, will not give you any cause for reproach. You will not lose the freedom you hold so dear, if you behave discreetly. But do not think I wish to constrain you. You may choose for yourself if you wish, and if you can.'

'How can I? You have forbidden me to tell anyone that I am expecting a child and I could not deceive anyone like that.'

'If there is a man, worthy of you and your name, who loves you enough to marry you in these circumstances, I should not oppose it. I will inform you where and when you are to come to me so that the marriage can take place. If you are accompanied by a man of your own choice, I will marry you to him. If you are alone, you will take the person I offer you.'

'Who will that be?'

'No more questions. I will say nothing more. You will have to trust me. You know I love you like my own daughter. Do you agree?'

Marianne nodded slowly, all her joy and pride evaporating in the face of grim reality. Ever since her discovery that she was pregnant, she had been carried along on the tide of exaltation that came from knowing she carried the Eagle's son within her and for a little while she had believed that this would enable her to hold her own before the world. But now she knew that her godfather had reason on his side, for however much she might scorn the opinion of others for herself, had she the right to force her child to carry the stigma of illegitimacy? There were those in society, she knew, who were not the children of those whose names they bore. The charming Flahaut was the son of Talleyrand and all the world knew it, but he owed his brilliant military career to the fact that his mother's husband had obliterated the stain that would have closed society's doors to him. Had not Marie Walewska returned to the snows of Walewice in order that her husband, the old count, might be able to acknowledge her unborn child? Marianne had sense enough to know that her own heart and her love must bend before necessity. She had, as the cardinal had said, no alternative. Yet at the very moment of acceptance which would seal her fate as surely as that final 'I will', she made one last effort to fight.

'I implore you, let me see the Emperor at least, speak to him … He may find a solution. Give me a little time.'

'Time is the one thing I cannot give you. We must act very quickly, and I can tell from your expression that you do not know when you will see Napoleon again. Besides, what is the use? I have told you: when you tell him, he will solve the problem in the only way possible, by marrying you to one or other of his own people, some fellow of dubious lineage, the son of an innkeeper or groom, and you, a d'Asselnat whose ancestors rode into Jerusalem with Godfrey of Bouillon and into Tunis with St Louis, will have to thank the creature humbly for taking you! The man I have in mind will ask nothing of you, and your son will be a prince.'

This harsh reminder of her position struck Marianne like a blow. She had a sudden vision of her father's proud, handsome face, the noble bearing of the portrait in the gilded frame, and then, set against the misty background of childhood, the less handsome but kindlier features of her Aunt Ellis. Surely their ghosts would be justified in turning their backs with anger on a child who could not accept the sacrifices which honour demanded? They had subdued their whole lives to that same sense of honour, even to the ultimate sacrifice. Marianne saw, as clearly as if they had risen suddenly out of the shadows of the library, the long line of her forbears, French and English, all of whom had fought and suffered to preserve intact their ancient name and the principle of honour. In that moment, she gave in.

'I agree,' she said firmly.

'In good time! I was sure you would.'

'Let it be understood clearly,' Marianne added quickly. 'I agree in principle to be married in a month, but between now and then I shall do all I can to find a husband of my own choosing.'

'I see no objection, providing always that you choose one who is worthy of us. All I ask is that you come, alone or otherwise, at the place and time I shall appoint. Let us call it a bargain, if you like. I will release you from Francis Cranmere, and you will protect your honour or pledge yourself to accept the man I shall bring you. Is it agreed?'

'A bargain is a bargain,' Marianne said. 'I pledge myself to honour this one.'

'Very well. In that case I shall set about fulfilling my part of the bargain.'

He moved to a tall writing desk which stood open in a corner, and taking a sheet of paper and a pen, wrote a few words. Meanwhile, Marianne poured herself another cup of coffee. She had no thought of going back on the words she had uttered, but one disturbing possibility occurred to her which she hastened to put into words.

'Supposing that I fail to find someone, may I ask one favour, godfather?'

He looked round at her without speaking, waiting to hear what she would say.

'If I must accept the husband of your choice, please, I beg of you, think of the child and do not make him bear the name of one who is his father's enemy.'

The cardinal smiled and dipped his pen in the standish with a tiny shrug.

'Not even my loyalty to the king would tempt me to anything so base,' he said with gentle reproach. 'You know me well enough. No such thought should ever have occurred to you.'

He finished what he was writing, sanded it, then folded it and affixed a wafer. He held it out to Marianne.

'Take this. I shall be leaving Paris in a few minutes and I do not like to leave you in this perilous situation. Tomorrow morning, take this letter to Lafitte, the banker. He will give you the fifty thousand livres which this English devil demands. That will grant you a breathing space, and allow you to recover that foolish Adélaïde who seems to have grown no wiser with age.'

Amazement took away Marianne's breath as nothing else in that extraordinary interview had been able to do. She stared at the letter as if it were something miraculous, hardly daring to touch it. Her godfather's magnificent generosity left her speechless, especially as it forced her to overcome her resentment at his severity. She had thought him to be acting solely from a sense of duty and now, with a stroke of the pen, he had made his protection something warm and real. Her eyes filled with tears because for a while it had seemed as if he no longer loved her.

'There, take it,' the cardinal said gruffly, 'and don't ask unanswerable questions. You may have known me as poor as a church mouse but that does not mean I cannot find the money to save your life.'

There was, in fact, no time for any questions. The library door opened to admit a second cardinal. The newcomer, who was dressed in the robes of his office, was as small as the Cardinal San Lorenzo but his face, which was extremely handsome, had a pronounced air of nobility and bore a striking resemblance to the portrait over the fireplace.

'The coach and escort are at the door, my poor friend. We must go. Your horse is ready in the stable with your saddle-bags and such clothes as you need.'

'I am ready.' Gauthier de Chazay spoke almost joyously, gripping the newcomer's hands warmly. 'My dear Philibert, I can never thank you enough for sacrificing yourself like this. Marianne, I want to introduce you to Canon de Bruillard who, not content with offering me the shelter of his house, has carried friendship to the point of taking my place tonight.'

'Good heavens!' Marianne exclaimed. 'I had forgotten. You are to be sent to Rheims. But —'

'But I am not going. While my friend Philibert, accompanied by the Abbé Bichette, is travelling peacefully to Rheims in the coach, escorted by the Duc de Rovigo's men, I shall be disguised as a servant and riding hard for Italy where the Holy Father is waiting for me to report to him about a certain mission.'

Still clutching the precious letter which spelled a year of freedom to her, Marianne stood speechlessly staring at the two cardinals, the real and the false, wondering if she had ever really known Gauthier de Chazay. Who was this man who had fought with such determination to save her as a baby, who, although he certainly possessed no fortune of his own, was able with a stroke of the pen to pay out a prince's ransom, and who travelled the roads on horseback dressed as a servant?

Evidently the one-time Abbé had noticed his goddaughter's bewilderment, for he went to her and kissed her affectionately.

'Do not try to understand what is outside your comprehension, Marianne. Just remember that you are still my beloved child and that I want you to be happy, even if the means I use to procure your happiness do not meet with your approval. God keep you, my child. I will pray for you as I have always done.'

He blessed her quickly and then turned away to open the window.

'This is the swiftest way to reach the stables without meeting anyone,' he said. 'Good-bye, my dear Philibert. Send Bichette back to me, you know where, when you can spare him. I hope you will not have to suffer for our little deception.'

'Have no fears. The escort will notice nothing. I will hide my face as far as possible, and fortunately neither of us is well known. Your brethren of the Sacred College may be a trifle surprised but I will explain matters to them and in a few days, I shall find the means to return here, in my real identity. Have a good journey, my dear Chazay, and convey my filial regards, respect and obedience to the Holy Father.'

'I will. Marianne, farewell. My regards to that silly creature Adélaïde when you find her. We have never seen eye to eye but I have a fondness for her just the same.'

Whereupon his Eminence threw one leg over the window-sill and jumped down into the courtyard. Marianne saw him vanish swiftly through the darkened doorway of the coach house below the tower. Canon de Bruillard made her a little bow.

'Do not worry about him. He will leave by way of the Seine. And now permit me to leave you also. The Abbé Bichette is outside and the escort is waiting below.'

He was donning a voluminous cloak as he spoke, turning up the collar to conceal the greater part of his face. Then, with one last nod of farewell, he left the library. As the door opened, Marianne caught sight of the Abbé Bichette, looking more like a frightened chicken than ever. Crossing to a barred window, she saw a large travelling coach with lighted lamps drawn up in the street below, surrounded by a platoon of mounted men in black cocked hats with red cockades, the horses' hooves striking sparks from the ancient cobbles. This display of military strength for the sake of two peaceable servants of God struck her as absurd and at the same time intolerable. But when she remembered the casual way in which Gauthier de Chazay had climbed out of the window and felt the letter in her hand, she thought again. Surely the little cardinal, so frail and harmless to all appearances, represented an infinitely more active and formidable power than she could ever have imagined? He seemed to command men and events like God himself. In a month a man would be prepared, at his command, to marry her, Marianne, a total stranger and pregnant into the bargain. Why? What for? By what authority?

A dash of arms outside called Marianne from her thoughts and she saw the small, red figure of the pseudo-cardinal climb into the coach, followed by the tall, lean one of the Abbé who crossed himself several times at the sight of the captain in charge of the escort, as if he had seen the devil. She heard the door slam shut in the darkness, the crack of the whip, and then with a thunderous roar the coach and its escort swept away down the Rue Chanoinesse. Behind her, Marianne heard the measured tones of the footman who had admitted her earlier.

'If madame will allow me to see her to her coach? I must shut the house now.'

She picked up her cloak, which she had laid over the back of a chair, and put on her gloves, stowing the precious letter carefully in an inner pocket.

'I am ready' she said.

Now that her godfather had gone and she was alone Marianne felt the full weight of her misery. A month! In a month she would be married – to a complete stranger perhaps. It was true that she was free to choose for herself if she wanted to avoid giving her hand to the unknown man whose name, true to the love of mystery which she had always found in him, her godfather had refused to divulge. The Abbé de Chazay had been the most secretive of men and it seemed that the Cardinal San Lorenzo shared his uncommunicative habit. No, at all costs, she must find someone, someone who did not fill her soul with loathing, a man for whom she might feel, if not love, at least respect. She had always known that girls of her station married, often, without meeting their betrothed. It was a matter for their families. It might have been expected, after all, that this would be her own fate, but the independence she had acquired through the blows fate had dealt her made it impossible for her to yield without a struggle. She wanted to choose for herself. But who?

As she followed the footman with his heavy candlestick through the darkened rooms, Marianne was mentally reviewing the men to whom she might turn. Fortunée had told her that the whole of the Imperial Guard was in love with her but she was unable to identify a single face, a single person to whom she might turn for help. She hardly knew them and there was no time now to further an acquaintance. Moreover, some were no doubt married and others had no desire to be, especially under such conditions; Marianne was wise enough to know that it was a long way from paying court to her to marriage. Clary? The Austrian prince would never marry an opera singer. In any case, he was already married to the daughter of the Prince de Lignes, and even if he were not, Marianne would never willingly become a fellow-countrywoman of the hated Marie-Louise. What then? It was out of the question to ask Napoleon to find her a husband, for the reasons put forward by the cardinal, and besides her feelings revolted at the idea of being bestowed by the man she loved on someone who could only be a complaisant husband. Better the unknown chosen by her godfather, who had at least promised that he would be irreproachable.

It occurred to her momentarily that she might marry Arcadius but even in her misery the idea was enough to make her smile. No, she could not imagine herself as Madame de Jolival. It would be like marrying her own brother, or perhaps an uncle.

Then, when she reached the street and saw Gracchus-Hannibal Pioche in the act of letting down the steps of her carriage the answer came to her in a sudden, blinding flash. Side by side with the boy's chubby face and thatch of carroty hair she saw, by association, another face. The vision was so clear that she said out loud: 'He! He is the man I need.'

Gracchus turned, hearing her voice. 'What is it, Mademoiselle Marianne?'

'Nothing, Gracchus. Tell me, can I count on you?'

'Need you ask, mademoiselle? Only tell me what I must do.'

Marianne did not hesitate. She had made her choice and she felt a sudden sense of relief.

Thank you. Indeed, I did not doubt it. Listen, when we get home, I want you to change into travelling clothes and saddle a horse. Come to me then and I will give you a letter which I want carried as quickly as you can.'

'I will stop for nothing but to change horses. Is it far?' To Nantes. But first, home, Gracchus, as fast as you can.'

An hour later, Gracchus-Hannibal Pioche, heavily booted and enveloped in a thick riding cloak that would withstand the heaviest downpour, a hat pulled down over his eyes, clattered through the gates of the Hôtel d'Asselnat. Marianne watched him go from an upstairs window and it was not until Augustin, the porter, had shut the heavy gates behind him that she left her post and made her way back to her own room where the smell of hot wax still hovered in the air.

Automatically, she went straight to her small writing-table and closed the blue Morocco folder, first carefully extracting the single sheet of paper, signed only with an 'F', which had lain there. This letter, which had been waiting for her when she returned from the rue Chanoinesse, appointed a meeting for the following evening to hand over the fifty thousand livres. Marianne had an impulse to burn it but the fire in the hearth had gone out and then it crossed her mind that she should perhaps show it to Jolival, who at that late hour had still not come in. She thought he was probably trying to find the money for the ransom. The few words in Francis's handwriting had no power to wrest a shiver from Marianne. She read them indifferently, as though they did not really concern her. All her thoughts, all her anxieties, were concentrated on the letter she had just written and which Gracchus was at that moment carrying on its way to Nantes.

It was, in fact, two letters. One was addressed to Robert Patterson, United States consul, requesting him to speed the second letter to its destination with the utmost urgency. Even so, Marianne did not attempt to conceal from herself that the second letter was a little like the message in a bottle cast by a shipwrecked mariner into the waves. Where was Jason Beaufort at that moment? Where was the vessel whose name Marianne had refused to ask? A month was such a short time and the world so wide. Yet, however hopeless the odds, Marianne had been unable to prevent herself from writing that letter summoning to her side the man she had so long believed she hated and who now seemed to her the one being strong, reliable and true enough, the one man she dared ask to give his name to Napoleon's child.

Jason, accustomed from childhood to take life by the horns, to fight it with his bare hands, Jason, who acknowledged no master but the sea, he would be able to guard and protect her and her child. Had he not begged her to go with him once before to find peace and rest in that vast, free country of his? Had he not written: 'Remember I am here, and that I owe you a debt …'? Now, Marianne meant to ask him to repay that debt. He could not refuse because it was to some extent through him that fate had brought Marianne to her present pass. Once before, he had snatched her by night from the quarries of Chaillot and the talons of Fanchon Fleur-de-Lys. Now he must come again and snatch her from the mysterious stranger to whom her godfather meant to marry her.

He must! It was her only chance of a marriage which would not make her shrink with horror.

Yet Marianne knew that by summoning Jason to her side she was committing herself to the bitter sacrifice which she had rejected with despair in her interview with her godfather. She was renouncing Napoleon, committing herself to part from him, perhaps for ever. Jason might agree to give his name to Marianne's child, but he was not the man to accept the undignified role of a complaisant husband. Once he had married her, even if, as Marianne meant to persuade him, he refrained from exercising his rights as a husband, she would still be obliged to go with him and live where he wished, which would certainly be in America. The width of the ocean would divide her from the man she loved, she would no longer be beneath the same sky, breathing the same air. But then, was she not divided from him already by the woman whose rights over him made her an impassable barrier between them? Only the child was left and Marianne knew that through him she would always be united with her lover by ties more binding than those of the flesh.

As for Jason, Marianne dared not examine herself too closely on her feelings for him. Affection, respect, tenderness or merely friendship? It was not easy to be sure. Trust, certainly, complete and absolute trust in his courage and his qualities as a man. In him, the child would have a father capable of inspiring respect, admiration, perhaps even love. And with him, Marianne herself would be able to find, if not happiness, at least security. The solid wall of his determination and his stout shoulders would stand between her and all those who threatened her. There would be no Napoleon for Marianne and her child, but no more Francis Cranmere either, nor any other unwelcome sire.

Tired of meditating by the dead fire, Marianne got up and stretched and went towards her bed. All she wanted now was to sleep, and dream perhaps of the distant land about which Jason Beaufort had once talked to her with such compelling enthusiasm, in the little pavilion in the garden of the Hôtel Matignon.

Marianne let fall her dressing-gown and was about to climb into bed when someone knocked at her door.

'Are you asleep?' said a voice in a half-whisper.

It was Arcadius, home at last and certainly unsuccessful in his search for money. There was to be no sleep yet awhile. Marianne sighed at the thought that she would have to tell him all that had occurred, except for what concerned the child and the plans for her marriage. That must remain her secret.

'I am coming,' she said aloud. Then, scooping up her dressing-gown from the floor, she slipped it on and went to open the door.

# CHAPTER SEVEN
# The Mountebanks

The dreadful moment had come. It was time to meet Francis to hand over the money. Yet there was nothing to distinguish Marianne and Arcadius from the rest of the Parisian crowd as, in the late afternoon of the following day, they mingled with the people strolling among the open air theatres, showmen's booths and cafés that filled the boulevard du Temple for most of its length. Wearing a walking dress of chestnut-brown merino trimmed with matching velvet ribbon and a narrow *fraise* of pleated white muslin, a deep poke bonnet of the same velvet and a light brown pelisse over her shoulders, Marianne looked calm enough, despite the agitation which possessed her. Her appearance was that of an ordinary young woman of good family walking out to observe the sights of the famous boulevard. Arcadius, in beaver hat, black cravat and grey coat and pantaloons gravely offered his arm.

They had left the carriage at the back of the gardens by the Café Turc. The afternoon was fine and a good many people were strolling up and down beneath the elm trees of the boulevard, drinking in all the sights and sounds of the permanent fairground which had established itself there.

The entertainment they were offered, against a constant background of music and shouting, showman's patter, trumpets, drums and cries of 'Roll up, roll up, see the show', included the Fire-Eating Spaniard, a thin, olive-skinned youth in a suit of spangles who drank boiling oil and walked on hot coals without apparent discomfort, the Intelligent Dog, able to select cards from a pack to order, and performing fleas drawing miniature coaches and fighting duels with pins. A tall old gentleman with a patriarchal beard stood on a wooden dais calling out: 'Roll up, ladies and gentlemen, roll up and see an entirely new performance, put on by special request, of that celebrated comedy in five acts, "The Triumph of Peter, or the Atheist Confounded", complete with Transformation Scene, Rain of Fire in Act Five, Grand Finale and Ballet featuring the world-famous dancer, Mademoiselle Malaga, as Don Juan with Innumerable changes of costume! See her in Act Four in a suit of bronze velvet with ruffles of Flemish lace! And, ladies and gentlemen, to prove to you that accounts of her Great Beauty are in no way Exaggerated, we proudly present to you – Mademoiselle Malaga in person!'

Fascinated, by the showman's technique and by the whole colourful scene, Marianne saw a young girl spring on to the stage like some exotic comet in a swirl of multicoloured silks. Her long, dark hair was bound with strings of sequins and she acknowledged her audience with a charming grace that won her instant applause.

'How pretty she is!' Marianne exclaimed involuntarily. 'What a shame that she should be obliged to appear on such a pitiable stage!'

'There is a great deal more talent than you might think to be seen in these booths, Marianne. Malaga herself is reputed to be of good, even noble birth. The old fellow drumming up custom is her father, a *declasse* nobleman of some kind; as you can see, he still has some traces of the grand manner about him. We will come back some evening and see the show, if you care to. I should like you to see Malaga dance with her partner, Mademoiselle Rose. Few dancers at the Opera are so graceful. But for the present, our business is elsewhere.'

Marianne coloured. In that atmosphere of cheerful, carefree gaiety she had temporarily forgotten the real reason for their expedition to the boulevard du Temple.

'You are right. Well, since we must, where is this waxworks where we have to meet –' She broke off, finding it increasingly difficult to utter Francis Cranmere's name. Arcadius shifted under his arm the wallet containing the fifty thousand livres in banknotes which Marianne had collected that morning from Lafitte, the banker, and pointed to a large building a little way ahead of them. Its neo-classical façade towered above the host of tents and smaller booths.

'You see the Olympic Circus, there, where Monsieur Franconi mounts his equestrian spectacles? Monsieur Curtius's Hall of Waxworks is the old house just beyond it, with the balcony and four Corinthian columns. It is a strange place, as you will see, but take care where you walk. The ground here is very muddy.'

Indeed, to avoid the queues forming in front of the Gaîté and Ambigu Comique theatres, where posters in gaudy colours solicited the customer as imperiously as the hucksters, they had to fight their way towards the cover of the trees, where the ground, soaked by a heavy rain that fell towards morning, was as muddy as they could wish.

A group of small boys passed by, shouting a refrain from Désaugiers, which was very fashionable at the time:

'The only prom'nade that's worth anything,
The only one I'm in love with,
The only one where I give myself, where I laugh,
Is the boul'vard of the Temple in Paris.'

Jolival, doing his best to protect Marianne from the dirt splashed up by their feet, murmured apologetically:

'I am sorry to subject you to this but I think it is better than remaining in the open.'

'Why so?'

For answer, Jolival nodded towards a low building crammed in between the waxworks and a little wooden theatre with a large, canvas pediment announcing its name: the Pygmy Théâtre. The ground floor of the house was taken up by a spacious tavern, the sign over the doorway representing an ear of corn being cut by a sickle.

'That delightful spot is the Épi-Scié, owned by our friend Fanchon Fleur-de-Lys. We shall be wiser to keep well away from there.'

The mention of Francis's sinister associate was enough to make Marianne shiver, agitated as she was by the thought of the impending meeting. She quickened her pace and, in a few moments, they had reached their destination. Outside the waxwork hall was the magnificent figure of a Polish Lancer, so lifelike that Marianne had to go close to it to be certain that it was really only a dummy. Meanwhile Arcadius, the wallet still tucked firmly under his arm, was paying their entrance money at the gate. The inevitable barker exhorted the good people of Paris to 'Step-up and see the figures of the great and famous, more real than in life.'

Marianne went forward nervously into the large, gloomy hall. The only light came from windows which could have done with a good cleaning; for all the bright afternoon outside, grey twilight reigned within. The wax figures loomed ghostly and unreal in the murky dimness and would have been frightening but for the presence of the visiting public, laughing and exclaiming over the show.

They stood for a moment, ostensibly admiring a warlike effigy of the late Marshal Lannes, their eyes busy searching for Francis among the crowd of people, real and waxwork. Marianne shivered.

'It is cold in here.'

'Yes,' Jolival agreed, 'and our friend is late.'

Marianne made no answer. Her nervousness was increasing, possibly from the unnerving presence of so many all-too-lifelike wax dummies. The principal group, occupying the very centre of the room, represented Napoleon himself seated at table with all his family, with footmen in attendance. All the Bonapartes were there: Caroline, Pauline, Elisa and their stern Mama in her widow's weeds. But it was the wax Emperor himself that

Marianne found most disconcerting. She had the feeling that his painted eyes were looking at her, seeing her conspiratorial air, and shame mingled with the fear of finding Francis suddenly before her made her want to turn and run.

Guessing her trouble, Arcadius stepped up to the imperial table and laughed.

'You have no idea how this dinner-table has reflected the history of France. It has seen Louis XV and his august family, Louis XVI and his august family, the Directorate and their august families and now here is Napoleon with *his* august family – although you will observe that the Empress is missing. Marie-Louise is still unfinished and besides, I have an idea they were going to cannibalize some parts of the Pompadour, who is now obsolete. What I do know is that this fruit has been here since Louis XV, and I should think that may well be the original dust!'

Jolival's commentary raised no more than a faint smile from Marianne. She was wondering what had become of Francis for, little as she wished to see him, she was also anxious to get the interview over and turn her back on a place she found depressing in the extreme.

Then, suddenly, he was there. Marianne saw him emerge from the darkest corner, behind the bath in which the dying Marat lay, struck by Charlotte Corday's knife. He, too, was dressed soberly, a brown hat pulled down low over his brow and his coat collar turned up to hide his face. He came quickly towards them and Marianne, who had never known him anything but confident and self-assured, was surprised to see him cast a swift, furtive glance around him.

'You are in good time,' he said curtly, without troubling to bow.

'You, on the other hand, are late,' Arcadius retorted drily.

'I was detained. You must forgive me. You have the money?'

'We have the money.' Again, it was Jolival who answered, and his grip on the wallet tightened a little. 'It does not appear, however, that you have Mademoiselle d'Asselnat.'

'You shall have her later. The money first. How can I be sure it is indeed in that wallet?' His hand went out towards the leather satchel.

'What is so delightful in dealing with persons of your sort, my lord, is the sense of trust which exists. See for yourself.' Arcadius slipped open the leather case, exposing the fifty notes, each for one thousand livres, then shut it swiftly, and tucked it back securely under his arm. 'There,' he said coolly. 'Now show us your prisoner.'

Francis moved irritably. 'I said later. I will bring her to your house tonight. For the present, I am in haste and may not linger here. It is not safe for me.'

That much was clear. His eyes were shifting continually, never meeting Marianne's. Now, however, she decided to take a hand. Laying her fingers on the wallet as if she feared that Arcadius might be overcome by some impulsive act of generosity, she said clearly: 'The less I see of you, the better I shall like it. My doors are closed to you, and you will gain nothing by coming to my house, alone or otherwise. We struck a bargain. You have seen that I have fulfilled my part of it. I call on you to fulfil yours. If not, we are back where we started.'

'Your meaning?'

'That you will get no money until you have restored my cousin to me.'

Lord Cranmere's grey eyes narrowed and began to glitter dangerously. His smile was unpleasant.

'Are you not forgetting something, my lady? If my memory serves me correctly, your cousin was only a part – a very small part of that bargain. She merely guaranteed that I should be undisturbed while you collected the money which will ensure that you in turn shall be left undisturbed.'

Marianne did not flinch before the barely concealed menace. Now that the swords were out, she had recovered all her poise and confidence, as she always did when a fight was in prospect. She permitted herself a small, contemptuous smile.

'That is not how I see it. Since the delightful conversation which you forced on me, I have taken steps to ensure that I shall be left in peace. I am no longer afraid of you.'

'You are bluffing,' Francis said roughly. 'You need not. I am stronger at that game than you. If you did not fear me, you would have come here empty-handed.'

'I came only to recover my cousin. As for what you call bluffing, let me tell you that I have seen the Emperor. I spent several hours in his private office. If your information is as good as you pretend, you should have known that.'

'I do know it. I know also that you were expected to leave it under arrest.'

'Instead, I left it to be politely escorted to my coach by his majesty's own valet,' Marianne countered with a coolness she was far from feeling. Determined to carry it through to the end, she went on: 'Distribute your pamphlets, my friend, they will not hurt me. And you will not get a penny from me until you return Adélaïde.'

She knew his twisted nature too well not to feel deeply anxious, for he was not to be defeated so easily. Even so, Marianne could not help rejoicing a little inwardly as he hesitated, and when she saw a look of something very close to admiration on Arcadius's face, she was sure that she was gaining an important advantage. It was vital that Francis should be made to believe that nothing mattered to her now but Adélaïde, not to save the money, which Arcadius was still holding on to so grimly, but in order to render Lord Cranmere harmless in future. It was true that her future from now on would probably belong to Jason Beaufort but, just as she had recoiled in horror from the thought of involving Napoleon in a scandal of her making, so did she jib at offering Beaufort a wife who was an object of public infamy. It was bad enough to bring him one already pregnant by another man.

Lord Cranmere spoke suddenly.

'I wish I could return the old battle-axe to you. Unfortunately, I have not got her.'

'What!'

Marianne and Arcadius spoke simultaneously. Francis shrugged sulkily.

'She has vanished. Slipped between my fingers. Escaped, if you prefer it.'

'When?' Marianne asked.

'Last night. When her supper was taken to her – her room, she was not there.'

'Do you expect me to believe this?'

All Marianne's hidden fears and anxieties exploded suddenly in one outburst of anger. That was too easy! Did Francis take her for a fool? He would collect the money and give nothing in return, except a dubious promise.

Equally angry, Francis flung back at her: 'You have no choice! I was obliged to believe it. I swear to you that she had vanished from the place where she was kept.'

'You are lying! If she had escaped, she would have returned home.'

'I can only tell you what I know. I learned of her flight only a moment ago. And I swear, on my mother's grave –'

'Where had you hidden her?' Jolival interposed.

'In the cellars of the Épi-Scié, next door to here.'

Jolival gave a shout of laughter. 'With Fanchon? I had not thought you such a fool! If you want to know where she is, ask your accomplice. I'll swear she knows. No doubt she thinks her share of the profits are unworthy of her appetite!'

'No,' Lord Cranmere said curtly. 'Fanchon would not try such tricks on me. She knows that I should know how to punish her, once and for all. In any event, her anger at the old fidget's escape told its own tale. If you care for her, my dear, take care she does not fall into Fanchon's hands again. She certainly did her best to drive her to a fury.'

Marianne was well enough acquainted with Adélaïde to guess how she had taken her abduction and imprisonment. Bold and cynical Fanchon Fleur-de-Lys might be, but it was, after all, possible that the unconquerable old maid had succeeded in making her escape. But if so, where was she? Why had she not made her way back to the rue de Lille?

Francis was growing impatient. For some time, he had been glancing with increasing frequency towards the entrance where an enormous grenadier of the guard had now appeared, his head in its tall, red-plumed shako adorned with such a luxuriant growth of beard, such long, drooping moustaches, that it seemed to belong to some strange, hairy animal.

'An end to this,' Francis growled. 'I have wasted enough time already. I do not know where the foolish creature may have got to, but you will surely find her. The money!'

'No,' Marianne said firmly. 'You shall have that when I have my cousin.'

'Is that so? I think that you will give it to me now. Come, hand me that wallet, little man, at once, or it will be the worse for you.'

Marianne and Jolival had a sudden glimpse of the black muzzle of a pistol aimed from the shelter of Francis's coat directly at the girl's stomach.

'I knew you would make trouble over the old woman,' Lord Cranmere muttered grimly. 'Now, the money, or I fire. And do not move, you.' He nodded at Jolival.

Marianne's heart missed a beat. She read death in Francis's suddenly haggard face. Such was his lust for gold that he would not hesitate to kill, yet she refused to let him see her fear. She took a deep breath and drew herself up to her full height.

'Here?' she said scornfully. 'You would not dare.'

'Why not? There is no one here but that soldier, and he is too far off. I should have time to get away.'

The tall grenadier was ambling peacefully among the wax figures, his hands clasped behind his back. At that moment, he was making for the imperial table and his head was turned away from them. Francis would have time to fire more than once.

'Suppose we strike a bargain,' Arcadius said suddenly. 'Half now and half when we have Mademoiselle Adélaïde again.'

'No. It is too late and I have no more time. I must have the money to return to England. I have business there. So, hand it over quickly, before I take it by force, and before I distribute my little yellow pamphlets. We'll see what their effect is. It is true, of course, that it will not interest you very much, being dead.'

The pistol waved menacingly in Francis's hand. Marianne looked round desperately. If she could only shout to the soldier – but he seemed to have disappeared. Francis had won. They would have to give in.

'Give him the money, Arcadius,' she said helplessly. 'And then let him go to hell.'

Arcadius held out the wallet in silence. Francis seized it eagerly and thrust it inside his driving coat. To Marianne's relief, the pistol also vanished. For an instant she had read madness in Francis's eyes and feared that he would shoot anyway. She did not want to die, least of all so needlessly. For some reason, life had grown very dear to her. She had still too much to give, beginning with the child, to resign herself to dying like this, by the hand of a maniac.

'Don't count on it,' Francis said with a sneer, answering her last words. 'I am the sort that clings to life, as you should know. We shall meet again, Marianne my sweet. Remember, this grants you a year of peace, no more. Make the most of it.'

Insolently, he raised the brim of his hat a fraction, then turned and began to move away between the waxen figures, frozen in their ceremonial attitudes, when all at once he staggered and fell under the weight of the grenadier, who had stepped suddenly from behind the massive figure of Marshal Augereau.

Marianne and Arcadius gazed in astonishment as the two men rolled on the ground, locked in a desperate struggle. The grenadier had the advantage of height and weight but Francis, like most Englishmen of his class, was a skilled sportsman and possessed above average strength and agility. He fought, moreover, with all the fury and desperation of a man cornered with a fortune in his grasp, just as he was about to return home to enjoy the fruits of his labour. He uttered short, inarticulate cries of rage but the other man fought in silence, using his superior weight to hold down an adversary who was as slippery as an eel. Both men were on their feet now, heads together, arms locked inextricably, panting and groaning like two fighting bulls.

A treacherous thrust with his knee gave the Englishman his chance. The grenadier folded up with a grunt of agony and collapsed on his knees, holding his stomach. Before he could recover his breath, Francis had made a grab for the wallet which was lying near the door and struggled, gasping, out into the open. Instantly, Marianne and Arcadius ran to the assistance of his unfortunate opponent, but the man was already putting a whistle to his lips and blowing a shrill blast before he had even risen to his feet.

'I must be getting rusty, or drinking too much,' he remarked cheerfully. 'At all events, he won't get far. Still, I should have preferred to pick him up myself. That was a foul blow, not to mention the dance he's led me up to now. Well, never mind. It's good to see you again, my pretty.'

Marianne stared at him unbelievingly as he rose, recognizing with incredulous joy the familiar voice emerging from the whiskery apparition before her.

'It can't be?' she said uncertainly. 'Am I dreaming?'

'No, no. It's me all right. So you've not forgotten your Uncle Nicolas? I don't mind telling you, it came as a surprise to me to see you here just now. I wasn't expecting that.'

'Nicolas! Nicolas Mallerousse!' Marianne sighed happily as the 'grenadier' began to divest himself of his superfluous hair. 'But where have you been? I have thought of you so often.'

'And I of you, little one. As for where I have been, why, in England, as always. I have spent a long time trailing the little rat who has just slipped so neatly through my fingers. But I dare say my colleagues will be holding him fast by now. He's clever, though, and cunning. To tell you the truth, I'd lost him in England and I had some trouble picking up his trail here.'

'Why were you after him?'

'I have a score to settle with him, a heavy score and one I mean to make him pay in full. There! What did I tell you. Here they come, now.'

Francis Cranmere had re-entered the hall of wax figures, but this time firmly in the grip of four stout police officers. Even with his wrists bound, he was still fighting like a demon and the men were having to half-carry him. He was white-faced and foaming with rage, his eyes glaring murderously at the crowd which had gathered round the entrance as the policemen pushed their way inside.

'Got him, chief,' said one.

'Nice work. Take him to Vincennes, and keep a close watch on him, eh?'

'I'd advise you to release me,' Francis said furiously. 'You'll regret this.'

Nicolas Mallerousse, alias Black Fish, strolled over to him and bent to thrust his face close into his.

'You think so, eh? It occurs to me, my friend, that by the time I've finished with you, you are going to regret that you were born. Take him away.'

One of the men spoke. 'We found this on him. It is full of money.' He held out the wallet.

To judge by the hunger on his face as he looked at it, it seemed to Marianne that the money mattered even more to Francis than his freedom and that if he were deprived of it, he would, in the event of his escaping, become deadly dangerous. Remembering the relationship which Arcadius had uncovered between Lord Cranmere and Fouché and the desperate lengths to which Francis had gone to obtain the money, perhaps the wisest course would be to let him keep his ill-gotten gains. But then again, surely the luck which had brought Black Fish to them at the very moment when she was handing over the ransom was a sign of fate? The formidable Breton was not likely to permit Francis to escape what was clearly going to be an unenviable fate. Locked up inside the medieval towers of Vincennes, he would cease to be a danger to her. Besides, the temptation to indulge her revenge now that it was offered was too strong. With a smile, she held out her hand towards the wallet.

'That money is mine,' she said quietly. This man took it from us at gunpoint. No doubt you will find the weapon on him. May I have it?'

'I saw the prisoner take the wallet from this gentleman,' Black Fish corroborated, indicating Arcadius. 'Since it is merely money, there is no reason why it should not be returned to you. I thought at first that it was something a deal more dangerous and, to be honest with you, little one, it was lucky for you that we had met before. It might have gone hard with you. Search him, you men.'

While the policemen searched the angrily protesting Francis and quickly found the gun that he was carrying, Marianne asked: 'Why might it have gone hard with me?'

'Because before I recognized you, I took you for a foreign spy.'

'She?' Francis burst out furiously. 'You know well enough what she is! A trull! A spy of Bonaparte's and his mistress besides!'

'And what of you?' Marianne said caustically. 'What should I call you, besides a spy? Blackmailer? And —'

'You'll suffer for this one day, you little whore! I should have known that you would spring a trap on me. It was your doing, was it not?'

'How could I? Who arranged this meeting, you or I?'

'I, to be sure. But you set these bloodhounds on, regardless of my warnings.'

'It is not true!' Marianne cried hotly. 'I did not know; how could I have known that they were following you?'

'Enough of these lies,' Francis said, raising his bound hands as if he would have struck the girl before him. 'You have won this time, Marianne, but don't rejoice too soon. I shall not stay in prison forever – and then look to yourself!'

'Enough!' Black Fish let out a sudden roar, his eyes bulging at this revelation of Marianne's relations with the Emperor. Take him away, I said. Gag him if he won't be quiet. Don't you upset yourself, my pretty. I know enough about him to put a rope around his neck, and what the dungeons of Vincennes once hold they do not lightly give up.'

'In six months, I'll be even with you!' Francis shrieked before one of the men stuffed a dirty chequered handkerchief in his mouth and stifled his threats.

Yet even gagged and bound, Marianne watched him as they dragged him away with a kind of horror. She knew the power of evil that inhabited the man and the deadly, consuming hatred that he felt for her, a hatred which would surely grow now that he believed her guilty of betraying him. But she had known, ever since their wedding night, that there was a fight to the death between them which would not end while both remained alive.

Divining his friend's thoughts, Jolival slipped his arm through hers and gripped it firmly, as though to reassure her that she was not alone. But when he spoke it was to Black Fish, who was standing with hands on hips watching his men remove the prisoner.

'Setting aside the fact that he is English, what has he done? And why have you trailed him from England?'

'He is a dangerous man, one of the Red Herring's spies.'

'The Red Herring?' Marianne echoed in astonishment.

'Lord Yarmouth, if you prefer, the present chief of the Home Office in Perceval's cabinet. His wife, the beautiful Maria Fagiani, still lives in Paris, amusing herself very pleasantly with a little court of whom our fine game-bird is one. But I've another reason apart from his spying for swearing to bring this Cranmere to book.'

'What's that?'

'His interest in the French prisoners in the hulks at Portsmouth. It seems the gentleman's fond of hunting and he's got himself a pack of hounds to specialize in tracking down escaped prisoners. I've seen some of those poor devils after Cranmere's beasts have been at them – or what was left of them.'

Black Fish's voice was hoarse with rage, his teeth clenched and his hands opened and closed convulsively. Marianne closed her eyes to shut out the nightmare vision he had conjured up. What kind of creature was this man to whom she was bound? What depths of evil and sadistic cruelty lay behind that handsome face and princely bearing? She had a brief recollection of the bargain she had struck with the Cardinal San Lorenzo and for the first time her thoughts went out to her godfather with gratitude. Anything rather than remain tied to this monster!

'Why didn't you kill him, with your bare hands?' she asked softly.

'Because I am first and foremost the Emperor's servant. Because I want him to stand trial and would not cheat the guillotine of his head. But if his judges do not send him to his death, then I swear that I will kill him, if I die in the attempt. Enough. They are letting in the public again and we must give way to the waxworks.'

Two or three people were already poking their heads curiously into the hall now that the policemen seemed to have gone. They were obviously far more interested in any traces of the drama which had taken place there than in the waxworks.

'All good things must come to an end,' Jolival said with a sigh. 'If you have no objection, I should be glad to leave this place – so many wax dummies, you know ...'

'No, no, there is no need for you to remain. Only tell me where I may find you. I have to stay because I did not find the papers I was expecting on the Englishman. Someone else may yet come, and I must wait for that someone.'

'Someone who is to come here?'

'So I imagine. You be off now, my pretty. What happens now is no concern of yours. And don't you worry about his threats. He will be in no case to carry them out.'

Marianne would have liked to ask many more questions. Ever since Black Fish had appeared on the scene the mystery seemed to have deepened, like the gloom in Monsieur Curtius's dimly-lit chamber, but she knew that it was not for her to meddle in state secrets, or in police matters. If what had taken place were to rid her of Francis that would be enough. She had complete trust in Black Fish. There was something indestructible about him, neither men nor the elements could touch him. Francis had met his match in him.

Arcadius was hastily scribbling their address on a leaf torn from his notebook when, without warning, one of the wax footmen at the imperial table exploded in a gargantuan sneeze which left no doubt of the human identity concealed beneath the wax disguise. The unfortunate individual continued to sneeze uncontrollably, his hand fishing desperately in his pocket for a handkerchief. In an instant, Black Fish had reached him and had snatched the dirty white wig from his head in a cloud of dust and ancient powder.

'Fauche-Borel! I might have guessed!'

With a wail of terror, the false footman sprang backwards, sending a waxwork crashing to the ground, and took to his heels, Black Fish in hot pursuit. The quarry was a small, spare man, well-designed for slipping through the growing crowd of visitors like the hunted creature that he was. Before any of the visitors could grasp what was happening, they were borne down by the charging bulk of Black Fish. Arcadius laughed outright and seizing Marianne by the hand tried to hurry her towards the door.

'Come and see! This should be fun.'

'But why? Who is this Fauche —?'

'Fauche-Borel? A Swiss bookseller from Neufchâtel who thinks himself the king of spies and devotes himself to the service of his mythical majesty Louis XVIII. He has always had a weakness for waxworks. In fact, he's hopelessly incompetent. Come on, I long to see what your picturesque friend will make of him.'

But Marianne had no desire to dash off in pursuit of the disguised grenadier and a waxwork footman. The taste left by her encounter was too bitter and for all her trust in Black Fish she could not recall without a shudder that last look the Englishman had cast at her above the handkerchief stopping his mouth. She had never met a glance of such pure, implacable hatred and when she compared it with what Black Fish had told her she felt herself go cold with horror. It was as if Francis had suddenly thrown off his splendid human shape and appeared before her as the monster he really was. Until then she had thought Lord Cranmere wicked, unscrupulous and cold-hearted, but Black Fish's words had opened up an abyss of sheer, sadistic cruelty before her eyes, the murky depths of a brilliantly cunning mind joined to the unpredictable violence of a dangerous madman. No, she wanted no distractions. All she wanted was to go home to her own quiet house and think these things out.

'You go, Arcadius,' she said in a tired voice. 'I will go back to the carriage and wait for you.'

'Marianne, Marianne! Wake up! That man frightened you, did he not? And the horror of what you heard was too much for you?'

She gave him a wan smile. 'You understand me so well, my friend.'

'Marianne, you have nothing more to fear. He will not escape, he is in the safest prison in all France.'

'Have you forgotten what you yourself told me? He has Fouché's ear. Black Fish knows nothing of the Minister's secret plans for peace with England. He may be in for an unpleasant surprise.'

Arcadius nodded and, taking Marianne by the arm, led her soberly towards the door, saying as they went: 'I have not forgotten. Fouché is certainly unaware of what his guest from across the channel has been up to. He cannot ignore the fact that he has been responsible for the hideous deaths of French prisoners. In my view, to release that monster now would be to sign his own death warrant. Napoleon's care for his troops is real and he would never forgive him. Some crimes cannot be passed over and Fouché is more likely to deal with Lord Cranmere so quietly that he may well vanish without trace. Money is not the only way to silence a dangerous man. So stop worrying and let us go home.'

She thanked him with a smile and leaned more heavily on his arm. Outside, darkness had fallen but the boulevard was bright as day with a profusion of lights of every description, from candles to lanterns. Every building, from the Circus down to the humblest stall, was illuminated. Only the Épi-Scié remained dark and silent with one faint light glimmering from its grimy window-panes. However, next door, in front of the Pygmy Théâtre, the crowd seemed to be surging to and fro in unusual excitement. The two actors on the boards had stopped their performance and were standing with arms akimbo watching the extraordinary scene that was being enacted on the ground below them.

'Here – there's a fight going on!' Jolival exclaimed. 'I'll lay you it's your friend and Fauche-Borel! Bobèche and Galimafré seem to be enjoying it at any rate.'

'Who?'

'The pair of clowns you see slapping their thighs up there.' Arcadius pointed with his stick. 'The pretty fellow in the red waistcoat, yellow trousers and blue stockings with the red wig and the big butterfly on the length of wire is Bobèche. The other one, the tall, gangling creature with the long face and vacant grin, is Galimafré. They are newcomers to the boulevard but already they have had a great success.'

The two buffoons were shouting robust encouragement to the combatants, accompanying their words with much witty downing, but Marianne only shook her head.

'Please come away. Black Fish knows where to find us, he will come and tell us the end of the story.'

'Oh, as to that, there can be no doubt. Fauche-Borel is not up to his weight – but you are tired, aren't you?'

'Yes, a little.'

Slowly, avoiding the crowds, they made their way back to the Jardin Turc where they had left the carriage. Jolival helped Marianne inside, flung the direction at the driver and then climbed in himself, taking care to stow the wallet safely between them.

'What do we do with this?' he asked. 'It is unwise to keep such a sum in the house. We have the Emperor's twenty thousand livres as it is.'

'Take it back to Lafitte tomorrow, but place it in our name. It may be we shall still need it. If not, then I will simply return it.'

Arcadius nodded agreement, then pulled his hat down over his eyes and settled back in his corner as if he meant to sleep. However, after a moment or two, he said softly: 'I should like to know what has become of Mademoiselle Adélaïde.'

'So should I,' Marianne said, feeling slightly ashamed that the dramatic scene with Francis had temporarily driven her elderly cousin from her thoughts. 'But surely the main thing is that she is no longer in the hands of Fanchon Fleur-de-Lys?'

'We should perhaps have made sure. But something tells me we would be wrong to worry too much about her.'

There was silence again, unbroken on either side until they reached the rue de Lille.

It was about eleven o'clock that night and Marianne was in the hands of her chambermaid, Agathe, who was brushing her long, black hair, when Arcadius tapped on the door of her room and asked to speak to her urgently, alone. She sent her woman to bed at once.

'What is it?' she asked quickly, alarmed by his mysterious behaviour.

'Adélaïde has come back.'

'She is here? But I heard nothing, no carriage —'

'I let her in. I was on the point of going out myself, just to walk down to the Seine and back, and saw her coming as I opened the gate. I must confess, I hardly recognized her at first.'

'Why?' Marianne cried in quick alarm. 'She is not hurt —?'

Jolival chuckled. 'No, no, nothing of the kind. But you shall see for yourself. She is waiting downstairs. I should add that she is not alone.'

Marianne paused in the act of darting through the door, clutching the broad pink ribbons that fastened her lace dressing-gown. 'Not alone? Who is with her?'

'One she refers to as her saviour. I may as well tell you at once — this guardian angel is none other than Bobèche, one of the two clowns I pointed out to you earlier in the boulevard du Temple.'

'What? Are you joking?'

'Far from it. Although his appearance tonight is perfectly respectable, I assure you. Would you like to see him?'

'This is absurd! Why has Adélaïde brought him here?'

'She will tell you herself. I think she is anxious for you to meet him.'

Marianne had had more than enough excitement for one day, but quite apart from her joy at having her cousin restored to her, she was possessed by a curiosity far stronger than her fatigue. Hastily twisting her hair into a knot and tying it as best she could with a ribbon, she hurried to her wardrobe, pulled out a dress at random and slipped it on in place of her dressing-gown. Returning to the bedroom, she found Arcadius waiting for her with a smile on his lips that instantly infuriated her.

'You seem to find all this amusing?'

'I do, I confess. And what is more, I think you will also when you take a look at your cousin. And a great deal of good it will do you, too. This house has been decidedly gloomy of late.'

In spite of this warning, Marianne started in amazement when she saw Adélaïde sitting calmly in a chair in the music room. She had to look twice to be sure that it was really her. A fantastic blonde wig peeped from beneath a hat of the very latest mode and her face was almost unrecognizable under a thick coat of paint. Only the blue eyes, bubbling over with life and happiness, and the commanding nose, were indisputably her own.

Adélaïde no sooner set eyes on her than she sprang up, oblivious of her cousin's stunned expression, and ran to embrace her warmly, transferring a good deal of paint to Marianne's cheeks in the process. Marianne returned her kisses automatically, exclaiming as she did so: 'But Adélaïde, where have you been? Surely you knew how dreadfully anxious we would be?'

'So I should hope!' Mademoiselle d'Asselnat declared happily. 'You shall have all the explanations you wish, but first – ' she turned and held out her hand to her companion ' – first, you must thank my friend Antoine Mandelard, otherwise known as Bobèche. It was he who rescued me from the hole where I was being kept prisoner, who hid me and defended me —'

'And encouraged you not to return home?' Jolival put in teasingly. 'Have you found your vocation on the boulevard, dear lady?'

'You speak more truly than you know, Jolival.'

All this time, Marianne had been gazing curiously at the tall, fair-haired young man who was bowing very correctly to her. She liked his frank, open face, laughing eyes and the suggestion of mischief in his smile. He was dressed in plain, dark clothes that were not without elegance. She extended her hand.

'I owe you more than I can put into words, monsieur.'

'No thanks are needed for helping a lady in distress,' he answered gallantly. 'I could do no less.'

'Such charm!' Adélaïde murmured with a sigh. 'And now, my dear, if you are glad to have your old cousin back again, suppose you offer us a bite to eat. I, for one, am half dead with hunger.'

'I should have guessed it,' Marianne said, laughing. 'All the servants are in bed but if you will set the table, Adélaïde, I will go down to the kitchen and see what may be found.'

It appeared that the cook was a woman of some forethought and Marianne soon assembled a palatable cold supper. In an amazingly short time, the four of them were seated round a table gleaming with silver and crystal.

In the intervals between disposing of a prodigious quantity of cold chicken and salad and shavings of smoked beef washed down with champagne, Mademoiselle d'Asselnat recounted her adventures. She described how a servant wearing Madame Hamelin's livery had arrived with a request for her to join her cousin at the Creole's house, and how she had no sooner got into the chaise that waited at the door than she was bound and gagged and blindfolded with a scarf, then transported across Paris to some unknown destination. When she recovered the use of her senses, she was in a small chamber divided by a ramshackle wooden partition from what seemed to be a large cellar. The only light came from a shaft set too high in the wall to be reached even by standing on the heap of coal which, with a few armfuls of straw, formed the chief furnishing of her prison.

'Through the gaps in the boards,' Adélaïde continued, helping herself liberally to her favourite Brie, 'I was able to obtain a glimpse of the rest of the cellar. It was piled with barrels and jars of all descriptions, bottles, full and empty, and everything else you would expect to find in a wine cellar. There was also a strong smell of onions, from the strings which were hanging from the ceiling, and from the noise of footsteps moving about my head and the clamour of intoxicated voices, I concluded that the cellar must belong to some kind of tavern.'

Arcadius grinned. 'I hope they didn't let you die of thirst amid such plenty?'

'Water!' Adélaïde's voice throbbed with indignation. That was all they gave me, and some bread that was very nearly inedible! Goodness, this Brie is delicious, I shall have some more.'

'But you must have seen someone in this dungeon?' Marianne said.

'Oh yes indeed! I saw a frightful old woman decked out like a queen whom they called Fanchon. She gave me to understand that my fate depended on you and on a certain sum of money which you must pay. The interview was far from friendly. I was not going to have that creature teaching me lessons about patriotism. Daring to vilify the Emperor, and crack up that windbag who calls himself Louis XVIII! I promise you, she will not soon forget the way I boxed her ears for her. I would have killed her if they hadn't got her away!'

Jolival laughed. 'I dare say that did nothing to encourage them to improve your diet, my poor Adélaïde, but I congratulate you with all my heart. Let me kiss this dainty but determined hand.'

'So much for your prison,' Marianne said. 'But how did you escape?'

'As to that, you had better ask my friend Bobèche. He will tell you the rest.'

'Oh, it was nothing really,' the young man said with a deprecating smile. The Épi-Scié is next door to us and I go there now and then for a drink with my friend Galimafré. They have a nice little wine from Suresnes which is not bad at all. I should add that we go to keep our eyes and ears open too, because we could not help but notice that the place had some remarkably strange customers. We soon began to find it very interesting. Myself, I take care not to be seen there too often but Galimafré spends hours at a time just sitting. No one takes any notice of him because he looks such a simpleton, but underneath he is by no means a fool. For all his drooping eyelids and sleepy air Galimafré is very wide awake, and, like myself, wholly at the Emperor's service.'

As he uttered the Emperor's name, Bobèche rose to his feet and raised his glass, a gesture which earned him a warm smile from Marianne. She liked this mountebank; without his make-up and his stage costume he had a kind of natural courtesy which appealed to her, besides which she was far from indifferent to his discreetly admiring gaze. It pleased her to be admired by a man who so straightforwardly declared his devotion to Napoleon. It occurred to her that Adélaïde was listening to the young man with an expression of such ardent enthusiasm that she had forgotten to eat. Could it be that she felt something more than gratitude towards him? But Bobèche was speaking again.

'The other night, Galimafré noticed them taking a loaf of bread down to the cellar where it had no business to be, unless it was intended for someone down there. Late that same night we did a little exploring in the lane, more of a tunnel really, which runs between our Pygmy Théâtre and the tavern. We already knew that there was a fanlight hidden behind a heap of rubbish which looked down into the cellar of the Épi-Scié and we were there in time to witness an angry scene between Mademoiselle and Fanchon Fleur-de-Lys which told us a good deal, then —'

'Then the following night,' Adélaïde finished triumphantly, 'they came back with tools and a knotted rope to open the window and help me out of the cellar. I would never have believed I could do it.'

'But why didn't you come straight here?' Marianne asked.

'Bobèche thought it wiser not to. Besides, I could never have crossed Paris all covered with coal as I was. And – well, I had begun to find the Épi-Scié and its environs very interesting. I may as well tell you, Marianne, that I am going back there with Bobèche. We have some business to attend to.'

Marianne frowned, and then shrugged lightly. 'This is absurd. What business can you have there? I am sure these gentlemen do not want you.'

It was Bobèche who answered with a smile for the elderly spinster.

'That is where you are wrong, mademoiselle. Your cousin has kindly agreed to keep the gate for us.'

'Keep the gate?' Marianne said in astonishment.

'Most certainly,' Mademoiselle Adélaïde's voice held the hint of a challenge. 'And I don't need you to tell me that such an occupation is quite unsuited to a woman of my condition. I have recently learned otherwise.'

Marianne blushed. It ill became her to reproach her cousin when she herself had taken to the boards. As theatres went, the Pygmy was no more to be despised than the elegant Feydeau. But the knowledge that Adélaïde wanted to go away again filled her with unexpected sadness. Marianne met Arcadius's eyes across the table and he smiled and winked, then, reaching for the bottle, he refilled Adélaïde's glass with more champagne.

'If that is your vocation, you would be wrong to fight against it. But do you really intend to keep the gate only – or will you venture to tread the boards?'

'Not yet, at all events,' she told him with a laugh. 'And, as I said, I shall be in no danger, whereas by remaining here I may run the risk of being kidnapped again and even putting you all in peril. That I could not endure! Besides, I am enjoying myself. I want to see if the Ambassador Bathurst's papers really will turn up at the Épi-Scié.'

'Papers? What papers are you talking about?' Marianne burst out at last. 'All day I have heard of nothing but papers. I don't understand it.'

Arcadius laid his hand gently over hers. 'I think I understand. Our business has become confused with another and much more important matter in which your – the Englishman, that is, was also involved. Hence the unexpected arrival of your friend the colossal grenadier, and possibly also the appearance on the scene of Fauche-Borel. Is that right?'

'Quite right,' Bobèche agreed. 'Forgive me if I do not explain further but it seems probable that certain papers stolen recently from an English ambassador may turn up at the Épi-Scié, which is something of a nest of foreign agents. The police never set foot there, or not officially. That is why there has been so much excitement in that neighbourhood of late and why one of those agents, believing himself recognized, had the idea of concealing himself among the waxworks.'

'By the way,' Arcadius said, 'was he captured?'

Bobèche nodded and became apparently absorbed in contemplation of the champagne in his glass, thereby indicating his wish to change the subject. Marianne was now looking at him in amazement coupled with no little admiration. It seemed strange to hear such grave words coming from a mouth so clearly fashioned for laughter. Who was this clown and for whom was he really working? He had proclaimed his devotion to the Emperor, but he did not seem to be one of Fouché's men. Could he be a member of that secret band, answerable to the Emperor alone, as they had been to the last kings of France, and who, it was said, formed a kind of special police force alongside the official one? His profession must surely give him many opportunities for observing without himself coming under suspicion and he was probably also an adept at disguise. Tonight, in his well-cut dark-green coat and faultlessly-tied cravat, his thick golden hair carefully brushed, he would not have seemed out of place in any drawing-room, and no one would have suspected the presence of the clown.

Marianne's puzzled gaze went from the young man to her cousin who was leaning back in her chair nibbling a crystallized citron without taking her eyes from her new friend. She was literally drinking in his words and there was a light in her blue eyes that Marianne had not seen before. Her cheeks were flushed a youthful pink. For all her forty years, her absurd wig, her paint and her long nose, Adélaïde was transformed. She looked almost young and very nearly beautiful.

It came to Marianne suddenly, with a flash of amazement. 'She is in love!' The thought saddened more than it amused her, for she was afraid that poor Adélaïde would give her heart in vain. Bobèche had been protective, even chivalrous, and he seemed to have a genuine admiration for Adélaïde's courage, intelligence and acting abilities, but between the wildest admiration and the most unexacting love there was such a vast distance! Because of this, Marianne was moved to protest when Adélaïde stood up and shook out her dress with a satisfied sigh, then said: 'There! Now you know everything, and I think it is time that we were returning to the theatre. We only came, you know, to let you know that I was safe. That is done, and I shall go away again.'

'This is ridiculous,' Marianne said unhappily. 'You will still be in danger and I shall be half-dead with worry.'

'Then you will be foolish, mademoiselle,' Bobèche said quietly. 'I promise you that I will care for Mademoiselle Adélaïde as if she were my own sister. She is in no danger while she is with Galimafré and me, I can assure you, and we are very happy that she should have chosen to honour us with her friendship.'

'Furthermore,' put in Mademoiselle d'Asselnat, who had listened to this little speech with obvious gratification, 'nothing on earth would prevent me from going back. For the first time in my life, I feel truly alive.'

Marianne was silent, her objections conquered. Truly alive? A woman who had been thrown into prison for daring to protest against Napoleon's divorce, had lived in hiding in the attics of the abandoned Hôtel d'Asselnat with only a portrait for company, and had tried one night to set fire to that same house because she believed it to have fallen into unworthy hands? What had she meant by living until then? It was with feelings of profound sadness that she allowed Adélaïde to kiss her good-bye.

Guessing her thoughts, Arcadius slipped his arm through hers and whispered: 'Let her go, Marianne. She is having such fun playing at secret agents, and indeed I wonder if she has not a talent for it. Besides, it is better for both of you that she should not come back here. The lad is right: no one, not even Fanchon, will ever think to look for her at the Pygmy Théâtre.'

'You are right, of course,' Marianne said with a sigh. 'But I shall miss her dreadfully.'

She had counted so heavily on Adélaïde for the hard days ahead, to help her when the child came and with her advice when she went to join the cardinal – supposing that Jason did not come. A small voice whispered: 'If she knew the truth, she would stay with you.' But Marianne could not tell her the truth because of her promise to her godfather. And even if Adélaïde knew how much Marianne needed her, would she have the heart to say good-bye to the dream she had made for herself, her chance of sharing briefly in the life of an attractive young man for whom she felt something more than kindness? No, Adélaïde must be allowed to follow the absurd road she had chosen for herself. There was nothing Marianne could do about it.

Her heart felt very heavy as she heard the great gate slam behind the departing guests. She was suddenly cold and shivered as she held her hands out to the blaze in the hearth. The room was very quiet, disturbed only by the tiny sounds of Arcadius taking snuff. The floor creaked as he came towards her, slowly.

'Why torment yourself, Marianne?' he said gently. 'After all, Adélaïde is in no real danger, although she may lose some illusions. Cheer up and smile. Life will seem good again, you'll see. Look at Adélaïde. She has found happiness in a theatre booth. Who knows what tomorrow may have in store for you?'

Marianne blinked back her tears and managed to smile. Dear Arcadius, so kind and so faithful. She felt ashamed of the secret which, for no good reason that she could see, she was obliged to keep from him for a month. But a bargain was a bargain. She must play her part.

'You are right,' she said softly. 'Let Adélaïde have her fun. After all, I still have you.'

'So I should think! Now go to bed and try and find sweet dreams.'

'I will try, my friend, I will try.'

They walked together towards the great staircase, which at this late hour was in darkness, and Arcadius took a branch of candles from a side table to light their way. They were about half-way up when he asked suddenly: 'By the way, where is Gracchus? No one has set eyes on him today and Samson is missing from the stables.'

Marianne felt herself blushing to the roots of her hair and blessed the darkness which concealed it, but she could not prevent her voice from sounding a shade too quick and strained as she replied.

'He – he asked me for – for leave to visit his family for a few days i – in the country. He had bad news –'

Marianne had always been a bad liar but this time the effort was terrible. She cursed her own clumsiness, convinced that Arcadius must smell a rat at once. Yet his voice was perfectly smooth as he observed: 'I was not aware he had any family in the country. I thought there was only his grandmother, a washerwoman, out at Boulogne, on the route de la Revoke. Where has he gone?'

'To – to Nantes, I believe,' Marianne said desperately, taking refuge in a half-truth. But Arcadius asked no further questions and merely remarked: 'Ah, I see…' in such a distracted voice that it seemed to her he was already thinking of something else. When they reached the door of Marianne's room he bowed gracefully as he wished her good night and went away in the direction of his own room, humming under his breath. He had not seemed so light-hearted for a long time. Marianne reflected, as she closed her door, that it was possible he really believed that Francis could do no further harm.

The thought brought with it a sense of relief, a new serenity, and that night Marianne slept like the child she had been so short a time ago. What was more blessed than peace of mind? And for three days and three nights Marianne enjoyed it to the full, together with a pleasurable feeling of having won a victory over both Francis and herself.

An idea came to her during those days and she hugged it to her lovingly. If Black Fish succeeded in removing Francis from the face of the earth, then there would be no need for an annulment, or for the threatened marriage. She would be a widow, free, with nothing more to fear from Francis Cranmere, free to join with the father of her child in seeking a less desperate remedy for her situation.

A hundred times she was on the point of picking up her pen and writing to her godfather but each time one thing stopped her. Where should she write? To the Pope at Savona? The letter would never reach him. It would surely fall into Fouché's hands. No, it was better to wait for word to come from the cardinal. Time enough then to tell him what had occurred and he might be the one to offer another solution. It was so good to dream, to make plans that were not dictated by necessity.

On the morning of the fourth day all these dreams were shattered into fragments. The blow came in the form of a single sheet of white paper, carefully folded and sealed, brought by Agathe to her mistress as she lay in bed. Marianne read it and flung back the covers with a cry of anguish. Barely pausing to catch up a dressing-gown in passing, she tore downstairs, barefoot, to where Jolival was peacefully enjoying his breakfast in the company of the morning's papers. When Marianne burst in on him, white-faced and clearly in a state of terror, he sprang to his feet so suddenly that the table at which he had been sitting tottered and fell with a crash, taking the breakfast things with it. Neither of them so much as glanced at this miniature cataclysm of broken China. Marianne was holding out the letter speechlessly. She dropped into a chair and signed to Jolival to read it.

In a few hurried, angry lines, Black Fish apprised his young friend of Lord Cranmere's escape from Vincennes. How he had contrived it was a mystery. His trail led to the Boulogne road and thence, no doubt, to England. The Breton added that he was about to set out in pursuit. 'And the devil help him when I get my hands on him,' he wrote. 'It will be him or me.'

Arcadius had himself more under control than Marianne but even he blanched. Crumpling the letter in his fist he cast it into the hearth, then turned his attention to the girl, who was lying back in her chair with closed eyes and livid complexion, breathing unevenly and apparently on the verge of fainting. Arcadius administered two or three brisk slaps to her cheeks before seizing her cold hands and rubbing them hard.

'Marianne!' He spoke in agonized tones. 'Marianne, don't. Open your eyes! Look at me! Marianne —'

She raised her eyelids, showing her friend eyes that were two dark pools of terror.

'He is free …' she muttered. 'They have let him escape – they have let that monster go free, and now he will give me no peace. He will come here, seeking vengeance – he will kill me. He will kill us all!'

Her voice was shrill with fear. Arcadius had never seen Marianne like this. She was always so brave, so ready to face any peril, yet these few words had driven her to the brink of madness. He realized that the only way to save her was to be cruel, make her ashamed of her panic. He stood up, letting fall the hand he held.

'Is it for yourself that you are afraid?' he said harshly. 'Don't you understand what Nicolas Mallerousse says? The man has escaped, yes, but he is making for England where I dare say he will return to his hobby of hunting down escaped prisoners. Since when have your fears been for yourself, Marianne d'Asselnat? You are in your own house, surrounded by faithful servants, men like Gracchus and myself who are your devoted friends! You can command the aid of the man who holds all Europe in his

148

hands and you know that the man you fear is hunted by an implacable enemy. And are you afraid for yourself? You should be thinking rather of those poor wretches who must once again face a hideous death in their efforts to escape ...'

As he spoke, using his voice like a whiplash, Jolival saw Marianne's eyes begin to clear and fill, first with disbelief and then, little by little, with the shame that he was waiting for. He saw the colour creep back into her white cheeks and deepen to a blush. She sat up and the hand she passed across her face barely trembled. Another moment and:

'Forgive me,' she said in a low voice. 'I am sorry. I lost my head. You are quite right – as always. But when I read that letter, just now, I felt as if my head would burst. I thought I was going mad. You can't understand.'

Slowly, Arcadius knelt beside her and placed both hands gently on her shoulders.

'Yes, I can guess. But I will not let you destroy yourself because of this man's shadow. By now he is probably a long way away and he must save his own life before he can attack yours.'

'He may come back very soon, in disguise.'

'We will be watching.'

'He is stronger than we are. See how he managed to escape – regardless of walls and chains, the massive gates, the guards and even Black Fish.'

Arcadius got up and began mechanically setting the table to rights. His mouselike countenance was grave.

'It is true. I was wrong. But how could anyone guess that Fouché would dare? What is the Englishman's part in the political web he is weaving?'

'A very important one, no doubt.'

'No political scheme is important enough to merit leaving a fiend at large, Marianne! The Emperor must be warned.'

'Warned? Of what? That a spy has escaped from Vincennes? He must know that by now.'

'I doubt it. He would want to know why. I hardly think it will be mentioned in Fouché's daily report. Go and see him – tell him everything – and trust in God!'

'The Emperor is away.'

'He is at Compiègne, I know. Go there —'

'No. When I said he was away, I was thinking of myself. He does not wish to see me at present – later, perhaps. I told you how we parted.'

'Go, even so. He loves you still.'

'Perhaps, but I do not care to risk it. Not just now. I should be too frightened, frightened of making another mistake. No, Arcadius, let us leave him to his honeymoon, let him make his tour of the northern provinces.

When he returns, maybe ... Wait and see how matters turn out. We must trust in Nicolas Mallerousse. He hates him too much to fail.'

With a sigh, Marianne rose and, kicking aside the fragments of the Sèvres coffee-pot, went to the mirror. Her face looked pale and hollow but her eyes had recovered their old assurance. The battle had begun again and she had tacitly accepted it. Fate would decide.

She was halfway to the door when Jolival asked, almost timidly: 'You really mean to do nothing? You will wait?'

'I have no alternative. You told me that these secret negotiations of Fouché's could be a blessing for France. That is worth the risk of a few lives – even mine.'

'I know you, Marianne. You will show a serene face to the world but inside you will be scared to death.'

She had reached the door before she turned to him with a faint smile.

'That may well be, my friend. But one grows accustomed to it, you know. One grows accustomed.'

# CHAPTER EIGHT
## The Long Wait

Time seemed to stand still. To Marianne, confined to the house as much from prudence as from a lack of any inclination to go out, day followed day unvaryingly. The only change was that each day seemed longer than the one before. Uncertainty gnawed at Marianne, like water wearing away a stone, making the waiting an agony.

Gracchus had been gone for more than a fortnight and the reasons for his continued absence were a mystery. If he had ridden day and night, as he had declared his intention of doing, he should have reached Nantes very quickly, in three days at most. After handing the letter to the United States consul, he should have been back within a week or so. Then why this delay? What had happened? Marianne spent her days at the window of the little sitting-room on the first floor overlooking the main courtyard and the Rue de Lille. The sound of a horse's hooves would set her heart beating faster, leaving disappointment behind when they passed on and died away. It was worse still when they stopped and were followed by the slightly cracked sound of the front door-bell. On these occasions Marianne would hurl herself at the window only to draw back at once with tears pricking at her eyes because it was not Gracchus.

The nights became steadily more terrible. Marianne slept little and badly. She spent the endless sleepless hours building up all kinds of fantastic theories, each wilder than the last, about what had happened to Gracchus. The worst of these, which left her trembling and bathed in sweat on her burning hot pillows, was that the unfortunate youth had been set on by the highwaymen who still infested the roads despite the vigilance of the imperial police. A solitary horseman was an easy victim and there were plenty of places where a body could be left unnoticed in the undergrowth for many weeks. Marianne was tormented by the thought that if anything had happened to her faithful coachman no one would come to tell her. She might be waiting in vain for the return of a loyal friend and for a reply which would never come.

There was only one bright spot in the prevailing gloom. Napoleon had sent her a short note from Compiègne and the handwriting quickened her blood although the contents were a disappointment.

'My dear Marianne, a brief word to let you know that you are still in my thoughts. Take care, your health is important to me, as is the voice which, when I return from my travels, shall once more alleviate the cares of State which weigh on your N.'

The weight of the cares of State, indeed! The Emperor's 'dear Marianne' knew from Arcadius, who was far from sharing her seclusion, that he was a great deal more occupied with his honeymoon and the pleasures of his court than with affairs of State. It was all balls, hunting, picnics, theatres and diversions of every kind, and apart from presiding once over the Council of the Imperial Household and one audience with Murat concerning affairs in Italy, the Emperor had done very little. It was kind of him to have written, of course, but Marianne merely tossed it on to the mantelpiece with a sigh and thought no more about it, a thing which would have been unthinkable a few weeks earlier.

Even her panic fear inspired by Lord Cranmere's escape took second place to her longing for Gracchus to return, bringing word of whether she could hope for Jason's arrival. She no longer shuddered at every strange sound in the night, no longer flinched at the sight of a stranger in the street who reminded her of the Englishman. She knew that Jason's coming would be the best cure for her fears. If he consented to take her under his protection for always, she would no longer fear the threats of ten Francis Cranmeres. Jason was strong and bold, the kind of man who could make one glad to be a woman. He must come, he must. But, oh God, the time of waiting seemed long!

There was one person, apart from the faithful Jolival, whom Marianne would have been glad to see and that was Fortunée Hamelin. The panic which had filled her at the news of Francis's escape had faded but Marianne had thought long and deeply about it. She had no details, but it was clear that it could not have happened without the tacit consent of the Minister of Police. Yet it seemed to her impossible that one of Napoleon's ministers could stoop so low, as to baulk the efforts of his own agents, and release a dangerous criminal who was also a deadly enemy of his country.

Fortunée, who knew so many things, might have been able to elucidate the mystery but Fortunée was not at hand: caught up afresh in her passionate affair with the handsome Fournier-Sarlovèze, she had vanished from sight just as her black butler Jonas had predicted.

Marianne thought dejectedly that both the women whom she really trusted, the only two she really cared for, had been swept off their feet by the irresistible power of love. She alone was left with a lover who was worse than useless and who seemed for the moment at least to have abandoned her.

Napoleon had said one day, quoting Ovid and laughing, that love was a kind of military service. For Marianne it was worse than that. It was like entering a convent with solitude and memory for her only companions.

Then one morning at breakfast-time, Monday the nineteenth of April by Marianne's calendar, Fortunée descended without warning on her friend. Haphazardly dressed, with her hair in disorder she embraced Marianne abstractedly, told her she was looking blooming, which was a manifest exaggeration, and sank down in a chair, calling Jérémie to send her a big pot of coffee, very strong with lots of sugar.

'You had better drink chocolate,' Marianne observed, alarmed by the possible effects of coffee on someone visibly suffering under strong agitation. 'Coffee is very stimulating to the spirits, you know.'

'I need stimulating. I want to be excited and enraged! I want to keep my anger on the boil!' Fortunée declared dramatically. 'I don't want to forget the perfidy of men. Remember this, my poor sweet. Believe what a man tells you and you may as well listen to the wind! Even the best of them are abject monsters and we are their pitiful victims.'

'Do I gather that your hussar has been making victims?' Marianne inquired, feeling Fortunée's fury like a breath of fresh air.

'He is a wretch!' Fortunée declared forcefully, helping herself to a substantial portion of scrambled egg and several slices of bread and butter. 'Just imagine, a man I have loved for years, whom I have nursed day and night with nun-like devotion, and to do that to me!'

Marianne bit back a smile. The last time she had seen Fortunée and the handsome Fournier, on the evening of the Emperor's wedding, her behaviour had been anything but nun-like.

'What?' she asked. 'What has he done?'

Fortunée gave a sharp, mirthless little laugh. 'A mere nothing! Can you credit it, he dared to bring that Italian female with him to Paris?'

'What Italian?'

'Some girl from Milan – I don't know her name! The stupid creature fell in love with him there and left everything, fortune and family, to go with him. I had heard that he had brought her back with him and installed her in a house of his at Sarlat, in Périgord, which is where he comes from, but I would not believe it. And now it seems that she was not only at Sarlat but has come here with him! It is too much!'

'How did you find out?'

'He told me himself! You can have no idea of the depths of his cynicism. He left me last night, merely saying that it was time he rejoined her as she must be in some anxiety about him! He had dared to send her a message from my house to the effect that he was hurt and was being cared for in a place where he could not send for her to come. I threw him out, as I hope she will do as well, the baggage!'

This time Marianne was unable to help herself. She dissolved in helpless laughter and was conscious of a feeling of strangeness as she did so. It was the first time she had laughed in three weeks.

'You should not fly into such a passion. If he has been shut up with you for a fortnight, he must need rest and sleep more than anything. And after all, he was still a sick man. Let him go back to his Italian. If they are living together, she must be in some sort his wife and yours is really the better part. You can abandon him to the delights of his fireside.'

'Fireside? Him? It is clear you do not know him. Do you know what he asked me as he left?'

Marianne shook her head. It was best that Fortunée should continue in ignorance of her encounter with Fournier.

'He asked for your address,' Fortunée said triumphantly.

'Mine? But why?'

'To call on you. He thinks that your "vast influence" with the Emperor will enable you to obtain his reinstatement in the army. In which he is greatly mistaken.'

'Why so?'

'Because Napoleon dislikes him enough already, without adding to his dislike with suspicions about the precise nature of his relations with you.'

That much was obvious, and moreover Marianne had no desire for a further meeting with the ebullient general with his bold eyes and over-ready hands. Considering the manner of their first meeting, it was decidedly impudent of him to have dared to think of asking her help. Besides, she was tired of men who always wanted something, who never gave anything for nothing. Consequently, it was with considerable dryness that she said: 'I am sorry to have to say this, Fortunée, but I should on no account do anything for your hussar. In any case, God alone knows when I shall see the Emperor again.'

'Good for you,' Fortunée approved. 'Leave my admirers to their own devices. You have little enough to thank them for, it seems.'

Marianne's eyebrows rose. 'What do you mean?'

'That I am perfectly aware of the despicable way Ouvrard behaved towards you. Well, Jonas has remarkably sharp ears you know, and he is not above listening at keyholes.'

The colour flamed in Marianne's face. 'Oh!' she said. 'You knew? You said something to Ouvrard?'

'Not a word! But it will keep. You need not worry, I shall find a way to take revenge for both of us, and before very much longer. As for you, I would go through fire for you if need be. You have only to say the word. I am yours, body and soul! Do you still need money?'

'No, not now. It is all right.'

'The Emperor?'

'The Emperor,' Marianne agreed, suppressing a twinge at this fresh lie. She did not want to tell Fortunée about her meeting with her godfather and what had followed.

She had given her word not to talk about her dreadful situation, about the child that was coming and the marriage to which she had been obliged to consent, and ultimately it was better so. Fortunée would not have understood. Her religious feelings were superficial, not far removed from paganism. She was a Creole, careless and shameless, and she would have flaunted an army of bastards in the world's eyes without a blink if nature had not decreed otherwise. Marianne knew that she would have opposed the cardinal's plans with all her strength and it was not difficult to guess what her advice would be. She would counsel her friend to tell Napoleon of the coming event and let him marry her off to the first man who was fool enough to take her – and then console herself with all the lovers she could get her claws in. But not even to save her honour and her child's would Marianne consent to give her hand to a man motivated by base self-interest. There was nothing base about Jason and she knew her godfather well enough to be sure that any man chosen by him would not marry her for the sake of any such calculations. From every point of view, it was better to say nothing to her friend. There would be time enough afterwards – or at least when Jason had come, if he came …

Lost in her own melancholy, Marianne had not noticed the silence that had fallen between them, or the scrutiny to which Fortunée was subjecting her, until her friend said abruptly: 'Something is troubling you, isn't it? Is it your husband?'

'He?' Marianne uttered a short laugh. 'He was arrested but it appears that he escaped three days later.'

'Escaped? Where from?'

'From Vincennes.'

'Vincennes!' Fortunée exclaimed. 'Nonsense! No one escapes from Vincennes. If he got away from there, then he was helped. And it takes the devil of a lot of influence to arrange that. Have you any ideas?'

'N-no.'

'Oh yes you have. And not only that, but you have the same idea as I have. This escape had been kept very quiet and I'll wager the Emperor knows nothing of it, as he probably knew nothing of the original arrest. Now, will you tell me who is powerful enough to arrange the escape of an English spy from Vincennes without anyone knowing and without the newspapers getting wind of it?'

'Well – there are the warders, the governor —'

'Would you be willing to bet that if we went to the prison, we would meet nothing but faces shining with innocence and the most complete denials? No one would know what we were talking about. No, to my mind, the matter is clear, but what I do not understand is Fouché's reason for letting slip an enemy.'

'Yes, but you do not know it all.' Swiftly Marianne recounted to her friend the events which had taken place in the waxworks and Black Fish's appalling revelations. Fortunée heard her attentively and when it was over, she sighed.

'This is ghastly. I hope for his own sake Fouché is not aware of all this.'

'How could he fail to be aware of it? Do you think Black Fish would have concealed it?'

'It is possible that he has not seen the minister since the arrest. Fouché might be at Compiègne or on his own estates at Ferrières. Certainly, he was in no hurry to investigate the arrest – which might have proved embarrassing. Our minister is a cunning fox, but I shall find out if he knows about this Englishman's hunting exploits, I promise you.'

'How will you do that?'

'That is my business. Just as I shall find out why there has been this curious leniency towards an English spy.'

'Arcadius says that Fouché has been negotiating with the English behind the Emperor's back, by means of the bankers Labouchère, Baring – and Ouvrard.'

Madame Hamelin's dark eyes gleamed suddenly.

'Well, well! That might explain a lot of things, my darling. I had noticed some very odd goings on around the Hôtel de Juigné recently, and in the vicinity of our friend Ouvrard's bank as well. If Jolival is right, and I trust his judgement, there must be a great deal of money in it for those gentlemen – quite apart from the benefit to France, which is no doubt a minor consideration. Well, I am inquisitive by nature and I shall bring this little business out into the open.'

'How will you do that?' Marianne asked, alarmed at the thought of her friend engaging in this dangerous form of warfare.

Fortunée rose and dropped a motherly kiss on Marianne's brow.

'Don't you bother your pretty head with all this complicated stuff. Let me deal with it in my own way. I promise you we will have a good laugh and that neither Ouvrard nor Fouché will get away with it. Now run and get dressed and come out with me.'

'Where to?' Marianne seemed to shrink back in her chair, as though daring her friend to drag her out of it.

'To do a little shopping. It is a beautiful day. And regardless of what I said, you look dreadful. It will do you a world of good to take a little fresh air.'

Marianne pouted obstinately. She was sure that if she went out for so much as a minute, Gracchus was bound to arrive.

'Come along,' Fortunée persisted. 'I am giving a little supper party tomorrow night and I must go to Cheret in the Palais-Royal and see if they have any oysters. Come with me, it will give you something else to think about. It is not good for you to stay cooped up like this, brooding, and frightening yourself. You are frightened, aren't you?'

'Put yourself in my place. Wouldn't you be frightened?'

'I? I should be terrified, but I think that would make me even more inclined to go out. It is much better to be in a crowd than all alone within four walls. Besides, what is it you fear from your Englishman? Do you think he will kill you?'

'He swore to be revenged on me —' Marianne stammered.

'Very well. But there are different kinds of revenge. You say he is intelligent —'

'More than that! He is a devil.'

'Then he is not going to kill the goose that lays the golden eggs. That would be too simple, too easy, too quick and, above all, unalterable. He would have every reason to suppose, moreover, that the Emperor would use every means to find out your murderer. No, I think he is much more likely to try and revenge himself by making your life a misery, perhaps even to the point of driving you to make an end of yourself, but he will not come and murder you in cold blood. The man is a monster, but he is not an idiot. Think of the money he could still get from you.'

As she spoke, Marianne's doubts began to fade before the logic of what she was saying. Fortunée was right. It was the loss of a huge sum of money, so easily come by, which had driven Francis to madness during his arrest, not the loss of his freedom. The man was too sure of himself to be daunted by prisons or gaolers. But gold, the gold that he hungered for, that was more vital to him than breathing. Marianne got to her feet.

'I will come,' she said finally, 'but don't ask me to come to your supper party, for I should not accept.'

'Well, as to that, I have not invited you. It is a supper *a deux*, my love.'

'Ah, I see. You are expecting your hussar to come back.'

This suggestion struck Madame Hamelin as so irresistibly funny that she broke into a peal of laughter, or rather her own particular cooing chuckle.

'You are wrong there! To the devil with Fournier. If you want to know, it is another hussar I am expecting.'

'But – who then?' Marianne could not help feeling slightly taken aback to hear that Fortunée, having arrived spitting fire and fury, could now talk so calmly about having supper the next day with another man. The Creole only laughed more than ever.

'Who? Why Dupont, Fournier's eternal adversary, the man who pinked him so prettily in the shoulder the other night! He is a charming fellow, you know? And you can't think how delightful he will make my revenge! Run and get dressed.'

Marianne did not wait for a second telling. Fortunée's logic was beyond her comprehension. To say nothing of her morals. She really was a most extraordinary woman.

An hour later, Marianne found herself tripping at her friend's side beneath the arcades of the Palais-Royal, where all the best food shops were to be found. The day was fine, the sun was shining brightly on the young green leaves, on the fountain and in the eyes of the pretty girls who always abounded in this place.

Marianne was beginning to feel better. They went first to Hyrment's where Fortunée ordered a basket of fresh truffles and a variety of condiments with the observation that it was always as well to encourage men in their amorous propensities. From there, they went to Cheret, the celebrated purveyor of game. Here customers were obliged to squeeze into the long, narrow shop between barrels of herring and fresh sardines, creels of oysters and crayfish, dodging the carcasses of deer hanging like sentinels on either side of the doorway. Marianne could not resist a smile at the sight of the famous Carême, Talleyrand's chef, flanked by a pair of wooden-faced footmen and trailing three kitchen boys bearing enormous baskets. He was dressed in the sober but expensive style of a well-to-do bourgeois and was selecting his purchases with all the solemnity of a diamond merchant examining an array of precious stones.

'This place is too crowded,' Fortunée declared,' and Carême will be here for ever. We will come back later. Let's go to Corcellet's.'

This fashionable emporium, a veritable paradise for all lovers of good food, occupied extensive premises at the far end of the Galerie de Beaujolais. Flocks of eager assistants hovered in readiness to serve discriminating clients with mortadella from Lyons, *foie gras* from Strasbourg and Périgord, sausage from Arles, pâté from Nérac, tongue from Troyes, larks from Pithiviers, fowls from Le Mans, to say nothing of gingerbread from Rheims and Dijon, sugar plums from Agen, and crystallized fruits from Clermont.

Fortunée pointed out discreetly for her friend's benefit two or three women of the first consequence who had come to place their orders. One of these, a dumpy, pleasant-faced lady seemed to be on excellent terms with all the staff.

'The wife of Marshal Lefebvre,' whispered Madame Hamelin, 'an excellent creature but hardly Duchess of Dantzig! They say she was a washerwoman and the sticklers of the court will not receive her but she doesn't care, and for all her washerwoman's hands, she has far more the heart of a duchess than some that I could name.' She pointed surreptitiously to a tall, dark woman, a trifle bony but with a pair of splendid black eyes, wearing a rather over-elaborate morning dress and giving her commands with an air of great self-importance. 'I could not say the same of her, for instance.'

'Who is she?' Marianne had seen the woman before but had already forgotten her name.

'Eglé Ney. She is so conscious of her great fortune and her husband's fame that she has become insufferably conceited. You see the pains she is taking not to appear to notice Madame Lefebvre? The men are brothers in arms but the wives cannot stand one another. That is typical of the Tuileries ...'

Marianne was no longer listening. She was standing by the window staring at a woman who had just come out of a nearby café and had paused for a moment in the doorway, a woman she seemed to know well.

'What is it?' Fortunée was saying curiously. 'What are you looking at? The Café des Aveugles is no place for you, I assure you. It is a place of very ill-repute, a haunt of rogues, pimps and prostitutes.'

'It is not the café – it is that woman, the one in the red shawl and the mouse-coloured dress. I am sure I know her. I – oh!'

The woman in the red shawl had turned her head and without another word of explanation, Marianne left her friend and darted out into the street, driven by uncontrollable impulse. She knew now who the woman was. It was the Breton girl, Gwen, the mistress of the wrecker, Morvan, who since that fateful night at Malmaison had once more become an inmate of one of the imperial prisons.

Perhaps, after all, it was not so surprising to find the wild creature of the Pagan rocks here in Paris, dressed as a respectable middle-class young woman. If Morvan were in Paris, even in prison, there was no reason why his mistress should not be there also, but a mysterious voice whispered in Marianne's ear that Gwen had other business in Paris than merely being near her lover. But what?

The Breton girl walked unhurriedly along the Galerie Beauvais. Her manner was modest, almost timid, and she kept her head lowered so that her face was almost hidden by the poke of her plain grey bonnet with its bunch of red ribbons. She was clearly anxious not to be mistaken for one of the numerous prostitutes who frequented the galleries of the Palais-Royal with their outrageously painted faces and their daringly low-cut gowns. Gwen concealed her very real beauty to avoid attracting the attentions of the gentlemen who sauntered there.

In the same pious hope, Marianne had quickly let down the full, almond green veil that draped her own hat, a manoeuvre which also enabled her to follow the Breton without running the risk of being recognized.

The two women traversed the gallery in turn as far as the former Théâtre de la Montansier. There, Gwen turned left along the arcade leading to the rue de Beaujolais. Before she reached it, however, she looked round once or twice in a way that instantly put Marianne on her guard, and each time she drew back into the shelter of one of the massive stone pillars, apparently engrossed in contemplation of the entrance to the famous Restaurant Véfour. After a moment she peered cautiously out into the street.

Gwen was standing not far away, next to a black chaise which reminded Marianne of one she had seen on another, disagreeable occasion. The driver's face was hidden by the turned-up collar of his coat but he and Gwen seemed to be engaged in animated conversation, as a result of which Gwen turned and made her way back to where Marianne was standing. Marianne saw her cast several glances at the tall, decorated windows of the famous restaurant, as if she were interested in something or someone inside the Grand Véfour.

Gwen paused and began to stroll up and down the arcade outside. Marianne at once retreated as far as the Galerie de Beaujolais, but without losing sight of her old enemy whose behaviour was beginning to appear increasingly odd. It was at this point that Fortunée Hamelin at last caught up with her friend.

'Do you mind telling me what happened?' she said. 'You shot out of Corcellet's as if the devil were after you.'

'No one was after me but I wanted to go after someone else. Would you mind if we strolled on a little way, Fortunée? I don't want to be noticed.'

'Well, you'll be out of luck, my dear,' the Creole informed her drily. 'You may have let your veil down but you're not exactly dressed to melt into the crowd, you know. Nor, I flatter myself, am I. But we'll walk on if you like. Are you still watching that girl in the red and grey? Who is she?'

In a few words Marianne told Fortunée what she knew and the Creole readily agreed that this was something worth investigating. She put forward one objection, however.

'You don't think that perhaps the girl is simply endeavouring to earn a living? She is pretty enough and there are girls here who put on airs of respectability.'

'It is possible,' Marianne conceded, 'but I do not think so. If so, what is the meaning of that carriage waiting in the street, and why is she hanging about outside the restaurant? She is waiting for someone and I mean to find out who it is.'

Fortunée sighed. 'Well of course, there are people who would be interested in the activities of such women – our friend Fouché among others. We'll see what happens. It might be interesting.'

Arm in arm, the two of them strolled idly towards the quincunx of lime trees which formed the centrepiece of the garden and back again to the point which they had left, apparently deep in conversation. Their words were lost in the babel from the countless cafés and billiard halls, booksellers and small shops of every kind which made the Palais-Royal a scene of animation for most hours of the day and night. As they walked, they kept a close watch on the Breton girl, who was also strolling slowly up and down the arcade between the gardens and the street. Suddenly, Gwen froze and her two watchers followed suit. The restaurant door was opening.

'Something is going to happen, I can feel it,' Fortunée hissed, her clutch on her friend's arm tightening.

A man had come out of the restaurant, a square-built man dressed in a blue coat with gilt buttons, a high-crowned beaver perched at a rakish angle on his head. He paused on the threshold, responded with a friendly wave of his hand to the bowing of the headwaiter, and then lit a long cigar. Marianne's heart beat faster as she recognized him.

'Surcouf!' she breathed. 'Baron Surcouf!'

'The pirate?' Madame Hamelin could scarcely contain her excitement. 'That fellow built like a battleship?'

'Yes, and now I know who it was the girl was watching for. Look!'

Gwen had slipped out from the shelter of her pillar and was about to pass the entrance to the Grand Véfour, dragging her feet suddenly, like a woman in the last stages of exhaustion.

'What is she going to do?' Fortunée whispered. 'Is she going to try and accost him?'

Marianne frowned. 'She is up to no good, that's for sure. Morvan hates Surcouf even more than he hates the Emperor. I wonder —' She broke off. 'Come on, quickly.'

She had a sudden fear that the girl might be concealing a weapon underneath her pelisse but no, as she came up with the king of the corsairs, she stopped and seemed to stagger. Then, putting one trembling hand up to her head, she swayed and fell in a little heap upon the ground.

Surcouf, seeing a young woman fainting at his feet, naturally sprang forward to aid her. He had his arms round her to raise her and Marianne, springing forward at the same instant, arrived in time to hear the Breton murmur faintly: 'It is nothing – for pity's sake, sir, help me to the carriage ... close at hand. I shall be ... cared for.'

As she spoke, she moved her hand a little, wearily, warding off the other persons who had drawn near. But Marianne knew now what she planned. Surcouf would require no assistance to carry this slip of a girl as far as the carriage where, no doubt, there would be men lying in wait for him. He would be whisked into the vehicle in a trice and neatly carried off. A valuable hostage against the release of the wrecker – supposing the bargain was ever kept. Moreover, Marianne was sure that Fanchon Fleur-de-Lys and her associates had a hand in the affair. She did not hesitate for an instant.

Stepping up to Surcouf, who was already lifting the pretended invalid in his arms, she laid her gloved hand on his sleeve and said crisply: 'Do not touch the woman, Baron, she is no more faint than you or I. Above all, do not go near that carriage.'

Surcouf looked in astonishment at the veiled woman who had made this remarkable statement, laying Gwen down again as he did so. The girl gave an angry exclamation. 'Who are you, madame?' Surcouf asked.

Marianne swiftly pushed back her veil. 'Someone who stands greatly in your debt and who is glad to have been by in time to prevent your kidnapping.'

The sight of her face called forth two exclamations, one glad, the other furious.

'Mademoiselle Marianne!' cried the pirate.

'You!' spat the Breton. 'Must you always interfere?'

'Such is not my intention,' Marianne said coldly. 'If you behaved yourself like anyone else it would not be necessary.'

'Well, you were wrong! Anyone can be taken ill —'

'And be well again just as quickly! My appearance has cured you fast enough.'

A crowd was already beginning to gather, attracted by the sound of the two women's angry voices. Seeing that she had failed in her mission, Gwen shrugged and would have slipped away but Surcouf's large, brown hand was laid heavily on her shoulder, preventing her.

'Not so fast, my pretty. You don't run away from this quarrel. You have been accused, now defend yourself.'

'I have nothing to explain.'

'I think you have.' Fortunée's lilting tones came to them as she made her way through the crowd with two men at her heels. 'These gentlemen are most anxious to hear what you have to say.'

Black coats buttoned to the chin, battered felt hats, stout shoes and truncheons, all proclaimed that the new arrivals were policemen. The crowd parted and drew back to make way for them and the two men ranged themselves with practised ease on each side of Gwen, who began to struggle like fury.

'I have done nothing! Let me go! What right have you to arrest me?'

'We are arresting you for the attempted kidnapping of the Baron Surcouf. Come along now, young woman, you can explain yourself to the judge.'

'You have no right to accuse me without proof! This is not justice —'

'In the absence of proof, we're holding your two accomplices: the men in the black chaise. This lady,' the policeman indicated Madame Hamelin, 'warned us in time. Two of our colleagues are dealing with them now, so come along quietly.'

Strong hands dragged Gwen away, kicking and screaming like a mad thing. Once, before she was out of sight, she turned and spat at Marianne.

'We'll meet again and I shall pay you out for this, you little bitch!'

When the policemen had gone, the crowd surged back again, surrounding Surcouf with a buzz of admiration. Everyone wanted to shake the famous sailor by the hand. He endeavoured to extricate himself with an unfeigned shyness, shook a few hands and finally succeeded in leading Marianne to the terrace of the Café de la Rotonde which jutted out into the gardens.

'Come and eat an ice with me and let us renew our acquaintance. After so much excitement, you must need some refreshment, and your friend also.'

When they were seated under the circular glass dome and Surcouf had given the order, his twinkling blue eyes moved from Marianne to Fortunée, who was displaying all her exotic plumage for his benefit, but returned always to Marianne.

'I was wondering, you know, what had become of you. I wrote to you several times, through Fouché, but I had no answer.'

'I did not remain with the Duke of Otranto,' Marianne said, attacking a vanilla sorbet with gusto, 'but he might have put himself to the trouble of forwarding your letters.'

'That is rather what I think. I was going to call on him before I go back to Brittany.'

'What? Do you go so soon?'

'I must. I came only on business and now that I have seen you all is well. I can leave with a quiet mind. Do you know, you are looking magnificent?'

His admiring gaze took in the fashionable *toilette*, lingering on the gold and jewels adorning her wrists, and Marianne felt herself grow hot with embarrassment. How could she tell him what had happened to her? Her liaison with the Emperor was so fantastic, so wholly unexpected that it must be hard for a man as simple and direct as the corsair to understand it. It was Fortunée who guessed her friend's dilemma and hastened to explain.

'But my dear Baron, you are looking at the queen of Paris.'

'What's this? Not that I would deny your right to have a kingdom at your feet, but —'

'You wonder how it came about so quickly? Marianne, let me tell you, is no more. Allow me to present to you the Signorina Maria Stella.'

'You? But all Paris is talking of nothing but your beauty and your talent. Then you are the Emperor's —' He broke off and the great, leonine face flushed suddenly under its tan. An identical flush mounted Marianne's cheeks. He was embarrassed by what he had nearly said, she by his abrupt and obvious silence. She knew that, short as his stay in Paris had been, Surcouf was familiar with the current gossip and was now well aware he was talking to Napoleon's mistress, and it seemed to her that he did not relish the thought. His blue eyes, so oddly reminiscent of Jason Beaufort's, had darkened. There was a short, pregnant pause. Even Fortunée seemed unwilling to break into it with her inconsequential chatter but had turned her attention instead to the consumption of her chocolate ice. In the end, it was Marianne who was the first to speak.

'You disapprove of me, don't you?'

'No ... I am only afraid for your happiness — if you love him. And there can be no doubt of that, I think.'

'Why do you say that?'

'Because there are some things a woman like you will not do without love. I can only add that he is a lucky man. I hope he realizes it.'

'I am luckier. But why do you think I may not be happy?'

'Because you are who you are, and because you love him. His marriage must have been painful for you.'

Marianne bowed her head. With the simple percipience of men who spend their lives dealing with nature as well as with men, the sailor had read her feelings like a book.

'Yes.' She managed a small, taut smile. 'It is painful but I would not have it otherwise. I have learned to my cost that everything in this world must be paid for and I am ready to pay the price of my happiness, however heavy.'

He rose and, bowing slightly, raised her hand to his lips. The hardness of his face frightened her suddenly.

'Are you going? Does this mean that - that you are no longer my friend?'

His rare smile swept for a brief instant across his face but there was a world of warmth in the blue eyes bleached by so many storms, so many nights spent gazing into the wind from a heaving deck.

'Your friend? I shall be that to my last breath, to the ending of the world. It is just that I am obliged to go. Here is my brother coming with two of our captains whom I had arranged to meet here in the gardens.'

Marianne clung a little to the roughened fingers that clasped hers. 'I shall see you again?'

'If it lies in my power. But where may I find you?'

'At the Hôtel d'Asselnat in the Rue de Lille. You will always be welcome there.'

Once again, he pressed his lips lightly to the small hand imprisoned in his own and smiled but this time with a boyish twinkle in his eye.

'Do not be too pressing in your invitation or you might never be rid of me. You can't think how persistent we nautical fellows can be.'

He moved away to join the three men and Fortunée Hamelin heaved a great sigh.

'He scarcely so much as glanced at me,' she said with a disappointed pout. 'Indeed, my love, when you are by none of us stand a chance. Yet I wish he might have noticed me a little. He is a man after my own heart.'

Marianne gave a gurgle of laughter. 'So are most men, Fortunée! Leave me my corsair, you have plenty more. What about Dupont, for instance?'

'There is a time for everything. This one is something special and if you do not tell me the moment he shows his face inside your house, I shall never speak to you again.'

'Very well. I promise.'

The little noon gun had just gone off in a neat puff of white smoke, and Marianne and her friend made their way out of the gardens to where the carriage was waiting for them in front of the Comédie Française. As they passed underneath the arcades of the erstwhile palace of the Dukes of Orléons, Fortunée remarked suddenly: 'I am worried about that Breton girl. I did not like that look of hers. You have enough enemies as it is.'

'I am not afraid of her. What can she do? I could hardly let her kidnap Surcouf. I should never have forgiven myself.'

'Marianne,' Fortunée spoke with unwonted seriousness. 'Never underestimate a woman's hatred. Sooner or later, she will try and be revenged on you for what you have done.'

'On me? What about you? Who fetched the police? And by the way, how did you manage that so quickly?'

Madame Hamelin shrugged her pretty shoulders and fanned herself idly with a corner of her scarf.

'Oh, as to that, there are always some in any public place and they are not hard to recognize, are they now?'

Marianne said nothing. She was thinking about the peculiar series of coincidences which seemed to have been conspiring to bring together all the people who, for good or ill, had played a part in her life since her ill-fated wedding day. She had heard of people on the point of death seeing the whole of their past lives unroll before their eyes. Was something of the same kind happening to her and was her life about to take a completely new direction? The short-lived existences of Lady Cranmere and the singer Maria Stella were passing before her eyes once more before they vanished, to make way for what? What name would Marianne d'Asselnat bear next? Mrs Beaufort – or that of some man, as yet a stranger to her?


The excursion to the Palais-Royal had certainly proved a distraction, but it seemed to Marianne that she had never known a day so long. She was filled with an overwhelming desire to go home, she was sure that there was something waiting for her there, but since she had no real excuse for returning to the Rue de Lille fear of Fortunée's mockery kept her at her friend's side throughout her interminable shopping expedition. Besides, what could there be awaiting her but empty silence?

Fortunée was in the throes of one of her periodical fits of extravagance. She had always taken a childish pleasure in spending money but there were times when she would throw it about with a kind of madness. Today was one of those days. She bought far more things than she could ever possibly need until the carriage was piled high with parcels and packages containing scarves, gloves, hats and slippers, each thing more expensive than the last. When Marianne finally voiced her astonishment at this renewal of her wardrobe, Fortunée burst out laughing.

'I told you I would make Ouvrard pay for the charming trick he played on you. This is only the beginning. He is going to be snowed under with bills.'

'Suppose he refuses to pay?'

'Oh, he is far too vain. He'll pay, my love, down to the very last farthing! Just look at that ravishing hat with the curled feathers! It is exactly the green to match your eyes. It would be a shame for anyone else to wear it. I shall buy it for you.'

Despite Marianne's protests a smart pink bandbox containing the green hat was added to the impressive collection already filling the barouche.

'Think of me when you wear it,' Fortunée chuckled, 'and let it take your mind off your cousin's antics! At her age, to lose her head over a play-actor! Not that I deplore her taste, mark you. That Bobèche is a very pretty fellow, very pretty indeed.'

'In another five minutes you will be asking me to go with you to see him perform,' Marianne cried. 'No, Fortunée. I love you dearly but the kindest thing you can do now will be to take me home.'

'Are you tired already? And I wanted to take you to Frascati's for some chocolate!'

'Another time, please. It will be a dreadful squeeze and I don't want to see anyone but you.'

'You are so old-fashioned!' Madame Hamelin grumbled. 'All this absurd fidelity! And meanwhile his majesty is hunting and dancing and gaming and playgoing in the company of his blushing bride!'

'I am not interested,' Marianne snapped.

'No? Not even if I tell you our dear Marie-Louise has already managed to put up the backs of half the ladies at court, and a good few men besides? She is thought stiff, awkward and far from amiable. A far cry from poor, darling Joséphine and her delightful manners! How Napoleon can fail to see it —!'

'She is a Habsburg. He probably still sees her with the Austrian eagle on her back and the crown of Charlemagne on her head! He is dazzled,' Marianne said automatically, unwilling to discuss Marie-Louise.

'Well, he is the only one! And I can't imagine that she will dazzle the good people in the north who are to have the honour of admiring her in a week's time. The court leaves Compiègne on the twenty-seventh —'

'I know,' Marianne said vaguely. 'I know.'

The twenty-seventh? Where would she be on the twenty-seventh? The cardinal had given her a month to prepare herself for the bridegroom he had chosen for her. Their last meeting had been on the fourth of April. That meant that she should join her godfather by about the fourth of May, and already it was the nineteenth of April, and Gracchus had not returned. The time was passing horribly fast.

Unconsciously translating her inward trouble into words, she said: 'Please, take me home.'

'As you wish,' Fortunée sighed. 'Perhaps you are right. I have spent enough money for one day.'

Marianne's impatience grew as they approached the Rue de Lille.

When the carriage reached her own house, she sprang down into the street before the driver could turn into the courtyard, and without even giving the footman time to let down the steps.

'Well really!' Fortunée exclaimed, gaping at her. 'Are you in such a hurry to be rid of me?'

'It is not you,' Marianne called over her shoulder. 'But I must get home. I have just remembered something important.'

As an excuse it was not brilliant but Fortunée was too well-bred to press her further. A shrug, a smile, a wave of her hand, and she gave her coachman the word to drive on while Marianne, with a feeling of relief, pushed open the little side gate and stepped into the courtyard.

The first thing she saw was Guillaume, one of the stable lads, leading a foam-flecked horse towards the stables, Marianne's heart missed a beat and she knew that her instinct had not misled her in urging her to come home. The horse was Samson. Gracchus had come back, at last. Marianne sped up the steps and practically fell over Jérémie, opening the door in his usual stately fashion.

'Gracchus?' she panted. 'He is back?'

'Yes, mademoiselle. About ten minutes ago. He desired to speak with mademoiselle but I informed him —'

Where is he?'

'He has gone to his room, no doubt to change his clothes. Should I —'

'No need. I am going to him.'

Ignoring his scandalized expression, Marianne picked up her skirts and ran to the servants' quarters. Speeding breathlessly up the wooden stairs that led to Gracchus's chamber, she burst in without knocking to be greeted by an anguished cry from her scantily-clad henchman, who dived rapidly behind the bed, making a grab for the quilt to cover his embarrassment.

'Mademoiselle Marianne! Lord, what a fright you gave me! I'm all of a dither —'

'Never mind that,' Marianne interrupted him briskly. 'Tell me what kept you so long. For days now I have been gnawing my fingers with anxiety. I thought you had been waylaid, murdered even —'

'Ah, and I was not far off it, either!' Gracchus scowled. 'And not by brigands but by the Emperor's recruiting sergeants who were determined to carry me off to fight for King Joseph in Spain. At Bayonne that was.'

'Bayonne! But I sent you to Nantes!'

'I went to Nantes to begin with but M'sieur Patterson told me M'sieur Beaufort was due in at Bayonne in a day or two with a cargo, so I took the letter and rode off there.' His voice took on a reproachful note. 'You might have told me, Mademoiselle Marianne, that it was M'sieur Beaufort you were writing to, and it would have saved me a journey. I could have gone straight to Bayonne.'

Marianne's jaw dropped. 'What's this?'

Gracchus blushed. He shrugged and shifted his gaze away from Marianne as though conscious under her steady gaze of his improvised toga.

'I'd better tell you, I suppose,' he said at last, uncomfortably. 'I've been keeping in touch with M'sieur Beaufort - it may seem strange to you, I dare say, but you see, well, the day he left - after that business in the quarries of Chaillot - he had me go to his hôtel and he gave me a bit of money, see, and he said to me: "Gracchus," he said, "I've got to go away, see, and I'm feared it may be a blow to Mademoiselle Marianne like. She'll forget me soon enough," he says, "but I'll not be at ease until I see her happy. So I'll find the means to let you know when I'm in France and you can send me word to where I'll tell you so as I'll be sure all's well and she's not in any trouble" —'

'Oh!' The exclamation burst indignantly from Marianne. 'So you've been spying for him, and he paid you to do it!'

Gracchus looked hurt and drew himself up, gathering up as much dignity as his unconventional garb allowed. 'No! It weren't like that at all! The money was a gift, for what I'd done at Chaillot. And the rest - well, if you must know, it was I who bought the flowers, that night at the Feydeau, and left them for you with the card like he told me.'

The bouquet of camellias! So that was how they had got into her dressing-room! Marianne remembered the shock of joy she had felt, seeing them there on her dressing-table, and her disappointment when she realized that Jason was not in the audience. And instead of the friend she sought, she had seen Francis …

The remembrance of her feelings at that moment made Marianne forget her momentary wrath. The little conspiracy between the two men was rather touching. It was also the best of omens for the demand she hoped to make of the American!

Her face relaxed a little. 'Well?' she said. 'So you heard from him. But where did the letters come?'

'To my grandma's,' Gracchus admitted, blushing harder than ever, 'the washerwoman in the route de la Révolte.'

'But if you knew he was to put in at Bayonne,' Marianne persisted, 'why did you not go there directly? Surely you must have guessed when I sent you to Monsieur Patterson?'

'Mademoiselle Marianne,' the young man answered gravely, 'when you give me an order, I don't question it. That's a matter of principle with me. I did think a bit, I'll own, but if you saw fit not to tell me straight out, then you had your reasons for it.'

Marianne could only bow before this proof of discretion and obedience.

'I am sorry, Gracchus. I was wrong and you were right. You are a good friend. Now, tell me quickly what Monsieur Beaufort said when you gave him my letter.'

Settling herself unceremoniously at the foot of the bed, she waited like an expectant child, but Gracchus shook his head.

'I never found him, Mademoiselle Marianne. When I got there, the *Sea Witch* had been at sea for twelve hours and left no word of her next port of call. All they could tell me was that she had been heading north.'

All Marianne's happiness melted away and misery came flooding back.

'What did you do then?' she asked through dry lips.

'What could I do? I hurried back to Nantes, thinking M'sieur Jason might put in there, and I gave the letter to M'sieur Patterson and I waited. But nothing came.'

Marianne bowed her head; overcome by a sudden bitter disappointment she had no power to hide.

'It is over then,' she said softly. 'He will not get my letter.'

'Why shouldn't he?' Gracchus protested, nearly dropping his quilt in his distress at the sight of the tears gleaming on Marianne's cheek. 'He will still have it quicker than if he was in America! M'sieur Patterson told me he generally puts in at Nantes when he is in those waters. He said the *Sea Witch* must have urgent business elsewhere but she would surely come there before long. I would have waited longer but I began to fear you would be fretting yourself. Besides' – he raised his voice in an effort to impress Marianne with his own confidence – 'the consul promised to pass the word to every captain sailing out of Nantes to tell the *Sea Witch*, if they met her, there was an urgent letter waiting, so you see!'

Marianne sighed and stood up. 'You are a good lad, Gracchus,' she said, feeling a little comforted. 'I will reward you as you deserve.'

'Not to worry about that. Are you happy now? Truly?'

'Truly. You did all you could have done. It is out of our hands now. Take this evening off, I shall not need you again tonight.'

Gracchus looked anxious. 'How have you managed without me all this time? You haven't got another man?'

Marianne smiled faintly. 'Simpler than that. I have merely stayed at home. You know I could not replace you.' And leaving the faithful Gracchus much comforted by this assurance, she went downstairs, only to find Jérémie waiting for her with an expression that seemed to presage the direst of catastrophes. Marianne was too well acquainted with his air of settled melancholy to be seriously deceived but tonight her nerves were on edge and Jérémie's long face was more than she could stand.

'Well?' she demanded. 'What is it now? Has one of the horses cast a shoe or has Victoire made an apple tart for supper?'

Instantly, the butler's mournful look changed to one of deep offence. With great solemnity, he turned and lifted a silver salver from a side table and proffered a letter to his mistress.

'If mademoiselle had not departed so hastily,' he murmured, 'I should have given mademoiselle this letter. A messenger, very dusty, brought it a short while before mademoiselle's coachman returned. I believe it to be urgent.'

'A letter?'

The single, folded sheet, sealed with red wax, had clearly travelled far, for the paper was stained and crumpled, but Marianne's fingers trembled as she took it. The seal was a simple cross but she recognized her godfather's hand. This letter was her sentence, a life sentence, crueller perhaps than a sentence of death.

Marianne walked slowly up the stairs; the letter still unopened in her hand. She had known that it must come one day but she had hoped against all hope that she would have her own answer. Now she was putting off the moment of opening it as long as possible, knowing that when she opened it and read it would seem like an implacable decree of fate.

Reaching her own room, she found her maid, Agathe, putting away some linen in a drawer. One glance at her mistress's white face made Agathe exclaim: 'Mademoiselle is so pale! Let me take your outdoor things off first. And after that, I will fetch you a hot drink.'

Marianne hesitated for a moment then she laid the letter on her writing-table with a sigh.

It meant a few minutes' respite, but all the time Agathe was removing her street dress and half-boots and replacing them with a soft house dress of almond-green wool trimmed with bronze ribbons and matching slippers, her eyes kept turning to the letter. She picked it up at last and retired with it to her favourite chair beside the fire, feeling slightly ashamed of her childish weakness. As Agathe slipped noiselessly from the room with the clothes she had discarded, Marianne slid a determined finger under the seal and smoothed out the letter. It was brief and to the point. In a few words, the cardinal informed his goddaughter that she was to be at Lucca in Tuscany on the fifteenth of the following month and should take rooms at the Albergo del Duomo.

'You will have no difficulty in procuring a passport to travel,' the cardinal continued, 'if you declare your object as being to take the waters at Lucca for the sake of your health. Ever since Napoleon made his sister Elisa Grand Duchess of Tuscany he has looked favourably on those who wish to visit Lucca. Do not be late.'

That was all. Marianne turned the letter over in disbelief. What? Nothing more?' she murmured incredulously. 'Not one word of affection! No explanation! Merely instructions to present myself and advice about procuring a passport. Not one word about the man I am to marry!'

The cardinal must be very sure of himself to write in such terms. This meeting meant that her marriage to Francis Cranmere was already dissolved but it meant, in addition, that somewhere under the sun a stranger was preparing to marry her. How could the cardinal have failed to realize the terrors this stranger must hold for Marianne? Was it so impossible to say a few words about him? Who was he? How old? What did he look like? What kind of man was he? It was as if Gauthier de Chazay had led his goddaughter by the hand to the entrance of a dark tunnel and left her there. It was true he loved her and desired her happiness but Marianne felt suddenly like a helpless pawn in the hands of an experienced player, an object to be manipulated by powerful forces in the name of the honour of her family. Marianne was beginning to find out that the freedom for which she had been fighting was nothing but an illusion, it had all been for nothing. She was once again the daughter of a great house, passively accepting a marriage which others had arranged for her. Centuries of pitiless tradition were dosing on her like a tombstone.

Wearily, Marianne tossed the letter into the fire and watched it burn before she turned to take the cup of hot milk Agathe brought for her, curling her cold fingers round the warm porcelain. A slave! She was no better than a slave! Fouché, Talleyrand, Napoleon, Francis Cranmere, Cardinal San Lorenzo: they could all do as they pleased with her. Life could use her as it would. It was pitiful!

Rebellion welled up in her. To the devil with that absurd promise of secrecy which had been extorted from her! She desperately needed a friend to advise her and for once she could do as she wanted! She felt choked with anger, misery and disappointment. She needed the relief of speech. She marched quickly to the bell-pull and tugged it twice, with decision. In a moment Agathe came running.

'Has Monsieur de Jolival returned yet?'

'Yes, mademoiselle, a moment ago.'

'Then ask him to come here. I wish to speak to him.'


'I knew there was something the matter,' was all Arcadius said coolly when Marianne had put him in possession of the facts. 'And I knew that you would have told me if it lay in your power to do so.'

'And you are not shocked? You are not cross with me?'

Arcadius laughed, although there was little gaiety in his laughter.

'I know you, Marianne. Your own distress when you are obliged to conceal something from a true friend makes it cruel as well as absurd to be angry with you. There was little else you could have done in the present case. Your godfather's precautions were fully justified. What are you going to do now?'

'I have told you: wait until the last possible moment for Jason and if he does not come – go to meet my godfather as he says. Do you see any alternative?'

To Marianne's surprise, Arcadius coloured violently, then rose and walked about the room in an agitated manner, his hands clasped behind his back. At last, he came back to her, looking embarrassed.

'There might have been an easier one for you. I know that my life has been unsettled but my family is a respectable one and you could have become Madame de Jolival without blushing for it. The difference in our ages would have protected you from any – any importunities on my part. I should have been more a father to you than a husband. Alas, it is no longer possible.'

'Why not?' Marianne asked gently. Arcadius's reaction had not taken her wholly by surprise.

Arcadius flushed scarlet and turned his back on her before he answered in a muffled voice. 'I am already married. Oh, it is old history now,' he added quickly. He turned back to her. 'I have always done my best to forget it but the fact remains that there is, somewhere, a Madame de Jolival who, whatever her title to that name, at least prevents me from offering it to any other.'

'But Arcadius, why did you never tell me? When I first met you in the quarries of Chaillot you were at odds with Fanchon Fleur-de-Lys because, if I remember rightly, she was trying to force you to marry her niece, Philomena. She was keeping you a prisoner on that account. Why did you not tell her that you were married?'

'She would not believe me,' Jolival said pathetically. 'She even said that if it were so it need present no obstacle. They would merely be obliged to remove my wife. Now, I dislike Marie-Simplicie intensely – but not as much as that! As for you, I did not tell you the truth at first because I did not know you very well and I feared that your principles might forbid you to keep me with you; and you are so exactly the daughter I would have wished to have.'

Much moved, Marianne rose at once and going to her old friend slipped her arm affectionately through his.

'We are both equally guilty of deception, my friend! But you need not fear. I would not have lost you for the world; no one, since my aunt died, has taken such care of me as you have. Will you let me ask you one question? Where is your wife?'

'In England,' Jolival said gruffly. 'Before that, she was at Mittau and before that in Vienna. She was one of the first to flee when the Bastille was attacked. She was a close friend of Madame de Polignac while I – well, our political ideas could not have differed more.'

'And – you had no children?' Marianne asked, almost timidly, but unexpectedly Jolival laughed.

'It is clear that you have never set eyes on Marie-Simplicie. I married her to please my poor mother and to settle an interminable family squabble, but I assure you that it went no further than my name! Besides, quite apart from her ugliness, her pride and her religion would probably have made her shy from such gross, animal contact as we call love. She is at present one of the ladies-in-waiting to the Duchess of Angoulême and, I am sure, perfectly happy, from what I hear of that princess. They can join in praying to God to confound the Usurper and restore France to the delights of an absolute monarchy, so that they can return to Paris to the cheerful clatter of chains as the leaders of the Empire are led off to the galleys! She is a very gentle, devout woman is Marie-Simplicie.'

Marianne dropped a light kiss on her friend's cheek. 'Poor Arcadius. You do not deserve that. I am sorry I raked up all these memories you were trying so hard to forget. Only tell me, how long will it take me to reach Lucca?'

'It is about six hundred miles,' Arcadius replied, with a speed that showed how glad he was to talk of something else. 'The road takes you by Mont Cenis and Turin. We should be able to cross the pass at this time of the year, with luck, and with good post horses, should cover between twenty-five and thirty leagues a day.'

'That is if we make halts every night,' Marianne said. 'What if we sleep in the coach and simply stop to change horses?'

'I should not advise it, especially for a woman. And you would need at least two coachmen. Gracchus could never do it alone. You must reckon on fifteen days at the best, Marianne. You cannot travel so fast in the mountains.'

'Fifteen days! That will mean leaving on the first of May! It does not leave much time for Jason to come. Suppose – suppose one were to travel on horseback?'

This time Jolival laughed outright.

'It would be much slower. You could not keep up a pace of sixty miles a day for very long. You would need to be in training, with a hide like a cavalryman's to stand such a journey. Have you heard the story of the courier of Friedland?'

Marianne shook her head. She loved Arcadius's stories.

'Of all the Emperor's couriers,' Jolival began, 'there was one who was especially swift, and he was the rider named Esprit Chazal, known as Moustache. On the day after the battle of Friedland, Napoleon wanted to send the news to Paris as fast as possible. To begin with, he decided to entrust it to his brother-in-law,

Prince Borghese, one of the best horsemen in the Empire, but twenty-four hours later he sent his famous Moustache off with the same news. After fifty leagues, Borghese changed his horse for a travelling coach and travelled day and night. Moustache, for his part, made do with what he had: post horses and his own endurance. He rode day and night and in nine days, would you believe it, he had covered the four hundred and fifty leagues between Friedland and Paris – and arrived before Borghese. A remarkable exploit! But it nearly killed him and Moustache is a giant, carved in granite. You are no Moustache, Marianne my dear, even if you have far greater courage and endurance than most women. I will procure as stout a carriage as I can and we will travel –'

'No,' Marianne said swiftly. 'I want you to stay here.'

Arcadius gave a start and his brows drew together.

'Here? Why? On account of this promise made to your godfather? Are you afraid that –?'

'Not in the least, but I want you to stay and wait for Jason as long as possible. He may come after I have left, and if there is no one here to meet him he cannot try to come after me. He is very strong, a sailor and I have no doubt an excellent horseman. It may be' – she hesitated and now it was her turn to blush – 'for my sake, he may try and emulate Moustache's exploit.'

'And ride from Paris to Lucca inside a week? I believe that he might do it, for you. Well, I will stay – but you cannot set out alone – the long journey –'

'I have travelled on long journeys alone before, Arcadius. I shall take my woman, Agathe, and with Gracchus-Hannibal on the box, I shall have little to fear.'

'Would you like me to find Adélaïde?'

Marianne hesitated. 'I have heard nothing from her,' she began.

'I have. I have been to see her several times. It is true that she shows no disposition to return. Without wishing to offend you, I really think that she is mad. I'll swear she is in love with that fellow Bobèche!'

'Well leave her then. I can do quite well without her. I did think of taking Fortunée but she could never resist talking. As far as the world is concerned, I am going to Lucca to take the waters – and I should be grateful if you would see to my passports, my friend.'

Arcadius nodded. He went slowly to the window, put aside the curtain and looked out. The little garden was shrouded in soft darkness. The cupid on the stone basin smiled faintly, mysteriously. Jolival sighed.

'If this road did not take you to your godfather, I would not let you go, Marianne. Have you thought of what the Emperor will say? Surely it would have been more natural to go to him first? After all, he is the person most concerned.'

'What else would he do?' Marianne said shortly. 'He would offer me a husband of his own choice – and I could not bear it. I would rather face his anger than submit to his giving me to another. It will be less painful.'

Arcadius de Jolival did not insist. He let fall the curtain and came back to Marianne. For a moment they stood looking at each other in silence, but with a world of affection and understanding in their eyes. Marianne knew that all her own fears about the strange prospect which the Cardinal de Chazay had laid before her had now passed to Arcadius and that he would suffer all the time she was away. Indeed, he was telling her so in a choked voice.

'I hope with all my heart – I hope that Jason Beaufort will come in time. He shall set out again the moment he arrives, and this time I will go with him. But until then, although I am not a religious man, Marianne, I will pray for you, I will pray with all my heart that he will come – come and –'

His feelings overcame him at last and Arcadius de Jolival ran from the room, tears streaming down his face.

# Part II

# THE MAN IN THE GLOVE

# CHAPTER NINE
# The Tomb of Ilaria

The rain which had been falling all night and for most of the morning ceased abruptly as the coach left Carrara after a change of horses. The sun broke through the clouds and sent them scudding back towards the mountains, giving way to a wide, sweeping canvas of blue sky. The mountains of white marble which had loomed so dully only a short while before now shone with the dazzling brightness of a glacier carved by some gigantic ice-axe. Blinding arrows of light glanced off every ridge but Marianne was too tired to have eyes for any of it. There was a marble everywhere at Carrara, in rough-hewn lumps, in squared blocks, in slabs, in the white dust lying over everything, even on the tablecloths at the inn where they had snatched a hasty meal.

'We supply every court in Europe, in the whole world in fact. Our Grand Duchess sends vast amounts into France. Every single statue of the Emperor comes from here!' The innkeeper spoke with simple pride but Marianne's answering smile was perfunctory. She did not doubt Elisa Bonaparte's willingness to bury her energetic family under tons of marble in the form of busts, bas-reliefs, and statues, but she was in no mood today to listen to tales about any of the Bonapartes, Napoleon least of all.

Everywhere on her long journey she had encountered towns and villages decked out, as they had been for a month past, in honour of the imperial wedding. It was an endless succession of balls, concerts and festivities of every description, until it began to seem as if the loyal subjects of his Majesty the Emperor and King would never be done with celebrating a union which Marianne regarded as a personal insult. Their road was lined with a depressing assortment of limp flags, drooping flowers, empty bottles and tottering triumphal arches only too well suited to her own journey, at the end of which lay a marriage to a total stranger which she could not contemplate without revulsion.

The journey itself had been appalling. Despite Arcadius's anxious protests, Marianne had delayed her departure until the last possible moment, still hoping that Jason would arrive in time. In the end it was not until dawn on the third of May that she climbed into her coach. As the four powerful horses drew the berlin over the cobbles of the Rue de Lille and Arcadius's troubled face and waving hand were lost in the morning haze, she felt as if she were leaving a part of herself behind. It was like leaving Selton all over again and this time too, the future looked grim and uncertain.

In order to make up for lost time and avoid being late at the appointed meeting place, she travelled at breakneck speed. For three days, until they reached Lyon, she refused to stop for anything except to change horses and for the briefest of meals, paying the postillions two or three times the normal rate to encourage them to make better speed. They galloped on regardless of deeply rutted roads that sometimes degenerated into a sea of mud, and still Marianne leaned perilously out of the window to look back at the road behind them. But whenever a horseman did come in sight, it was never the one she hoped for.

After a few hours' rest at Lyon, the coach began climbing towards the mountains and was forced to slow its killing pace. The new road across Mont Cenis, begun by Napoleon seven years before, had been advised by Arcadius because it shortened the distance considerably. But the work was only recently completed and the crossing was an uncomfortable one for Marianne, Agathe and Gracchus, who were obliged to go a good deal of the way over the pass on foot while the coach was drawn by mules. Yet for all that, thanks to the comforting welcome they received from the monks of the hospice, and thanks, still more, to the splendours of the mountain scenery, which she beheld for the first time in her life, Marianne found here a brief respite from her troubles. There was something a little intoxicating, perhaps, in the knowledge that her coach was, if not actually the first, certainly only the second or third to travel that way. She did not feel in the least tired and, forgetting the need for haste, she sat for a long time beside the blue waters of the lake at the top of the pass, conscious of a strange yearning to remain there forever breathing in the pure air and watching the slow flight of the jackdaws, black against the snowy majesty of the peaks. Time, here, stood still. It would be easy to forget the noise and deceits and complications of the world, its furies, and its heartbreaks. There were no faded banners here, no popular songs, no trampled flowers to destroy the harmony of the scene, only the blue stars of gentian in the crevices of the rocks, and the silver lace of lichen. The bare, almost barrack-like shape of the hospice, it too enlarged by the Emperor, seemed to take on a kind of nobility, a strangely mystical air, as if its stern walls were illumined by the prayer and charity that dwelt within. Not until one of the monks came and laid his hand gently on her arm to remind her that an exhausted maid and a half-frozen coachman were waiting for her by the coach, now ready for the descent, did she consent to continue her journey to Susa.

The same wicked pace was resumed. They clattered through Turin and Genoa with hardly a glance. Neither the sun, nor the flower-filled gardens, nor the indigo sea had any power to lift the black mood that settled more firmly on Marianne with every turn of the wheels. She was possessed by a demoniacal urge to travel faster and yet faster, causing Gracchus to look anxiously at her from time to time. He had never seen his mistress so coldly desperate, so tense and irritable. He could not know that as they drew nearer to their goal she was suffering increasingly from misery and self-disgust. Until this point, she had still hoped against all hope that somehow Jason would come to her, Jason whom she had come to look on as her natural protector. Now that hope was gone.

They had slept last night for a bare four hours in a wretched inn tucked away in a fold of the Apennines. Sleep to Marianne was a series of nightmares broken by feverish wakings which left her feeling so little rested that before cock-crow she was up from her lumpy straw mattress and calling for her coach. Dawn on the day that was to be the last of the journey saw the berlin with its occupants racing madly downhill to the sea. It was the fifteenth of May, the final day, but Lucca was not far ahead.

'Thirteen leagues or thereabouts,' said the innkeeper at Carrara.

Now the coach was travelling along a level, sandy road, almost as smooth as a private driveway, following the coast. Only the antique flagstones which stood out here and there showed that this was the ancient Via Aurelia, built by the Romans. Marianne closed her eyes and let her cheek sink on to the cushions. Beside her, Agathe was sleeping, curled up like a weary animal with her hat tipped forward over her face. Marianne wished she could do the same but, tired as she was, her taut nerves would not let her rest. The landscape of dunes and reeds, with a few distant umbrella pines standing out tall and black against a sky dotted with fleecy clouds, only served to depress her further. Her eyes would not stay shut and she found herself following the movements of a tartan that was flying seawards under its triangular sail. The tiny vessel looked so light-hearted, rejoicing in its freedom, and Marianne yearned to be out there with it, running straight before the wind, thinking of nothing else.

She realized suddenly what the sea could mean to a man like Jason Beaufort and why he remained so passionately faithful to it. She was sure that it was the sea which had come between them now to prevent him coming to her in her need. She knew now that he would not come. He might be on the other side of the world, far away in his own country perhaps, and Marianne's cry for help had gone unheard or, if it ever reached him, it would be too late, much, much too late.

A crazy idea came to her, born of a sudden panic and the sight of a dilapidated finger-post on which she read that Lucca was now a mere eight leagues distant. Why should she not escape, she too run away to sea? There must be ships, a harbour within reach. She could take ship and go herself to find the man who, perhaps just because she could not reach him, had suddenly become so strangely dear, so necessary, like the symbol of her threatened freedom. Three times he had asked her to go away with him and three times she had refused, in her blind pursuit of an illusory love. How could she have been such a fool!

Acting on this impulse, she called out to Gracchus who, carefree and tireless, was calmly whistling the latest popular tune from Désaugiers: 'Bon voyage, Monsieur Dumollet, safely land at Saint-Malo ...' with an aptness of which he was quite unaware.

'Do you know if there is a port on this road, somewhere with a fair-sized harbour?'

Gracchus's eyes opened wide beneath the dusty brim of his hat.

'Yes. The girl at the inn told me. There is Livourne but aren't we going to Lucca?'

Marianne did not answer. Her eyes strayed once again to the tiny tartan which was now setting course along a golden pathway straight into the setting sun. Gracchus reined in the horses.

'Whoa there!' The coach came to a stand and Agathe opened big sleepy eyes. Marianne shivered.

'Why have you stopped?'

'Because if we're not going to Lucca anymore, better say so at once. That's the road there, on the left. Straight on for Livourne.'

It was true. On the left, a road led away towards hills dotted with cypress trees among which blossomed here and there the red-brown walls of a small farm or the warm pink campanile of a church. On the other side, the tartan had disappeared, absorbed into the red sunset. Marianne shut her eyes and swallowed back an anguished sob. She could not do it. She could not go back on her given word. Besides, there was the child: he made all such escapades impossible. His mother had no right to expose that frail life to the perils of the sea. From now on it was her duty to sacrifice everything, even her own deepest feelings, even her most natural hopes and fears, for his sake.

'Are you ill?' Agathe was asking, watching her white face. 'It is this dreadful journey.'

'No, it is nothing. Drive on, Gracchus. Of course, we are going to Lucca.'

The whip cracked and the horses sprang forward. The coach turned its back resolutely on the sea and headed into the hills.

Dusk had fallen with a soft mauve haze by the time Lucca came in sight, and Marianne was feeling calmer. After leaving the Via Aurelia, they had crossed over a beautiful river, the Serchio, by a noble Roman bridge and driven over a peaceful, fertile plain towards a ring of hills in the centre of which the city had suddenly appeared before them, pink and charming within its bastion of walls, their sternness lightened by trees and greenery. Lucca, with its tracery of towers and Romanesque campaniles, all clothed in softest green, seemed to rise up towards the rounded hills where the last rays of light still lingered in the air.

Marianne sighed. 'Here we are. Ask for the Duomo, Gracchus. That is the cathedral and the inn where we are to stay will be in the square.'

The travellers' papers were in order and the guards placid and good-humoured. After the briefest of formalities, the berlin rumbled through the arched gateway just as the tinkling notes of the angelus floated from the belfries out over the surrounding countryside. A noisy band of children followed the coach, struggling to hitch a ride on the springs.

They passed along a street lined with tall, medieval houses. Lanterns were already burning here and there in the gathering dusk. Just as on every fine evening in Italy, the whole town seemed to be out of doors and the coach was obliged to travel at a walking pace. A good many of the crowd were men, groups of them arm in arm, heading towards the main squares of the town, but there were women also, dressed in sad colours for the most part but all of them enveloped from head to foot in big shawls of white lace. There was much talk and mutual greeting, occasional snatches of song, but Marianne noticed that many of the men wore uniform and concluded with a sigh that the Grand Duchess Elisa was probably in residence at her luxurious summer villa at Marlia. If news of the so-called 'cure' being undertaken by the *cantatrice* Maria Stella were to reach her, Marianne might well find herself the object of an embarrassing invitation which would please neither her godfather nor herself. In fact, Lucca would see the end of Maria Stella's brief career. Henceforth her new identity would surely make returning to the stage out of the question. Moreover, Marianne had to admit that she did not feel cut out for the theatre and would abandon it without regret. Her last public appearance at the Tuileries had been too painful. She would have to do her best to avoid the notice of Napoleon's sister.

The coach rolled on its way, still with its escort of shouting children, picking up speed as it crossed a broad, handsome square, tree-lined and dominated by a statue of the Emperor, and came to a halt at last before a splendid Romanesque church, the solemnity of its massive, crenelated tower alleviated by the lightness of the façade with its triple row of columns.

'There's your cathedral,' Gracchus said.

'Where's the inn?'

'Over there, of course. You can't hardly see anything else.'

Next door to a charming renaissance palazzo, the heavily barred but well-lighted windows of the Albergo del Duomo were plain to see. Honeysuckle twined about the sign which hung over its broad, arched door.

'It looks rather full,' Marianne said doubtfully.

A number of saddled horses stood outside with soldiers at their heads.

'Must be a regiment on the march,' Gracchus muttered. 'What do we do?'

'What should we do?' Marianne spoke impatiently. 'Go in! We cannot spend the night in the coach just because there are people at the inn. Rooms will have been reserved for us.'

Like a good servant, Gracchus asked no more questions but drove through the arched gateway and brought his steaming horses to a halt in the inn yard. Grooms and servants appeared as if by magic from every shadowy corner while the innkeeper himself, armed with a large lantern, came bustling through the door at the far end to bow and scrape before the owner of this elegant equipage.

'Orlandi, madame, at your excellency's service. Madame's visit honours the Albergo del Duomo but I venture to say that nowhere will madame find better board and lodging.'

'Have rooms been reserved for myself and my servants?' Marianne inquired in perfect Tuscan. 'I am the Signorina Maria Stella and —'

'*Si, si ... molto bene*! If the signorina will condescend to follow me. Signor Zecchini has been waiting since this morning.'

Marianne accepted this without a blink although the name was perfectly unknown to her. Some messenger of the cardinal's perhaps? It could scarcely be the man she was to marry. She gestured towards the uniformed figures that were visible through the smoky kitchen windows.

'The inn appears to be very full?' she said.

Signor Orlandi shrugged his fat shoulders and spat on the ground to show his contempt for the military.

'Pah! The men belong to her highness, the Grand Duchess. They make only a brief stay – or so I trust!'

'Manoeuvres, no doubt?'

Orlandi's round face, to which a flowing moustache like a Calabrian bandit's attempted unsuccessfully to impart a touch of ferocity, seemed to lengthen strangely.

'The Emperor has given orders for the closing of all religious houses throughout Tuscany. Some bishops of Trasimene have rebelled against authority. Four have been apprehended but it is thought that the others have fled into Tuscany. This is the result ...'

The same old story of the antagonism between Napoleon and the Pope! Marianne frowned. Why had her godfather brought her into these parts where the feud between Napoleon and the Church seemed hottest? It would scarcely lessen the difficulties she foresaw attending her journey back to Paris. Even now, she could not think without a shudder of what the Emperor's reaction would be when he learned that, without even consulting him, she had given herself in marriage to a stranger. The cardinal had certainly promised that the man would not be an enemy, the reverse indeed, but could anyone foresee the reactions of a man who was so obsessively jealous of his power?

Noise struck them in the face as they entered the main room of the inn. A group of officers were crowding round one of their number who had clearly just arrived. He was dusty and red-faced, his moustaches quivering with anger, and his eyes flashed as he spoke: '– a damned, cold-blooded fellow of a servant came and shouted through the bars, above the barking of the dogs, that his master never received visitors and it was no use looking for those confounded bishops in his house. And with that he simply turned his back on me and walked off just as if we were not there! I'd not enough men with me to surround the place but damn me if they'll get away with this! Come on, to horse. We'll show this Sant'Anna what he'll get for defying the Emperor and her Imperial Highness the Grand Duchess.'

This martial declaration was greeted with a chorus of approval.

Orlandi had turned pale. 'If the signorina will be kind enough to wait a moment,' he whispered hurriedly, 'I must interfere. Ho there, Signor Officer!'

'What d'you want with me?' growled the angry man. 'Fetch me a carafe of chianti and sharp! I've a thirst on me that won't wait!'

But Orlandi, instead of complying, shook his head.

'Forgive me saying so but, if I were you, signor, I should not try to see Prince Sant'Anna. In the first place you will not succeed, and in the second, her highness will be displeased.'

The noise ceased abruptly. The officer thrust aside his comrades and came towards Orlandi. Marianne shrank back into the shadow of the stairs to avoid notice.

'What do you mean by that? Why should I not succeed?'

'Because no one has ever done so. Anyone in Lucca will tell you the same. It is known that Prince Sant'Anna exists, but no one has ever seen him, except for the two or three servants closest to him. Not one of the others, and there are many, here and in the prince's other houses, have never seen more than a figure in the distance. Never a face or a look. All they know of him is the sound of his voice.'

'He is hiding!' roared the captain. 'And why should he hide, eh, innkeeper? Do you know why he hides? If you don't know, I will tell you, because I shall know soon enough.'

'No, Signor Officer, you will not know, or expect to feel the anger of the Grand Duchess Elisa, for she, like the Grand Dukes before her, has always respected the Prince's wish for seclusion.'

The soldier gave a shout of laughter but to Marianne, listening eagerly to this strange story, his laugh rang false.

'Is that so? Is he the devil, then, your Prince?'

Orlandi shivered superstitiously and crossed himself hurriedly several times while one hand behind his back, where the officer could not see it, pointed two fingers in the sign to ward off the evil eye.

'Do not say such things, Signor Officer! No, the Prince is not – not what you said. It is said that he has suffered since childhood from a terrible affliction, and this is why no one has ever seen him. His parents never produced him in public and not long after he was born, they went abroad and died there. He was brought back, alone – or at least with only the servants I spoke of who have been with him since his birth.'

The officer wagged his head, more impressed by this than he cared to admit.

'And he lives so still, shut away behind walls and bars, and servants?'

'Sometimes he goes away, to some other of his estates most probably, taking his major-domo and his chaplain with him, but no one ever sees him go or is aware when he returns.'

There was silence. The officer tried to laugh, to lighten the atmosphere. He turned to his friends who gaped uncomfortably.

'This Prince of yours is a joker! Or a madman! And we don't like madmen! If you say the Grand Duchess won't like it if we attack him, then we won't attack him. In any case, we've plenty of things to do besides that just at present. But we'll send word to Florence and' – his tone changed abruptly, the threatening note returned and he thrust his fist under poor Orlandi's nose –'and if you have been lying to us, we'll not only go and dig your night bird out of his hole, but you'll feel the weight of my scabbard on your fat carcass! Come on, all of you! Our next call is the monastery of Monte Oliveto – Sergeant Bernardi, you stay here with your section! They're a bit too pious in this damned town. As well to keep on eye on them. You never know ...'

The militia trailed out of the room in a great clatter of boots and sword belts. Orlandi turned to Marianne who had been waiting quietly, with Gracchus and Agathe peering avidly over her shoulder, for this bizarre scene to end.

'Signorina, excuse please, but I could not let these men attack the Villa Sant'Anna. It would have brought trouble for everyone, for them and for us.'

Curiosity impelled Marianne to find out more about the strange person whom the innkeeper had described.

'Are you really so much afraid of the Prince? Yet you yourself have never seen him?'

Orlandi shrugged and picking up a lighted candle from a side table turned to conduct the travellers upstairs.

'No, I have never seen him, but I have seen the good which is done in his name. The Prince is very generous to the poor, and who knows how far his power may extend? I would rather he was left alone. We know his generosity, we do not yet know his anger – and what if he should indeed be in league with the Evil One ...' Once again, Orlandi crossed himself three times in quick succession. 'This way, signorina. Your coachman's lodging shall be seen to and there is a small room for your maid next door to your own.'

In a moment he had thrown open a door and ushered Marianne into a chamber, simple but clean, with bare, whitewashed walls and furnished with a table, a pair of upright chairs and a long, narrow bed, its massive black wooden head so tall that it reminded Marianne uncomfortably of a tomb. There was also a large crucifix and a number of holy pictures. Except for the red, cotton counterpane and window curtains, the room might have been a convent cell. Jug and basin, made of thick green and white pottery, were shut away neatly in a cupboard and the whole room was dimly illuminated by a single oil lamp.

'My best room,' Signor Orlandi remarked with pride. 'I hope the signorina will be comfortable. Should I perhaps inform the Signor Zecchini?'

Marianne gave a little shiver. The story of the invisible Prince had in some degree taken her mind from her own troubles and from this mysterious individual who had been waiting for her since that morning. She thought she might as well find out at once who he was.

'Yes, tell him I am ready to receive him. Then you may bring us some food.'

'Does the signorina wish her baggage brought up?'

Marianne hesitated. She had no idea whether her godfather's plans for her included a lengthy stay at the inn, but she reckoned that her baggage would not suffer from one more night strapped to the coach.

'No, I do not know if I shall be staying. Just send up the big carpet bag from inside.'

When Orlandi had gone, Marianne took the precaution of despatching Agathe, who was practically asleep on her feet, to explore her own small chamber, a cubby-hole reached by a door in the corner of the room. Marianne told her not to come back until she was called.

'But – suppose I fall asleep?' the girl said.

'Then sleep well. I will wake you in time for supper. My poor Agathe, you had no idea this journey would prove such a penance, had you?'

Under her crumpled bonnet, Agathe smiled happily at her mistress. 'Oh it has been tiring, but ever so interesting. And I would go anywhere with mademoiselle. All the same, I can't say I think much of this inn. A nice fire would do no harm. It's that damp in here.'

Marianne's gesture of dismissal silenced her. There had been a light tap on the door.

'Come in,' Marianne called when the girl had gone.

The door opened slowly, so slowly that it seemed as if the person outside were nervous or embarrassed. A lanky figure appeared, dressed in a coat of cinnamon-coloured cloth with knee breeches and white stockings, big, buckled shoes and a round hat set atop a curious kind of cap. The hat was raised, the cap remained in place, after which the visitor clasped both hands and raised his eyes to heaven and sighed deeply.

'God be praised! You have come! I cannot tell you how anxious I have been all day with all these soldiers. But you are here, and that is all that matters.'

During the utterance of this thankful greeting, Marianne had time to get over her initial surprise at the realization that Signor Zecchini was none other than the Abbé Bichette. Even so, she could not help laughing a little at the poor man, he was so obviously ill-at-ease in his unfamiliar garb.

'Why, monsieur l'Abbé, how strange you look! Surely carnival time is long past now?'

'I beg you, do not laugh. I feel sufficiently uncomfortable, I can assure you. If it were not for the most urgent necessity, if His Eminence had not particularly requested it …'

Instantly, Marianne was serious again. 'Where is my godfather? I thought to find him here.'

'In these dreadful days you will understand that a Prince of the Church must be especially careful. We have been staying at the monastery of Monte Oliveto but we considered it wiser to leave there.'

'As indeed it was,' Marianne agreed, remembering what the angry captain had said not long before.

'Where is His Eminence now?'

'Over there,' the Abbé answered, indicating through the window the campanile of the cathedral opposite. 'He has been waiting for you in the verger's house since this morning.'

Marianne looked at the tiny gold-enamelled watch that she wore round her neck. 'It is late. The church will be closed – perhaps watched …'

'The evening service has only just begun. The Emperor's orders concern religious houses only. Church services are not affected. In any case, the verger was to leave a door open all night in case of need. His Eminence will be waiting for you after the service.'

'But where? The church is very large –'

'Enter by the left-hand door and go straight to the transept. Find the tomb of Ilaria. You will know it by the figure of a young woman lying with a little dog at her feet. The cardinal will meet you there.'

'Will you not come with me?'

'No. My orders from Monseigneur are to leave the inn during the night. He does not wish us to be seen together. My task is done and I have other business.'

'Thank you, monsieur l'Abbé. I will tell my godfather how faithfully you have carried out your trust. And now I must go to him.'

'May God keep you in His holy care. I will pray for you.'

Putting one long finger to his lips to enjoin her to silence and walking on tiptoe in his clumsy shoes, the so-called Signor Zecchini departed as quietly as he had come.

Marianne went quickly to her dressing-table and took off her hat. A swift glance at her hair and she turned to the carpet bag which Orlandi had sent up before the Abbés entrance and extracted from it a big, dark-red cashmere shawl. This she put over her head, wrapping it closely round her in imitation of the local women she had seen. She opened the door that led into Agathe's room. As she had expected, the maid was lying on her bed, fully dressed, and so sound asleep that she did not even hear the door open. Marianne smiled, knowing that Agathe would not wake while she was out.

On her way downstairs she encountered Orlandi carrying a tray loaded with plates, glasses and dishes.

'Bring supper in a little while, if you please,' she said. 'I – I wish to slip across to the church to say a prayer or two, if I may.'

Orlandi's professional smile became touched with a hint of something warmer.

'But of course you may! The evening service has just this moment begun! You run along now, signorina, and I will have supper for you when you return.'

'The soldiers – they will not hinder me?'

'Hinder you going to church?' The worthy landlord was indignant. 'I should think not indeed. We are good Christians here. The town would be up in arms if they tried to close the churches. Would you like me to go with you?'

'Thank you, but only as far as the inn door, I will go alone from there.'

Escorted by Orlandi, his moustaches bristling, Marianne passed through the main room of the inn without interference from the soldiers who seemed, in fact, little disposed to make trouble. The sergeant was playing cards with one of his corporals and the other men were quietly drinking. One or two had produced long clay pipes and were gazing up at the smoky ceiling, puffing away dreamily. The moment she was outside, Marianne hugged her shawl about her and set off running across the open square. It was quite dark by this time and only a lantern here and there served to illuminate the pale bulk of the ancient cathedral.

A light wind had got up, bringing with it the scents of the countryside, and Marianne paused for a second in the centre of the square to breathe in its odours. Above her head, countless stars twinkled softly in a blue-black arch of sky. Somewhere in the darkness a man was singing, accompanying himself on a guitar, while from the open doors of the church came the solemn notes of a psalm. The man's song was a love song, the psalm proclaimed the glory of God and the bitter joys of renunciation and humility. One was a call to happiness, the other to stern obedience, and for the last time, Marianne hesitated. Her hesitation was brief, because for her the choice between love and duty was no longer possible. Her love was not calling her, was not seeking for her. He was travelling the roads of the Low Countries, surrounded by the rejoicings of his people, smiling at his young bride, careless of the one he had left behind who was now, to her grief and shame, turning to a stranger to ensure that her child would have the right to hold up its head.

Resolutely turning her back on the song, she looked instead at the church. It loomed enormous in the darkness, with its squat shape and the tall tower reaching skywards like a cry for help. Yet God had allowed her own cry to go unheard: the friend to whom she looked for help had not come, and would not come. He too was far away, he too had forgotten her perhaps … Marianne's throat contracted, then she shook herself with a spasm of anger.

'You little fool,' she told herself through clenched teeth. When will you stop feeling sorry for yourself? You have made your own fate; you have brought it on yourself! You always knew you would have to pay for your happiness, however short it seemed. So now pay, and don't complain. You are going to meet someone who has always loved you, who cannot wish for anything but your happiness, or at least your peace of mind. Try and trust him as you used to …'

Resolutely, she made her way to the triple doorway, climbed the shallow steps, and pushed open the left-hand door. Yet still her mind was not easy. She could not quite bring herself to trust her godfather and the knowledge gave her pain and made her reproach herself. She longed to feel again the same blind trust she had known as a child. But this fantastic marriage! The submission it demanded of her whole being!

Except for the red sanctuary lamp and a few lighted candles, it was dark as night inside the cathedral. At the high altar, an aged priest with white hair and a tarnished silver chasuble was officiating before a handful of kneeling worshippers. Marianne could see only their bowed shoulders and bent heads, hear nothing but the murmur of their voices mingling with the sighing of the organ that floated up into the blue, Gothic vaults above.

She paused for a moment beside a holy water stoup, crossed herself and knelt to say a brief prayer, but her heart was not in it. It was more a formal gesture of politeness towards God. Her thoughts were elsewhere. Swiftly, making no more noise than a shadow, she glided down the aisle, past a delicate, octagonal edifice containing a weird figure of Christ crucified in long Byzantine robes, and finally reached the transept. A few figures knelt there, but she could not see the one she had come to find, and no one turned to look at her.

She had seen the tomb at once and she moved slowly towards it. It was so beautiful that her eye went to it immediately, ignoring even an exquisite painting of the Virgin and two saints, and remained fixed on it. She could never have believed that any tomb could be so lovely, so full of purity and peace. A girl in a long robe lay on the stone which was supported by cherubs bearing heavy garlands. Her hands were folded quietly on the delicate folds of her gown, her feet were resting on a little dog, and her hair, escaping from a wreath of flowers, framed a face so ravishing that Marianne found herself staring, fascinated by the young girl whom the sculptor had portrayed so lovingly. She did not know who she was, this Ilaria who had died four hundred years before, but she felt strangely close to her. There was no trace in the delicate features of the suffering which had brought her to the grave when she was hardly out of childhood.

Resisting an urge to clasp the dead girl's hands in her own, Marianne went and knelt a little way away. She rested her head on her hands and tried to pray, but her mind was too watchful. She did not start when someone came to kneel beside her. She raised her eyes and recognized her godfather despite the black collar turned up to hide his face. He saw her look at him and gave her a quick smile.

'The service is almost over,' he whispered. 'When they have all gone, we can talk.'

They did not have long to wait. In a few moments the priest left the altar, carrying the censer. The church emptied slowly. There was a sound of chairs scraping, then footsteps moving away. The verger came to extinguish the candles and the lamp. The only lights left burning were those standing before a fine statue of John the Baptist in the transept, the work of the same artist as the tomb. The cardinal rose and seated himself, with a gesture to Marianne to do the same. She was the first to speak.

'I have come, as you commanded …'

'No, not commanded,' Gauthier de Chazay corrected her mildly. 'I merely asked because I thought it best for you. You have come – alone?'

'Alone. As you knew I should, did you not?' There was an almost imperceptible shade of bitterness in her voice which did not escape the priest's subtle ear.

'No, God is my witness that I should have preferred to see you find a man in whom your duty and your inclination could combine. But I realize that you had little time, or choice, perhaps. And yet, it seems to me that you feel some resentment towards me for the situation in which you find yourself.'

'I blame only myself, godfather, be sure of that. But tell me, is everything arranged? My marriage ...'

'To the Englishman? Has been duly annulled, of course, or you would not be here. It was not difficult. The circumstances were exceptional and since the Holy Father's position was also somewhat unusual, we were obliged to make do with a small court to decide your case. I had counted on that to enable us to proceed so rapidly. I have, moreover, sent word of these proceedings to the consistory of the Church of England and written to the lawyer responsible for marriage settlements. You are quite free.'

'For so short a time! But thank you. I can never be sufficiently grateful to you for releasing me from a bondage that was hateful to me. You seem to me, godfather, to have become a remarkably powerful person.'

'I have no power but what comes to me from God, Marianne. Are you now ready to hear the rest?'

'I think I am.'

How strange it was, this conversation in the empty cathedral. They were alone, sitting side by side, gazing into a dark world in which, from time to time, a candle flame would spurt up to reveal a masterpiece. Why here, rather than the inn where the cardinal could have entered in disguise as easily as the Abbé Bichette had done, regardless of the soldiers? Marianne knew her godfather well enough to be sure that he had chosen his ground deliberately, perhaps in order to add to the solemnity of what he had to say. It may have been for the same reason that he seemed to pause now before going on. His eyes were closed and his head bent. Marianne guessed that he was praying but her nerves had been strained to breaking point by the journey and her mental anguish. She could not control the impatience in her voice as she muttered: 'I am listening.'

The cardinal rose and laid his hand on her shoulder. 'You are on edge, my child,' he said, with gentle reproach, 'and it is no wonder, but you see the responsibility for what is to come will be mine and it is only natural that I should feel the need for a moment's reflection. Listen, then, but remember, above all, that you must never despise the man who is about to give you his name. You will be joined in marriage but your union will never be complete and it is this that troubles me, for it is not thus that a man of God should contemplate a marriage. Yet each of you has something to give the other. He will save you and your child from dishonour and you will give him a happiness for which he had ceased to hope. Thanks to you, the great name which he had doomed to die with him will yet survive.'

'Can this man not have children? Is he too old?'

'He is neither old nor impotent but for him the idea of having children is unthinkable, fraught with terror even. It is true that he could have adopted a child but he recoils in horror at the thought of grafting a common shoot on to his ancient stock. You bring him the best blood of France and mingled with it the blood, not merely of an emperor, but of the one man he admires most in all the world. Tomorrow, Marianne, you are to be married to Prince Corrado Sant'Anna —'

Forgetting her surroundings, Marianne uttered a faint cry. The man whom no one has ever seen?'

The cardinal's face was stony. His blue eyes flashed.

'What do you know of him? From whom have you heard this?'

Briefly, Marianne described the scene which she had witnessed at the inn. At the end, she added: 'They say he suffers from some terrible disease and that is why he hides himself away, they say even that he is mad —'

'People will talk and if they do not talk, still they will think. No, he is not mad. As for why he chooses to live in seclusion, that is not for me to divulge. It is his secret. He may reveal it to you one day, if he sees fit – although I should be surprised. All you need to know is that his motives are not merely honourable but very noble.'

'But – surely I must see him – if we are to be married?' Unconsciously, Marianne spoke hopefully.

The cardinal shook his head. 'There is no curbing feminine curiosity. Listen to me, Marianne, for I shall not say this again. Between you and Corrado is a new pact, like the one you and I have made together. He will give you his name and acknowledge your child, who will one day inherit all his titles and possessions, but it is unlikely that you will ever look upon his face, even during the wedding ceremony.'

'But you know him?' Marianne cried, galled by this mystery to which the cardinal appeared to be a party. 'You have seen him? Why does he hide himself like this? Is he a monster?'

', I have seen him, many times. I have known him ever since the dreadful day of his birth. But I have sworn on my honour and on the Gospels never to speak of his person. Yet God knows, I would give much to make it possible for your marriage to be a real one in the sight of all, for I have met few men of such worth. But as things are, I believe that in bringing about this marriage I am acting in the best interests of both of you, by joining together, as it were, two people in trouble. As for you, you must repay him for what he gives to you, for in future you will be a very great lady, by conducting yourself honourably, with due respect for the ancient family to which you will belong. Its roots go back as far as classical times and she who lies in this tomb was not unconnected with it. Are you prepared for this? For make no mistake, if you have come seeking nothing but a cover that will allow you to live as you please with any man, you had better go away and look elsewhere. Never forget that what I am offering you is not happiness but the honour and dignity of a man who will not be beside you to defend them, that and a life free from all material cares. In short, I expect you to behave as befits your birth and breeding. If these conditions seem too hard to you, you may still draw back. I will give you ten minutes to think whether you will remain the singer Maria Stella or become the Princess Sant'Anna.'

He made a move as if to leave her alone to her thoughts but Marianne, seized with a sudden panic, gripped his arm.

'One thing more, godfather, I beg of you. I must make you understand what this decision means to me. I know it is not for the daughter of a great house to raise objections to the match made for her by her family, but you must admit the circumstances are unusual.'

'I do admit it. Yet I thought you had done with objections.'

'It is not that. I do not object. I trust you and I love you as I should my own father. All I ask is that you explain a little more. You tell me that I must live henceforth as befits a Sant'Anna, respect the name I bear?'

The cardinal's voice hardened. 'I did not think to hear such a question from your lips.'

'I do not know how to say it,' Marianne said desperately. 'What I mean is: what will be my life when I have married the Prince? Shall I be obliged to live in his house, under his roof — ?'

'I have already told you, no. You may live precisely where you choose, in your own house, at the Hôtel d'Asselnat or where you will. You may also reside whenever you wish to in any of the houses belonging to the Sant'Annas, either in the villa you will see tomorrow or in any of their palaces, in Venice or in Florence. You will be perfectly free and Sant'Anna's steward will ensure that your life is not merely free from practical cares but as magnificent as befits your station. I only mean that you should live up to that station. No scandals, no passing fancies, no —'

'Oh, godfather!' Marianne cried, hurt. 'What right have I ever given you to think that I could sink so low —'

'Forgive me. I too am expressing myself badly. That was not what I meant to say. I was still thinking of your chosen profession. You may not have been aware of its dangers. I know you have a lover, and who he is. I may deplore the choice of your heart, but I know that he can call you back to him whenever he will. You cannot fight both him and yourself. All I ask, my child, is that you should remember the name you bear and be discreet. Never do anything that may give your child – now the child of both of you – any cause to reproach you. Indeed, I believe that I may trust you. You are still my own dear child. Only you have been unlucky. Now I will leave you to think.'

The cardinal moved away quietly to kneel before the statue of St John, leaving Marianne alone by the tomb. She turned to it instinctively, as if those stone lips could give the answer for which the cardinal was waiting. Dignity, that must have been the story of the girl who lay there. She had lived and died in dignity, and in what grace she clothed it! Marianne had to confess, moreover, that she did not honestly care for adventures, not at least for those she had encountered, and she could not help thinking that if things, and especially Francis, had been different, she would at that very moment have been living a life of peace and dignity amid the grandeurs of Selton Hall.

Stepping softly up to the tomb, she laid her hand on the marble folds. Their coldness surprised her. Was it an illusion, or had there been a suggestion of a fleeting smile on the narrow face with its closed eyes, resting so quietly in its high, framing collar? As if Ilaria were trying from beyond the grave to give encouragement to her living sister.

*I must be going mad*, Marianne told herself furiously. *I am seeing things! This has gone on long enough.*

She turned her back firmly on the statue and went to her godfather where he was praying, his head bowed on his hands. She did not kneel but said in a small, clear voice: 'I am ready. Tomorrow I will marry the Prince.'

The cardinal did not turn or look up. With his eyes still on the statue, he answered softly: 'It is well. Go home now. Leave the inn at noon tomorrow and tell your coachman to take the road leading to the Baths of Lucca. It is some twelve or fifteen miles. This will cause no surprise since you are supposed to have come for the purpose of taking the waters, but you will not go all the way. About three miles from here you will see a small wayside shrine. I will be waiting for you there. Go now.'

'You are staying? It is so dark – and cold.'

'I am staying here. The verger is one – is a friend. Go in peace, my child, and God be with you.'

He seemed suddenly tired, and anxious for her to be gone. With one last look at the statue of Ilaria, Marianne left by the way that she had come, her mind busy with a new idea. There seemed no end to her godfather's capacity to surprise her. What was it that he had started to say about the verger? That he was one of what? Was it possible that a Roman cardinal, a prince of the Church, could belong to a secret society? And if so, which? This was a fresh mystery which might be better left alone. Marianne was tired of all these secrets which were creeping into her life.

After the smell of cold wax and moist stone inside the cathedral the night air was delicious, soft and fragrant, and the sky was beautiful. To her surprise, Marianne found that she was at peace with herself now that her decision had been made. She felt almost glad that she had finally agreed to this strange marriage, and indeed it would have been madness to have rejected a match which guaranteed her the kind of life she had been born to and understood while at the same time leaving her fully her own mistress. All she had to do was to be worthy of the name of Sant'Anna.

Even the momentary thought of Jason could not disturb her new-found serenity. She had probably been wrong to persist in looking to him for help. Fate had chosen for her and perhaps it was better so. All things considered, the only person she really missed was her dear Arcadius.

Everything was always so much easier when he was there.

As she crossed the dark square she was struck by the silence. No sound was to be heard there now, no love songs hung in the air. There was only the night with its disquieting shadows beyond which lay another dawn whose colours she could not foresee. Marianne shivered, without quite knowing why.

# CHAPTER TEN
# The Voice in the Mirror

It seemed to Marianne that she was entering a new world as her coach passed through the huge wrought-iron gates set between high walls, their heraldic bearings a fantastic tracery of black and gold. Its guardians, the two stone giants that stood upon the entry piers, one bearing a lance, the other a drawn bow, seemed to challenge all who would enter these forbidden precincts. The gates swung open as if by magic at the horses' approach. No gatekeeper appeared, nor was there any sign of the dogs which had so alarmed the militia captain. Not a soul was in sight. Within, a long, sanded avenue lined with tall, black cypresses and lemon trees in stone urns, gave on to a wide expanse of green, a peaceful prospect stretching away until the view was closed by the tall, misty plumes of fountains rising from a lake.

As the carriage advanced up the smooth drive, park-like vistas opened up with glimpses of a romantic landscape peopled with statues, massive trees and soaring fountains, a world where water reigned supreme but from which flowers were absent. Marianne stared about her, holding her breath as if time had stood still, a prey to a terror she could not control. Opposite her was Agathe, her pretty face fixed in a faintly apprehensive expression. Only the cardinal, absorbed in his own thoughts, seemed unconscious of his surroundings and immune from the strange melancholy of the place. Even the sun, which had been shining as they left Lucca, had disappeared behind a thick bank of white cloud, pierced now and then by broad shafts of light. The day had grown suddenly oppressive. No birds sang, there was no sound at all but the melancholy song of the water. Within the carriage, no one spoke and even Gracchus on his box forgot to sing or whistle as he had been in the habit of doing all through that endless journey.

The berlin rounded a bend, past a grove of gigantic thuyas trees and emerged into a dream. A long lawn adorned with statues of prancing horses, and where white peacocks trailed their snowy plumes, led up to a palace whose ordered serenity was mirrored in still waters and backed by blue

Etruscan hills. White walls, surmounted by balustrades, tall windows gleaming around a great loggia, its columns interspersed with statues, an old dome rising above the central body of the house crowned by a figure mounted on a unicorn: this was the dwelling of the unknown Prince, renaissance with touches of baroque magnificence, on the threshold of a legend.

Arrows of sunlight shot through the great trees massed on either side of the vast lawn, illuminating here and there in the depths of a glade the graceful lines of a colonnade or a leaping waterfall.

Out of the corner of his eye, the cardinal watched the effect of all this upon Marianne. Wide-eyed, with parted lips, she sat as if drinking in the beauty of this enchanted domain through every fibre of her being. The cardinal smiled.

'If you like the Villa dei Cavalli, it is in your power to remain here for as long as you wish – forever if you will.'

Marianne ignored the subtle hint but asked instead: 'The Villa dei Cavalli? Why that?'

'That is the name given to it by the people hereabouts. The villa of the horses. It is they who are the real masters here. The horse is king. For more than two centuries the family of Sant'Anna has possessed a stud which, if any of its products ever left it, would no doubt rival the fame of the Duke of Mantua's celebrated stables. But, except for occasional magnificent gifts, the princes of Sant'Anna have never parted with their animals. Look –'

They were nearing the house. To one side Marianne saw yet another fountain, the water spouting from a huge conch shell. Beyond it, between a pair of noble pillars marking, perhaps, the way that led to the stables, a groom was holding three superb horses whose snowy whiteness, flowing manes and long, plumed tails, might have been models for the statues that filled the park. From her earliest childhood, Marianne had always loved horses. She loved them for their beauty. She understood them better than she had ever understood any human being and even the most fiery-tempered had never been known to frighten her. It was a passion which she inherited from her Aunt Ellis who, before the accident which had left her a cripple, had been a notable horsewoman. The sight of these three magnificent animals seemed to her the most comforting of all welcomes.

'They are superb,' she said with a sigh, 'But how do they adapt themselves to an invisible master?'

'He is not so for them,' the cardinal said abruptly. 'For Corrado Sant'Anna they are life's one real joy. But we have arrived.'

The coach swept round in a stylish curve and came to a halt at the foot of an impressive flight of marble steps on which the palace servants were drawn up to welcome it. Marianne beheld an imposing array of white and gold footmen, their powdered wigs accentuating the olive tints of their impassive faces. At the top, where the perron joined the loggia, three figures in black stood waiting. They were a white-haired woman, the severity of whose garments was relieved by a white collar and the bunch of gold keys hanging at her waist, a bald, shrivelled priest who might have been almost any age, and a tall, well-built man with roman features and thick, black, lightly grizzled hair, dressed with impeccable neatness but without real elegance. There was about this latter personage an indefinable air of the peasant, a kind of toughness which only the earth could give.

'Who are they?' Marianne whispered with some alarm as two of the footmen stepped forward to open the carriage door and let down the steps.

'Dona Lavinia has been housekeeper to the Sant'Annas for many years. She is some kind of poor relation. It was she who brought up Corrado. Father Amundi is his chaplain. As for Matteo Damiani, he is both the Prince's steward and his secretary. Get out now, and remember your birth. Maria Stella is dead – once and for all.'

Marianne descended from the coach. As though in a dream, she climbed the marble steps between the double row of motionless footmen, supported by her godfather's suddenly iron hand, her eyes on the three people above. Behind her, she could hear Agathe's awe-struck gasp. It was not hot, although the sun had come out again, but Marianne felt suddenly stifled. The strings of her bonnet seemed to be choking her. She hardly heard her godfather perform the introductions or the words of welcome spoken by the housekeeper who curtsied low to her as if to a queen. Her body felt as if it were controlled by some mechanism outside herself. She heard herself replying graciously to the chaplain and to Dona Lavinia but it was the secretary who fascinated her. He too seemed to be moving like an automaton. His pale eyes remained fixed stonily on Marianne's face. He seemed to be scrutinizing her every feature, as if he could read there the answer to some question known only to himself, and Marianne could have sworn that there was fear in that relentless stare. She was not mistaken: Matteo's silence was heavy with suspicion and warning. It was clear he did not look with favour on the intrusion of this stranger and Marianne was certain, from the very first, that he was her enemy.

With Dona Lavinia it was quite otherwise. Her serene face held, despite the marks of past sufferings, nothing but gentle kindness and her brown eyes expressed complete admiration. Rising from her curtsey, she kissed Marianne's hand and murmured: 'Blessed be God for bringing us so lovely a princess.'

As for Father Amundi, he might carry himself nobly enough, but he did not appear to be in possession of all his faculties. Marianne was quick to notice his habit of mumbling to himself, a rapid, low-pitched gabble that was perfectly incomprehensible and very irritating to listen to. But the smile he bestowed on her was so beaming, so innocent, and he was so clearly pleased to see her that she found herself wondering if he were not by any chance some old friend whom she had forgotten.

'I will take you to your room, Excellenza,' the housekeeper told her warmly. 'Matteo will take care of His Grace.'

Marianne smiled and her eyes went to her godfather.

'Go, my child,' he told her, 'and rest. I will send for you this evening, before the ceremony, so that the Prince may see you.'

Marianne followed Dona Lavinia in silence, repressing the question that sprang instinctively to her lips. She was consumed with a curiosity greater than anything she had ever known, she felt a devouring urge to 'see' this unknown Prince herself, this master of a fairy-tale domain who kept such wonderful creatures in it. The Prince was to see her. Then why should she not see the Prince? Was the malady with which he was afflicted, as she now suspected, so terrible that she could not approach him? Her eyes rested suddenly on the housekeeper's straight back as she led the way, her keys chinking softly. What was it Gauthier de Chazay had said? It was she who had brought up Corrado Sant'Anna? Surely none could know him better than she – and she had seemed so glad to see Marianne …

*I will make her talk,* she told herself. *She must be made to talk!*

The interior of the villa was no less magnificent than the gardens. Leaving the loggia, which was decorated in baroque plasterwork with gilded lanterns of wrought iron, Dona Lavinia led her new mistress through a vast ballroom that shimmered with the dull gleam of gold, then through a series of apartments, one of which was especially sumptuous, with delicate red and gold carvings setting off the dark shine of black lacquer panels. This, however, was the exception. The general colours of the house were white and gold, with floors of a black and white marble mosaic on which their feet slid silently.

The bedchamber assigned to Marianne, which was situated in the lefthand wing of the house, was decorated in a similar style. Even so, she found it startling. Here, too, all was white and gold except for a pair of red lacquer cabinets which added a warmer note to the room. The ceiling, however, was painted with *trompe-l'œil* figures, who appeared to be leaning over the cornice, as though from a balcony, observing the movement of whoever was in the room below. The walls were covered in a profusion of mirrors. On every side, the two dark forms of Marianne and Dona Lavinia were reflected over again into infinity, along with the great Venetian bed hung with rich brocades. The bed was raised up on three steps like a throne and flanked by a pair of torches in the shape of two women dressed in oriental style, bearing clusters of tall red candles on their heads.

Marianne gazed at this magnificence with a kind of appalled wonder, while the servants carried in her trunks.

'Is – is this my room?'

Dona Lavinia threw open a window and applied a deft touch to the massive spray of orange blossoms dripping from an alabaster vase.

'It has belonged to every Princess Sant'Anna for two hundred years. Do you like it?'

To avoid the necessity of answering, Marianne asked another question.

'Why all these mirrors?'

At once, she had the feeling that the question was an unwelcome one. The housekeeper's worn features tensed a little, and she turned away to open a door leading into a small room apparently hollowed out of a block of white marble. A bathroom.

'Our Prince's grandmother,' she said at last, 'was a woman of such remarkable beauty that – that she desired to contemplate herself continually. It was she who ordered the mirrors put in here. They have been allowed to remain –'

Her tone intrigued Marianne who found her curiosity about this family increasing all the time.

'There is no doubt a portrait of her somewhere in the house,' she said with a smile. 'I should like to see her.'

'There was one – but it was destroyed in the fire. Would your ladyship care to rest, a bath, perhaps, or a little refreshment?'

'All three, if you please. But first, a bath. Where have you put my maid? I should like to have her near me.' This was to the obvious relief of Agathe who, ever since entering the villa, had been walking on tiptoe as though in a church or a museum.

'In that case, there is a small room at the end of this passage.' As she spoke, Dona Lavinia pressed a knob on one of the carved panels. The join was so fine that the door was wholly invisible. 'A bed shall be set up there. I will prepare the bath.' She was about to leave the room when Marianne stopped her.

'Dona Lavinia –'

'Excellenza?'

Her green eyes gazing directly into those of the housekeeper, Marianne asked quietly: 'Whereabouts in the palace are the Prince's apartments?'

The question was a perfectly natural one but clearly Dona Lavinia was not expecting it. Marianne could have sworn that her face paled.

'When he is here,' she said with an effort, 'his highness resides in the right wing – the room equivalent to this.'

'Very well. Thank you.'

Dona Lavinia curtsied and went away, leaving Marianne and Agathe alone. They looked at each other. The maid's pretty face was crumpled with fright and all her pert, Parisian assurance had deserted her. She clasped her hands together in a gesture of childish entreaty.

'Oh, mademoiselle – are we going to stay here long?'

'No, Agathe, not very long, I hope. Don't you like it?'

'It's very beautiful ...' She cast a doubtful glance around her. 'But – no, I don't like it. I don't know why. I'm sorry, mademoiselle, but I don't think I could ever feel at home here. It's all so different ...' Marianne smiled.

'Well, go and unpack my things,' she told her kindly, 'and don't be afraid to apply to Dona Lavinia, she is the housekeeper, you know, for anything you might need. She will be kind to you, I think. Now, be a brave girl, Agathe. There is nothing to be afraid of here. It is just the fatigue of the journey, and being in strange surroundings ...' As she spoke, Marianne became aware that in trying to comfort Agathe it was to herself that she was really talking. She, too, had been conscious, ever since entering the gates of this strange and splendid mansion, of an indefinable sense of oppression, all the stranger in that she could perceive no tangible signs of danger. It was something more subtle, like a bodiless presence, the presence, perhaps, of this man who kept himself so closely guarded. But there was something else besides and that, Marianne could have sworn, emanated from this very room, rather as if the ghost of the woman who had hung these mirrors still roamed here, intangible but supreme, as though in a shrine of which the great, gilded bed was the altar and the fantastically dressed figures on the ceiling a host of attentive worshippers.

Marianne moved slowly to a window. Perhaps it was her English blood that made her believe in ghosts. She could feel something now, here in this room.

The opposite wing of the house was hidden from view behind the jutting central block, but the windows commanded the whole extent of the peacock lawn, which ended in an immense cascade down which the water foamed and tumbled from pool to pool to fill a wide basin framed by two groups of plunging horses. It seemed to Marianne that these churning waters, in such strong contrast to the green and peaceful gardens, were a symbol of some powerful, hidden force penned beneath a surface of deceptive calm. But then, after all, those boiling waves, the restless plunging of the horses, these things were life itself, the passion to be and to act which Marianne had always felt fretting within herself. It may have been that which made this place, with its uncanny silence, strike her like a tomb.

Dusk found Marianne standing in the same place. The green park had melted into indistinct shades of grey, the cascade and the statues were pale blurs and the regal birds had gone. Marianne had bathed and nibbled half-heartedly at a light collation but she had found it impossible to sleep for an instant. The blame for this could probably be assigned to the preposterous bed, which made her feel like a victim offered up to the sacrificial knife.

Now she was dressed in a gown of heavy, creamy-white brocade, stiff with gold embroidery, which Dona Lavinia had brought to her, spread out in both arms as solemnly as if it had been some precious relic. Her head was crowned for the first time with a weighty diadem of gold set with outsize pearls, the fellows of the ones that made up the collar and bracelets of almost barbaric splendour which adorned her neck and arms. She stared out into the darkening garden, trying to quell the nervous fears that mounted in her as the hour drew near.

She saw herself, so short a time before, standing in another place, looking out at a different park, on the brink of another marriage. That was at Selton, on the eve of her wedding to Francis. Good God, was it possible that it was scarcely nine months ago? It felt like several centuries! She had stood at the windows of the marriage chamber, clad in a flimsy wisp of cambric, her girlish body quivering with mingled fear and anticipation, staring out as darkness shrouded the familiar landscape. How happy she had been that night! It was all so simple and beautiful. She loved Francis with all her youthful being and hoped to be loved by him, and she waited with passionate intensity for the moment when, in his arms, she would learn the overwhelming joys of love.

It was another who had taught her love and every fibre of her body trembled even now with intoxicating gratitude at the memory of those white-hot nights at Butard and the Trianon. Yet it was this love also which had given birth to the woman whose image she had contemplated only a moment past in those ridiculous mirrors: a statue of almost Byzantine majesty and splendour, huge eyes in a set, pale face, Her Serene Highness the Princess Sant'Anna. Serene … most serene … ineffably serene, while her heart was wrung with grief and anguish. What a mockery!

Tonight, there was no question of love, only of a marriage, positive, realistic, implacable. A union of two people in trouble, Gauthier de Chazay had called it. Tonight, no man would come knocking at the door of this room, no desire would come to claim her body in which life, secret as yet, but already all-powerful, was growing … no Jason would appear to demand payment of a debt, fantastic yet disturbing …

Marianne leaned on the bronze window hasp, fighting off the giddiness which overwhelmed her, thrusting back the mariner's image as she suddenly thought that if he had come, she might have felt a real happiness. But he was not there and the world was strangely empty. She wanted to cry out, and she pressed her be-ringed fingers into her mouth to keep back that absurd call for help. Decked in jewels an empress might have envied, she had never felt more miserable.

She was shaken out of her morbid state when the double doors of her room were flung wide open and the shadows were dispelled by the appearance of six footmen holding branched candlesticks aloft. Aureoled in the sparkling light of the dancing flames, his robes of red watered silk sweeping the polished floor, the cardinal entered in all the splendour of the Church of Rome and at the glory of his entrance Marianne blinked like a night bird brought suddenly into the light. The cardinal's gaze rested thoughtfully on her for a moment but he made no comment.

'Come,' he said, merely. 'It is time.'

Whether it was his words or the blood red of his garments, Marianne could not have said, but she felt like one condemned, being summoned to the scaffold. She went to him, nonetheless, and laid her bejewelled hand on the red gloved fingers he held out to her. Their two trains, the sweeping *capa magna* and the queenly gown, whispered in concert over the marble surface of the rooms.

As they walked through them, Marianne saw with amazement that every room was lighted as if for a ball, yet nothing could have been less festive than this huge, magnificent emptiness. She thought, for the first time in years, of the fairy stories she had loved as a child. Tonight, she was Cinderella, Donkeyskin and the Sleeping Beauty all rolled into one, but for her there was no Prince Charming. Her prince was a phantom, invisible.

In this way, in slow and solemn procession, they traversed the entire palace. It was as though the cardinal were proudly presenting the newcomer to the assembled shades of all those who had once lived, loved and, perhaps, suffered in this place. At last, they came to a small saloon, hung with red damask, in which the principal article of furniture was a tall mirror of the French regency period, set on a gilt console and framed by a pair of bronze girandoles bearing clusters of lighted candles.

Bidding Marianne with a gesture to be seated, the cardinal stood beside her in silence with the air of one waiting for something. His eyes were on the mirror, which Marianne was sitting facing, but he had retained her hand in his, as if for reassurance. Marianne felt more oppressed than ever and she was already opening her mouth to ask a question when he spoke.

'My friend, here, as I promised, is Marianne d'Asselnat de Villeneuve, my goddaughter,' he said proudly.

Marianne shivered. It was to the mirror he had spoken, and now it was the mirror that answered.

'Forgive my silence, my dear cardinal. I should have spoken first, to welcome you, but I must confess that I was dumb with admiration. Madame, your godfather endeavoured to describe your beauty to me but, for the first time in his life, his eloquence has proved unequal to the task; so far unequal that only the fact that none but a poet could find words to express such divinity can excuse him. Let me say how deeply – humbly grateful I am to you for being here – and for being yourself.'

The voice was low and muffled. Its very tonelessness gave it a note of weariness and profound sadness. Marianne tensed, to control the excitement which was quickening her breath. She too looked at the mirror from where the voice seemed to come.

'Can you see me?' she asked softly.

'As clearly as if there were no obstacle between us. Let us say, I am the mirror in which you see yourself reflected. Have you ever seen a mirror happy?'

'I wish I could be sure of that – your voice is so sad.'

'That is because it is little used. A voice that has nothing to say comes to forget that it could sing. In the end, it is crushed by silence. But your voice is pure music.'

It was strange, talking to someone who remained invisible, but little by little Marianne acquired confidence. She decided it was time she took her own fate in hand. The voice was that of one who had known suffering, or was suffering still. She determined to play this game for herself. She turned to the cardinal.

'Godfather, would you leave me for a moment? I should like to talk to the Prince, and I should find it easier alone.'

'It is natural. I will wait in the library.'

No sooner had the door closed behind him than Marianne rose but instead of moving closer to the mirror she turned away towards one of the windows. It unnerved her to sit face to face with herself, hearing the bodiless voice speaking, as it was speaking now, with a shade of hesitation.

'Why did you send the cardinal away?'

'Because I must speak to you. There are some things, which must, I think, be said.'

'What things? I understood that my eminent friend had explained the precise nature of our agreement?'

'And so he has. It is all perfectly cut and dried; at least, I think so.'

'He told you that I shall not interfere in your life? The only thing he may not have said – but which I will ask …'

He paused and Marianne was aware of a slight break in his voice, but he recovered himself almost at once and continued: 'I will ask you, when the child is born, to bring him here sometimes. I should like him to learn to love this land, in my place, to love this house and its people, for whom he will be a real person – not a furtive shadow.' Again, there was the slight, almost imperceptible break and Marianne felt her heart swell suddenly with a rush of pity. At the same time, another part of her mind was saying that all this was absurd, fantastic, and most of all this desperate veil of secrecy in which he wrapped himself. Her voice, when she spoke, was imploring.

'Prince – pardon me, I beseech you, if my words give you pain, but I do not understand and I want to, so much. Why all this mystery? Why may I not see you? Surely, I have the right to know my husband's face?'

There was a silence, so long and heavy that for a moment she was afraid that she had driven her strange interlocutor away. She was afraid that her impulsiveness had made her go too far, and too soon. But at last, the answer came, slow and final as a judgement.

'No. That cannot be. In a little while, we shall be together in the chapel and my hand will touch yours – but we shall never be as close again.'

'But why, why?' she persisted. 'My birth is as good as your own and I fear nothing – however terrible – if that is what restrains you.'

There was a brief, low, mirthless laugh.

'You have been here so short a time and already you have heard men talk, have you not? I know – they have all sorts of theories about me, of which the most agreeable is that I am the victim of a hideous disease, leprosy or something of that kind. I am not a leper, madame, or anything of the kind. Nevertheless, it is impossible for us to meet face to face.'

'But in the name of God, why?'

This time it was her voice that broke.

'Because I would not risk becoming an object of horror to you.'

The voice was silent, and this time the mirror did not speak for so long that Marianne realized she was truly alone. Her hands, which had been gripping the thick, shiny leaves of some unknown plant in a Chinese vase, relaxed and she let out her breath in one long sigh. The disturbing presence had gone, to Marianne's great relief, for now she thought she knew what she was dealing with. The man must be a monster, some wretched semblance of humanity, doomed to darkness by repulsive disfigurement, too hideous to be endured by any eyes but those which had known him from birth. That would explain Matteo Damiani's stony countenance, the pain in Dona Lavinia's and perhaps also the childishness of Father Amundi's old features. It would explain, too, why he had broken off their interview when so many things were still to be said.

*I was clumsy*, Marianne reproached herself. *I was in too much of a hurry. I should have approached the subject more cautiously, not rushed in at once with the question I wished to ask. I should have tried to penetrate the mystery little by little, by careful hints. And now I daresay I have frightened him.*

One other thing which surprised her was that the Prince had asked her nothing about herself, her life, her tastes. He had merely praised her beauty, as if that were the only thing that mattered in his eyes. Marianne reflected a little bitterly that he could scarcely have shown less curiosity if she had been a handsome filly destined for his precious stables. Indeed, it was more than likely that Corrado Sant'Anna would have made inquiries into the health and habits of such an animal. But, after all, for a man whose sole object in life was the possession of an heir to carry on his ancient name, the physical characteristics of the mother were bound to be of paramount importance. Why should Prince Sant'Anna concern himself with the affections, feelings and habits of Marianne d'Asselnat?

The door of the red *salon* opened to admit the cardinal once more, but this time he was not alone. Three men were with him. One was a little, dark fellow with a face that seemed entirely made up of nose and whiskers. The cut of his coat and the big, leather folder which he carried under his arm proclaimed the notary. The other two might have stepped straight down from a gallery of ancestral portraits: two venerable gentlemen in velvet suits dating from the time of Louis XV, and bob wigs. One leaned on a stick, the other on the cardinal's arm and both their faces were expressive of extreme old age.

They bowed with an exquisite, old-fashioned courtesy to Marianne who curtsied deeply in return. They were presented to her as the Marquis del Carreto and Count Gherardesca, kinsmen of the Prince, and they were there to witness the marriage. The last-named, the one who walked with a stick, was also, in his capacity as the Grand Duchess's chamberlain, to register the marriage officially.

The lawyer seated himself at a small table and opened his brief-case. Everyone else sat down. At the far end of the room were Dona Lavinia and Matteo Damiani, who had come in after the witnesses.

Marianne was so nervous and distraught that she hardly listened to the long, pedantic reading of the marriage contract. The endless convolutions of legal terminology were irritating. All she wanted now was to get it over, quickly. She was not in the least interested in the enumeration of the possessions which Prince Sant'Anna was to settle on his wife, any more than in the truly royal sum of her allowance. Her attention was divided between the silent mirror facing her, behind which the Prince might once more be watching, and the unpleasant sensation that she herself was the focus of an insistent gaze.

She could feel that gaze between her bare shoulders and on the back of her neck where her hair was piled up into a heavy chignon to support the diadem. It slid over her skin, dwelling on the soft curve of her neck with an almost magnetic force, as if someone were trying, by sheer force of will, to attract her attention. At last, her overwrought nerves could bear it no longer. She turned quickly but met nothing but Matteo's frozen stare. He seemed so indifferent that she thought she must have been mistaken but no sooner had she turned back than the sensation was renewed, more distinctly than ever.

Her discomfort increased until she welcomed with relief the end of this obligatory ceremony. She signed, without so much as glancing at it, the act of settlement which the lawyer presented to her with a low bow, then her eyes went to her godfather's and he smiled at her.

'Now we can go to the chapel,' he said. 'Father Amundi is already waiting for us there.'

Marianne had expected the chapel to be situated somewhere in the building but she realized that she was mistaken when she saw Dona Lavinia coming towards her with a long, black velvet cloak which she placed on her shoulders, taking care to put up the hood.

'The chapel is in the park,' she explained. 'The night is warm but it is chilly under the trees.'

As he had done when leading her from her room, the cardinal took his goddaughter's hand and led her solemnly to the great marble steps where footmen armed with torches awaited them. The remainder of the little procession formed up behind them. Marianne saw that Matteo Damiani had offered his arm to the aged Marquis del Carreto, next came Count Gherardesca with Dona Lavinia, who had thrown a black lace shawl hastily over her head and shoulders. The lawyer and his brief-case had vanished.

In this way they descended into the park. As they emerged, Marianne saw Gracchus and Agathe waiting in the loggia. They were staring at the approaching procession with such flabbergasted expressions that Marianne suddenly wanted to laugh. They had clearly not yet taken in the incredible news which their mistress had imparted to them before she dressed, that she was here in order to marry an unknown prince, and if they were too well-mannered to make any comment, the dismay on their honest faces gave a good idea of their thoughts. Marianne smiled at them as she passed and indicated that they were to follow after Dona Lavinia.

*They must think I am mad*, she thought. *Agathe does not matter. She is a nice girl but she has no more brain than a linnet. But Gracchus is a different matter. I shall have to speak to him. He has a right to know a little more.'*

The night was black as ink. The sky was starless and invisible but a slight wind blew the torches carried by the lackeys. A low, distant rumbling presaged a storm but the Cortège advanced at a slow, solemn pace which set Marianne's teeth on edge. She muttered under her breath. 'This is more like a funeral procession than a marriage! There ought to be a friar chanting the *Dies Irae*!'

The cardinal's hand tightened on hers until it hurt.

'A little more conduct!' he chided softly, without looking at her. 'It is not for us to impose our wishes here. We must obey the Prince's orders.'

'They indicate his joy at this marriage!'

'Do not be bitter. And above all, do not be stupid and cruel. No one could desire the joy of a true wedding more than Corrado. For you, this is no more than a formality – for him it is a source of bitter regrets.'

Marianne accepted the reproof without protest, aware that she had deserved it. She gave a sad little smile and asked in a different tone: 'All the same, there is one thing I should like to know.'

'And that is?'

'My – Prince Corrado's age.'

'Twenty-eight, or a little more, I believe.'

'What? Is he so young?'

'I thought I told you he was not old.'

'Yes, but – so young!'

She forbore to add that she had pictured a man in his forties. To one like Gauthier Chazay on the brink of old age, forty was the prime of life. But now she discovered that the unfortunate whose name she was to bear, whom a cruel fate had condemned to perpetual seclusion was, like herself, young, with all the same youthful aspirations towards life, and happiness and freedom. The recollection of that muffled voice, with its weight of sadness, filled her with an immense pity, joined to a real desire to help him, to lighten as far as might be possible the sufferings she could imagine.

'Godfather,' she whispered. 'I would like to help him – give him, perhaps, a little affection. Why does he so stubbornly refuse to let me see him?'

'You must leave it to time, Marianne. In time Corrado may perhaps come to think differently – although I do not expect it. Remember only, if it will make it easier for you, that you are bringing him the thing he has always dreamed of: a child to bear his name.'

'Even though he will not be its real father! He asked me – to bring him here from time to time. I will do it gladly.'

'But – were you not listening to the marriage contract? You have pledged yourself to bring the child here once a year.'

'I – no, I did not hear,' she confessed, a slow flush spreading over her face. 'I must have been thinking of something else.'

'It was hardly the time,' the cardinal said gruffly. 'You signed, at all events –'

'And I will keep my word. After what you have told me I shall even be glad to do it. Poor – poor Prince! I would like to be a friend to him, a sister. Indeed, I should!'

'God grant that you may,' the cardinal sighed. 'But I do not hope for it.'

The avenue that led to the chapel lay behind the right wing of the house, a little way beyond the gateway leading to the stables. As she rounded the corner of her new home, Marianne saw that the mirror-like sheets of water surrounded it on all four sides, but that stretching almost the whole length of the rear of the building was an elaborate grotto, built around the entrance to a cavern.

Bronze lanterns attached to every pillar illuminated the whole of this remarkable edifice and were reflected in long, gold streamers in the water, giving to the whole the air of a Venetian carnival. Then the way leading to the chapel passed under the shade of a small grove of trees and the elegant grotto was lost to sight. Soon, even the lights of the villa disappeared, showing no more than an occasional glimmer between the leaves.

The chapel itself, raised up in a small clearing, was a low, dumpy building of considerable age. In style, it was a very early Romanesque, expressed in massive walls, pierced by few apertures, and rounded arches.

Its primitive solidity contrasted with the somewhat artificial elegance of the palace and its encircling waters, like some obstinate, cross-grained elderly relative, sternly disapproving the follies of youth.

The small, arched doorway was open, allowing a glimpse of lighted candles within, an ancient altar stone covered with an immaculate white cloth and the golden cope of the old priest waiting there. There was also a curious, black shape which Marianne was unable to make out clearly from outside. It was only when she stood on the threshold of the church that she saw what it was. Black velvet curtains had been hung from the low vaulted roof, cutting off half of the choir, and she realized that the brief hope which she had cherished of being allowed at least a glimpse of the Prince's figure during the ceremony had failed. He was, or would be, concealed within that velvet alcove, next to which were a chair and a *prie-dieu*, the pair, no doubt, to others placed behind the curtains.

'Even here —' she began. The cardinal nodded.

'Even here. Only the priest will be able to see both parties, for the curtains are open on the altar side. It is necessary that he should be able to see both husband and wife as they make their vows.'

With a weary sigh, Marianne allowed herself to be led to the place prepared for her. Close by, a huge white wax candle burned in a silver sconce standing on the floor but, apart from the sacred vessels and the altar cloth, no other preparations had been made for the ceremony. The little chapel was cold and damp, with the musty smell of buildings that are never aired. Along the walls of the nave, long dead Sant'Annas slept in effigies of stone upon their ancient tombs. It was a cheerless place and Marianne was reminded of a play she had seen once, in London, in which the hero, under sentence of death, was allowed to marry the heroine in the prison chapel on the night before his execution. There, too, the prisoner had been separated from his bride by an iron grating, and Marianne recalled how vividly the sombre and dramatic scene had impressed her. Now she herself was to play the part of the bride and the union to be solemnized here would be just as brief. When they left the chapel, they would be divided as surely as if the executioner's axe were to fall on one of them. Indeed, the man waiting silently behind the frail wall of velvet was also under sentence in his way. His youth sentenced him to Life, when life was an abomination.

The cardinal and the witnesses had taken their places a little way behind but Marianne saw to her surprise that Matteo Damiani had gone to the altar to assist the priest. He was now wearing a white surplice over his massive shoulders from which his bull neck emerged with a plebeian strength in curious contrast to certain traits of nobility in his features. It was a Roman face, beyond a doubt, but not a handsome one: perhaps it was the mouth that was too full, too heavily sensual, or the eyes, fixed and unblinking, whose gaze so soon became an intolerable burden. All through the service, Marianne was conscious of those eyes on her and when at last she turned on him a glance sparkling with anger and disdain the steward's bold stare did not waver and it seemed to her that there was even a cold, fleeting smile on his ugly lips. It so enraged her that for a moment she forgot the man who stood on the other side of the curtain, so near and yet so far away.

Never in her life had she given so little of her attention to the mass. Her whole being was taken up with the already familiar voice which she now heard praying almost uninterruptedly, praying aloud with a fervour and devotion that she found strangely disturbing. It had not occurred to her that the master of a domain of such sensual beauty could be the ardent Christian those prayers revealed. She had never heard such an agonizing combination of melancholy resignation and entreaty on any human lips. Surely, such prayers belonged only to the most strictly enclosed orders, places where the pitiless monastic rule foreshadowed the final annihilation of the grave? Little by little, she forgot Matteo Damiani in listening to that astonishing voice.

The time for the marriage vows had come. The chaplain descended the two stone steps and stood before the strange couple. As if in a dream, Marianne heard him put the ritual question to the Prince, and in a moment the voice answered him with unexpected strength.

'In the sight of God and of men, I, Corrado, Prince of Sant'Anna, do here take as my lawful wedded wife ...'

The sacred words rang out like a challenge, filling Marianne's ears like the rumble of a storm, and they were given a sinister emphasis by the violent clap of thunder which just then burst directly over the chapel. She blenched as if struck by a premonition of disaster and her own voice shook when her turn came to utter the formal vows. Then the priest said quietly: 'Join your hands.'

The black curtains parted. Wide-eyed Marianne saw a black velvet sleeve, a lace cuff and a hand, gloved in white kid, extended towards her. It was a very large hand, strong and long-fingered, and the glove moulded it perfectly: the hand of a very tall and active man. Trembling suddenly at this real, tangible object Marianne stared, fascinated, not daring to place her own within it. There was something about that open palm, those extended fingers, which was both attractive and alarming. It was like a trap.

'You must place your hand in his,' whispered the cardinal's voice in her ear.

All eyes were on her. Father Amundi's held surprise, the cardinal's a mixture of command and entreaty, Matteo Damiani's were sardonic. It may have been the last which decided her. She placed her hand firmly in the one held out to receive it. The fingers closed on it gently, almost delicately, as if they feared to hurt her. Marianne felt, through the glove, the firm, living warmth of the flesh. The words she had heard so short a time before came back to her.

'We shall never be as close again,' the voice had said.

Now, the old priest was pronouncing the final blessing, the words half drowned by a second peal of thunder.

'I declare you man and wife, for better for worse, until death do you part.'

Marianne felt the hand that held hers quiver. Another hand appeared through the crack in the curtains, for just long enough to slip a broad gold band on her finger, then both hands were withdrawn, taking hers with them. A tremor ran through her. Two lips were pressed to her fingertips before her hand was released.

The brief, physical link was broken. There was nothing behind the wall of velvet, only a sigh. Father Amundi knelt in prayer at the altar, his back beneath his chasuble so bent that he looked like a bundle of cloth, reflecting the light from its folds. Another thunderclap, more violent than either of the two preceding ones, made the very walls reverberate with the din. At that moment, the heavens opened. Water poured down, drumming on the roof like a cataract. Within seconds, the chapel and those inside it had become an enclosed world, cut off by the storm. The old priest trotted away to the tiny sacristy, bearing the altar vessels, but Matteo almost flung off his surplice.

'A carriage must be fetched!' he exclaimed. The princess cannot return to the villa in this.'

He was already making for the door when Gracchus suggested diffidently: 'May I come with you, to help?'

The steward looked at him. 'There are plenty of servants to do that, and you are not familiar with our horses. Stay here.'

Beckoning authoritatively to two of the servants who had carried the torches, he opened the door and plunged out, head down, into the storm, hurling himself into the wind like a charging bull. After one bewildered glance at the black curtains, behind which there was now no sound of movement, as if the Prince had vanished miraculously into thin air, Marianne sought refuge beside her godfather. This sudden storm, breaking out at the very moment of her marriage, was more than she could bear.

'It is an omen,' she breathed. 'An evil omen.'

'Have you grown superstitious now?' he scolded her in an undertone. This was not the way you were brought up. I suppose you have caught this from the Corsican? They say he is inordinately superstitious.'

She recoiled before his ill-concealed anger. She could think of no reason for it, unless it was that he too had been struck by the storm and was trying to counteract his own feelings. He might have hoped to crush Marianne's childish fears beneath his own adult contempt but the result he achieved was quite different. The reminder of Napoleon was a salutary one for Marianne. It was as if the all-powerful Corsican had suddenly come into the chapel with his eagle eye and that unyielding hardness against which even the strongest broke themselves in vain. She heard his mocking laughter and the evil spell was broken. It was for his sake that she had been forced to accept this curious marriage, for the sake of the child that he had given her. Very soon, tomorrow, she would set out again for France, to him, and all this would be no more than a bad dream.

In a few minutes, Matteo reappeared. Without a word, but with a gesture so full of pride that it dared her to refuse him, he offered his hand to Marianne to lead her to the carriage. But she ignored him and, with an icy stare, made her own way to the door. She had entered the chapel on her godfather's arm: since there was no husband there to give her his arm, she intended to leave it alone. This man with his bold stare must learn to know that from now on she meant to be treated as sovereign mistress here.

Outside, the carriage was waiting with the steps already let down and the door held open by an expressionless and dripping lackey. But between it and the little porch stretched a large puddle, fed by a heavy curtain of water. Marianne swept the train of her precious gown over her arm.

'If your highness permits ...' said a voice. Before she could utter a word of protest, Matteo had picked her up bodily in his arms and lifted her over the obstacle. She gave one squeak and then stiffened, shrinking from the hateful touch of his broad hands damped firmly round her thighs and under her arms, but his grip only tightened.

'Your highness should take care,' he said blandly. 'Your highness might fall in the mud.'

Marianne was obliged to let him place her on the cushioned seat of the carriage but she had hated feeling herself, even for an instant, pressed to that man's chest and she merely thanked him curtly, without a single glance. Not even the sight of the little cardinal, all bundled up in his red robes, being transported in the same fashion had the power to erase the angry frown from her brow.

'Tomorrow,' she said through her teeth, as soon as he was set down beside her, 'I am going home!'

'So soon? Is that not a little – hasty? I should have thought that you owed it to – to your husband, and the consideration he has shown you, to remain for, shall we say, a week, at least?'

'I do not feel comfortable in this house.'

'Yet you have promised to return here once a year. Come now, Marianne, is it so difficult to do as I ask? We have not seen one another for so long. I had hoped that you would have been willing to spend these few days with me?'

The green eyes, beneath lowered lids, looked sideways at Gauthier de Chazay.

'You will stay?'

'But of course! My child, don't you think I am looking forward to having my little Marianne again, for a little while, who used to come running to meet me under the trees at Selton?'

The unexpected reference brought tears to Marianne's eyes.

'I thought – I thought you had forgotten that.'

'Because I did not speak of it? It is all the dearer to me. I keep the memory of those days hidden away in the most secret corner of my old heart and, now and then, when I feel very depressed, I open it up and peep inside.'

'Depressed? Nothing ever seems to depress you, godfather.'

'Because I do not let it appear? I am getting old, Marianne, and tired. Stay a little while, my child. We both need to be together again, to forget, in each other's company, that there are such things as kings and wars and intrigues, especially intrigues. Do this for me – in memory of other days.'


The warmth of renewed affection had its influence on the dinner-party which took place shortly afterwards in the ancient banqueting hall of the villa. This was a vast room, lofty as a cathedral and paved with black marble beneath a marvellous ceiling composed of repeated representations of the curious arms of Sant'Anna, a gold snake and a unicorn on a field of sable. These arms amused Marianne, who, by comparing them with those of her family, which included the lion of the Asselnat's and the hawk of their Montsalvy cousins, noticed that they made up a very singular heraldic menagerie.

The walls of the hall were painted with frescoes by an unknown artist depicting the legend of the unicorn, executed with great freshness of colouring and a charming naivety. This was the first room in the villa which really appealed to Marianne. Except for the table, which was lavishly spread and decorated, there was less gold to be seen than elsewhere and the effect was, overall, restful.

Seated at the long table with the cardinal facing her at the other end, she did the honours of the meal as gracefully as if she had been in her own house in the Rue de Lille. The aged Marquis del Carreto, who was somewhat hard of hearing, was not the most enlivening of conversationalists. Count Gherardesca, however, conversed with ease and wit. During the meal, Marianne learned from him all the latest gossip of the court of Florence, including that of the Grand Duchess Elisa's intimacy with the handsome Cenami and of her more turbulent affair with Paganini, the satanic violinist. A gentle hint was also allowed to drop that Napoleon's sister would be pleased to welcome the new Princess Sant'Anna at her court, but Marianne declined the invitation.

'I have little taste for court life, Count. Had my husband been able to present me himself to her imperial highness, it would have been a great joy to me. But, as matters stand ...'

The old nobleman directed at her a glance full of understanding.

'In marrying my unhappy cousin, Princess, you have performed an act of great charity. But you are young and beautiful, and there are limits to devotion. There are none, among the nobility of this country, who would condemn you should you choose to go into society without your husband, since, alas, Prince Corrado's temper leads him to live the life of a recluse.'

'I thank you for saying so but indeed, just at present, I am not tempted to do so. Later, perhaps – and I should be grateful if you will convey my apologies, and my respects to her imperial highness.'

While her lips were almost mechanically framing the polite, formal words, Marianne's eyes were studying the Count's pleasant features to guess how much he knew of his cousin. Did he know what it was that forced Corrado Sant'Anna to lead this terrible existence? He had spoken of his 'temper' when the Prince had himself confessed that he did not wish to give her a horror of him. She might have questioned him more closely but the cardinal, as though guessing her intention, turned the conversation into other channels by asking the Count about the recent measures which had been taken against the religious houses and the meal ended without an opportunity to return to the subject that she most wished to know about.

The two witnesses took their leave immediately on rising from table, putting forward their age as their excuse for not remaining longer. One was bound for his palace at Lucca, the other for a villa he owned in the country nearby, but both used their exquisite, old-world courtesy to express their hope of soon meeting again 'the prettiest of princesses'.

'Well, you have made two conquests,' Gauthier de Chazay remarked with a mischievous smile. 'One must make allowances, of course, for the excitability of the Italian temperament, but even so ... Not that I am altogether surprised. But,' his smile faded, 'I trust the ravages of your beauty will stop there.'

'What do you mean?'

'That I should infinitely have preferred it if Corrado had not seen you. You see, I wished to give him a little happiness. I should be deeply distressed to cause him any pain.'

'What makes you suddenly say this? You knew I was not precisely repulsive.'

'It is a very sudden thought,' the cardinal admitted. 'Do you know, Marianne, that Corrado did not take his eyes off you all through the meal?'

She shivered. 'What? But – how could he? He was not present!' Then, as she recalled the red damask salon: There was no mirror ...'

'No, but there are places in the ceiling where the carving can be put aside to allow a view of what is passing in the room, old spy holes which had a certain usefulness in the days when the Sant'Annas were involved in political life. I know them well. I saw a pair of eyes – which could have belonged to no one else. If this unfortunate should fall in love with you –'

'You see, it is best that I should go.'

'No. That would appear like flight and you would wound him. After all – we may give him that small happiness. And who knows? It may encourage him one day not to conceal himself so completely from you, if not from others.'

But Marianne's momentary relaxation had gone and her discomfort returned. Despite the cardinal's comforting words, she felt a kind of horror at the idea that the owner of that sad voice could fall in love with her. She tried with all her might to cling to the terms of the bargain, for that was all it was, a contract, and that was all it must ever be. And yet, what if Gauthier de Chazay were right and she had brought this unseen man a new burden of pain and regrets? Remembering the kiss that had been pressed on her fingers, she shivered.

She regained her own bedchamber to find Agathe in a state of complete bewilderment. The strange ceremony which she had witnessed, added to the terror already inspired in her by the palace, had plunged the poor girl into total disarray. She stood beside Dona Lavinia, who was as imperturbable as ever, trembling like a leaf and at her mistress's entrance sank into a curtsey so deep that it landed her on the floor. This was all that was needed to put her in hysterics and the housekeeper's reproving eye finished the matter. Without even attempting to get up, Agathe burst into tears.

'Tut!' said Dona Lavinia. 'Has the girl lost her wits?'

'No,' Marianne answered calmly, 'she is merely frightened. You must forgive her, Dona Lavinia. I had told her nothing and it has all been such a shock to her. The journey, too, was very trying.'

Between the two of them, they managed to get Agathe to her feet, mumbling desperate apologies.

'Oh mad – madame – your highness – forgive me. I – I don't know what came over me. I – I –'

'Her highness is perfectly right,' Dona Lavinia said briskly, thrusting a handkerchief into her hand. 'You are hysterical, my girl. What you need is a good night's rest. With your permission, madame, I will see her to bed and give her a sedative. She will be better tomorrow.'

'Thank you, Dona Lavinia, if you will.'

'I will be back immediately to help your highness to undress.'

While the housekeeper bore off the still weeping Agathe, Marianne walked over to a big Venetian mirror in front of which was a low, Chinese lacquered table bearing innumerable bottles and toilet articles in crystal and solid gold. She felt horribly tired and all she wanted now was to go to bed.

Now that the covers had been drawn back, revealing clean, white linen sheets, the great gilded bed looked much more welcoming. A soft night light was burning below the huge, curtained baldachin and the big, down-filled pillows were an irresistible invitation to sleep.

She could feel one of her headaches coming on and the diadem seemed to weigh very heavy on her temples. Not without difficulty, for it was firmly anchored with pins, she managed to rid herself of it, laid it on the table without so much as a glance and finished letting down her hair. The dress, too, with its crusted embroidery and long train, was beginning to irk her and Marianne set about getting it off without waiting for Dona Lavinia. With a twist of her slim waist, which gave, as yet, no hint of her approaching motherhood, she unfastened the hooks, then wriggled it off her shoulders and, with a sigh of relief, allowed the heavy fabric to fall to the floor. She stepped out of it, picked up the dress and threw it over a chair, stripped off stockings and petticoats and then, wearing only her flimsy cambric shift with its trimmings of Valenciennes lace, she stretched like a cat and sighed happily. But the sigh was choked off in a scream of terror. There, in the mirror opposite, was a man, his eyes devouring her greedily.

She swung round but saw only the other mirrors on the wall reflecting nothing but the quiet candlelight. There was no one in the room. Yet Marianne could have sworn that it was Matteo Damiani who had been there, watching her with lustful eyes as she undressed. But there was nothing there. The silence was absolute. Not a sound, not a breath.

Her legs felt weak and she subsided on to the brocade-covered stool that stood before the dressing-table and passed a trembling hand across her face. Had it been an hallucination? Had the steward made such an impression on her that she was beginning to see him everywhere? Or was it simply fatigue? She could no longer be quite sure that she had really seen him. She had heard that nerves strained to breaking point could conjure up phantoms, bring forms and faces into being where none existed.

Dona Lavinia returned to find her lying on the stool, half-naked and white as a sheet. She wrung her hands agitatedly.

'Your highness should not have done it,' she exclaimed reproachfully. 'Why did you not wait for me? See, you are trembling all over. You are not ill?'

'No, just exhausted, Dona Lavinia. I can't wait to get into bed, and sleep. Won't you give me some of whatever it was you gave to Agathe? I want to be sure to sleep well.'

'It's only natural after such a day.'

In a very few moments, Marianne was lying in bed while Dona Lavinia brought her a warm tisane, its pleasant scent already beginning to relax her tired nerves. She drank it gratefully, longing to escape from her wild imaginings. She was sure that, without some outside aid, she would never manage to get to sleep, however tired she was, while she could still see that face. As though guessing something of her trouble, Dona Lavinia sat down on a chair near the bed.

'I will stay here until your highness is asleep,' she promised, 'and be sure that nothing disturbs you.'

Relieved, although she would not admit it, of a weight on her mind, Marianne closed her eyes and let the tisane take its soothing effect. Within minutes, she was fast asleep.

Dona Lavinia sat still in her chair. She had taken a set of ivory beads from her pocket and was quietly saying her prayers. Quite suddenly, there came a sound of horses' hooves galloping in the darkness, softly at first, then growing louder. The housekeeper rose noiselessly and went to the window, pulling one of the curtains a little aside. Outside, in the thick darkness, a white shape appeared, moved swiftly across the grass, and vanished as fast as it had come: a white horse going at full gallop, bearing a dark figure on its back.

Dona Lavinia let fall the curtain with a sigh and returned to her place at Marianne's bedside. She felt no desire for sleep. On this night, more than any other, she felt the need to pray, both for the sleeper in the room and for that other whom she loved like her own child; if happiness were impossible, she prayed that heaven would grant them at least the gentle numbness of peace.

# CHAPTER ELEVEN
# Night of Enchantment

When Marianne awoke after a night's uninterrupted slumber to a room flooded with brilliant sunshine, she was fully herself again. The previous night's storm had washed everything clean and such debris of broken branches and wind-tossed leaves as it had left about the park had been already swept up by the gardeners of the villa. Grass and trees put forth their brightest green and all the sweet fresh smells of the warm countryside were wafted in at the open windows, bringing the mingled scents of hay and honey-suckle, cypress and rosemary.

Just as when she closed her eyes, she opened them to find Dona Lavinia standing by her bedside, smiling as she arranged a huge armful of roses in a pair of tall vases.

'His highness desired that the first thing you saw this morning should be the loveliest of all flowers.' She hesitated. 'There is this, also.'

'This' was a sandalwood box and several black leather cases stamped with the arms of Sant'Anna but all bearing the unmistakable signs of wear inseparable from old things.

'What are they?' Marianne asked.

The jewels of the princesses of Sant'Anna, my lady. Those which belonged to Dona Adriana, our Prince's mother, and – and those of the other princesses. Some of them are very old.'

There was, in fact, jewellery of every description, from ancient and very lovely cameos to an assortment of curious oriental objects, but the greater part was made up of heavy renaissance ornaments, huge baroque pearls made to look like sirens and centaurs in settings of multicoloured gems. There was jewellery of more modern workmanship also; ropes of diamonds to adorn a décolletage, dusters of brilliants, collars and necklaces of gold and precious stones. There was also several unset stones and when Marianne had examined everything, Dona Lavinia produced a small silver casket lined with black velvet on which reposed twelve incomparable emeralds. They were huge, rough-cut stones of a deep, translucent green and intense luminosity, certainly the finest Marianne had ever seen. Even those which Napoleon had given her could not begin to match their beauty. And suddenly, the housekeeper echoed the Emperor's words.

'His highness said that they were the same green as my lady's eyes. His grandfather, Prince Sebastiano, brought them back from Peru for his wife, but she did not care for the stones.'

'Why ever not?' Marianne was holding the perfect gems up to watch the play of light upon them. 'They are beautiful!'

'They were thought in earlier times to be a symbol of peace and love. Dona Lucinda believed in love – but she hated peace.'

So it was that Marianne heard for the first time the name of the woman who had been so enamoured of her own reflection that she had covered the walls of her room with mirrors. But there was no time to ask more. Dona Lavinia informed her with a curtsey that her bath was prepared and the cardinal awaited her company at breakfast. Before the new Princess could summon up courage to ask her to stay and answer her questions, she had gone, leaving her to Agathe's ministrations. A shadow had undoubtedly passed over the old woman's face, a faint darkening of her eyes as if she regretted having uttered that name, and she had certainly been in a hurry to be gone. Clearly, she was anxious to avoid the questions that she sensed were coming.

When Marianne joined her godfather in the library, where he had ordered breakfast to be served, she lost no time in asking the question which had put Dona Lavinia to flight. She began by describing how she had been presented with the ancestral jewels.

'Who was the Prince's grandmother? I gather that her name was Lucinda but no one seems anxious to talk about her. Do you know why?'

The cardinal spread a thick layer of delicious-smelling tomato sauce over his pasta then added cheese and mixed the whole carefully together. At length, having tasted the resultant combination, he said coolly: 'No. I have no idea.'

'Oh come, that is surely impossible! I know you have been acquainted with the Sant'Annas for ever. Otherwise, how does it come about that you are permitted to share the secret which surrounds Prince Corrado? You must know something of this Lucinda. Say, rather, that you will not tell me.'

The cardinal chuckled. 'You are longing to know so much that in a moment you will be calling me a liar,' he said. 'Well, my dear, let me tell you that a prince of the Church does not tell lies, or at least, no more than a simple parish priest. It is quite true that I know very little, beyond the fact that she was a Venetian, of the noble family of Soranzo, and extremely beautiful.'

'Hence the mirrors! But the mere fact of being beautiful and over fond of her own reflection does not explain the kind of reserve which everyone here seems to feel about her. Even her portrait seems to have vanished.'

'I should add that, by what I have heard, Dona Lucinda's reputation was – er – unsavoury. There are those among the few people still alive who knew her who claim that she was mad, others say that she was something of a witch, or at least in league with the devil. Such things do not make for popularity here – or elsewhere.'

Marianne had an idea that the cardinal was being deliberately evasive. For all the trust and respect in which she held her godfather, she could not help having an odd suspicion that he was not telling her the truth, or at any rate not the whole truth. Determined, however, to drive him as far as possible, she asked innocently, while pretending to be absorbed in the selection of cherries from a basket of fruit: 'Where is she buried? In the chapel?'

The cardinal choked as if he had swallowed a mouthful the wrong way but it seemed to Marianne that his subsequent fit of coughing was not altogether accidental and that it was designed to cover up the sudden flush which coloured his cheeks. However, she smiled prettily and offered him a glass of water.

'Drink this. It will help.'

'Thank you. Her grave – hmm – no, there is not one.'

'No grave?'

'No. Lucinda died tragically in a fire. Her body was never recovered. No doubt there is, somewhere in the chapel, an inscription – er – commemorating the fact. Now, do you care to step outside and look at your new estate? The weather is perfect and the park is looking its best. There are the stables, too. You will certainly be impressed by them. You used to be so fond of horses as a child. Did you know that the animals here are of the same stock as those in the famous Imperial Riding School in Vienna? They are Lipizzaners. The Archduke Charles, who founded the famous stud at Lipizza in 1580, presented the Sant'Anna of the period with a stallion and two mares. Ever since then, the princes of this house have devoted themselves to the perfecting of the breed.'

Once the cardinal had begun on this subject it was impossible to stem the flow, much less to bring him back to one which, like Dona Lavinia, he clearly preferred to avoid. This flood of eloquence was intended to prevent Marianne from getting a word in and at the same time give her thoughts another direction. In this it was to some extent successful for as soon as the two of them entered the vast stable yard, Marianne temporarily forgot the mysterious Lucinda in abandonment to her lifelong passion for horses. She found, too, that her coachman, Gracchus-Hannibal Pioche, was there before her, apparently as happy as a pig in clover. Although he spoke no Italian, he had succeeded in making himself perfectly understood with his Parisian street urchin's capacity for mime. He was already friends with all the grooms and stable lads who instantly recognized a fellow worshipper at the shrine of the horse.

'This place is heaven, Mademoiselle Marianne!' he exclaimed joyfully as soon as he set eyes on her. 'I never saw finer animals!'

'Well, if you want to be allowed in here much longer, young man,' the cardinal observed, half-angry, half-amused, 'you will have to learn to say your highness – or even your serene highness, if you prefer.'

Gracchus blushed violently and stammered: 'Ser – you'll have to be patient with me, mad – I mean your highness. I'm not sure I'll find it easy to get it right first off.'

'Just call me madame, Gracchus, and that will do very well. Now, show me the horses.'

They were in truth magnificent, full of fire and blood, with powerful shoulders and strong, slender legs. Nearly all of them had pure white coats. A few were pitch black, but no less beautiful. Marianne had no need to feign admiration. She had an excellent eye for the points of a horse and within an hour had succeeded in convincing all the inhabitants of the stables that the new Princess was altogether worthy of the family. Her beauty did the rest and by the time she returned to the villa, late in the afternoon, Marianne left behind her one small world irrevocably won, much to the cardinal's satisfaction.

'Do you realize what you are going to mean to them? A real, live mistress, someone visible who can understand them. Your coming is a real relief to them.'

'I am glad of it, although they will have to continue to do without me for a great part of the time. You know that I must go back to Paris – if only to explain my new position to the Emperor. You do not know him in his rages.'

'I can imagine it. But you are under no compulsion to go. If you were to remain here ...'

'He would be quite capable of sending an armed guard to fetch me, just as he escorted you – or your double – to Rheims. No, I thank you. I have always preferred to stand and fight and this time I mean to explain myself in person.'

'What you mean is that you would not for the world lose this opportunity of seeing him again.' The cardinal sighed. 'You are still in love with him.'

'Have I ever denied it?' Marianne retorted proudly. 'I do not think I ever pretended otherwise. Yes, I do love him still. I may regret it as much as you, although for different reasons, but I love him and that is all there is to it.'

'I know. We need not quarrel about that again. There are times when you put me very much in mind of your Aunt Ellis. The same impatience and the same relish for a fight! And the same generosity. Never mind. I know you will come back here, and that is what matters.'

The sun was going down behind the trees in the park and Marianne watched its descent with a sense of foreboding. The coming of twilight wrapped the domain in an indefinable sadness, as if life as well as light were being withdrawn.

Marianne shivered suddenly as they made their way back to the house and hugged the muslin shawl that went with her simple white dress more closely about her shoulders. Walking slowly beside the cardinal, she stared up at the white mass of the house as it loomed up before them. They were approaching it now from the right, the side where Prince Corrado had his apartments. The tall windows were dark. Possibly the curtains were already drawn but if so no chink of light showed through.

'Do you think,' she said suddenly, 'that I ought to thank the Prince for the jewels he sent me this morning? Surely it would be the merest politeness?'

'No. It would be a mistake. As far as Corrado is concerned, they are rightfully yours. You are their keeper, in much the same way as the French king was keeper of the crown jewels. One does not return thanks for such a charge.'

'But the emeralds —'

'Are doubtless a personal gift – to the Princess Sant'Anna. You will wear them, display them – and hand them on to your descendants. No, it is useless to try and approach him. I am sure he does not wish for it. If you would please him, wear the jewels he has given you. That will be the best way to show him your pleasure.'

For dinner that night, which she took sitting opposite the cardinal in the vast dining-room, Marianne clasped a large, antique brooch of pearls and rubies in a gold setting to the low-cut bosom of her high-waisted dress. Heavy, matching ear-rings hung from her ears. But although she kept glancing discreetly at the ceiling throughout the meal she saw no sign of movement and no eyes watching her, and she was surprised to note a small pang of disappointment. She knew that she was looking beautiful and she would have liked her beauty to be a silent tribute to her unseen husband, a kind of thank you. But she saw no one, not even Matteo Damiani on whom she had not set eyes all that day. When she met Dona Lavinia later, on her return to her own room, a question sprang naturally to her lips.

'Has the Prince gone away?'

'Why, no, your highness. Why should you think so?'

'I have seen no sign of his presence all day, not even his secretary or Father Amundi.'

'Matteo has been seeing some tenants at some distance and the chaplain has been with his highness. He rarely leaves his own apartments, unless for the chapel or the library. Do you desire me to inform Matteo that you wish to see him?'

'By no means,' Marianne said, rather too quickly. 'I was merely asking.'

That night in bed she found it hard to sleep and lay for several hours unable to close her eyes. Round about midnight, just as she was beginning at last to fall into a doze, she heard a horse galloping across the park and roused for a moment to listen. Then, reflecting that it was most probably Matteo Damiani returning home, she relaxed and, closing her eyes, fell into a deep sleep.

The next few days passed quietly, in much the same way as the first. Marianne explored the estate, accompanied by the cardinal, and drove out several times to see the surrounding countryside in one of the many carriages which belonged to the villa. She paid a visit to the baths of Lucca, and also to the gardens of the Grand Duchess Elisa's sumptuous villa at Marlia. The cardinal, dressed in plain black, attracted little attention but Marianne's beauty aroused admiration and a good deal of curiosity, for the news of the marriage had spread fast. People in the villages and country lanes came out to catch a glimpse of her, bowing deeply as she passed and regarding her with an admiration touched with compassion that drew a smile from Gauthier de Chazay.

'Do you know, they look on you practically as a saint?'

'Me? A saint? How absurd!'

'The general belief in these parts is that Corrado Sant'Anna is a desperately sick man. They are impressed that you, who are so young and beautiful, should give yourself to one so afflicted. When the birth of the child is announced you will be hailed almost as a martyr.'

'How can you make a joke of it!' Marianne was shocked by the prelate's lightly cynical tone.

'My dear child, if one is to get through life without being too much hurt, the best way is to look for the funny side of things. Besides, it was necessary for you to know the reason why they regard you in this way. Now it is done.'

Most of Marianne's time, however, was spent in the stables, despite the cardinal's remonstrances. He did not consider the stables a proper place for a great lady, besides which it alarmed him that in her condition she should spend long hours in the saddle, mounting each animal in turn in order to discover at first hand its merits and defects. Marianne laughed at his fears. She was in the best of health. No sickness troubled her, and the open-air life suited her to perfection. Rinaldo, the head groom, followed her everywhere, like a large dog, as with the skirts of her habit flung over her arm (she had not dared to adopt the masculine dress which she preferred for riding for fear of causing a scandal), she tramped for miles over the fields where the horses were pastured.

On her return from these exhausting treks, she would eat a hearty dinner and then tumble into bed to sleep like a child until sunrise. Even the curious sadness which descended on the villa each night with the gathering darkness no longer affected her. The Prince had made no further sign, except for a message to express his delight at her interest in his horses, and Matteo Damiani appeared to be keeping his distance. On those occasions when he chanced to meet Marianne, he merely bowed deeply, inquired after her health, and then effaced himself.

The week slipped by, swiftly and without incident, and so pleasantly that she was hardly aware of it until it dawned on her at last that she was not particularly anxious to return to Paris. The deadly weariness of the journey, the unbearable nervous tension, her agonies and fears had all vanished.

'After all,' she thought, 'why not stay here for a little while? There is nothing for me to do in Paris. The Emperor is unlikely to return for some time.'

Even Napoleon's honeymoon journey had ceased to trouble her. She was at peace with herself and so thoroughly enjoying the tranquillity of her new home that it even crossed her mind to spend the whole summer there and write to Jolival to join her.

But the end of the week brought the Abbé Bichette, back at last from his mysterious mission, and with him came a change. The cardinal, who had shown himself the most delightful and affectionate of companions, was closeted for hours on end with his secretary. He emerged wearing a deep frown, to inform Marianne that he was called away and must leave her.

'Must you really go?' she said, feeling disappointed. 'I was hoping that we should be able to prolong our stay here. It was so good to be together. But, since you are going, I will pack also.'

'But why? I shall only be away for a few days. Can you not wait for me here? I, too, have enjoyed being with you like this, Marianne. Why should we not make it last a little longer? When I return, I shall certainly be able to give you another week.'

'What shall I do here without you?'

The cardinal laughed. 'Why, just as you have done with me. Don't you think it might be a good idea to grow accustomed to, well, to reigning alone? It seemed to me that you enjoyed yourself here.'

'Yes, indeed, but ...'

'Well? Can you wait a few days for me? Five or six, at most. Is that really too much?'

'No.' Marianne smiled, 'I will wait for you. But next time, when you go, I shall go too.'

On this understanding, the cardinal left the villa that afternoon accompanied by the Abbé Bichette, as busy as ever and still bowed beneath a load of secrets, real or imaginary. But almost as soon as the carriage had rolled out through the gates Marianne was regretting her decision to stay. All the oppressive sensations of the first day returned, as if only the cardinal's presence had been keeping them at bay.

Turning, she saw Agathe standing behind her, her eyes full of tears. When she expressed surprise at this, Agathe clasped her hands together piteously.

'Aren't we going to go away as well?'

'Why should we? Aren't you happy here? I thought that Dona Lavinia was being very kind to you?'

'Oh yes. She is kindness itself. I am not frightened of her.'

'Of whom then?'

Agathe gestured vaguely, taking in the whole house.

'Of all this – this house which gets so sad at night, the silence when the fountains are turned off and the shadows that make you think something is going to jump out at you, and of his highness that no one ever sees – and the steward!'

Marianne frowned, disconcerted to find that her own uneasiness was shared by her maid, but she forced herself to answer lightly to avoid adding to Agathe's fears.

'Matteo? What has he done to you?'

'Nothing – but I feel as if he is stalking me. It's the way he has of looking at me when we meet, brushing against my dress when he passes by. I'm scared of him, my lady! I want to go away.'

Agathe was looking very white-faced and, remembering her own sensations, Marianne tried to laugh away her alarms.

'Come, Agathe, there is nothing so very dreadful in that. You won't tell me this is the first time a man has made up to you? I seem to recall that you were not short of admirers in Paris. What about the butler at the Hôtel de Beauharnais? Or even our own Gracchus? And you did not appear to mind them?'

'In Paris it was different,' Agathe persisted, her eyes downcast. 'Here, it is all so funny, not like other places. And that man scares me,' she added obstinately.

'Well, you had better tell Gracchus. He will look after you, and stop you worrying. Would you like me to speak to Dona Lavinia?'

'No – she will only think I am being foolish.'

'And she would be right! A pretty girl should be able to take care of herself. Don't worry, anyway, we shall not be here much longer. His Eminence is coming back in a few days, but only for a short while this time, and when he goes away again so shall we.'

All the same, Agathe's fears had infected Marianne, adding to the uneasiness which she already felt. She did not like the idea of Matteo Damiani hanging round Agathe. He was a fine figure of a man and did not look his age, but the fact remained that he was well past fifty and Agathe not yet twenty. She made up her mind to put a stop to it, discreetly, but with the greatest firmness.

That evening, feeling unequal to dining alone in the huge dining-room, she gave orders that she should be served in her room. She begged Dona Lavinia to keep her company and put her to bed while Agathe took a turn about the park, with Gracchus for protection, on the excuse that the girl was looking peaked. But as soon as Marianne broached the subject which was occupying her mind the housekeeper seemed to retreat into herself like a sensitive plant.

'Your Highness must forgive me,' she said, with evident embarrassment, 'but I cannot undertake to say anything to Matteo Damiani.'

'Why ever not? Surely you are the person who has always had charge of the household, the servants and the running of the house?'

'That is so – but Matteo's position here is a special one and it is not for me to interfere in his concerns. For one thing, he is not a man to take kindly to criticism and, for another, he is deep in his highness's confidence, for he too served the Prince's parents. If I were to venture to offer the smallest hint, I should get nothing but a scornful laugh and a recommendation to mind my own business.'

'Indeed?' Marianne gave a tiny laugh. 'I imagine that I need have no such fears, however privileged the fellow may be.'

'Oh, your highness —!'

'Well, go and fetch him to me. We shall see who will have the last word. Agathe is my personal maid, she came with me from France and I will not have her life made a misery. Go, Dona Lavinia, and bring the steward to me at once.'

The housekeeper sank into a deep curtsey and departed, to return a few minutes later, but alone. She said that Matteo was nowhere to be found. He was not with the Prince or anywhere else in the house. It might be that he had been detained in Lucca, where he often had occasion to go, or at one of the farms …

Dona Lavinia spoke very fast, her words falling over one another, like a woman trying to sound convincing, but the more reasons she produced for the steward's absence, the less Marianne believed her. Something told her that Matteo was not far away but that he did not wish to come.

'Very well,' she said at last. 'We will forget it for tonight, since he is not to be found, but tomorrow morning we shall see. Let him know that I shall expect him here first thing, or I shall ask the Prince – my husband to listen to me.'

Dona Lavinia said nothing but looked increasingly unhappy. While she performed Agathe's task of unpinning her mistress's black hair and brushing it for the night, Marianne could feel that her hands, usually so deft, were trembling. But she did not take pity on her. On the contrary, in an effort to shed some light on the mystery surrounding this unassailable steward, she did her best to press Dona Lavinia, almost cruelly, questioning her closely about Damiani's family and his connection with the Prince's parents. Dona Lavinia twisted and turned, returning such evasive answers that in the end Marianne was goaded into begging the housekeeper to go away and leave her to put herself to bed. Dona Lavinia made no secret of her relief and hurried from the room without waiting to be asked twice.

Left alone, Marianne took two or three restless turns about the room before she flung off her dressing-gown, blew out the candles and threw herself down on her bed. Ever since that morning, the country had been basking in a heat-wave and darkness had brought very little relief. Despite the cooling effect of the many fountains, the heat, heavy and stifling, had during the day invaded the villa's large rooms and now it clung to the skin until Marianne, stretched out under the gilded hangings of her bed, was drenched with perspiration.

At last, she sprang out of bed and drew back the curtains, flinging the windows wide open in the hope of a little relief from the feverish heat. The gardens, bathed in white moonlight, looked magical and unreal, deserted but for the musical rustle of the fountains. The shadows of the great trees stretched deep black over the colourless grass. Beyond the gardens, the countryside lay wrapped in silence, all nature seemed turned to stone. That night, the whole world seemed dead.

Marianne's throat was parched and she was just about to go back to her bed to pour herself a glass of water from the carafe on her night table when she stopped suddenly and turned back to the window. The distant sound of galloping hooves had reached her ears, a soft drumming that came slowly nearer, growing louder and sounding clearer. Something like white lightning flashed out from a grove of trees. In a moment, Marianne's sharp eyes had recognized Ilderim, the finest stallion in the stables and the most difficult to mount, a snow white thoroughbred of unbelievable beauty but capricious temper whom, for all her skill, she had not yet dared to try. She could see now the dark shape of a rider on his back but could not recognize him. He seemed tall and well-made but at that distance it was difficult to be sure of anything. One thing was certain: it was not Matteo Damiani or Rinaldi or any of the grooms. A second later, horse and rider had crossed the expanse of turf and were swallowed up once more in the shadow of the trees. The rhythmic hammering of the hooves died away and ceased altogether. But Marianne had had time to marvel at the rider's incomparable horsemanship. The dark, ghostly figure on the white horse had seemed one with his mount. Proud Ilderim recognized his master.

A sudden thought entered Marianne's mind and settled there, tormenting her until, unable to wait until morning for an answer, she strode over to the bell-rope hanging by her bedside and tugged it furiously, as if it were a matter of life and death. Dona Lavinia appeared almost at once, clad in her shift and a nightcap on her head, quite clearly terrified and fearing the worst. Finding Marianne out of bed and to all appearances perfectly cool, she let out a sigh of relief.

'Dear God, you frightened me! I thought your highness must be ill —'

'Do not alarm yourself, Dona Lavinia, I am quite well. I am truly sorry to have woken you but I want you to tell me something, at once, and as clearly as you can.'

The candle in Lavinia's hand trembled so violently that she was obliged to set it down.

'What is it you wish to know, my lady?'

Marianne gestured towards the open window by which she still stood and her eyes fixed themselves imperiously on the housekeeper's face which had turned chalk white in the moonlight.

'You know quite well, Dona Lavinia, what it is I wish to know, or you would not look so pale. Who was the man I saw just now, riding like the wind across the park? The horse he rode was Ilderim, whom I have not so far known anyone to mount. Tell me, who was he?'

'My lady – I —'

The unfortunate woman seemed scarcely able to stand. She clutched at a chair back for support but Marianne advanced on her relentlessly and seized her arm in a painful grip.

Who – was – it?'

'P-prince Corrado.'

Marianne's pent-up breath was released in a long sigh. She felt no surprise. Ever since she had first set eyes on the blurred figure of the rider, she had been prepared for this answer. But Dona Lavinia had dropped into a chair, and was weeping softly, her head in her hands. At the sight of her grief, Marianne was instantly filled with remorse and fell on her knees beside her, trying desperately to calm her.

'Calm yourself, Dona Lavinia. I did not mean to hurt you by questioning you like that, but you must see how dreadful it is for me to find myself amid all this mystery!'

'I know – I do understand,' sobbed Lavinia. 'I knew, of course, that some night you were bound to see him and to ask me, but I hoped – God knows what I hoped.'

'That I would not remain long enough to see him, perhaps?'

'Perhaps. But it was a childish hope, because sooner or later … You see, my lady, he goes out like this nearly every night. He gallops for hours on

Ilderim whom only he can mount. It is his greatest joy – the only one he permits himself.' The housekeeper's voice broke. Marianne took both her hands and held them gently.

'Surely, he is too hard on himself, Dona Lavinia?' she said softly. 'The man I saw is not crippled or an invalid, if he were he could not ride Ilderim. He did not seem to me in any way abnormal. I thought he looked tall and, to all appearances, strong. Why should he hide himself like this, why condemn himself to this dreadful seclusion, why bury himself alive?'

'Because it is impossible for it to be otherwise. Impossible! Believe me, Princess, it is no morbid love of mystery or any wish to be eccentric which makes my poor boy hide himself from the world like this. It is because he cannot help himself.'

'But, the person I caught a glimpse of was in no way repulsive. He looked – he looked perfectly normal.'

'Perhaps it is – otherwise with his face.'

'That could only be an excuse. I have seen men with ghastly faces, disfigured by injuries, men one could hardly bear to look at, yet they still lived openly. I have even known men to wear masks,' she added, remembering Morvan and his scarred face.

'Corrado wears one when he goes out like this. Darkness and the shadow of a hat and cloak he does not think enough to hide him. But in the full light of day, even the mask would not be enough. I beg you, my lady, believe me, and do not try to find out, or to see him. He – he might die of shame!'

'Of shame?'

Dona Lavinia rose, painfully, and drew Marianne to her feet also. She was no longer crying and her face had become very calm. She seemed in some way relieved to have spoken. Looking Marianne straight in the eyes, she continued, with great earnestness: 'You see, Corrado is the victim of a curse which once fell on this house that was formerly so strong and powerful, a curse that bore the face of an angel. Only the child that you will give him can exorcise it, not Corrado himself, for his sufferings there is no cure, but at least the house of Sant'Anna, so that it may shine once more among men. Good night, your highness. Try and forget what you have seen.'

This time, Marianne, defeated, did not insist. She let Dona Lavinia go without a word. She felt wearied to her very soul, and utterly depressed. The mystery of Corrado filled her whole being, obsessed her, like an insoluble torment. Her excited curiosity urged her to commit the wildest follies, such as hiding where she could watch the phantom horseman ride by or throwing herself under Ilderim's hooves so as to force him to stop. But something she could not explain held her back. It might have been Dona Lavinia's words: 'He might die of shame...', words as heavy with sadness as the voice that spoke out of the depth of the mirror.

To soothe her nerves and cool her burning head, she went into the bathroom and bathed her face and hands and sprinkled her whole body with eau-de-Cologne but when she lay down again sleep still refused to come. The oppressive heat and the thoughts that jangled wildly in her head drove it relentlessly away. Her ear was still tuned to the vague sounds of the night, listening for the distant sound of a horse galloping. But the hours passed and no sound came until at last Marianne sank, exhausted, into a kind of torpid doze that was neither sleep nor waking. Strange images passed through her mind, as in a dream, and yet it seemed to her that she was not asleep. There were vague, cloudy forms and sometimes the characters on the ceiling seemed to have come down to dance around her, grinning and gibbering, or strange, unnatural flowers leaned over her and turned into faces, and then it was the wall of her bedchamber that opened suddenly to reveal a head, and the head belonged to Matteo Damiani …

Marianne woke abruptly with a cry. The final impression had been so strong that it had ripped through the mists of sleep and jerked her back into reality, gasping and pouring with sweat. She sat up in bed, tossed back the long, damp strands of hair that had fallen over her face and stared about her. Dawn was breaking, filling her room with a pale, mauve light that was already beginning to be tinged with the rosy colour of sunrise. Away in the countryside, cocks were beginning to crow, their harsh cries taken up from one farm to the next. Cool air was coming in from the garden and Marianne felt suddenly chilled in her damp bed with her nightshirt clinging to her body. She got up to take it off and find a dry one and a dressing-gown, when suddenly her eyes fell on the place where, in her nightmare, she had seen Matteo's head appear and she uttered a cry of amazement. There, just below the gilt edge of one of the mirrors, was a dark line on the wall, a dark line she had never seen before.

Making no more sound than a cat in her bare feet, Marianne crept up to it with a pounding heart, and felt a faint draught. The panel yielded quietly to her hand, revealing the black opening of a narrow spiral stair, cut in the thickness of the wall.

At once, everything fell into place in her mind. So she had not been dreaming! As she lay there half-asleep, she really had seen Matteo Damiani's face look through that opening. But why? What did he want? How many times already had he dared to come into her room like this while she slept? At that moment, she recalled the face which she had caught sight of in the mirror on the night of her wedding, while she was undressing. So that, too, had not been a dream! He had indeed been there, and at the recollection of the naked lust in his face, Marianne's own cheeks flushed scarlet, with anger as much as injured modesty. She was seized with a furious rage. So, not content with persecuting Agathe, that vile creature had dared to enter her room, the room of his own master's wife, and pry into her most private moments! What was his object in creeping in like a thief in the night? What mad act might he not have committed one day, this very morning perhaps, if she had not discovered the panel which, in his hurried retreat, no doubt, he had forgotten to close properly.

'I'll make sure he never wants to try it again,' she muttered furiously. Without stopping to think, she slipped on a dress at random, pushed her feet into a pair of light sandals and quickly tied the strings, then went to her portmanteau and fetched one of the pistols which Napoleon had given her and which she had brought with her from Paris. One swift check to make sure of the priming and she slid it into her belt and lighted a candle. Thus armed, she marched determinedly to the still-open panel and began to descend.

The draught made the candle flame waver but did not extinguish it. Carefully, without making the smallest sound, she descended the worn steps, protecting the candle flame with her free hand. The stairway was quite short, no more than a single storey. It came out at the back of the house, the exit masked by thick, leafy bushes. Peering through the branches, Marianne was suddenly aware of the calm waters of the grotto stretching before her, rosy in the dawn. She also saw Matteo just disappearing into the cavern, the entrance to which lay within the central colonnade. She determined to follow him. Quickly blowing out the candle, she set it down under the bushes ready to pick up on her return.

Her anger was touched now with the excitement of the chase, and a certain feeling of triumph. She did not know what the steward was about, but she knew that he would be caught there in a trap and could not escape her now. She was familiar with the grotto for she had explored it with her godfather. It was a pleasant place in hot weather. The lake continued inside the grotto, making a kind of room with a pool in the centre. The rock walls of the cavern had been hung with silk and carpets and cushions set out around the pool in oriental profusion.

Marianne sprang lightly in pursuit of the steward. She ran along the colonnade, pausing for a moment at the entrance to the cave to flatten herself against the rocky wall and draw her pistol from her belt. Slowly, with infinite caution, she crept forward and turned the corner. Then she gave a gasp of astonishment. Not only was there no one in the cave, but one of the silken panels that covered the walls had been lifted to reveal the entrance to a tunnel which seemed to pass right through the hill, for there was a glimpse of daylight at the end.

Not hesitating for an instant, only tightening her grip a little on the weapon in her hand, Marianne stepped into the tunnel. It was quite wide and the floor was covered with a fine sand, pleasant to walk on and silent underfoot. Little by little, some of her anger had faded, giving way to excitement, the kind of excitement she had felt out with the hounds at Selton, but here she was dealing with something more dangerous than any fox and the nearness of danger filled her with exaltation. There was also the thought that she had, in so short a time, begun to penetrate some of the secrets of the Sant'Annas. But when she reached the end of the passage, she stood, pressed close to the rock in the shadow of the opening, staring at the spectacle which met her eyes.

The tunnel opened into a narrow clearing, no more than a steep cleft in the rocks, closed in at the top on both sides by a tangled mass of trees and undergrowth. Down below, leaning at crazy angles in niches cut in the rock walls, was a weird population of statuary, clothed in brambles and rampant bines, their limbs frozen in attitudes of frantic gesticulation which gave a tragic emphasis to the burnt-out ruins of a building that occupied the centre of the dell.

Nothing was left but a confused heap made up of stumps of charred and broken columns, tumbled stones and shattered carvings, all overgrown with matted brambles and bitter-smelling ground ivy. The fire which had destroyed it must have been uncommonly fierce, for rubble and rock walls alike showed the long, blackened streaks caused by the flames. Yet, standing among the ruins, as though preserved by a miracle, was a single, gleaming statue of pure white marble. Marianne caught her breath in wonder at the scene.

A few steps had been roughly hacked out of the pile of ruins and on the top step, kneeling with both arms clasped about the knees of the statue, was Matteo Damiani.

The statue itself was the strangest and most beautiful that Marianne had ever seen. It was the life-sized figure of a naked woman, shaped with such sheer, sensual perfection as to be almost demoniacal in its beauty. The woman was standing with her arms spread backwards, away from her body; her head was flung back, as if drawn by the weight of her unbound hair and she seemed, with her closed eyes and parted lips, as if on the point of giving herself to some unseen lover. The sculptor had rendered every detail of the female form with an uncanny accuracy and the skill with which he had delineated the features, the narrowed eyes and voluptuously swollen lips, an ecstasy of pleasure so agonizing that it was almost pain, was close to genius. Disturbed by that breathing image of desire, Marianne thought that the artist must have loved his model with a torturing intensity.

The sun was rising and one golden beam slipped over the cliff and lighted on the statue. At once the cold marble glowed and came to life. The polished grain of the unfeeling stone took on a golden sheen, softer than any human skin, and for a moment it seemed to Marianne that the statue was truly living. Matteo had risen to his feet and was standing on the pedestal, clasping the marble woman in his arms. He was kissing the lips that offered themselves in a frenzy of passion, as if he were trying to infuse his own warmth into them, and murmuring an incoherent stream of words, words in which insults and endearments were strangely mixed, a curious litany of love and rage and the crudest expressions of lust. At the same time his hands roved feverishly over the marble body which seemed, in the warm light of morning, to be quivering in response to his caresses.

There was something so unnerving about this love scene with a statue that Marianne stepped back with an instinctive revulsion into the tunnel, forgetting that she had come there to confront the man and cow him. The pistol hung uselessly from her shaking hand and she restored it to her belt. The man was mad, there could be no other explanation of his insane behaviour, and Marianne was suddenly afraid. She was alone with a madman in a secret place which might well be unknown to most of the inhabitants of the villa. Even the weapon she carried seemed a puny defence. Matteo's strength was certainly prodigious. If he once realized her presence, he could overpower her before she had a chance to defend herself. Or else she would be compelled to shoot, and she did not wish to kill him. She had suffered enough, and suffered even now, from having involuntarily caused the death of Ivy St Albans.

She could hear the man making delirious promises to return that night to his insensate mistress.

'The moon will be full, my she-devil, and you shall see that I have not forgotten.'

Marianne's heart leaped. He was coming away, he would find her. Without waiting for more, she fled back along the tunnel and out through the cavern and the grotto with the speed of a hunted hare. She darted in amongst the bushes but turned, before plunging into the staircase passage, to take one last look through the leaves. She was only just in time. Matteo was coming out of the grotto and once again Marianne asked herself if she had not been dreaming. The man who a moment before she had surprised in a state of total erotic frenzy was now strolling quietly along the path that lay between the colonnade and the water, his hands clasped behind his back and his coarse features seemingly lifted to enjoy the light breeze that ruffled his grey hair. He might have been anyone taking an early morning walk in the cool, dew-fresh gardens before starting the day's work.

Marianne ran quickly up the stairs and stepped through the open panel but before she closed it again, she took careful note of its inner and outer workings. It was, in fact, possible to open it from either side, by means of a handle on the stair or by pressing a boss on the gilded moulding within the room. Then, seeing that it was nearly time for Agathe to bring her morning tea, she slipped hurriedly out of her dress and sandals and got into bed. The last thing Marianne wanted was for Agathe to find out about this morning's expedition.

Snuggling down among the pillows, she tried to think calmly but this was not easy. The discovery, in quick succession, of the secret panel in the wall and then of the temple in the dell, the statue and Matteo's madness was enough to overcome a far more robust nervous system than Marianne's. In addition, there was that curious and highly ominous assignation he had made with his marble mistress. What was the meaning of his strange words? What was it he had not forgotten? What did he mean to do that night in the ruins? Most of all, what was that monument, gutted by fire, on whose ruins the statue stood? A villa? A temple? To what cult had it been dedicated, and was perhaps dedicated still? To what dark ritual of madness did Matteo Damiani mean to offer sacrifice that night?

Marianne turned all these questions over in her mind without finding the slightest answer. At one moment, she thought of questioning Dona Lavinia again, but she knew that her questions caused the poor woman pain and she would hardly have recovered from the previous night's ordeal. Besides, it was quite possible that she knew nothing, either of the steward's insanity or of the strange goddess to whom he meant to make his secret sacrifice. She wondered whether even the Prince knew how his steward and secretary passed his nights and, if he did, whether he would answer her questions, even supposing that she were able to ask them. Perhaps the best way was still to question Matteo himself, although this would naturally have to be done cautiously. In any case, she had ordered Dona Lavinia the night before to send him to her first thing in the morning.

'Well, we shall see,' she muttered under her breath.

Her mind made up, Marianne swallowed the scalding tea which Agathe brought in at that moment, then got up and dressed. The day promised to be as hot as yesterday and she selected a morning dress of sulphur-yellow jaconet embroidered with a design of big, white daisies and a pair of matching slippers. Dressing in light, gay colours seemed to her a good way of combating the unpleasant memories of the night. Then, when Dona Lavinia came in to tell her that the steward was awaiting her pleasure, she made her way to the small sitting room adjoining her bedchamber and rang for him to be admitted.

She sat at a small desk and watched him enter, doing her best to conceal her dislike of him. The scene in the dell was still too fresh in her mind for her to feel anything but distaste but if she wanted to find out anything it was necessary to control herself. He appeared in no way disconcerted at her summons and anyone seeing him, standing before her in a deferential attitude, would have sworn that he was a model servant and not a man so base that he could steal, like a thief, into the very same woman's bedchamber while she lay helplessly asleep.

To keep her fingers from trembling, Marianne had picked up a long goose quill from the desk and was fiddling with it absent-mindedly. When she said nothing, Matteo took it on himself to open the conversation.

'Your highness sent for me?'

She glanced up indifferently.

'Yes, Signor Damiani, I sent for you. You are the steward of this estate and I imagine there is very little you do not know about it?'

He smiled faintly. 'I think I may claim to know it, yes.'

'Then you will be able to tell me. Yesterday afternoon was so hot that even the gardens were stifling. I sought refuge, and coolness, in the grotto…' She paused, her eyes never wavering from the steward, and thought that she saw his thick lips tighten a little. With a pretence at carelessness, but measuring every word, she went on: 'I noticed that one of the hangings was a little awry and that a draught was coming through. I found that there was an opening behind it. I should not be a woman if I were not inquisitive and I entered the passage, and found the remains of some burnt-out monument.'

She had deliberately refrained from mentioning the statue but this time she was sure that Matteo had paled under his tan. There was a darkling look in his eyes as he answered:

'I see. Permit me to tell your highness that the Prince would not be pleased to know that you had discovered the little temple. For him, it is a forbidden subject, and it would be best for your highness —'

'I am the only judge of what is best for me, Signor Damiani. Naturally, the reason that I have spoken of this to you is because I do not intend to ask – to ask my husband about it, and with more reason if the subject is a disagreeable one to him. But you will answer me.'

'Why should I?' the steward retorted, more insolently than he may have meant.

'Because I am the Princess Sant'Anna, whether you like it or not.'

'I did not say —'

'Have the goodness not to interrupt me. When I ask a question, let me tell you, I expect an answer. All my servants,' she leaned a little on the word, 'know this. You have yet to learn it. Moreover, I fail to see why you should not give me an answer. If the place were not meant to be seen, if its associations for your master are unpleasant, why has the passage not been walled up?'

'His highness has not ordered —'

'And you never act without precise instruction, is that it?' Marianne spoke with heavy irony.

He stiffened but appeared to accept defeat. His eyes met hers, coldly.

'Very well. I am at your highness's service.'

Recognizing that she had won, she permitted herself the luxury of a smile.

'Thank you. Then just tell me about this "little temple" and, more particularly, about the woman whose statue stands among the ruins. It is an astonishing and magnificent piece of work. And do not tell me that it is antique because I shall not believe you.'

'Why should I not tell the truth? The statue, my lady, is that of Dona Lucinda, our Prince's grandmother.'

'Surely, she is somewhat, er, scantily clothed for a grandmother. They are not commonly found so in France.'

'No, but the Emperor's sisters are,' he said forcefully. 'Did not the Princess Borghese commission Canova to immortalize her beauty in stone? Dona Lucinda did likewise. You cannot conceive how beautiful she was! It was terrible, beyond bearing. And she knew how to use it, like a devil she knew. I have seen men at her feet, I have seen men go mad and kill themselves for her – even when she was forty-five years old and more! But she was possessed of the devil!'

Matteo was talking now, the words pouring out of him like a pent-up flood released and Marianne listened, fascinated, her loathing and resentment temporarily forgotten.

'You knew her?' she murmured softly.

He nodded and his eyes shifted slightly, as if her intent gaze irked him. Then he went on in a voice thick with anger.

'I was eighteen when she died – died by fire, burned to death in that temple which, in her folly, she had erected to her own glory. There, she used to entertain her lovers, most of them taken from among the peasantry, or sailors, for her worship of her own beauty was only equalled by her lusts.'

'But – why from the common people?'

He rounded on her at that, with sudden violence, his head lowered like a bull about to charge, and Marianne shivered for she heard the fires of hell roaring in his voice and guessed that Lucinda had ignited them.

'Because she could then dispose of them without awkward questions. There were men of her own rank who gratified her and them she kept, safe in the knowledge that they were her slaves and would not live without her. But how many young men vanished without trace after giving all their youth and ardour to the insatiable she-wolf in one night of love? No one – no one can imagine what that woman was like. She could awaken the basest instincts, the ultimate madness, and she liked to see death as the end of love. Perhaps, after all, the legend was right –'

'What legend?'

'Men said that her deathless beauty was the outcome of a pact with the devil. One night, as she was studying herself anxiously in the mirrors of her bedchamber, a handsome young man dressed in black appeared to her and offered her, in exchange for her soul, thirty years of unfading beauty, thirty years of pleasure and power. They say that she agreed but that time passed and she had made a fool's bargain because before the thirty years were up her servants entered her room one morning to find only a carcass, crawling with worms.'

Marianne sprang to her feet with a cry of horror but he gave her a contemptuous smile.

'It is only a legend, my lady. The truth was quite different for, as I told you. Dona Lucinda perished in the fire which ravaged the temple – a fire she lighted with her own hands the night she found a wrinkle at the corner of her mouth. I dare say, Princess, you may be wondering why she should choose so terrible a death. Well, I will tell you. She did not wish that marvellous body which she had cherished with such care to rot slowly in the ground with all the horrors of decay. She preferred to see it consumed by fire! That was a dreadful night. The fire burned so fiercely that the flames were seen far off and the peasants still swear in terror that it was the fires of hell opening for her. I can still hear her screams … like a wild beast howling … But I know that she is not wholly gone. She lives on.'

'What do you mean?' Marianne cried, struggling to shake off the horror which threatened to overwhelm her.

Matteo turned glazed eyes on her. He smiled, drawing his lips back over his strong, yellow teeth. His answer came in a voice of mysterious, incantatory power.

'She still walks in this house – in the gardens – in your chamber, here she used to stand, naked, watching herself in the mirrors, always comparing her beauty to that of the statue which she had placed there. She brought a curse to this place and she is watching over that curse, which is her revenge. You will not stop her!'

His tone changed abruptly. Almost obsequiously, he asked: 'Is there anything more your highness wishes to know?'

Marianne wrenched herself out of the spell in which the steward's words had held her enthralled. She coloured violently under the insolent gaze which seemed to be studying her boldly in every detail and, striving to hold her own, she returned his gaze haughtily and answered: 'Yes. Since she had such a predilection for peasants – were you also one of her lovers?'

He did not hesitate. With triumph in his voice, he answered her.

'Why, yes, my lady. And believe me, I can never forget the hours I owe her.'

Unable to control her anger any longer, Marianne merely indicated to him with a gesture that she had no further need of him. But, left alone, she sank down, prostrate, on her chair and remained so for a long time, fighting down the panic terror that filled her. All the beauty of the place where, for a short while, she had found peace and happiness had been destroyed, smirched, and defiled by the memory of the she-devil who had left her mark on it. The recollection of the dark figure of the man bestriding Ilderim in the night made her heart ache with pity; it seemed to her that between the Prince and the curse which lay upon him, was an unceasing struggle, a battle lost and always recommenced. It took all her resolution not to send for her coach and her baggage at once and fly back to France without a moment's delay. Even the sound of the fountains now seemed charged with menace.

But she had promised to wait for the cardinal, and there was also the curious promise which Matteo had made to the ghost of Lucinda. Marianne meant to find out the exact nature of the promise and, if need be, to intervene. Could it, perhaps, be the means of exorcising the devil that haunted the house of Sant'Anna at last? Her eye fell on the family crest embroidered on the back of a chair and she was suddenly struck by the powerful symbol which it represented. The snake and the unicorn. The venomous, crawling beast, silent and deadly, and the creature of legend, clothed in white light. This strife must cease before her child was born. She did not mean him to rule a world in Lucinda's image. Her maternal instinct awoke, violently opposed to the slightest shadow on her child's future. She, Marianne, must make an end of the devils. Even if she had to risk her life to do it, she would be present that night to see what those ties were which bound Matteo to the evil dead. Afterwards, she would do as her conscience dictated, even if it meant forcing herself on her unseen husband.

Yet, when night returned to cover the villa and its gardens, all Marianne's heroic plans melted away before the most primitive of all terrors, the terror of the unknown perils that lurk in darkness. The thought of going back to that ill-omened glade, and looking again on that devilish statue now that she knew the truth, chilled her to the marrow. Never in all her life had she known such fear, not even in that moment after Francis Cranmere's escape when she feared for her own life. Francis was, after all, only a man, whereas Lucinda belonged to the unseen, immeasurable world of the supernatural.

In her fear of being obliged to meet the steward again, she had spent the better part of the day shut up in her own rooms. Not until the afternoon, when she had seen him set off in the direction of the main road, did she venture down to the stables and there she spent a long time meticulously examining Ilderim, as if by some sign the beautiful stallion could give her the key to the mystery of his master. She said nothing to Rinaldo who had watched with some surprise the Princess's long colloquy with the thoroughbred.

Indoors again, she had waited for the night in a state of utter indecision. Curiosity urged her to go back to the ruins of the unholy temple but all that Matteo had told her of Lucinda filled her with an uncontrollable disgust and she feared the sight of that shameless statue almost as much as that of the fanatical servant.

She partook of a light supper, soon over, and then allowed her women to undress her for the night, but she did not go to bed. Her rich bedchamber, her splendid bed, now filled her with horror. She seemed to see the statue still standing there and hardly dared to turn her eyes to the mirrors for fear of seeing the ghost of the evil Venetian woman reflected there. Although it was still very hot, she had had all the windows tightly closed and the curtains drawn, prompted by an impulse of childish terror of which she was secretly ashamed. She had stared for a long time at the moving panel and ended by piling up a table and some chairs in front of it, reinforced by a few heavy metal objects, such as candlesticks, so that it was quite impossible for anyone to open it from the other side without causing a resounding crash.

Before sending Agathe and Dona Lavinia away, she had requested the housekeeper to send Gracchus to her. Her idea had been to make her youthful coachman sleep on a mattress in the short passage connecting her room with Agathe's, but Gracchus, unaware of his mistress's terrors, had gone to spend the evening with Rinaldo, with whom he had struck up a great friendship, at the farmhouse where he lived on the far side of the estate. Marianne was obliged to deal with her fears alone, fears which a hundred times that day had sent her hand creeping to the bell to send for her coach. Her will had prevailed but now she was obliged to live through a night which seemed fraught with dangers. The few hours that must pass before the sun rose again seemed an eternity.

*The best thing I can do,* she told herself, *is to go to sleep, fast asleep. Then I shan't be tempted to go back to the glade.*

With this object, she had asked Dona Lavinia to make her some of the tisane which had worked so well the first night, but on the point of drinking it, she had set it back, untouched, on the table by her bed. Suppose she were to sleep too soundly even to hear the collapse of the barrier she had erected in front of the panel?

No, even if the night were to be a hideous nightmare, she must endure it all, with all her wits about her.

With a sigh, she laid both her pistols within reach of her pillow, picked up a book and settled back to try and read. The book was a moving novel by Monsieur de Châteaubriand telling of the love of two young Indians, Chactas and Atala. Marianne had been enjoying it very much but that night her mind was not on it. Her thoughts were wandering far away from the banks of the Meschacebé to the glade where some unspeakable ritual was to take place. Gradually, her old curiosity revived, insidious and tormenting. At last, she threw aside her book.

'This is impossible,' she said aloud. 'If this goes on, I shall go mad.'

She reached out and tugged at the bell which rang in Agathe's room, intending to ask the girl to come in and spend the night with her. With someone else there, she would be better able to combat her fears, and Agathe herself, still in a state of nerves, would be delighted to stay with her mistress. But although she rang again and again, no one came.

Thinking that the girl might have taken one of Dona Lavinia's potions, she got up and, slipping on a cotton dressing-gown and pushing her feet into a pair of slippers, she made her way to Agathe's room. Light was showing under the door and Marianne tapped softly, then, getting no answer, she turned the handle and went in. The room was empty.

A lighted candle stood on the bedside table but the bed itself was empty, the sheets lying half on the floor as if they had been dragged there as the maid got out of bed. Worried, Marianne glanced up at the bell communicating with her own room which hung above the bed. An exclamation of surprise and irritation escaped her: the bell had been effectively muffled with a cloth. This was too much. Not content with leaving her room in the middle of the night, Agathe had even had the effrontery to silence the bell. But where had she gone? Whom had she gone to meet? Not Gracchus, he was with Rinaldo, and certainly none of the other servants, for Agathe had little to do with any of them. When she was not with her mistress, she was hardly ever out of sight of Dona Lavinia, the only person in the house she trusted. As for —

On the point of going back to her own room, Marianne paused and, turning back towards the bed, stood thoughtfully regarding the curious condition of the sheets. That was precisely the way they would have fallen had the girl been lifted bodily out of her bed. No one dragged the bedclothes off like that getting out of bed in the ordinary way, but when a body was lifted, asleep or awake … Marianne's heart almost stopped beating as a terrible idea struck her. The muffled bell, the disordered bedclothes, the candle left burning – and there was a cup, too, on the table by the bed, an empty cup that still smelled faintly and unmistakably of the familiar tisane, and with it another, more subtle odour. Agathe had not gone of her own accord. She had been carried off, and Marianne shrank from guessing by whom.

She hesitated no longer. In the same instant, the fear which had been lurking in the pit of her stomach all evening vanished. She sped back to her room and began feverishly dismantling the barrier which stood before the panel. With a scarf tied hastily around her waist to confine her billowing robe, a candle in one hand and a pistol in the other, a second pistol stowed safely in her waistband, she descended the staircase for the second time.

This time, she accomplished the descent swiftly, without hesitation, buoyed up by a rage which banished even the most elementary caution. She had no need to blow out her candle when she reached the entrance: the wind did it for her. It had been rising steadily all evening but behind her curtained windows she had not been aware of it. It was also very much cooler. As she took a deep breath of the night air, she thought that it must have been raining somewhere. The sky was quite light, for the moon was full, but clouds were scudding across it, every now and then hiding the silver disc. The brooding silence had vanished. The park was alive with the rustling of numberless leaves and the creak of swaying branches.

Marianne plunged resolutely into the cave and hurried through it but in the passage underneath the hill she moved more slowly in order to make no sound. A red light showed from the clearing beyond. The draught in the passage chilled the air and Marianne shivered and clutched the thin cotton of her robe closely to her throat. As she approached the end of the tunnel, her heart began to beat faster but she settled the gun more firmly in her hand and, flattening herself against the wall, ventured to put her head outside. Instantly, it seemed to her that she had been transported back in time, out of the noisy, fast-moving era of Napoleon with all its military glories and its busy, bustling life, back into the darkest, medieval night.

The statue stood gleaming in the light of a pair of tall black wax candles. More light, the strange, ruddy glow she had seen from the tunnel, came from a pair of low vases which also gave off a powerful, acrid smoke. Between them, a kind of altar had been set up on the ruins. On it, motionless and apparently unconscious since she remained perfectly still although evidently unbound, lay the figure of a naked woman. A receptacle resembling a chalice stood on a small board laid across her stomach. With mingled horror and amazement, Marianne saw that it was Agathe. Even so, she managed to hold her breath, for the silence was so deep that it seemed as if the smallest sound would precipitate disaster.

Matteo was on his knees beside the motionless girl, but a Matteo whom Marianne hardly recognized. He was wearing a kind of long, black dalmatic decorated with weird signs and unfastened over his chest. There was a gold circlet on his grizzled locks. This was no longer the Prince of Sant'Anna's taciturn steward but a necromancer preparing to celebrate one of the most ancient and unhallowed rites of all time. Suddenly he began reciting Latin prayers at the sound of which Marianne was left in no more doubt as to what he was doing.

'The black mass!' The thought appalled her, and her eyes went from the kneeling man to the statue which, in that sinister light, seemed clothed in blood. Once, long ago, she had unearthed a dusty volume from a long-forgotten shelf in the library at Selton and read, with growing horror, the details of that abominable rite. Soon, when he had reached the end of his sacrilegious orisons, Matteo would offer up his chosen victim to his goddess who, here, stood in place of Satan himself. Having first possessed her, he would then sacrifice her, so much was clear from the long knife which lay, gleaming ominously, at Lucinda's feet.

Matteo seemed to have fallen into a kind of ecstasy. It was no longer possible to distinguish what he was saying. The words had degenerated into a form of mumbling chant which filled Marianne with horror. With eyes wide with dread, she saw him rise and remove the chalice which he set down beside him. She watched him covering the unconscious form with kisses. He seized hold of the knife and Marianne's senses swam but, by some miracle, her fear had gone. Leaving the shelter of the tunnel, she stepped out into the clearing, raised her right arm, took careful aim and fired.

The report seemed to fill the narrow space. Matteo sprang up, letting fall the knife, and gazed about him with a bewildered air. He was unhurt, for Marianne had aimed at the statue, but at the realization that the lower half of Lucinda's uplifted face had disappeared he uttered a dreadful, choking cry. He was about to spring at her, but pulled up short at the sound of Marianne's icy voice.

'Stay where you are, Matteo,' she said, throwing aside the now useless pistol and taking the other from her waist. 'I could have killed you, but I saw no reason to deprive your master of an excellent servant. However, I have another ball ready for you if you do not do as I say. As you have seen, I am not in the habit of missing. I have decapitated your she-devil there. The next will be for your own head. Carry Agathe away from here and put her back in her room. I shall not tell you twice.'

It did not seem that he had even heard her. He was on his hands and knees, crawling over the ruins, wild-eyed, slack-lipped, but struggling to get to his feet. He seemed to be in a trance, the sharp edges of the stones and the thorny brambles might not have existed for him. As he advanced towards her Marianne felt her flesh, shrinking at the thought that, to defend herself from this man she was going to be compelled to fire, almost at point blank range.

'Stop!' she commanded him. 'Go back, I tell you. Do you hear me, go back!'

He did not listen to her. He had succeeded in staggering to his feet and was lurching towards her, hands outstretched, still with that frightening, sleepwalker's face. Instinctively, Marianne stepped back, then back again, unable to bring herself to fire. It was as if a power stronger than her own will had paralysed her arm. Matteo, with his contorted face, his black robes and his torn and bleeding hands, truly resembled some demon cast up out of the pit. Marianne felt her strength ebbing. She took another step backwards, feeling behind her with her free hand for the entrance to the tunnel, but she must have changed direction without knowing it and met nothing but rampant weeds and branches. The undergrowth? Could she push through and hide? But even as she stepped back again, her foot struck against some obstacle and with a scream she staggered backwards into a bush. Still Matteo advanced, with outstretched hands. She saw him growing huge, out of all proportion. The pistol had slipped from her hand as she fell and Marianne gave herself up for lost.

She screamed again but the scream died in her throat. There was a sound like thunder and a fantastic apparition burst out of the thicket at the far end of the clearing. A tall white horse and black-clad rider, a rider who reared over Matteo with upraised whip, seeming enormous to the terrified girl. She screamed at the sight. Before consciousness left her, she had caught one glimpse of a broad hat brim and, below it, a blank face, white, dead and featureless, in which the eyes were black, glowing holes, a shapeless thing, hidden in the folds of a flying, black cloak. The rider mounted on Ilderim was a phantom, a spectre risen from the terrors of darkness about to ride her down ... Marianne gave one desperate moan and fainted.

Marianne never knew how long she remained unconscious. When she opened her eyes, with the sense of awakening from some interminable nightmare, she saw that she was in her own room, in her own bed, and as the mists cleared from her brain, she thought for a moment that it had indeed been nothing but a dream. Outside, a wind was blowing but everything else was quiet. Surely it had all been a bad dream: Agathe's room, the clearing, Matteo's insane attack on her and the fearsome rider bestriding Ilderim? The thought was deeply reassuring. It was all so strange. She must be suffering from an overactive imagination to have dreamed up that ghastly scene.

At that moment, Agathe was no doubt peacefully asleep in her own little bed, very far from thinking of the part that she had played in her mistress's nocturnal fantasies.

She decided that it would do her good to get up and wash her face in cold water. Her head felt heavy and her thoughts were still confused. But when she threw back the bedclothes, she realized that she was lying naked in her bed which had been strewn by some unknown hand with sprigs of sweet-smelling jasmine. Then she knew that she had not been dreaming. It was all true: the clearing and the black mass, the shot that she had fired at the statue, Matteo's murderous rage and the final irruption of the terrible horseman.

She felt her flesh creep and her hair stand on end at the memory. Was it he who had brought her back here? It could scarcely have been Matteo – Matteo had tried to kill her and she was sure that she had seen him go down beneath the rider's flailing whip. Then it was the Prince who had carried her back, who had undressed her and put her to bed – and who had strewn these fragrant blossoms about her unconscious and defenceless body – had even perhaps – no, that was impossible. Besides, why should he have done so when, according to his own word and the cardinal's, the last thing he desired was to make their marriage a reality? And yet, struggling desperately to pierce the mists that had enveloped her brain since she fainted, she seemed to find there a memory of kisses and caresses …

A wild feeling that was very close to panic jerked her from her bed. She wanted to escape, at all costs and at once, she wanted to leave this house where madness lurked in wait for her, and where her godfather's departure had left her a prey to all the perils of a house whose inhabitants made secrecy their daily bread. She wanted to go back to daylight and sunshine and the quiet countryside of France, less romantic perhaps but so much more comfortable. She wanted her pretty, peaceful house in the Rue de Lille, Arcadius's twinkling eyes, Napoleon's rages, yes, even that would seem wonderful now, even the threat of Francis Cranmere. Yes, anything rather than this atmosphere of morbid sensuality which seemed to be dragging her down and against which all her young, healthy soul revolted.

Without stopping to put on her clothes, she ran to Agathe's room for the second time that night and found, to her immense relief, that she too was back in her bed. She would waste no time on questions. Who had brought the girl back and what had become of Matteo were things that could be left unasked. She shook the girl so hard that at last she managed to bring her to some semblance of consciousness, but when Agathe, who was clearly still suffering from the effects of the drug, sat swaying in her bed, staring at her with eyes clouded with sleep, Marianne picked up the water jug from the dressing-table and flung the contents hard in Agathe's face. The girl jumped and spluttered, but finally came fully awake.

'At last!' Marianne cried. 'Get up, Agathe, and hurry. You must pack our things, and go and wake Gracchus and tell him to put the horses to at once!'

'But – ma – my lady…' the girl stammered, disturbed as much by the sight of a naked Marianne with her hair tumbling down her back as by the shock of finding herself rudely awakened in the middle of the night with a jug of water. 'My lady – are we going away?'

'This minute! I want us to be on the road by sunrise. Come along, up with you. Faster than that!'

While Agathe was extricating herself from her soaking bed, Marianne, possessed now by a furious energy, ran back to her room, and started emptying chests and cupboards, dragging out trunks from the box room and stuffing things inside pell-mell, just as they came to hand. By the time her maid appeared a few minutes later, dry and dressed, she found her working like a demon in the middle of the worst chaos she had ever seen. After one look, Agathe snatched up a dressing-gown and ran to wrap it round Marianne's bare shoulders.

'You'll catch your death of cold, my lady,' she said in a tone of strong disapproval, but dared ask no further questions.

'Thank you. Now, help me get these things into the trunks, or rather, no, go and wake Gracchus – no, on second thoughts, I'll go myself.'

But here Agathe rebelled. 'You can't do that, my lady! You just get dressed quietly while I go and find Gracchus. You can't be seen in the servants' quarters, going about in your dressing-gown! I'll send Dona Lavinia to help you.'

Much to Marianne's surprise, Agathe had scarcely left the room before the housekeeper appeared, fully dressed, as if she had not been to bed at all. It might have been the din raised by her mistress which had wakened her but she certainly showed no surprise at finding her surrounded by trunks and boxes and scattered heaps of clothes. Her curtsey was as calm and correct as if it had been eight or ten in the morning.

'Is your highness leaving us?' was all she said.

'Yes, Dona Lavinia. And I can't say you seem particularly surprised.'

The housekeeper's blue eyes surveyed Marianne's flushed countenance mildly. She smiled a little sadly.

'I have been afraid that it would be so, ever since his Eminence left us. Alone here, you could not help but wake the forces of evil which still hold sway over this house. There were too many things you wanted to know – and yours is the beauty that inspires tragedy. Do not take it amiss when I say that I am glad that you are going. It will be best for everyone.'

'What do you mean?' Marianne's brows contracted. Dona Lavinia's calmness amazed her. It was as if the housekeeper were fully aware of the night's events.

'His highness came in a little while ago and sent urgently for Father Amundi. He is closeted with him now. Matteo Damiani is locked up in the cellars and it appears that lightning must have struck behind the hill at the back of the grotto, for I saw a great light there and heard a sound like falling rocks. For the present, it is best you should go, my lady. When you return –'

'I shall never return!' Marianne declared but the violence of her tone had no effect on Dona Lavinia's composure. She merely smiled.

'Indeed you will. You have pledged your word. As I was saying, when you return, many things will have changed. I – I think there will be nothing more to fear. The Prince –'

'I saw him,' Marianne broke in. 'It was dreadful! I thought it was a ghost. I was terrified – that white face –'

'No,' Dona Lavinia said quietly, 'merely a mask, that is all, a mask made of white leather. You must not blame him. He is more than ever to be pitied. He has suffered cruelly tonight. I will see to the baggage.'

Marianne watched speechlessly as she came and went about the room, folding dresses and underwear, putting away shoes in boxes and stowing everything neatly in the open trunks. When she made a move to include the jewel cases, Marianne intervened.

'No, not those. I do not wish to take them.'

'Indeed you must! They are your highness's property now. Do you wish to cause our master further pain? He would be deeply wounded, believing that your highness held him responsible ...' She left the sentence in mid-air. Defeated, Marianne acquiesced. She no longer knew what to think. She was even a little ashamed of the panic which had gripped her but lacked the courage to change her mind and prolong her stay. She must go now.

Once outside the bounds of this uneasy domain, she would be herself again, able to think calmly and clearly and come to some conclusions, but for the present, she had to go away. It was the only way to stop herself from going mad and not until she had put a considerable distance between herself and the Villa Sant'Anna would she be able to look back on that night's events without endangering her reason. She needed to be a long way from the rider of Ilderim.

When, at long last, she was ready, her luggage packed, and the sound of the coach outside at the foot of the broad steps, she turned to Dona Lavinia.

'I promised my godfather that I would wait for him,' she began unhappily, 'yet I am going ...'

'Do not fret, Princess. I will explain – or rather I and the Prince together will explain everything.'

'Tell him also that I am returning to Paris, that I will write to him here, since I do not know where he will go after this. And tell him that I do not blame him. I know he believed that he was acting for the best.'

'As indeed he was. You will see that one day. Bon voyage, your highness. Never forget that this house is your own, like all our master's houses. You need not doubt that in future he will know how to keep you safe in it and, when you return, do so confidently, without fear.'

Marianne was sorry for the old woman who was clearly doing her best to remove the unpleasant associations from her mind. She knew that later she would probably regret her unheroic behaviour but she knew also that when she returned, since return she must, she would never do so alone. Either the cardinal or Arcadius, or both together, must come with her. But she kept this thought to herself as she held out both hands affectionately to Dona Lavinia.

'Don't worry, Dona Lavinia. Say good-bye for me to your master. And thank you, thank you for everything! I shall not forget you. When I come back, there will be the child and all will be well. Tell the Prince that.'

When at last she climbed into her coach, the morning mist was already lying over the park, giving to it a strange, dream-like quality. The wind of the previous night had dropped and the air was grey and moist. There would be rain later but, sitting with Agathe in the coach, Marianne felt safe, secured against all the spells, real or imagined, contained within that fair domain. She was going home, back to those she loved. Nothing could touch her now.

The whip cracked. With a chink of harness and a faint creaking of springs, the coach moved off. The wheels crunched on the sanded avenue. The horses broke into a trot. Marianne laid her cheek against the cold leather headpiece and closed her eyes. Her fluttering heart was stilled but, just then, she felt tired to death.

As the cumbersome berlin ploughed through the early morning mist on the first stage of the long, long journey back to Paris, she pondered on the absurdity of fate, and its cruelty in condemning her to this eternal wandering in pursuit of an impossible happiness. She had come here fleeing from an evil and unworthy spouse, she had come in order that the child conceived in the likeness of an emperor might hold his head up in life, she had come, last of all, in the secret hope of exorcizing forever the fate that seemed bent on destroying her. She was leaving rich, bearing a princely title, a great name, an unassailable position, but with her heart stripped more than ever of illusions and affections. She was going back – to what? To the leavings of love which Marie-Louise's husband could offer her, to the sadness of a solitary life because in future she must not lose face, and because Jason could not, or would not come. In the end, all that awaited her at her journey's end was an old house, inhabited only by a portrait and by one faithful friend. The unborn child, the future, was without shape or colour yet. She was going, once again, into the unknown.

# CHAPTER TWELVE
# The Fontainebleau Gate

The coach swept through the Porte d'Aix and clattered down the narrow, dark streets of ancient Avignon. The sun was still high enough to gild the ramparts, picking out the sharp edges of towers and battlements and glancing off the yellow waters of the indifferent river flowing idly under the wide-spaced arches of the old, half-ruined Pont Saint-Bénezet The statue of the Virgin on the topmost turret of the formidable papal palace shone like a star. Marianne had let down the dusty window for a better view and was revelling in the scents of the warm air, laden with the spicy fragrance of Provence, of sun-warmed olives, thyme and rosemary.

It was fifteen days since she had left Lucca. They had travelled by the coast road and then up the valley of the Rhone, making easy stages, partly in order to spare Marianne herself, since she was now in her fourth month of pregnancy and obliged to exercise prudence, and partly to avoid overtaxing the horses. These were no longer the common post horses which had drawn the berlin on the outward journey but four splendid animals out of the Sant'Anna stables. They proceeded on average some forty miles a day, stopping each night at one of the posting houses with which the route was provided.

The journey had given Marianne an opportunity to measure just how great was the change in her status. The magnificence of her team, the crest and the crown surmounting it on the berlin's panel assured her everywhere of prompt and deferential service. She had discovered that there was something to be said for being a very great lady. As for Gracchus and Agathe, they were clearly bursting with pride at serving a Princess and allowed no one to forget it. One had only to see Gracchus stalking into the inn where they had stayed each morning and announcing grandly that her serene highness's carriage awaited. The one-time errand boy of the rue Montorgueil was developing all the airs and graces of an imperial coachman.

Marianne, for her part, was rather enjoying the leisurely journey. She was not looking forward greatly to returning to Paris where, apart from the pleasant prospect of seeing her dear Arcadius again, she expected little but trouble. The threatening shadow of Francis Cranmere loomed large in her thoughts but she had some anxiety to spare also for the welcome that awaited her from the Emperor. While she was still on the road, her perils were confined to the possibility of an encounter with brigands but so far, no alarming figures had appeared to bar the passage of the coach. At least the rural scene had succeeded in washing her mind clear of the mists and fantasies of the Villa Sant'Anna, although it had taken all her willpower to keep her thoughts from dwelling on the evil face of Matteo Damiani and the fantastic figure of the rider in the white mask. She would think about them, later, when she had come to terms with the new life that lay ahead for her. For the present, she had no idea what this would be. She was in Napoleon's hands. It was he who had mapped out the career of the singer, Maria Stella, but what would he make of the Princess Sant'Anna? Certainly, the Princess herself was none too sure what to make of her. Here she was, married again, married but without a husband.

Marianne was enchanted by Avignon. It might have been the sun or the broad, lazy river, the warm colour of the old stones or the geraniums that clung to every iron balcony. Perhaps the silky murmuring in the silvery-olive trees had something to do with it, or the musical voices of the women in their striped petticoats gossiping and commenting on the passage of the coach. Whatever it was, it made her want to stay there for a few days before finishing her journey to Paris. She leaned out of the window.

'Gracchus, see if there is a good hostelry here. I should like to stay for a day or two.'

'We can try. There's a large inn over there with a handsome sign.'

The Auberge du Palais, one of the oldest and best-appointed in the region, nestled its thick, ochre-coloured walls and roof of semi-circular Roman tiles up against the Porte de l'Oulle. That it was also a staging post for the *diligence* was attested by the presence in the yard of that vast, unwieldy vehicle, liberally coated with dust, in the process of disgorging its load of stiff and yawning passengers amid a babel of clanging bells, shouting postillions and joyful cries of greeting from those meeting or being met.

One of the postillions, standing on the roof of the coach, was engaged in handing down boxes, portmanteaux and parcels belonging to the passengers to one of the inn servants. When all the luggage had been unloaded, he picked up several bundles of newspapers and tossed them down also. They were copies of the *Moniteur* from Paris; one of the bundles burst when the ostler failed to catch it, scattering the papers on the ground.

A stable boy sprang forward to retrieve them but, as he did so, his eye fell on the news contained in the front page and he let out a shout.

'Holy Virgin! Napoleon has sent old Fouché packing. How's that for news!'

There was uproar as patrons and inn servants began talking at once.

'Fouché dismissed? Surely not!'

'Bah! The Emperor must have had enough of him at last.'

'No, you're wrong there. The Emperor's done it to please his new Empress. She wouldn't want to be meeting him every day, not one of the old regicides from the Revolution who sent her uncle to his death!'

Some were delighted at the news, others merely amazed. Provence had never wholly supported the new regime. The region had remained royalist at heart and Fouché's fall was greeted overall as a hopeful sign.

Gracchus had remained on his box, observing the little scene, but now Marianne leaned out and called to him again.

'Go and fetch me one of those newspapers,' she said, 'and hurry!'

'At once, my lady. As soon as I have secured your lodging.'

'No. This minute! If these people are right, we may not be staying here after all.'

The news concerned her closely. It seemed almost too good to be true that her old persecutor Fouché, the man who had dared, by threats, to introduce her into Talleyrand's household as a spy, who had failed to save her from falling into the hands of Fanchon Fleur-de-Lys and who, worst of all, had permitted Francis Cranmere to roam Paris at liberty, should really have lost the dangerous power which had made him the secret master of the whole country. Marianne could scarcely believe it.

Yet, when she held the paper in her hands, yellowed and dusty from its long journey, she was obliged to accept the evidence of her eyes. Not content with the bare announcement that the Duke of Otranto had been succeeded as head of the Ministry of Police by Savary, the Duke of Rovigo, the *Moniteur* also published the text of the Emperor's official letter to Fouché.

'The services which you have rendered me on various occasions,' the Emperor wrote, 'have led us to entrust to you the governorship of Rome until such time as Article 8 of the Constitution Act of 17 February 1810 shall come into effect. We expect that you will continue, in this new post, to give further proof of your zeal in our service and devotion to our person ...'

Crumpling the paper nervously between her hands, Marianne allowed the joyful news to sink in. It was better even than she had hoped! Exiled! Fouché had been exiled! For there was no mistaking the real meaning of his appointment as governor of Rome; Napoleon wanted Fouché away from Paris. Another item of news, placed at a sufficient distance from that of Fouché's dismissal to ensure that no connection between the two should occur to the man in the street, caught Marianne's eye. On the very day of Fouché's 'retirement', the banker Ouvrard had been arrested in the *salon* of a

251

brilliant Parisienne hostess, on charges of malversation and acting against the interests of the state. Marianne's thoughts went instantly to Fortunée and the threats which she had uttered against her lover. Had she been responsible for Ouvrard's arrest? And, if that were so, was it through her that Napoleon had learned of Fouché's secret negotiations with England? She was perfectly capable of it, for she was as vindictive to her enemies as she was loyal to her friends.

'What is your highness's will?'

Gracchus's everyday tones broke in on her reverie. After such news there could be no more question of dawdling on the way. She must get back, quickly. Now that he had lost his ally, Francis had ceased to be a danger. She favoured her youthful coachman with the most radiant smile seen on her lips since leaving Lucca.

'Drive on, Gracchus, as fast as you can! I want to be in Paris as soon as possible.'

'Your Highness has not forgotten we are not driving post horses now? If we drive the way we did on the outward journey, these will be done in well before Lyon. And that, if I may say so, would be a downright shame.'

'I don't mean to kill my horses but I want you to make the stages as long as you can. We will go on further tonight. Drive on.'

With a resigned sigh, Gracchus-Hannibal Pioche mounted his box and began taming the berlin round, watched with a jaundiced eye by the landlord who had stepped out to welcome such an elegant equipage. Then, whipping up the horses, he set the coach bowling along the road to Orange.

It was nightfall when, after a striking demonstration of the stamina of Marianne's horses, the travelling berlin, so splashed with mud and coated with dust that even the colour, let alone the crest, was scarcely to be seen, drew up at the Fontainebleau guard post.[3] Marianne could not repress a sigh of relief when she saw the lights in the doorways of the elegant buildings designed by Ledoux which marked the outer limits of the city of Paris. She had arrived at last.

The initial surge of joy which had swept over her at Avignon and sent her speeding along the road to Paris had, it was true, abated somewhat, as it had seemed to do also in the minds of the people she met as she approached the capital. As the towns and staging posts swept by, Marianne had very soon made the discovery that Fouché's dismissal was regarded for the most part in the light of a catastrophe. This was not so much out of any affection for Fouché himself as from a universal dislike of his successor. People feared Savary for his blind devotion to his master; he was the imperial policeman, a man capable of carrying out any order, however monstrous, without blenching. As a result, Marianne had learned to her amazement that, in their

---

[3] The present day Place de L'Italie.

alarm and bewilderment, the people of France had begun to think of the slippery Fouché as almost a saint, and regret his departure.

*Well, I at least will never regret him*! she told herself, remembering bitterly all that she had suffered at his hands. *Besides, this Savary has never done me any harm. I have never met him, and I can't see that I need have anything to fear from his appointment.*

However, she could not repress a certain irritation when she saw the men on duty at the guard post paying unwontedly close attention to her coach.

'May I ask what you expect to find?' she snapped sharply. 'I suppose you imagine I am carrying a keg of brandy concealed under my cushions?'

'Orders are orders, madame.' The reply came from a gendarme who emerged at that moment from the guardhouse. 'All carriages entering Paris to be searched, especially those coming from a distance. Where are you from, madame?'

'From Italy,' Marianne said tartly. 'And I promise you I have no contraband goods, or conspirators in my coach. I am merely returning home.'

'Then I daresay you'll have a passport,' the gendarme said, smiling unpleasantly and revealing in the process a set of startlingly white teeth framed in the bristly thatch of his moustache. 'A passport in the name of the Duke of Otranto, perhaps?'

It did not appear that such passports would be well received and Marianne blessed the fate that had made her, henceforth, a loyal subject of the Grand Duchess of Tuscany. Proudly, she produced the passport which Count Gherardesca had presented to her three days after her marriage.

'This bears the signature of her Imperial Highness, Princess Elisa, Grand Duchess of Tuscany, Princess of Lucca and Piombino – and sister to his Majesty, the Emperor and King, as you may perhaps be aware,' she added ironically, taking a sardonic pleasure in retailing the impressive list of titles. However, the gendarme was impervious to irony. He was heavily engaged in spelling out the name inscribed on the official document by the light of the lantern.

'Marianne Elizabeth d'Assel... nat de Villeneuve... Princess... Sarta – no, Santa Anna...'

'Sant'Anna,' Marianne corrected sharply. 'Now may I return to my coach and continue my journey? I am extremely tired – and it is starting to rain.'

Big, round drops, heavy as coins, were beginning to fall, making small craters in the dust around the coach, but the gendarme in his cocked hat appeared not to notice it. He was eyeing Marianne suspiciously.

'You can get back in, but don't move on. I've got to check something.'

'Just what, I'd like to know?' Marianne raged, as the man vanished into the guardhouse with her passport. 'Does the oaf imagine that my papers are false?'

The answer came from an old market gardener with a cart full of cabbages who had drawn up alongside the berlin.

'No use getting impatient, m'dame. It's the same for everyone, every bloody day standing in the bloody rain! They've got so ruddy nosey you wouldn't believe! I can tell you, I've been made to unload a whole cart of cabbages, just in case I might be hiding some bleeding conspirator.'

'But, what is it all about? Has there been an attempt at assassination? Has a criminal escaped? Or are they looking for robbers?'

'Nothing like that, m'dame. It's all that bloody Savary, thinks he's the only one as knows how to serve the Emperor! So, he goes on searching and nosing and asking questions. Who hatched it? Who laid it? Wants to know it all, he does.'

The farmer's confidences might have continued indefinitely but for the reappearance of the hairy gendarme, preceded this time by a sub-lieutenant, a dapper, beardless youth who approached the coach and bowed perfunctorily, taking in Marianne with an eye of insolent appreciation.

'You are Madame Sant'Anna, it appears.'

Outraged at the tone the young whipper-snapper had used to her, Marianne felt herself stiffen.

'I am the Princess Sant'Anna,' she said, very distinctly. 'It is usual to address me as Serene Highness, lieutenant. Apparently, they do not teach you manners in the gendarmerie?'

'It is enough that we are taught to do our duty,' the young man said, in no way discomposed by her disdainful tone. 'My duty, Serene Highness, is to conduct you forthwith to the Minister of Police – if you will be good enough to ask your maid to make room for me.'

Before the outraged Marianne could say a word, the lieutenant had opened the door and climbed into the coach. Agathe rose automatically to relinquish to him her place beside Marianne, but her mistress laid a firm hand on her arm.

'Stay where you are, Agathe. I did not tell you to move and I am not in the habit of allowing any Tom, Dick or Harry to sit beside me. As for you, sir, I believe I must have misunderstood you. Will you repeat what it was you said?'

The lieutenant, obliged to maintain an uncomfortable stooping posture in the absence of anywhere to sit down, spoke in a voice of stifled anger.

'I said that I was to conduct you forthwith to the Minister of Police. Your name has been circulated to every guard post for more than a week. These are my orders.'

'Whose orders?'

'Whose orders would you expect? The Minister of Police, his grace the

Duke of Rovigo, and therefore of the Emperor.'

'That remains to be seen,' Marianne retorted. 'Very well, if that is what you want, we will go to the Duke of Rovigo. I should not object to telling him what I think of him, and of his subordinates. Until then, however, I intend to remain mistress of my own coach. Have the goodness to take a seat next to my coachman, young man. And while you are about it, you may show him the way. Under no other circumstances will you get me to budge from this spot.'

'Very well. I will go.'

With a very bad grace, the young gendarme climbed out and went to join Gracchus, who welcomed him with a sardonic grin.

'Nice of you to come and bear me company, lieutenant. You'll find it's well enough up here. A little damp, maybe, but you get more fresh air than inside. Now, where is it we're going exactly?'

'Straight on, and none of your sauce my lad, or you'll be the worse for it. Drive on.'

For answer, Gracchus touched up his horses and began to bawl out a lusty, street urchin's version of the soldiers' march from Austerlitz:

'When we break through their line
Ta rum ta ra, ta rum ta ra,
When we break through their line
Then how we'll laugh …'

Laugh? Marianne, hunched up inside the coach, felt no desire to laugh but even so the infectious rhythm of the march and the warlike gaiety of the voice suited something in her mood. She was far too angry to be afraid, even for an instant, of this Savary or of his reasons for ordering her arrest at the very gates of Paris.

When, a little later, they arrived at the Hôtel de Juigné, Marianne saw that there had been changes here also. The place was clearly being redecorated. Everywhere there was scaffolding, buckets of plaster and paint pots left about by the workmen at the end of the day. Despite this, and of the lateness of the hour (ten o'clock had not long sounded from Saint-Germain-des-Prés) the forecourt and antechambers were filled with footmen in glittering liveries and with visitors from every class of society. Instead of conducting Marianne upstairs to the dusty waiting-room on the first floor which led into the tiny, ill-furnished office that had belonged to the Duke of Otranto, the young lieutenant handed her over to a towering major-domo in red plush and powder. He flung open the doors into a *salon* on the ground floor furnished with an unswerving obedience to the known tastes of the Duke's imperial master. The room was filled with solid mahogany furniture and trophies made of ormolu, there were hangings of dark green with embroidered bees, a Pompeian chandelier and warlike allegorical scenes executed in stucco upon the walls. The final touch was given by an outsized bust of the Emperor, crowned with bays, sprouting from a marble plinth.

In the middle of all this, a lady in a gown of mauve taffetas, with a black pelisse and a rice-straw hat, was pacing up and down in an agitated manner. She was middle-aged, and her noble features and wide, thoughtful brow suggested a temper of mingled gentleness and austerity. It was a face that Marianne knew already from having seen it often in the house of Talleyrand: the Canoness de Chastenay, an aristocratic and intellectual lady who, it was said, had once entertained a certain partiality for the young General Bonaparte.

At Marianne's entry, she stopped her feverish pacing and regarded the newcomer in some surprise before uttering a joyful cry and hurrying to meet her with hands outstretched.

'Dear Muse of Song – oh, forgive me, dear Princess, I should say, what a joy and comfort to find you here!'

It was Marianne's turn to be surprised. How could Madame de Chastenay have known of the change that had occurred in her station. The Canoness gave a nervous little laugh and drew the younger woman over to a sofa guarded by a pair of forbidding bronze victories.

'But no one in Paris talks of anything else but your romantic marriage! That and the unfortunate Duke of Otranto's fall from grace are almost the only topics of conversation. Did you know that he is not to be governor of Rome after all? It seems the Emperor is perfectly furious with him on account of his making a bonfire of all the secret files and papers belonging to his ministry. He has been exiled, really exiled! It scarcely seems possible! But – where was I?'

'You were saying, madame, that people are talking about my marriage,' Marianne murmured, stunned by this flow of words.

'Ah, yes. Oh, it is quite extraordinary! You know, my dear, you are a real little slyboots! Hiding one of the greatest names in France like that! So romantic! Although, you must know, I was never really taken in. I guessed long ago that you were truly of noble birth and when we heard the truth —'

'But from whom did you hear it?' Marianne asked quietly.

The Canoness paused for a moment and appeared to reflect, then she was off again, more volubly than ever.

'How was it, now? Ah, yes – the Grand Duchess of Tuscany wrote to the Emperor about it as though it were something altogether remarkable! And so deeply moving! The beautiful young singer consenting to marry an unfortunate so dreadfully deformed that he could never bear to show himself in public! And, to crown it all, the great artiste then reveals that she is of noble race! My dear, I should think your story must be all over Europe by now.'

'But – the Emperor? What did the Emperor say?' Marianne persisted, feeling both bewildered and alarmed to discover so much talk about a marriage which she had believed secret. The court of Tuscany must be a hive of gossip indeed for the ripples of gossip started there to have spread so far and so fast.

'Goodness, I hardly know,' the Canoness answered. 'All I know is that his Majesty mentioned it to Monsieur de Talleyrand and roasted the poor Prince most unkindly for making the Marquis d'Asselnat's own daughter reader to the erstwhile Madame Grand.'

That was very like Napoleon. He must have been furiously angry at the marriage and had chosen to take out his wrath on Talleyrand. By way of changing the subject, Marianne asked: 'But what brings you here, madame, at this late hour?'

Instantly, Madame de Chastenay's sophisticated playfulness left her and she began to look as agitated as she had when Marianne had first entered.

'Oh, don't speak of it! I am still quite distracted! There I was in the Beauvaisis, with friends who have such an enchanting estate there and who – well, this very morning along comes a great lout of a gendarme to say that the Duke of Rovigo commands my presence instantly. And the worst of it is that I have not the least idea why, or what I could have done! I left my poor friends in the utmost anxiety and passed a terrible journey wondering all the time why I had been, not to put too fine a point on it, arrested. I was so wretched that I went first to call on Councillor Réal to ask him what he thought and he urged me to come here without delay. Any delay, he said, could have the most serious consequences! Oh, my dear, I am in such a state – and I dare swear that you are just the same –'

'No, not quite the same.' Marianne forced herself to maintain an icy calm. She had her own reasons for thinking that the order concerning her came from a higher source, although she would never have believed that Napoleon would go so far as to have her arrested for daring to marry without his consent. However, there was no time to disclose her own fears to her companion. The majestic usher reappeared to inform Madame de Chastenay that the minister was ready to receive her.

'Oh God!' the Canoness exclaimed. 'What will become of me? Say a little prayer for me, my dear Princess.'

The mauve taffeta dress vanished into the Minister's office, leaving Marianne alone. The room was extremely warm, for the windows were hermetically sealed. For coolness's sake, Marianne unfastened the full dust-coat which she had been wearing over her light gown of green silk, and untied the satin ribbons of her hat. She felt tired, sticky and dirty, certainly in no condition to confront a Minister of Police, and she would have given anything for a bath. But when would the opportunity to bathe be hers again? Would she even be allowed to go home? What was she to be accused of? It was like the Emperor to deal harshly with those against whom he had reason for anger, and remembering the stormy scenes which had already taken place between them, Marianne could not help but feel anxious.

The door opened again.

'If madame will follow me.'

The usher had reappeared and was holding open the door of a large, well-appointed office that was a far cry from Fouché's. Within, seated at a mahogany table decked with roses placed directly underneath a huge, full-length portrait of the Emperor, a good-looking man with dark hair and velvety eyes was working, or pretending to work, on a large file. His air of lofty complacency and invincible self-satisfaction was of the kind that always grated on Marianne, and the fact that he had not so much as looked up at her entrance only increased her irritation. If this were a piece of calculated rudeness, it hardly augured well for her; all the same, Marianne decided it was time to remind him of the respect due, if not to her person, at least to her rank and the name she bore. Besides, she was past caring.

Advancing coolly into the big room, she walked across and seated herself in a chair facing the desk. She spoke very smoothly.

'Pray, do not disturb yourself on my account, but when you can spare a moment, sir, perhaps you will be good enough to inform me to what I owe the honour of this summons?'

Savary let fall his pen with a start of surprise which, genuine or not, at least did credit to his histrionic talents.

'Great heavens! My dear Princess! I had not realized —'

'So it would seem.'

He leaped up from his chair and coming round the desk took the hand which she had not held out to him and carried it devoutly to his lips.

'Allow me to express my sincerest apologies – and also my delight that you have returned to Paris at last. You cannot imagine how eagerly you have been awaited.'

'I think I can imagine it very well,' Marianne said wryly. 'If, that is, I am to judge by the way your men pounced on my coach at the Fontainebleau guard post. But now, let us have no more beating about the bush, if you please. I acquit you of the social formalities. I have travelled a long way and I am very tired, so tell me quickly where I am to be imprisoned and, incidentally, why.'

Savary's eyes widened and this time Marianne could have sworn that his surprise was not assumed.

'Imprisoned? You? But, my dear Princess, why should you be? It really is most strange, no one this evening seems able to talk of anything else. Only a moment ago, Madame de Chastenay —'

'—was also ready to swear that you were going to send her there. Good heavens, what can you expect, if you will have people arrested?'

'But neither of you have been arrested. I merely indicated to my people that when you returned to Paris I should very much like to see you, and the same with the Canoness de Chastenay. You see, when my predecessor left this house, he made what I can only call a clean sweep of all the files and documents. The result is that I know no one.'

'A clean sweep?' Marianne said, beginning to be amused. 'You mean that he ...'

'Everything! He burnt everything!' Savary said pathetically. 'In my innocence, I trusted him. He offered to remain here for a few days, to put all in order, as he said, and for three days he shut himself up here putting all his secret files, all the dossiers compiled by his agents, all his correspondence, even the Emperor's letters, into the fire! Indeed, it was this which made his Majesty so angry.

'Monsieur Fouché is now exiled to Aix and he had to move quickly to escape the Emperor's righteous anger, while I am left trying to rebuild the machine which he has smashed. That is why I am asking people to come and see me. I am contacting all who have been thought to have some dealings with this house in the past.'

A deep flush, part anger and part shame, mounted to Marianne's cheeks. She understood now. Faced with an almost impossible task, this man was ready to do anything to prove to his master that his worth was at least as great as that of Fouché the Fox. If he thought that she was going to fall into the clutches of any policeman again, even a minister, he was mistaken. However, in order to make her own position perfectly clear, she asked quietly: 'You are quite certain that the – the invitation which was pressed on me at the Fontainebleau guard post has nothing to do with the Emperor?'

'Nothing in the world, my dear princess! Only my own desire to make the acquaintance of someone who has been the talk of Paris for fifteen days past led me to give orders which, I see now, have been greatly misconstrued, for which I hope you will forgive me.'

He had eased his chair very close to Marianne's and now took her hand, imprisoning it between his own. At the same time his velvet eyes took on a languorous heaviness that made Marianne wary. She knew that Savary was accounted successful where women were concerned, and there was nothing to be gained by raising false hopes. Gently withdrawing her hand, she asked:

'So everyone is talking about me?'

'Everyone! You are the heroine of the hour.'

'I am honoured indeed. Does everyone include the Emperor?'

Savary flung up his hands in horror. 'Oh, madame! His Majesty stands alone!'

'Very well,' Marianne said sharply. 'So the Emperor has said nothing to you concerning me?'

'No, I promise you! What else did you expect? I do not believe there is at present any woman in the world who could engage his Majesty's attention. The Emperor is deeply in love with his young bride and devotes all his time to her. There never was a more devoted couple. Indeed —'

Marianne got up quickly, unable to listen to any more. It seemed to her the interview had lasted long enough. If this nincompoop had brought her here merely to listen to him describing the Emperor's wedded bliss, he was even more of a fool than she had thought. Was he ignorant of the talk which had linked her name with Napoleon's? Fouché would never have been guilty of such clumsiness, or not without good reason.

'With your permission, sir, I leave you. I am, as I have already told you, very tired.'

'Yes, yes, by all means very natural, I am sure. I will see you to your coach. My dear Princess, you cannot conceive how delighted ...' His voice wandered on, losing itself in compliments which only served to increase Marianne's irritation. She could see only one reason for them: Napoleon no longer cared for her, for if he had Savary would not have permitted himself such liberties. She had been prepared for his anger, had been prepared for some shattering act of revenge, even to be thrown in prison, persecuted, but nothing of the kind had happened. He had merely listened, with one ear no doubt, to the gossip about her, and she had been brought here solely to indulge the curiosity of a raw new minister, eager to make contacts. Her heart swelled with anger and disappointment, there was a furious roaring in her ears through which she was vaguely conscious of Savary saying that his wife was at home on Mondays and would be most happy to entertain the Princess Sant'Anna to dinner one of these days. The last straw!

'I hope you have invited Madame de Chastenay also?' she said with irony as he stood waiting to hand her into her coach. The minister's eyes met hers with an expression of innocent surprise.

'But of course. Why should you ask?'

'Oh, curiosity merely. It is my turn, wouldn't you agree? Good evening to you, Duke. I too have been delighted to meet you.'

The coach moved off and Marianne sank back among the cushions, torn between the impulse to scream with rage, to burst into tears and shout with laughter. Was there ever anything so absurd? Tragedy that ended in farce! She had imagined herself, like a heroine of romance, going to meet a tragic fate, and instead she had received an invitation to dine!

'I am so glad to see you again, madame,' said Agathe at her side. 'I was frightened when that man brought us here.'

Marianne glanced at her maid and saw that the girl's cheeks were wet with tears and her eyes swollen.

'And you thought I should come out under an armed guard, in chains, on my way to Vincennes? No, my poor Agathe, I am not so important. I was sent for merely for the sake of seeing what I looked like. We must resign ourselves, my child, we are no longer the Emperor's beloved mistress! We are only a Princess.'

And Marianne promptly demonstrated her resignation by bursting into tears and thus completing poor Agathe's bewilderment. She was still crying when the coach entered the forecourt of the Hôtel d'Asselnat but her tears ceased abruptly at the sight that met her eyes. The old house was lit up from the basement to the handsome mansard roof.

Candlelight blazed in every window, most of which were open, revealing rooms filled with flowers and an elegantly dressed assembly moving about to the strains of violins. Marianne stared in amazement, recognizing the notes of a piece of ballet music by Mozart. It even occurred to her to wonder if she had not mistaken the house, but no, it was her own house, her own house with a party going on inside, and those were her servants lining the steps in splendid livery with branches of candles in their hands.

Every bit as flabbergasted as his mistress, Gracchus had brought the horses to a standstill in the middle of the courtyard and was staring with bulging eyes, incapable of bringing the coach up to the steps, or even of dismounting from the box. However, the clatter of hooves and iron-shod wheels on the cobbles must have penetrated through the music. From somewhere in the house, there came a shout.

'Here she is!'

In a moment, the entrance was packed with ladies in ball gowns and men in evening dress and, in their midst, the smiling, pointed face, goatee beard and bright black eyes of Arcadius de Jolival himself. But it was not he who came forward to the coach. Instead, a very tall man, dressed with great elegance, detached himself from the group and came down the steps, a man with a slight limp who leaned on a gold-knobbed stick. The haughty features and the cold blue eyes were illumined by a smile full of warmth and Marianne watched stupefied as Monsieur de Talleyrand put aside the footmen with a gesture and, advancing to the coach, himself flung wide the door and held out his gloved hand to her, saying in a loud voice as he did so: 'Welcome to the home of your ancestors, Marianne d'Asselnat de Villeneuve, and welcome also among your friends and your peers! You have returned from a journey longer than you know, but all of us are assembled here tonight to tell you of our sincere rejoicing.'

Marianne gazed at the brilliant crowd before her. Her face had gone suddenly very pale and her eyes dilated. She saw Fortunée Hamelin, laughing and crying at once. She saw, too, Dorothée de Périgord, in white,

261

and Madame de Chastenay in her mauve taffetas, waving to her. There were other faces, as well, which had been scarcely known to her until now but which she knew belonged to the greatest names of France: Choiseul-Gouffier, Jaucourt, La Marck, Laval, Montmorency, La Tour du Pin, Bauffremont, Coigny, all those whom she had met in the Rue de Varennes when she was merely a humble companion to the Princess Benevento. It came to her in a flash that Talleyrand had brought them here tonight, not only to welcome her home, but also to restore her at last to the position which by birth was rightfully hers and which she had lost only through misfortune.

The vision of pale gowns and glittering jewels was strangely blurred. Marianne placed her fingers, which seemed to be trembling suddenly, in the waiting hand. She stepped out of the coach, leaning heavily on that friendly arm.

'And now,' Talleyrand cried, 'make way, friends, make way for her Serene Highness, the Princess Marianne Sant'Anna, and allow me, in all our names, to wish her every happiness in the future.'

With the whole of society looking on and clapping, he kissed Marianne warmly on both cheeks and then bowed over her hand.

'I knew you would come back to us,' he whispered in her ear. 'You remember what I said to you, one stormy day in the Tuileries? You are one of us and that is something you can never alter.'

'Do you think – do you think the Emperor is of the same opinion?'

The Emperor, always the Emperor! Despite herself, Marianne could not rid her mind of its obsession with the man whom she knew that she still loved. Talleyrand's mouth twisted.

'You may expect a little trouble in that quarter, but come, they are waiting for you. We will talk later.'

Triumphantly, he led her to her friends. In a second, she was surrounded, petted, kissed, congratulated, passing from Fortunée Hamelin's lavishly rose-scented arms to the tobacco-smelling ones of Arcadius de Jolival. She abandoned herself, unresistingly, too dazed even to think. It was all so sudden, so unexpected. In the ballroom, while Talleyrand proposed a toast to her return, she took Arcadius aside.

'This is all very touching, and very pleasant, my friend, but I wish I understood. How did you know I was coming back? You seem to have been expecting me?'

'I was expecting you. I was quite sure you would come today, even before this came.'

'This' was a large, sealed envelope at the sight of which Marianne's heart beat faster. The Emperor's seal! But the contents, brief and to the point, held little of comfort.

'His Majesty the Emperor and King commands the attendance of the

Princess Marianne Sant'Anna on Wednesday the twentieth of June at four o'clock in the afternoon at the Palace of Saint-Cloud ...' It was signed: Duroc, Duc de Frioul, Grand Marshal of the Palace.

'Wednesday the twentieth is tomorrow,' Jolival observed, 'and you would not have been asked if it had not been known that you were on your way. Consequently, that meant you would be here today. Besides, Madame de Chastenay came straight here from the Duke of Rovigo's.'

'How could she have known I should not be detained?'

'She asked Savary, that is how. Now, Marianne, my dear, I must not monopolize you like this. Your guests are calling for you. You cannot think what a celebrity you have become since we had the news about your marriage from Florence.'

'I know – but, oh, I would so much rather have been alone with you, at least for tonight. I have so much to tell you!'

'And I have so much to hear,' Arcadius responded, pressing her fingertips affectionately. 'But Monsieur Talleyrand made me promise to tell him as soon as I knew anything. He was determined that your return should be triumphant.'

'That is one way of drawing me, willy-nilly, into his circle, is it not? All the same, he will have to recognize that I have not changed at all. My heart does not alter quite so fast.'

She looked thoughtfully at the imperial summons which she still held in her hand, trying to work out the meaning behind those brief, almost menacing words. She wagged it slowly under Jolival's nose.

'What do you think of this?'

'To be honest with you — nothing at all. Who can tell what is in the Emperor's mind? But I'll wager he's not best pleased.'

'I'll not take you. You would win,' Marianne said with a sigh. 'Dear Arcadius, be kind and take care of my guests while I change and freshen up a little. As this is the first time, I do think I should play the hostess worthily. I owe them that.'

Halfway to the stairs, she paused and turned: 'Tell me, Arcadius, have you heard anything of Adélaïde?'

'Nothing,' said Jolival with a shrug. 'The Pygmy Théâtre is closed for the while and I did hear that it had moved to the spa at Aix-la-Chapelle for the present. I suppose she has gone also.'

'How stupid it all is. Well, that is her affair. And —' There was a tiny pause before Marianne continued: 'Jason?'

'No news of him either,' Arcadius answered easily. 'He must be on his way to America and your letter still awaits him at Nantes.'

'Oh.' It was almost a sigh, a tiny ghost of a sound that yet betrayed the odd jerk at her heart-strings. It was true, of course, that the letter left with Patterson no longer mattered, the die was cast and there was no going back, but weeks of hope had ended in a void. The ocean was vast and a ship no more than a straw upon it: she had sent out her cry for help into infinity and no echo came back. There was nothing Jason could do for her now, and yet, as she mounted slowly to her bedchamber, Marianne found that she felt the same longing to see him again. It was strange when only the next day she would be facing the anger of Napoleon, waging one of those exhausting battles in which her love made her so vulnerable. It would not be easy, and yet her mind refused to worry about it. Instead, her thoughts obstinately kept going back to the sea. Strange, too, how insistently the memory of the sailor returned. It was as if all Marianne's youth, filled with wild dreams and the deep, almost visceral longing for adventure, were clinging to him, the supreme adventurer, as a last means of survival.

The time for adventure was past, however. Listening to the babble of aristocratic voices that mounted to her through the open window, against a background of an air from Mozart, the new Princess reflected that this was the beginning of a quite different life, adult, full of calm and dignity in which the child could share. Tomorrow, when she had arranged matters with the Emperor, there would be nothing left to do but let the days flow past, and live like everyone else, alas.

# CHAPTER THIRTEEN
# The First Rift

Four o'clock was striking from the clock set in the central pediment of the palace of Saint-Cloud as Marianne ascended the great staircase, built in the previous century. She felt ill at ease, not so much at the glances which had followed her ever since she entered the courtyard as at the thought of what awaited her in this unfamiliar place. Two and a half months had passed since the dramatic scene in the Tuileries and this would be the first time she had seen him since. It was enough to make her heart quake.

A brief note accompanying the imperial command had informed her that full dress was not worn, the court being in mourning for the Crown Prince of Sweden, and that she should appear in a round gown and 'fanciful head-dressing'. She had therefore selected a dress of thick white satin with no train and with no other ornament than a single gold and pearl pin just below the bosom. Her thick, black hair was dressed with a turban of the same material, trimmed with black and white ostrich plumes that curled softly on her neck. She carried a long black and gold cashmere shawl draped negligently over one shoulder and caught up on the other arm. Baroque pearls hung in her ears and gold bracelets, worn over long white gloves and reaching up almost to her sleeves, completed a *toilette* which roused envy in the breast of every woman who beheld it. Marianne suffered no qualms on this score. She had thought out every detail, from the deliberate simplicity of the dress which did full justice to her long, slender legs to the absence of jewels at her throat so as not to mar the smooth line of her slender neck, melting gracefully into her rounded shoulders. Even the snowy edge of her daringly low-cut bodice was designed to show off the golden warmth of her skin which, as Marianne well knew, had always been irresistible to Napoleon. As far as appearance was concerned, she was a complete success, her beauty was perfect. On the moral plane, however …

She had scarcely slept that night for thinking of the coming interview and there had been ample time to decide on her attitude. She had reached the conclusion that to betray the least consciousness of guilt would be the greatest foolishness. Napoleon had nothing to blame her for except for having taken steps to safeguard the future of his child without consulting him. It was therefore as a woman certain of her own power, a mistress determined to have her lover again, that she meant to go to him. She was tired of all the raptures she had heard since her return to France depicting Napoleon and Marie-Louise as a pair of turtle doves. Only last night, Talleyrand had whispered to her, with a hint of his rakish smile, that the Emperor spent the best part of his time either in his wife's bed or at least closeted with her.

'He is present at her *toilette* every morning and selects her gowns and jewels for her. He thinks that nothing can be too splendid for her. Our Mars has become a Mars in love.'

Marianne was set on causing a diversion in these amorous skirmishes. She had endured too much since the announcement of this marriage, suffered too much from the ravages of an almost animal jealousy at the thought of their nights together. She knew that she was beautiful, far more beautiful than that other woman, and well able to turn the head of any man. She was out to conquer. It was not the Emperor she was going to see but a man she meant to keep at any cost. It may have been this which made her heart beat so fast when she reached the waiting room on the first floor where, by custom, the palace chamberlain and four of the Empress's ladies were on permanent duty whenever their majesties were giving audience.

Marianne knew that today she would find Madame de Montmorency and the Countess de Périgord there, for the latter had told her the evening before that she was on duty.

'The custom is,' Dorothée had added, 'for one of the palace ladies to present you to the chief lady-in-waiting and to the palace chamberlain before you are admitted to the audience chamber. The chamberlain, the Marquis de Bausset, is a charming man but to my mind the lady-in-waiting, the Duchess de Montebello, is a perfect harpy. Unfortunately, the Empress can think of no one else, listens to no one else, loves and trusts no one else. But never mind. I shall be there and I will present you to her. Madame de Montebello handles me with kid gloves.'

That Marianne could well believe, knowing the young countess well enough to be sure that she would never allow Madame de Montebello to forget that she was born Princess of Courlande. It was therefore with a smile of perfect ease that she advanced to meet her friend Dorothée. But before the two young women could utter more than greetings, a third person intervened.

'Is it a ghost come back to us?' It was Duroc's gay voice that spoke. 'And what a ghost! My dear, it is a real pleasure to see you again! And in such beauty! Such elegance! You are – I cannot find words for what you are.'

'Say "imperial" and you will not be far from the truth,' said Dorothée in her rather mannish tones, while Duroc bowed low over Marianne's hand. Dropping her voice a little, she added: 'There is no denying that she takes the shine out of our beloved sovereign, and I have always maintained that Leroy's gowns cannot be worn by everyone!'

'Come, come,' the Grand Marshal protested. 'Countess, your tongue will get you into trouble one of these days.'

'Say rather my imperfect French,' Dorothée retorted with her abrupt laugh. 'I meant of course that they do not suit all figures. One must be slim and lithe, and long-legged,' she added, throwing a complacent glance at her own reflection in a nearby mirror as she spoke. 'And her majesty is a little too fond of pastries.'

Madame de Périgord's own elegance was beyond question. Marianne had been struck the night before by the change in her. The thin, gawky girl with the huge eyes had blossomed into a real beauty. Not even Marianne herself was better able to carry off Leroy's creations. Today, she was displaying a robe made of alternating bands of black velvet and heavy white lace. She slipped her arm through Marianne's in a friendly fashion.

'It is wonderful to see you again,' she said with a happy sigh. We are a long way now from Mademoiselle Mallerouse and from the Signorina Maria Stella!'

For all her self-command, Marianne felt herself blushing.

'I seem to be a kind of chameleon,' she sighed. 'And I can't help worrying a little about what people in general will think of me.'

Madame de Périgord's fine black brows rose sharply. 'People in general will not presume to judge you, my dear. As for those who are your equals, well, they have seen worse. Did you never hear that my grandfather was a groom in the Czarina Elizabeth's stables before he became her lover and married the Duchess of Courlande? Yet that does not prevent me from being extremely proud of him – in fact he is my favourite of all my forbears. Moreover, I know a good many of émigrés who have engaged in infinitely less respectable occupations than acting as companion to a princess and giving concerts! Now, stop tormenting yourself and come and be presented to our Cerberus.'

'One moment,' Marianne said. She turned to Duroc. 'Can you tell me, Duke, the reason for my summons? Why am I here?'

The Grand Marshal's round, slightly flabby face creased into a broad smile.

'Why – to be presented to their Majesties, that is all. It is the usual custom. In the normal way, this would have taken place at an evening party, but as we are in mourning ...'

'Is that really all?' Marianne said doubtfully. 'You are quite sure?'

'Indeed it is. The Emperor commanded me to invite you and I issued the command in his name. In fact,' consulting his watch, 'it is already time to go into the drawing-room and Madame de Montebello has not yet arrived. The Empress must have detained her. However, I am equally privileged to present new arrivals, so come, madame …'

Two liveried footmen flung open the double doors and the guests moved slowly into the next room and took up positions around the walls, the women in front and the men behind. Duroc, however, remained by Marianne whom he had placed a little apart, not far from the door by which the imperial couple were to enter. There were a great many people present but Marianne hardly gave them a glance, she was too absorbed in her own nervous anticipation and in her eagerness to see again the man whom she still loved. To her, they were merely a faceless mass of gowns and glittering uniforms. She was content with a glance at one of the tall mirrors, in passing, to check that her own appearance was in order. There was room for only one thought in her mind: what would her reception be?

She had thought at first that she was to see him alone, that he would have her brought to his own room, without witnesses. It had not occurred to her that she was in for a formal presentation, and she was bitterly disappointed. It was as though Napoleon were telling her that she was no longer anything to him, merely a woman like any other. Was it really possible that he could have fallen so deeply in love with that fat German? Moreover, Napoleon's reputation for bestowing public insults on several ladies was too well established to allow her to welcome the prospect of coming face to face with him in the presence of so many watching eyes and avidly listening ears.

'Their majesties, the Emperor and Empress!' The voice of the master of ceremonies rang out and Marianne shivered. Her nerves tensed. The great doors opened and her heart missed a beat. Napoleon, hands clasped behind his back, trod briskly into the room.

More slowly, a little behind him, Marianne saw Marie-Louise come in, looking pinker than ever in a white gown trimmed with roses of the same colour but edged with silver.

*She is fatter than ever!* was Marianne's first, maliciously gleeful thought.

A few important people entered in their wake but these remained at one end while the Emperor and Empress made their progress round the room, to a rippling wave of silken gowns and braided uniforms that dipped in endless homage. Marianne recognized Napoleon's sister, the enchanting Pauline, and the Duke of Würzburg, Marie-Louise's uncle. She was third in line after two haughty-looking dames considerably older than herself but she could not have recalled their names or repeated what Napoleon said to them for the buzzing in her own ears. Only Duroc's deep voice penetrated it.

'In response to your majesty's commands, allow me to present her

Serene Highness, Princess Corrado Sant'Anna, Marquise d'Asselnat, de Villeneuve, Countess Cappanori and Galleno ...'

The long list of the titles which she had acquired by her marriage fell with the weight of doom on Marianne. At the same time, her knees folded in the deep court curtsey which was far more demanding in grace, suppleness and sense of balance than merely kneeling. The blood was pounding in her temples and there was a mist before her eyes as Marianne heard the last of her titles. Her field of vision was limited to a pair of legs clad in white silk and silver-buckled shoes. There was silence. The Emperor was so close that she could hear him breathing but a sudden terror stopped her from raising her eyes. What was he going to say?

A hand she knew well was stretched out suddenly to raise her and Napoleon's cool voice said: 'Rise, madame. This is, I think, a long-awaited pleasure.'

She dared to look at him then and, meeting the grey-blue eyes, read in them no anger but rather a kind of amusement and wondered suddenly if he were mocking her gently. Certainly, the smile he bestowed on her was full of laughter.

'We are pleased, also, to felicitate you on your marriage, and to note that it has not altered you. You are as beautiful as ever.'

It was hardly a compliment. Merely a statement of fact. His gaze flickered rapidly from the charmingly flushed countenance to the uncovered shoulders and the breast that rose and fell so close to him but she could read nothing there. Already he was turning away to present the young princess to Marie-Louise and, like it or no, she was obliged to repeat her curtsey to the one woman whom she detested above all others. But before sinking into her reverence, she had time to note the discontented pout that accentuated the famous Habsburg lip.

'How do you do?' said the Empress sulkily.

That was all. Had she recognized the woman who had made the shocking scene at the Tuileries on the day following her wedding? The woman she had found sobbing at the Emperor's feet and called 'that wicked woman'? Marianne could have sworn that she had. As she rose, she could not prevent her eyes from meeting those of Marie-Louise in a silent challenge. A fierce joy surged up in her. There was an almost electric shock. Marianne was certain that the Austrian woman loathed her and she felt a delirious sense of triumph at the thought. Hatred vibrated between the two women, hatred which gave the measure of the fear which inspired it. Marianne was aware of people around her holding their breath in cruel anticipation. Was this the first encounter between the new bride and the latest mistress to become a confrontation?

No. With a nod, Marie-Louise passed on to join her husband who, in this brief interval, had managed to traverse half the room.

'There!' Duroc's voice murmured in her ear. 'That went off better than I hoped. As soon as this is over, you are to come with me.'

'What for?'

'Why – because you are now to be granted a private audience. The Emperor instructed me to take you to his private office after the reception. You did not imagine that a few polite words would be the end of it, did you?'

*Alone.* She was to see him alone. Marianne's heart leaped joyfully. All this had been merely a formality, a necessary ceremony due to her new rank, but now she was to be alone with him again, have him to herself for a little while. Perhaps all was not lost.

The amused Duroc found himself gazing into a pair of eyes bright with a thousand stars. He laughed.

'I knew that would please you better. All the same, do not hope for too much. The name you bear has protected you from an open scandal. That does not mean that all will be honey in private.'

'Why should you think that?'

Duroc took out his snuff-box, helped himself to a pinch and nicked the fallen grains off his splendid suit of purple velvet and silver. Then he gave another laugh.

'The best answer to that question, my dear, is in the fragments of one of the finest Sèvres vases in the palace, shattered by his majesty's own hand on the day he learned of your marriage.'

'Are you trying to frighten me?' Marianne said. 'Far from it, you cannot think how happy you have made me! I was frightened, I confess, but that was just now…'

It was true. She had been frightened of his formal politeness, his social smile, his indifference. The worst of his rages, yes, but not that! It was the one thing before which Marianne felt helpless.


The Emperor's office at Saint-Cloud opened directly on to the great terrace, gay with roses and geraniums. Striped awnings were stretched outside the windows and ancient lime trees cast a gentle shade which made the sunlight that lay full on the wide lawns seem more dazzling by contrast. The furnishings were little different from those in the Tuileries, but the business-like atmosphere was softened by the summery scents and the beauty of the green and golden gardens, laid out for a pleasure-loving age.

Dropping her shawl over the arm of a chair, Marianne walked over to one of the tall French windows, seeking in the view before her a distraction from what she imagined would prove a long wait. In fact, she had hardly reached the window before the Emperor's brisk step was heard on the tiled floor of the corridor outside. The door opened, clicked shut, and Marianne sank once again into her curtsey.

'There is no one who can curtsey like you,' observed Napoleon.

He was still standing by the door, hands clasped in the familiar way behind his back, watching her. But there was no smile on his face. As before, he was merely stating a fact, not paying a compliment designed to please. In any case, before Marianne could think of an answer, he had crossed the room and seated himself at his desk, motioning her to a chair as he did so.

'Sit down,' he said briefly, 'and tell me.'

Feeling a little breathless, Marianne sat down mechanically while he rummaged among the heaps of maps and papers that cluttered his desk, apparently paying no further attention to her. Now that she could see him better, it seemed to her that he was looking both fatter and tired. His smooth, pale skin had a yellowish tinge, like old ivory. His cheeks had filled out, stressing the dark shadows under his eyes, the rather weary curl to his lip.

That royal progress through the northern provinces must have been terribly tiring, Marianne thought, resolutely putting away the memory of Talleyrand's hints about the principal occupation of the imperial pair. But his eyes had glanced up at her for a moment.

'Well? I am waiting ...'

'What should I tell?' she asked quietly.

'Everything, of course. This astonishing marriage! I do not ask the reason. I know it.'

'Your majesty – knows it?'

'Naturally. It appears that Constant has a fondness for you. When I heard of this marriage, he told me everything, meaning, I am sure, to spare you the chief part of my anger.' It may have been the remembrance of this anger that made Napoleon bring his fist down suddenly on the desk. 'Why did you say nothing to me? I believe I had a right to be told, and that at once.'

'Certainly, sire, but may I ask your majesty what difference it would have made?'

'Difference to what?'

'To the course of events, shall we say? And after the way we parted, on the night of the concert, I can hardly see how I could have approached your majesty for another audience to tell you the news. I should have feared to intrude on the festivities attending your marriage. It was better for me to disappear and make my own arrangements in view of the coming event.'

'Your arrangements would appear to have been adequate to the occasion,' he said with a sneer. 'A Sant'Anna! Confound it! No mean achievement for a –'

'Permit me to interrupt you, sire,' Marianne said coldly. 'Your majesty seems in danger of forgetting that the character of Maria Stella was no more than a mask. It was not she who married the Prince Sant'Anna but the daughter of the Marquis d'Asselnat. Among our kind, such a union was merely natural. Indeed, your majesty is the only person to express surprise at it, to judge what I have heard since my return. Paris society has been much more surprised by –'

Again, the imperial fist came down with a crash.

'Enough, madame! You are not here to teach me what may or may not be the opinions of the Faubourg Saint-Germain-des-Prés. I know them better than you! What I wish to hear is how your choice came to fall on a man whom no one has ever seen, who lives shut up on his estates, hidden even from his own servants, like a kind of living mystery? I do not imagine he came here to find you?'

Marianne could feel the anger in him throbbing in her own veins. She lifted her chin and clasped her gloved hands together in her lap as she always did in moments of stress. Outwardly calm, despite the alarm within her, she answered him: 'A kinsman of mine arranged the match, for the honour of the family.'

'A kinsman? But I thought – oh, I see! I'll wager by that you mean the Cardinal San Lorenzo, that impertinent fellow to whom the fool Clary gave his carriage to please you, against my expressed commands. A plotter, like all the rest.'

Marianne permitted herself a smile. Gauthier de Chazay was out of reach of the imperial wrath. The admission she was about to make could do him no harm.

'Wager, by all means, sire, for you will win. It is quite true that it was my godfather who, as head of my family, made the choice for me. That, too, was natural.'

'There I cannot agree with you.' Napoleon rose abruptly and began to stride up and down the carpet of his office in one of his characteristic nervous pacings. 'I cannot agree with you at all,' he said again. 'It was for me, the father, to choose the future of my child. Unless,' he added cruelly, 'unless I am mistaken in thinking myself the child's father!'

Instantly Marianne was on her feet, her cheeks on fire, her eyes blazing.

'I never gave you the right to insult me, or to doubt me either! And I should like to know what arrangements your majesty could have made for the child other than to have forced his mother into some marriage or other!'

There was silence. The Emperor coughed and shifted his eyes away from the sparkling gaze fixed on him in almost insolent interrogation.

'Naturally. Unfortunately, it could not have been otherwise, since it was not possible for me to acknowledge the child. At least I could have entrusted you to one of those I trust, a man I knew intimately and could be sure of.'

'Someone who would shut his eyes and take Caesar's mistress – and the dowry that went with her. For you would have given me a dowry, would you not, sire?'

'Naturally.'

'In other words: a complaisant husband! Don't you understand,' Marianne cried passionately, 'that that was precisely what I could not have borne: to be given away, sold would be more accurate, by you to one of your people! To be obliged to accept a man from your hands!'

'Your noble blood would have rebelled, I take it,' he said, scowling, 'against giving your hand to one of those upstart heroes who make up my court, men who owe everything to their gallantry, to the blood they have shed ...'

'And to your generosity! No, sire, as Marianne d'Asselnat I should not have blushed to wed one such, but I would have died rather than that you, whom I loved, should give me to another. By obeying the cardinal, I did no more than follow the noble custom which requires a girl to accept blindly the husband chosen for her by her family. In that way I suffered less.'

'So much for your reasons,' Napoleon said, with a chilly smile. 'Now let me have your – husband's. What made a Sant'Anna take to wife a woman already with child by another?'

Marianne snapped back at him instantly:

'The fact that that other was yourself! Prince Corrado married the child of Bonaparte's blood.'

'I understand less and less.'

'Yet it is very simple, sire. The Prince is, by what they say, a victim of some malady which he is determined not to pass on to his posterity. He had therefore condemned himself of his own will to seeing his ancient name die with him, until, that is, Cardinal San Lorenzo told him of me. His pride was too great to allow him to consider adopting a child, but that pride did not apply in your case, sire. Your son will bear the name of Sant'Anna and ensure that it shall survive!'

There was silence again. Slowly, Marianne made her way over to the open window. She felt suddenly stifled, overcome by the weird knowledge that she had lied in her portrait of Corrado Sant'Anna. Sick? The man she had seen mounting Ilderim with such mastery? It was impossible! But how could she explain to the Emperor what she could not explain even to herself? His voluntary seclusion, the mask of white leather which he wore on his nocturnal rides? She saw again that tall, energetic figure glimpsed beneath the flowing black cloak billowing out with the speed of his gallop. Sick, no! But some mystery there was and it was never wise to present Napoleon with a mystery.

It was he who broke the silence.

'Very well,' he said at last. 'I accept that. It is a valid reason and one that I can understand. Moreover, we have nothing against the Prince. He has always behaved as a loyal subject since our accession to power. But one thing you said just now struck me as strange.'

'What was that?'

'You said: by what they say, the Prince is a victim of some malady. That suggests that you have never seen him.'

'Nothing could be truer. I have seen nothing of him, sire, beyond a gloved hand which emerged from a black velvet curtain and was joined to mine in the marriage ceremony.'

'You have never seen Prince Sant'Anna?'

'Never,' Marianne assured him, aware once again that she was not telling the truth. She meant, at all costs, to keep from him the knowledge of what had taken place at the villa. No good could come of telling him about the phantom rider, much less of her strange awakening after that enchanted night in a bed strewn with jasmine flowers. She was rewarded for her lie at once for at last Napoleon smiled. He came towards her, slowly, until he was almost touching her, and looked deeply into her eyes.

'So,' he said, and his voice was low and husky, 'he has not touched you?'

'No, sire. He has not touched me.'

Marianne's heart trembled. The Emperor's eyes were as soft now as a moment before they had been cold and implacable. She saw again, at long last, the look that he had worn in their days at the Trianon, the look she had so longed to see again, the charm that he could use to such good effect when he wished and the caressing expression in his eyes before they made love. For days, and nights too, she had dreamed of that look. How came it, then, that now it gave her no joy? Napoleon laughed suddenly.

'Don't look at me like that. Good God, anyone would swear you were afraid of me! Don't worry, there is nothing more to fear. All things considered, this marriage will do very well indeed and you have carried off a master stroke! By heaven, I couldn't have done better myself! A splendid marriage and, what is more important, a marriage in name only. You have made me suffer, you know.'

'Suffer? You?'

'Yes, I! I am jealous of what I love, am I not? Well, I imagined so many things?'

*And what about me?* Marianne thought, with the bitter memory of that terrible night at Compiègne vividly in her mind. *Thinking I should go mad when I learned that he could not wait even a few hours to get the Austrian into his bed.*

The sudden spurt of resentment was so strong that she did not realize that he had taken her in his arms and was murmuring words in her ear that grew ever huskier and more passionate.

'You, my green-eyed witch, my beautiful siren, in another man's arms, another man kissing and fondling your body… I almost hated you for doing that to me and just now, when I saw you again … so beautiful, more beautiful even than I remembered … I wanted to …' The words were lost in a kiss, a kiss that was greedy, demanding, almost brutal, full of selfish passion, the caress of a master to his willing slave, yet even so, Marianne could not resist it. The mere touch of this man whom she had made the centre of all her thoughts, all her desires, still acted on her senses like the most relentless and demanding of tyrants. In Napoleon's arms, Marianne melted as completely as on that first night at Butard.

Already he had released her and had moved away, calling: 'Roustan!'

The magnificent Georgian's turbanned head appeared, shining and expressionless, to receive the Emperor's curt command.

'Let no one in here until I call. On your life!'

The Mameluke bowed his understanding and withdrew. Napoleon grasped Marianne by the hand.

'Come,' was all he said.

He almost ran with her to a door cut in one of the panels of the wall, disclosing a small, spiral staircase up which he hurried her at a breathless pace. They emerged into a small apartment furnished with the tasteful luxury generally associated with rooms designed for love. The predominant colours were a glowing yellow and soft, rather faded blue. However, Marianne had little time to look at her surroundings, hardly time to think of those who had been before her in this discreet love nest. As deftly as the best of lady's maids, Napoleon had already taken out the pins that held the white satin turban and unfastened the dress. It slid to the ground, followed almost at once by the shift and petticoats. All this at incredible speed. This time, there was no question of the slow, tender preliminaries, the skilled, voluptuous process of undressing of that night at Butard, which had made Marianne a more than willing prey, and had given such delight to the early stages of their love-making in those days at the Trianon. In no time, the Serene Princess Sant'Anna found herself clad only in her stockings, sprawled across the sunshine yellow counterpane in the grip of a man bent only on ravishing her, like some marauding trooper, without a word spoken, merely covering her lips with frantic kisses.

It was so brutal and so swift that this time the famous charm was given no chance to work. In a few minutes it was all over. His majesty popped a kiss on the end of her nose, and patted her cheek.

'My good little Marianne,' he said, with a kind of sentimental fondness. 'You are truly the most delicious woman I have ever met. I fear you will be able to make a fool of me all my life. You make me mad.'

These kind words, however, were powerless to comfort his 'good little Marianne' who, in addition to her frustration and fury, had a disagreeable sensation of being made ridiculous. She discovered angrily that, just when she had believed that she had really found her lover again she had merely served to slake the sudden, violent passion of a married man, who was probably dreading being caught at any moment by his wife and already regretting his loss of control. Outraged, she snatched up the yellow counterpane to cover her nakedness and stood up. Her hair fell loose to below her waist, enveloping her in a shining black mantle.

'I am infinitely obliged to your majesty, I am flattered that your majesty is still pleased with me,' she said coldly. 'May I hope for your continued goodwill?'

He frowned, then he too rose and grinned.

'So you're sulking now, are you? Come now, Marianne, I know I have not been able to give you as much time as I used to, but you are a sensible girl and I think you must realize that many things have changed here, that I cannot be as I once was with you ...'

'As a bachelor! I know,' Marianne retorted, turning her back on him to restore some order to her hair in the glass over the fireplace. He followed her and, putting his arms round her, dropped a kiss on her bare shoulder. Then he laughed.

'You should be very proud. You are the only woman who could make me forget my duty to the Empress,' he said, clumsily making bad worse.

'Indeed, sire, I am proud,' Marianne said gravely. 'I am only sorry that I can make you forget for so short a time.'

'Duty, you understand ...'

'And the desire to get an heir soon!' she finished for him, thinking to goad him, but to no effect. Napoleon bestowed a radiant smile upon her.

'I hope he will not make me wait too long! Of course I want a boy. I hope you will give me a fine boy, also. We will call him Charles, if you agree, after my father.'

Marianne was dazed. He was talking of children now, and as naturally as if they had been married for years. She had a perverse urge to contradict him.

'It may be a girl,' she said. It was the first time such a possibility had occurred to her. Until then, she had always been convinced for some reason that the coming child would be a boy. But tonight, it was quite impossible for her to put him out of temper. He answered gaily.

'I should be delighted to have a girl. I have two boys already, you know.'

'Two?'

'Why, yes. Young Léon, who is some years old now, and little Alexandre, born last month, in Poland.'

Marianne was silent at this, more deeply hurt than she cared to show. She had not been aware of the birth of Marie Walewska's son and she was inexpressibly shocked to find herself put on the same level as the Emperor's other mistresses, her child placed firmly in a kind of nursery for imperial bastards.

'Congratulations,' she said grittily.

'If you have a daughter,' Napoleon went on, 'we will call her by a Corsican name, a pretty name! Letizia, like my mother, or Vannina – I like those names! Now, hurry up and get dressed or people will start to wonder at the length of this audience.'

Now he was worrying what people would say! Oh, he had changed, he had thrown himself wholeheartedly into his role of married man! Marianne dressed herself with angry haste. He had left her alone, perhaps out of gallantry but more probably because of his own impatience to be back in his office. He merely told her to come down when she was ready. Marianne's haste was as great as his. She was eager now to be gone from this palace where, she knew in her heart, a perilous rift had occurred in her great love. She would find it hard to forgive him for this hurried interlude.

When she returned to the office, Napoleon was waiting for her, her shawl over his arm. He settled it tenderly about her shoulders, asking in a voice that was suddenly coaxing, like a child asking to be forgiven: 'Do you still love me?'

She merely shrugged and smiled a little sadly.

'Then, ask me for something. I want to make you happy.'

She was about to refuse when all at once she remembered something Fortunée had told her the night before, something which was much on her mind. Now or never was the moment to do something for her most faithful friend, and also to annoy the Emperor a little. Looking him very straight in the eye, she gave him a wide smile.

'There is someone you could make very happy through me, sire.'

'Who is that?'

'Madame Hamelin. It appears that when the banker Ouvrard was arrested in her house, the men also arrested General Fournier-Sarlovèze who chanced to be in the house.'

If Marianne had hoped to annoy Napoleon, she had succeeded abundantly. The smiling face of a moment before was instantly transformed into the mask of Caesar. He did not look at her but turned back to his desk, saying curtly:

'General Fournier had no business to be in Paris without permission. His home is Sarlat. Let him stay there.'

'It would seem,' Marianne said, 'that your majesty is unaware of the ties of affection which exist between him and Fortunée. They are deeply in love and –'

'Rubbish! Fournier is in love with every woman he meets and Madame Hamelin is besotted about men. They can perfectly well do without each other. If he was in her house, there was probably some other reason for it.'

'But of course,' Marianne said blandly. 'He desires quite desperately to be restored to his place in the army, as your majesty well knows.'

'I know he is a troublemaker, a mischievous hot-head – and one that hates me and will not forgive me because I wear the crown.'

'But one that dearly loves your glory,' Marianne said softly, astonishing herself by her ability to produce arguments in favour of a man whom she personally detested. But Fortunée would be so happy.

Napoleon's eye was turned on her in sudden suspicion.

'This man – how do you come to know him?'

A devil came to tempt Marianne. What would he do if she were to tell him that on the night of his august nuptials, Fournier had tried to ravish her behind a garden gate? No doubt he would be furious, and his rage would repay her for many things, but Fournier might well pay with his life or by perpetual disgrace, and he had not deserved that, however odious and impossible he was.

'Know him would be rather too much to claim. I saw him one evening at Madame Hamelin's. He had come from Périgord to beg her to intercede for him. I did not stay long. I had the impression that the general and my friend were anxious to be alone.'

The Emperor's shout of laughter told her she had succeeded. He came to her and took her hand, kissed it and, still holding her, led her to the door.

'Very well! You win. You may tell that urchin in petticoats that she will have her handsome cockerel back soon. I will have him out of prison and he shall have his command again before the autumn. Now, be off with you. I have work to do.'

They parted at the door, he bowing slightly, she sinking once again into the deep, formal curtsey, as stiff and impersonal as if nothing had occurred behind that door but a polite conversation. Marianne found Duroc waiting in the Apollo gallery to escort her to her carriage. He held out his hand.

'Well? Happy?'

'Extremely,' Marianne said in a tight voice. 'Emperor was – charming!'

'The whole thing has been a complete success,' the Grand Marshal agreed. 'You are wholly restored to favour. You do not yet know how far! But I can tell you that you will certainly receive your appointment before long.'

'My appointment? What appointment?'

'As lady-in-waiting, to be sure! The Emperor has decided that as an Italian princess you will join the group of great ladies from foreign countries who are now attached to the Empress's person in this capacity. It is your right.'

'But I do not want to!' Marianne cried helplessly. 'How dare he do this to me? Attached to his wife, obliged to serve her, keep her company? He is mad!'

'Hush!' Duroc spoke hastily, casting an anxious glance around him. 'Do not fly into a panic. The appointments have already been made but, for one thing, the decree is not yet signed, although Countess Dorothée has already taken up her post; and for another, if I know anything of the Duchess of Montebello's exclusiveness, your duties will not take up much of your time. Apart from grand receptions, at which you will be obliged to attend, you will see little of the Empress, you will not enter her bedchamber, or converse with her, or ride in her carriage. It is, in fact, largely an honorary appointment but it will have the advantage of silencing busy tongues.'

'If I am obliged to have a post at court, could I not have been given to some other member of the imperial family? Princess Pauline, for instance? Or, better still, the Emperor's mother?'

At this, the Grand Marshal laughed quite openly.

'My dear Princess, you don't know what you are saying! You are a great deal too pretty for our charming, scatter brained Pauline, while as for Madame Mother, if you want to die a speedy death of boredom, then I advise you to join the company of grave and pious ladies who make up her entourage.'

'Very well,' Marianne said with a sigh of resignation. 'I admit defeat once more. I will be a lady-in-waiting. But for the love of heaven, my dear Duke, do nothing to hasten the signature of that decree! There will be time enough.'

'Oh, with a bit of luck, I can drag it out until August, or even September.'

*September*? Marianne's smile returned at once. By September her condition would be sufficiently obvious to excuse her from appearing at court since, according to her calculations, the baby should be born early in December.

They had reached the steps and Marianne extended her hand impulsively for the Grand Marshal to kiss.

'My dear Duke, you are a darling! And, and what is more to the point, a very good friend.'

'I preferred your first,' he told her, with a comical grimace, 'but I will be content with friendship. Good-bye for the present, fair lady.'

The sun was setting in a blaze of orange light that made the sky behind the hills of Saint-Cloud, where the windmills gently turned, seem on fire. The promenade de Longchamp was full of people, a gay, colourful crowd of gleaming carriages, handsome men on horseback, light-coloured gowns and brilliant uniforms. It was all feathers, lace, jewels and gilding as it had become the fashion for the people to parade in long lines of carriages which, at a walking pace, went up and down the promenade, often until late in the evening. Visitors included beautiful coquettes and opera girls, as well as

*Merveilleuses*, or rebellious women, who liked to dress to impress following the turmoil of the Revolution.

The evening was so mild that Marianne was glad not to hurry home. She was trying out a new carriage that day, an open barouche which Arcadius had ordered as a surprise for her homecoming. With its green velvet cushions and gleaming brass-work, it was both luxurious and comfortable. This splendid equipage attracted a good deal of notice, as also did its occupant. Women stared curiously, and men with an admiration divided equally between the ravishing young woman who reclined on the cushions and the four snowy Lippizaners handled with superb aplomb by Gracchus, glowing with pride in his new livery of black and gold.

The carriage was being turned around. Some walkers, seeing Marianne, greeted her or smiled. Marianne recognized Mme Récamier, the Baroness de Jaucourt, and the Countess Kielmannsegge, and Mme de Talleyrand, who, on passing her carriage, sent her a frantic salute with a proprietorial look. Obviously the excellent woman considered herself the discoverer, as it were, of this new star of Parisian high society.

A few men approached, hat in their hands, to kiss her hand, but Marianne had no desire to chat and was content to offer them a smile and a kind word, she did not detain them. Even the charming Prince Poniatowski, on his way to Saint-Cloud and expected by the Emperor, turned his head back as he passed, seemingly ready to spend time with her.

Marianne lay back, lulled by the gentle movement of her carriage, and breathed in the warm air, heavy with the sweet scent of acacia and chestnut trees in bloom. Her dreamy gaze took in just enough of the brilliant, passing throng to enable her to recognize a face or return a bow.

At one point, however, the two lines of vehicles were brought to a halt to allow a passage to the numerous retinues of Prince Cambacérès, rushing as usual in an over-decorated suit on which his triple chin of too much good living and the white powder from his 1780 wig were spread out. During the enforced halt, Marianne's wandering attention was caught and held by a man on horseback who stood out oddly in the colourful crowd. Riding a beautiful chestnut at a gentle trot along the grass track beside the road, he seemed to take no notice of the blockage, merely bowing from time to time to one of the many women, who all smiled at him.

Marianne could tell from his dark-green uniform with red flashes, from the Cross of St Alexander on his high collar and the peculiar shape of his black cocked hat with its knot of ribbons, that the man was a Russian officer, although the Cross of the Legion of Honour gleamed on his breast. No doubt he was one of the attachés to the Tzar's ambassador, the old Prince Kurakin, whom she had often seen at Talleyrand's house. But she had never seen this officer, while other faces, those of Nesselrode or Roumiantsoff, were already familiar to her. However, it was not easy to forget this face once you had seen it.

He was a superb horseman. That much was clear from his easy seat, combining gracefulness with strength, and from the muscular thighs, beautifully moulded by white buckskins. His figure, also, was distinctive: his shoulders were extremely broad but his waist as slim as a young girl's. The most extraordinary thing about him was his face which was very fair with narrow side-whiskers that grew like faint slivers of gold on his cheeks. The features had the absolute regularity of a Greek statue but the eyes, set at a slant, were fierce and of an intense green which betrayed Asiatic blood. The man had some Tartar in him. He was coming towards Marianne's carriage and as he neared it, he rode more slowly.

At last, he stopped altogether, only a few paces away from Marianne, but it was to look curiously and with great attention at her horses. He examined each one carefully, from head to tail, moved slightly back to study the effect, and then edged closer again. Then his eyes turned to her. The same procedure was repeated. The Russian officer sat on his horse two yards away, inspecting her with the attentive look of an entomologist discovering some rare insect. His eye roved in insolent appreciation from her thick, dark hair to her face, already flushed deep red, to the slender column of her neck, her shoulders and her breast, which Marianne hastened to cover with the black and gold cashmere. Bursting with indignation and feeling unpleasantly like a slave put up for sale, Marianne glared at him, but, lost in his contemplation, he seemed not to notice. More, he extracted a glass from his pocket and put it to his eye the better to scrutinize her.

Marianne leaned forward hastily and dug the tip of her sunshade smartly into Gracchus's arm.

'I do not care how you do it,' she said, 'but get us out of here! This person seems determined to stay where he is until Judgment Day.'

The youthful coachman glanced over his shoulder and grinned.

'It would appear your Serene Highness has an admirer. I'll see what I can do. In fact, I think things are beginning to move.'

The long line of carriages was indeed beginning to move again. Gracchus flicked the reins but still the Russian officer did not stir. He merely turned slightly in the saddle in order to follow the carriage and its occupant with his eyes. This was enough: 'Boor!' Marianne flung at him.

'Don't you upset yourself, Highness,' Gracchus told her. 'He's a Russian and everyone knows Russians don't know what's what. They're all savages. I dare say that one doesn't speak a word of French. It was his only way of telling you he thought you were beautiful.'

Marianne said nothing. There could be no doubt of the man's ability to speak French. The language was part of the normal education of all noble Russians and this one was evidently not born in a hovel. He was a thoroughbred, for sure, but his behaviour merely went to prove that it was possible to belong to the Russian nobility and remain horribly ill-bred. Oh well, she told herself, the important thing was to have got rid of him! It was lucky he had not been going her way.

But when her carriage passed through the handsome triple iron gate of the Porte Mahiaux she heard her coachman say casually that the Russian officer was still there.

'What? Is he following us? But he was going towards Saint-Cloud?'

'Maybe he was but he's not going there now. He's right behind us.'

Marianne looked round. Gracchus was right. The Russian was there, a few yards behind, following the carriage as calmly as if that had always been his place. When he saw her looking at him, he even had the audacity to give her a beaming smile.

'Oh!' Marianne cried aloud. This is too much! Spring 'em, Gracchus! As fast as you can!'

'Spring 'em?' Gracchus said in horror. 'We'll have someone over if I do.'

'You can avoid them. Spring them, I said. Now is the time for those horses to show their paces, and you your skill!'

Gracchus knew that it was useless to argue with his mistress when she spoke in that tone. The whip cracked. The carriage set off at a spanking pace along the route de Neuilly, traversed the place de l'Étoile, and thundered down the Champs-Élysées. Gracchus, standing up on his box like a Greek charioteer, shouted out warnings with the full force of his lungs whenever he perceived a pedestrian. All these, indeed, stopped in their tracks and stared, spellbound, at the sight of the smart barouche tearing past, drawn like the wind by four snow-white horses, with a horseman riding hell for leather in pursuit. The Russian's quiet following after the carriage had turned into a mad race. When the officer saw the barouche break into a gallop, he set spurs to his horse and set off in enthusiastic pursuit. His cocked hat was gone but he showed no sign of caring. His fair hair streamed in the wind as he urged on his mount with barbaric cries that matched Gracchus's shouts. It was not a sight to pass unnoticed.

With a thunderous roar, the barouche swept over the Pont de la Concorde, and rounded the corner of the Palais du Corps Législatif. The Russian was gaining on them, and Marianne was almost bursting with rage.

'We'll never shake him off before we reach the house,' she cried. 'We are nearly there.'

'Don't lose hope!' Gracchus yelled back. 'Help is coming!'

He was right. Another horseman was converging on their path, a captain of Polish Lancers who, seeing the smart barouche evidently pursued by a Russian officer, instantly decided to intervene. Marianne watched with delight as he cut across the Russian's path, forcing him to stop in order to avoid a collision. Gracchus's hold on the reins slackened instinctively and the carriage began to slow down.

'My thanks, monsieur,' Marianne called out, while the two men faced each other with obvious hostility.

'A pleasure, madame,' the lancer responded gaily, raising a gloved hand to his hat. A moment later, the same hand was applied to the Russian officer's cheek.

'That looks like the beginnings of a nice little duel.' Gracchus observed. 'Well, a sword thrust is a lot to pay for one smile.'

'Suppose you mind your own business,' Marianne snapped back. 'Take me home quickly and then come back and find out what has happened. Try and discover who both these gentlemen are. I will do what I can to prevent the duel.'

In a very few moments, she was standing in the forecourt of her own house, having despatched Gracchus to the scene of the quarrel. But when he returned not many minutes later, her young coachman could tell her nothing more. The two parties to the quarrel had already disappeared and the small crowd attracted by their altercation had melted away. Fearing the incident would attract a good deal more notoriety than it deserved and might even reach the Emperor's ears, Marianne did what she had always done in such a case and waited for Arcadius to come home to confide her troubles to him.

Since the previous day, the position of the Viscount de Jolival in Marianne's house had undergone change following a long interview during which he had been informed of the latest events in Italy: from the impresario of a singer, Jolival had been promoted to the double post of knight of honour and secretary to the new princess, a situation which suited his universal spirit as much as the strong affection which attached him to the young woman. He would thus have the upper hand in all the affairs of the house and particularly in financial matters and relations with Lucca. With him, Marianne would have nothing to fear from the strange machinations of Matteo Damiani, assuming that the Prince Sant'Anna had the weakness to keep him as secretary, or from any other steward put in his place.

'It is quite certain,' Arcadius had added after this conversation, 'that you must set up a more important house than that of Maria Stella. Among other things, you would need a lady to accompany you, or a reader.'

'I know,' said Marianne, 'but I won't have any. Apart from the fact that I hate people reading to me, I have no need of a lady to accompany me, especially if our dear Adélaïde will one day stop her madness and remember that we exist.'

The debate had been settled on this point, and Arcadius found himself with a mission of trust on his first day in office: to try to prevent an absurd duel between an officer of the Imperial Guard and a foreign officer, a mission he accepted with an amused smile, merely asking Marianne which of the two opponents she preferred.

'How can you ask!' she exclaimed. 'The Pole, of course! Didn't he rescue me from a man who was molesting me, at the risk of his life?'

'My experience of woman, my dear,' Arcadius retorted calmly, 'has not shown me that rescuers inevitably receive the gratitude they deserve. It all depends on who has done the rescuing. Take your friend Fortunée Hamelin. Well, I would stake my right arm that not only would she have felt not the faintest desire to be rescued from your pursuer, but she would have regarded any man who was fool enough to try it as a deadly enemy.'

Marianne shrugged.

'Oh, I know. Fortunée adores all men in general and anyone in uniform. She would think a Russian a great prize.'

'Not all Russians perhaps, but this one, most certainly.'

'Anyone would think you knew him,' Marianne said, staring. 'Yet you did not see him, you were not there.'

'No,' Jolival agreed pleasantly, 'but if your description is correct, I know who he is. Particularly as Russians who wear the Legion d'Honneur are not exactly two a penny.'

Then who —?'

'Count Alexander Ivanovitch Chernychev, Colonel of Cossacks of the Russian Imperial Guard, aide-de-camp to his majesty Tzar Alexander I and his customary emissary to France. He is one of the finest horsemen in the world and one of the most inveterate womanizers of two hemispheres. Women adore him.'

'Do they? Well, not this one!' Marianne cried, reacting with fury to Jolival's complacent introduction of the insolent rider of Longchamp. 'If this duel does take place, I hope very much that the Pole will skewer your Cossack as neatly as a tailor sewing thread. Attractive or no, his manners are atrocious.'

'That is what pretty women generally say of him the first time. It is odd, though, how often they tend to change their minds later. Come now, don't be cross,' he added, seeing her green eyes grow stormy. 'I will go and see whether I am able to prevent a massacre, although I doubt it.'

'Why?'

'Because a Russian and a Pole have never yet been known to renounce such a splendid opportunity for killing one another.'

In the event, ten o'clock was striking the next morning as Arcadius, who had gone out well before daylight, returned to inform Marianne that the duel had taken place that very morning at the Pré Catelan. The two parties had fought with swords and had returned unreconciled, one, Chernychev, with a thrust through his arm, the other, Baron Kozietulski, with a wound in the shoulder.

'You need not pity him too much,' Jolival added, seeing Marianne's distressed face. The wound is not severe and it will have the advantage of saving him from a tour of duty in Spain, where the Emperor would most certainly have sent him. And don't worry, I will send to inquire how he does. As for the other ...'

'The other does not interest me,' Marianne interrupted curtly.

The faintly sardonic smile which was Jolival's answer to this so offended Marianne that she turned her back on him without a word and went out into the garden. *Why*, she wondered, had her old friend smiled like that? *What was he thinking?* Did he imagine that she did not mean what she said when she declared that the Russian did not interest her? Did he think she was like all those other women who had fallen such easy victims to the handsome Cossack?

She strolled a little way along the sanded paths, all leading to the little pool with its murmuring fountain. It was a small garden, made up of no more than a few lime trees and masses of roses basking in the summer sun. The fountain was also small, in the form of a bronze dolphin clasped in the arms of an enigmatically smiling cupid. It was certainly nothing to compare with the marvels of the Villa dei Cavalli. Here, no proud stallion made the ground echo at night to the thunder of his furious galloping hooves, no phantom rider streaked through the shadows on his lonely way, carrying with him to the end of the night some terrible secret, some awful despair. Here, all was peace and cheerfulness, ordered, companionable, as a small Parisian garden should be.

The cupid on the dolphin smiled through the shower of falling crystal drops and it seemed to Marianne that she read a kind of irony in his smile. *You are mocking me*, she thought. *But why? What have I done to you? I believed in you and you betrayed me cruelly. You have never smiled at me except to take away what you have given. I entered into marriage as other women enter religion, yet you made marriage nothing but a mockery to me. And yet, here I am, married for the second time, and still as lonely. The first was a villain, the second is no more than a shadow – while the man I love is merely another woman's husband. Will you never have mercy on me?*

But no, the cupid remained silent and his smile did not change. With a sigh Marianne turned her back and went to sit down on a bench of mossy stone where a climbing rose dropped its crimson petals. Her heart felt empty, like one of those deserts created in a night by a hurricane gust of wind, carrying everything away with it, obliterating even the memory of what was there before. And when she tried to revive the fire that was slowly going out within her by remembering the madness of her love, the delirium of joy, the blind despair which the very name, the very picture of her lover had once had power to evoke. Marianne found to her distress that not even the echo of her cries remained. It was as if – yes, it was as if it were a story she had heard, but a story of which someone else was the heroine.

From a great distance, as though at the end of a long series of vast, empty rooms, she seemed to hear Talleyrand's persuasive voice saying: 'This was never made to last ...' Could he have been right, after all? Was he proved right already? Could it be that her great love for Napoleon was dying, leaving behind it only the small change of tenderness and admiration that remains after the burning, golden flood of passion has withdrawn?

# About the Author

Juliette Benzoni was born Andrée-Marguerite-Juliette Mangin on 30 October 1920 in Paris, France. She spent her childhood in Saint-Germain-des-Prés until she was almost 15 years old, when her family went to live in Saint-Mandé. She was educated at College d'Hulet, then at the Institut Catholique, where she studied philosophy, law and literature. In 1941 she married a doctor from Dijon, Maurice Gallois, and was soon mother of two children, Anne and Jean-François. In her twenties, she spent many hours in libraries, studying the history of Burgundy in Medieval times. One day she came across the legend of the Order of the Golden Fleece, which would later inspire her to write the Catherine series.

After her husband died in 1950, she went to Morocco to visit a relative of his, and ended up staying for two years, joining the editorial staff at a radio station called Radio-International. She then met Colonel André Benzoni, who in 1953 became her second husband. After her return to Paris, France, she launched into journalism, writing for several newspapers. At the beginning of the 1960s, a literary editor who had seen her make a television appearance invited her to write a historical romance in the style of Anne Golon's *Angelique*. The outcome was *Catherine: One Love is Enough* (original title, *Catherine, Il Suffit d'un Amour*), the hugely successful first entry in what was originally intended to be a five book series.

Next came another big success with the *Marianne* series, set during the Napoleonic period, beginning with *Marianne: A Star for Napoleon* (original title, *Marianne: Une Étoile Pour Napoléon*). Juliette was then asked if she would write two additional *Catherine* books, due to their sensational popularity. She agreed, and the series' seventh and final entry, *La Dame de Montsalvy*, appeared in 1979.

In 1983, the French station Antenne 2 adapted *Marianne: A Star for Napoleon* for television, directed by Marion Sarraut. This led on three years later to a television adaptation of all seven books in the *Catherine* series, again directed by Sarraut; the end result pleased Juliette far more than a substandard movie version produced in 1968.

Juliette continued to write up to her death on 7 February 2016.

For more information about Juliette and the *Catherine* books visit the official website: www.catherinedemontsalvy.ch.

# Also by Juliette Benzoni

**CATHERINE SERIES**
1: Catherine: One Love is Enough
2: Catherine
3: Belle Catherine
4: Catherine: Her Great Journey
5: Catherine: A Time For Love
6: A Trap for Catherine
7: Catherine: The Lady of Monsalvy

**MARIANNE SERIES**
1: Marianne: Napoleon's Star
2: Marianne: The Stranger from Tuscany
3: Marianne: The Privateer
4: Marianne: The Rebels
5: Marianne: Lords of the East
6: Marianne: Laurels of Flame

Printed in Great Britain
by Amazon

23042024R00161